BORN TO DIE

He walked to a file drawer and pulled it open. Inside were slim folders, information gathered over time on each of the pretenders. He opened the first one, and his gut twisted as he glared at the picture tucked within his notes.

Dr. Kacey Lambert.

She was special.

Until the mistake.

When he'd gotten too bloodthirsty, too hungry, too eager to destroy the one person who could ruin everything.

And the job had been botched.

Kacey had lived.

This time, there wouldn't be a mistake; this time he'd take care of her himself.

A slow-burning fury ran through his veins as he studied her picture. He'd watched her. Followed her. Learned her routine.

But she would have to wait.

There were others he had to deal with first.

He flipped open a few more files and sorted them. None of them knew each other; none of them realized that he was watching them, collecting all the ones that were in close proximity to Kacey.

He wondered if any of them were aware of each other.

If so, they hadn't guessed the one thing they had in common.

Each was born to die before her time.

And it was his mission to make it happen. . . .

Books by Lisa Jackson

Stand-Alones

SEE HOW SHE DIES
FINAL SCREAM
RUNNING SCARED
WHISPERS
TWICE KISSED
UNSPOKEN
DEEP FREEZE
FATAL BURN
MOST LIKELY TO DIE
WICKED GAME
WICKED LIES
WITHOUT MERCY

Anthony Paterno/Cahill Family Novels
IF SHE ONLY KNEW
ALMOST DEAD

Rick Bentz/Reuben Montoya Novels
HOT BLOODED
COLD BLOODED
SHIVER
ABOLUTE FEAR
LOST SOULS
MALICE
DEVIOUS

Pierce Reed/Nikki Gilette Novels
THE NIGHT BEFORE
THE MORNING AFTER

Selena Alvarez/Regan Pescoli Novels
LEFT TO DIE
CHOSEN TO DIE
BORN TO DIE

Published by Kensington Publishing Corporation

LISA JACKSON

BORN TO DIE

KENSINGTON BOOKS
www.kensingtonbooks.com

KENSINGTON BOOKS are published by

Kensington Publishing Corp.
119 West 40th Street
New York, NY 10018

All Kensington titles, imprints, and distributed lines are available at special quantity discounts for bulk purchases for sales promotion, premiums, fund-raising, educational, or institutional use.

Special book excerpts or customized printings can also be created to fit specific needs. For details, write or phone the office of the Kensington Special Sales Manager: Attn. Special Sales Department. Kensington Publishing Corp., 119 West 40th Street, New York, NY 10018. Phone: 1-800-221-2647.

Kensington and the K logo Reg. U.S. Pat. & TM Off.

Library of Congress Card Catalog Number: 2011928759

ISBN-13: 978-0-7582-5221-0
ISBN-10: 0-7582-5221-8

First Hardcover Printing: May 2011

10   9   8   7   6   5   4   3   2   1

Printed in the United States of America

ACKNOWLEDGMENTS

As always there are many people who helped me while I wrote this book. It's a case of the usual suspects, for the most part, and they're great: Nancy Bush, Alex Craft, Matthew Crose, Niki Crose, Michael Crose, Kelly Foster, Marilyn Katcher, Ken Melum, Robin Rue, John Scognamiglio, Larry Sparks, and more. Of course, there may be some errors in the book, and they are all mine.

BORN
TO DIE

PROLOGUE

Sometimes you win; sometimes you lose.

Tonight, Shelly Bonaventure thought, she'd come out the loser. Make that a loser with a capital *L,* the kind kids made with their thumb and forefinger held up to their foreheads.

She unlocked the door of her apartment, threw her purse onto the entryway table, and felt a sudden searing pain scream through her guts.

Gasping, she doubled over, her insides on fire.

Suddenly.

Out of the blue.

"Oooh," she moaned as the pain subsided enough that she could stumble to the couch. "What the hell?"

Still queasy, the pain in her abdomen slightly lessened, she took in several deep breaths. Was the pain bad enough to call 9-1-1, or should she head to the ER herself?

"Don't be silly," she whispered, but an uneasy feeling that something was very, very wrong stuck with her. "Pull yourself together," she said and kicked off her high heels. Either she'd drunk too much, eaten the wrong thing, or her period was coming a few days early.

No way. Not with pain like that.

She closed her eyes for a second, beads of perspiration collecting on her upper lip. She would take some Pepto if she had it and, if not, just suffer through until morning. As she swiped at the sweat, she glanced around for her cat. "Lana?" she said and heard no response. Odd. The cat usually trotted out of whatever hiding spot she'd claimed when she heard the front door's lock spring open.

Huh.

"Lana? Come on, kitty. . . ." Again she listened; again she heard nothing. Oh, well, maybe the calico was just playing games with her and would spring out from a darkened hallway to scare the liver out of Shelly. It had happened before.

Yet . . .

Slowly she made her way to the bathroom, nearly tripping on the rug she'd bought. . . . Oh, God, had it really been seven years ago? "Come out, come out, wherever you are!" she singsonged to the cat. "Momma's home."

Clunk!

The sound came from the patio.

Startled, Shelly whipped around.

Was there a shadow on the patio?

Heart in her throat, she stepped forward and peered through the sliding door where she saw that the shadow was only that of a palm frond catching in the wind and dancing in front of the porch light.

"Idiot! Stop being paranoid."

So what was the noise . . . ?

The cat? Where?

Her nerves still stretched a bit, Shelly convinced herself it was nothing. Probably the old guy in the unit above hers, Bob . . . whatever. He was always dropping something.

Another wave of nausea swept through her, and she clenched her teeth until the pain subsided. God, what was wrong with her?

Holding on to the back of the couch, she let out her breath, then glanced around the living area. Had she lived in this one-bedroom apartment for nearly a decade, watching as the years tumbled past, the lines in her face becoming more pronounced and the roles she'd hoped to land slipping through her fingers?

Ever since her divorce from Donovan . . .

She wasn't going to dwell on *that* piece of ancient history. Not tonight. A positive attitude, that was what she needed. And maybe something to calm her stomach. She'd just had a little too much to drink at Lizards, the bar named more for its clientele than any real reptile, which was less than two blocks down the street. Cutting loose, telling herself she was going to embrace the big three-five, which was bearing down on her, she'd overindulged.

But just a bit.

Right?

How could she help it when the guy she'd met at the bar had heard about her birthday, then had bought her several mai tais and had seemed really interested? *Really* interested. He was handsome and sexy and spoke in a voice so low, it caused her spine to tingle a bit. He'd almost seemed familiar, and when he'd touched the back of her hand, she'd experienced a definite tingle of anticipation. His gray eyes were intense, striated a deep midnight blue, his lips blade thin, the slight shading of his jaw only emphasizing how male he was. And then that smile, crooked and most definitely sexy as he'd talked to her. Yeah, he definitely had the bad boy routine down pat. She'd even mentioned to him that he had a killer smile, and he'd found that comment amusing. He'd said he'd never heard it described that way and chuckled deep in his throat.

She'd had fantasies of what he would look like without his shirt, how it would feel to have his lips press hot and urgent against hers, how she would tumble, oh, so easily into bed with him as his strong arms caught her.

Yeah, but you left him in the bar, didn't you?

To come back here. Alone.

Of course she'd walked away. She didn't know him from Adam. And getting out when she did was probably a good idea, really, considering the fact that she was feeling ill and had a five o'clock wake-up call that she wasn't about to miss.

Her agent had weaseled an audition for a role on a new drama to be aired on Fox in the fall. The casting call was being held early tomorrow, and she intended to look her best. Better than her best. Because if she didn't land this role, it was over . . . well, at least until she wangled her way onto *Dancing with the Stars* or some other reality vehicle that would help jump-start her flagging career.

If she could just shake this lousy feeling. Good Lord, was she actually perspiring? That wasn't good, not good at all.

After all, this television series could be her last shot, considering Hollywood's attitude about age.

How depressing was that?

Shelly Bonaventure had to make it, she *had* to. She couldn't very well go back to that Podunk town in Montana with her tail between her legs. Hadn't she been prom queen of Sycamore High, voted "most likely to be famous" her senior year? Hadn't she taken off, shaking the dust of that small town from her shoes as quickly as possible? And hadn't, in the beginning, her star shined brightly, rising with promise and a few plum roles? A recurring role in a soap opera before she was twenty! Hadn't she worked with the Toms—Cruise and Hanks—and Gwyneth and Meryl and . . . and even Brad Friggin' Pitt? Okay, so they were small parts, but still, they were legit! And she'd been a double for Julia Roberts! Then there was the vampire series *What's Blood Got To Do With It* on cable. She'd paid her dues, by God. But, she realized, those flashes of fame had been a while back, and lately she'd been relegated to corpses on *CSI,* a few commercials, and voice-overs for low-budget animated films.

If she didn't land the part of Estelle in this new series, she could kiss her B-listed career good-bye and open her arms to a reality show for has-beens. She shuddered at the thought.

Hollywood, she thought miserably, *the land of worn-out casting couches and broken dreams.*

She winced against another jab of pain that nearly buckled her knees. "Sweet Jesus," she whispered, then half crawled, half stumbled, to her small galley kitchen, where she dragged open her refrigerator door, saw the sparse contents inside, and felt depressed all over again. After retrieving the half-full bottle of Pepto, she unscrewed the cap and took a swallow of the pink ooze. Quivering, she replaced the top, put the remainder of the bottle back on the shelf, then sat on the floor, her legs extended, as she took in long, deep breaths.

God, she felt bad.

Maybe she should call her doctor, at least leave a message with his answering service. Slowly, she pulled herself to her feet and wondered, again, where was Lana?

Well, certainly not on the counter, where three days' worth of coffee cups, dirty glasses, and Lean Cuisine trays littered the chipped tile.

Her stomach still aching, she made her way to the bathroom, told herself she couldn't let this town beat her down.

Hadn't she suffered through bulimia?

Hadn't she done whatever it took?

And even if she wasn't classically beautiful, she'd been told her face had "character" and "intelligence." Her auburn hair was still vibrant; the skin around her green eyes and full lips without too many telltale lines.

With a glance in the mirror over the sink, she cringed as she wedged herself into the tiny bathroom. Despite the pep talk to herself, the years were beginning to show, if only a little. She used a ton of products to keep her complexion flawless, and she wasn't into Botox. Yet. Though she wasn't ruling it out. Then again, she wouldn't rule anything out that might force Father Time back a step or two.

But he was a persistent son of a bitch, she thought and pushed the flesh on the sides of her jaw backward in an attempt to see if she really needed to be "tightened up."

Not yet, thank God. She didn't have the money for any kind of "work." And she wasn't ready to write some kind of trumped-up tell-all book, which her agent had mentioned. She wasn't even thirty-five yet, for God's sake, at least not for a few more days; she wasn't ready to spill her guts just yet. And truth to tell, she didn't have that much to write about; her life had been pretty dull compared to a lot of her peers.

Noticing the whites of her eyes were a little bloodshot, she removed her contacts, then found the bottle of Visine she kept in the medicine cabinet. After unscrewing the bottle cap, she tilted her head back, blinked in the drops, and resealed the bottle. She closed the mirrored front of the cabinet and caught a glimpse of a shadow behind her.

What?

Her heart clutched and she jerked around. The room was empty; the door behind her open to the living room and the sliding door to her patio.

Her flesh prickled.

"Lana? Is that you?" she called as she stepped into the living area again, the edges of the room blurry from her myopia and the drops that hadn't quite settled. "Kitty?" Where was the damned cat, a calico she'd named after her favorite movie icon? "Come out, come out, wherever you are," she sang again but decided the cat, who often played a game of hide-and-seek, was lurking in the shadows somewhere, ready to pounce. More than once Lana had leapt from behind the framed pictures set upon the bookcase, scattering the photos, breaking the glass, and, plumping up to twice her size, had startled Shelly. Scaring her was the cat's favorite pastime. "Here, kitty, kitty . . ."

True to her independent temperament, Lana didn't appear.

Shelly stood barefoot in the living room. There was something about the apartment, a stillness that suggested no one, not even the cat, was inside.

Which didn't make sense.

Shelly had left Lana sleeping on the back of the couch when she'd gone out earlier. She was certain of it and remembered the cat desultorily flicking her tail as she lay curled in the soft cushions.

So why did it feel as if the rooms were empty, devoid of life? She heard dry leaves skittering across the patio, bits of brown and rust dancing eerily.

For the love of God, what was wrong with her? It was just the wind, nothing more than dead leaves, for crying out loud. Still, the hairs on the back of her arm lifted.

"Get over yourself."

Another sharp cramp to her midsection. "Ooh." She doubled over, the pain intense. This time she didn't wait. She crab-walked to her purse and fumbled for her cell phone.

The damned thing wasn't in its usual pocket. "Come on, come on!" This was no time for the phone to be missing. Fingers shaking, she fished through the interior of the purse, then as the pain increased, dumped the contents onto the tile floor. Keys, eyeglass case, wallet, receipts, coins, pack of cigarettes, tampon holder, and her tiny canister of pepper spray went skittering across the tile.

No phone.

What?

She'd had her cell at the bar. She remembered turning it to vibrate, and . . . hadn't she shoved it back into her purse? Or had she left it at Lizards, on the top of the sleek counter that was fashioned to look like snakeskin?

"Oh, God," she whispered, sweat breaking out on her forehead, her pulse jumping. She didn't have a landline; there was no way to call for help except for—

Sccrrraape!

The dry, rasping sound seemed to echo through her head.

What the hell was that?

The cat?

"Lana?" she said nervously, then noticed the sliding door was open, just the tiniest of cracks.

Hadn't it been shut?

Absolutely. She remembered sliding it closed, though, of course it didn't latch, because that stupid building super, Merlin, hadn't gotten around to fixing it.

Oh, Jesus! Her scalp prickled and her heart began to knock, though she told herself she was being paranoid. No one was in the apartment, lurking inside, lying in wait for her. *You've been auditioning for too many victims in those cheap horror flicks.*

Still . . .

Ears straining, heart thudding, she glanced toward her bedroom door, open just a crack. She had taken two steps in the direction of the open door when, from the corner of her eye, she saw movement, a dark figure at the edge of the slider, on the other side of the glass.

An intruder! Oh, no!

She opened her mouth to scream.

Then stopped when she recognized the guy from the bar. In his hand was her cell phone. Palm over her pounding heart, she declared, "You scared me half to death!" as she pushed the door open. "How'd you get my—?"

But she knew before he said, "You left it on the bar."

"So, how did you find me?"

Again the slow, crooked grin. "Your address is in the contact information. Under *home*."

"Oh. Yeah."

He really was a heart-stopper with that square jaw, dark hair, and eyes that showed a bit of the devil in their blue depths.

"Most people come to the front door and knock." She couldn't help but be a little irritated. Besides, she felt like hell.

His lips twitched. "Maybe I'm not most people."

She couldn't argue with that and wasn't about to try when another pain, sharp enough that she had to double over, cut through her. "Oh . . . oh . . . geez." She placed a hand against the glass-topped table and sucked in her breath. Again, she was perspiring, this time feeling a little faint.

"Are you okay?"

"No." She was shaking her head. "You'd better leave. I'm sorry— oh!" She sucked in her breath. This time her knees buckled, and he caught her, strong arms surrounding her.

"You need help."

Before she could protest, he picked her up and carried her unerringly to the bedroom. "Hey, wait a second. . . ."

"Just lie down," he said calmly.

She didn't have a choice. The bedroom was spinning, the bedside lamp seeming to swirl in front of her eyes. Man, she was sick. . . . Oh, wait . . . a new panic rose in her as he lay her on the mussed bedcovers. The mattress gave slightly with her weight.

"I don't think . . ." He left her for a second, and she thought about trying to escape. Something about his appearance at her back door was all wrong. She knew it now, despite the agony roiling through her insides. Her meeting him at the bar, the illness, him showing up on her patio . . .

Jesus, had he turned on the shower? She heard the rush of water and a creak as the old pipes were shut off. What was that all about?

Before she could move, he was back, holding her cell phone out to her. "I've already called nine-one-one," he said and she attempted to reach for the phone but couldn't. She tried to force her arm upward, but her fingers were limp and useless as her arm flopped back onto the mattress.

Oh, God, oh, God, she had to get away. . . . This was sooo wrong.

He set the cell next to her face, on the quilt her grandmother had pieced for her when she was ten. . . .

From the bed, with its tangle of blankets and sheets, she looked up at him and saw him grin again, and this time she was certain there was no mirth in his smile, just a cold, deadly satisfaction. His once handsome face now appearing demonic.

"What did you do?" she tried to say, though the words were barely intelligible.

"Sweet dreams." He walked to the doorway and paused, and she felt a chill as cold as death.

"Nine-one-one," a female voice said crisply from the phone. "Please state your name and emergen—"

"Help," Shelly cried frantically, her voice the barest of whispers. Her mouth wouldn't work, her tongue thick and unresponsive.

"Pardon me?"

"I need help," she tried to say more loudly, but the words were garbled, even to her own ears.

"I'm sorry. I can't hear you. Please speak up. What is the nature of your emergency?"

"Help me, please! Send someone!" Shelly tried to say, now in a full-blown panic. *Oh, God, help me!* The room was swimming around her; the words she wanted to cry out were trapped in her mind. She managed to jerk her arm toward the phone but it slid off the bed and to the floor.

Her head lolled to one side, but she saw him standing in the doorway, staring back at her. The "killer" smile had slid from his face, and he glared at her with pure, undisguised hatred.

Why? Why me?

Evil glinted in the eyes she'd found so intriguing just hours before.

She knew in the few last moments of her life that her death hadn't been random; for some godforsaken reason, he had targeted her. Theirs hadn't been a chance meeting in the bar.

God help me, she thought, a tear rolling from her eye, the certainty of death dawning. From the doorway, the mysterious stranger with his disturbing smile stared at her as she drew in a slow, shallow breath.

A voice was squawking from the phone on the floor, but it seemed distant, a million miles away. She watched as he came closer again and placed the vial of pills at her bedside. Then, while staring into her eyes, telling her silently that he was the cause of her death, he slowly and methodically began stripping her of her clothes. . . .

CHAPTER 1

Balancing a cup of coffee and a chocolate macadamia nut cookie from Joltz, the local coffee shop, in one hand and the case holding her laptop in the other, Dr. Acacia "Kacey" Lambert hurried along the sidewalk. Though it was nearly dawn, streetlights glowed, Christmas lights were strung and burning bright, dancing in the icy November wind that whistled through the small town of Grizzly Falls.

Winter had come early this year and with gale force, bringing early snow and ice, which was causing all kinds of electrical outages and traffic problems.

Just as it had a year earlier, she thought.

So much for global warming.

A steady stream of cars, this part of Montana's rush hour, was cutting through the surface streets on the way to the highway as people headed for work. Pedestrians in thick jackets, scarves, wool hats, and boots walked briskly past, their breath fogging, their cheeks red from the cold.

Winters here were harsh, much more frigid than they had been in Seattle, but she loved this part of the country and didn't regret for a second moving back to the small town where she'd grown up.

At the clinic, located in the lower level of the town, a few blocks from the courthouse and the river, she juggled her keys and unlocked the front door. Another blast of winter air cut through her down jacket as it raced along the river's chasm, rattling storefronts.

Colder than a witch's teat. Or so her grandfather would have said. Alfred Lambert, eyes a mischievous blue behind wire-rimmed glasses, had never given up his salty language, though his wife, Bess, had forever reprimanded him.

God, she still missed them both. Sometimes achingly so. She lived in the farmhouse where they'd spent over fifty years together, and consequently thought of them often.

A truck rolled by, and despite the cold, the passenger window was rolled down a bit, the nose of a hound of some kind poking out, the strains of "Jingle Bell Rock" audible.

"Still too early," she muttered as the door unlocked and she slipped into the empty reception area of the low-slung building that housed one of only two clinics in town. A row of slightly worn chairs rimmed the walls, magazines had been placed on the scattered tables, a dying betel palm filled a corner, and there were a few toys for the little ones stacked neatly near the reception window.

Lights were glowing from behind a wall of glass, and Heather Ramsey, the receptionist, was already planted at the long counter that served as her desk on the other side of the window. Nose to computer monitor screen, Heather was rapt, her eyes rapidly scanning the series of pages in front of her.

The images weren't patient charts, records, or anything remotely to do with the clinic's business.

As usual Heather was reading the latest on the gossip columns and blogs before she settled down to her work routine. "Brace yourself," she said, without even glancing up.

"For?"

"Your twin died," Heather said sadly. "Suicide."

"My twin," Kacey repeated, arching an eyebrow. "Since I'm an only child, who exactly would that be?"

"Shelly Bonaventure!"

"Shelly who? Oh, the actress who was in . . . Oh, God, I can't remember the film." But she did remember Shelly's face as pretty and even featured, with big green eyes, short nose, pointed chin, and high cheekbones. Heather's comparison was definitely a compliment.

"She was in lots of movies, just wasn't the star. Off the top of my head, there was *Joint Custody* and *Sorority Night,* but that was a few years back, and, oh, crap, what about *Thirty Going On Fifteen?*" Now she was scanning an article in the c-zine, getting her info from the computer screen. "Mainly she was known for her role on *What's Blood Got To Do With It,* you know, that vampire drama where Joey Banner got his start."

"Never saw it," Kacey admitted, but that wasn't surprising as she wasn't into television; just didn't have a lot of extra time. Between college, med school, residency, and her internship, she'd missed what seemed like a whole generation of pop culture.

"Wow, you missed out. But it's on DVD and Blu-ray. The whole series, starting with the pilot. It was great. *She* was great." Heather was really going now. Animated. "She was from around here, you know. Her real name was Michelle Bentley." Heather looked up, her brown eyes blinking with the adjustment to the light. "She was just thirty-five, or would have been this coming week."

Another thing in common. "And she committed suicide?" Kacey said. "A shame."

"Yeah, she didn't leave a note, either, or at least the police aren't copping to it . . . Oh, get it, 'copping' to it?" Heather's smile was wide, showing off adult braces as she caught her own joke.

"Got it." Kacey was already passing examination rooms and snapping on the lights in the short hallway. "Too bad."

"Yeah . . . weird. But she really does—did—look like you."

"Yeah, yeah, I know," Kacey said as she stepped into her office, a small room lined with bookshelves and one window overlooking the parking lot. Sleet was slanting from the still-dark sky, pinging against the window and drizzling down. Kacey set her computer on the desk, pulled it from its case, flipped it open, and plugged it in. As it warmed up, she adjusted the shade that allowed her to see out but no one to look into the office, then flipped through a stack of messages as she munched on her breakfast cookie and sipped her coffee.

Patients weren't due to arrive for nearly an hour, so she had time to catch up on paperwork, e-mail, and settle in for another day in the throes of flu season. She returned a couple of calls, heard the rest of the staff arriving, and through the window noticed steely clouds rolling in over the Bitterroot Mountains.

She'd just hung up from a consultation with a colleague in Spokane about a patient with breast cancer when Heather poked her head through the door, which Kacey kept ajar during most of the day. "Mrs. Ingles called and canceled, something about her nephew needing a babysitter."

"Okay." Helen Ingles was battling type 2 diabetes and had been scheduled for more blood work.

"Oh, and here. I ran off this article about Shelly Bonaventure."

Kacey looked over the tops of her reading glasses.

Heather dropped a couple of pages onto Kacey's desk. "Yeah, yeah, I know it's time to get to work, but"—she shrugged her slim shoulders—"she was a local celeb, and just look at how much she resembles you."

"Enough already," Kacey said, shaking her head, as she pushed the article to the side of her desk. For years, she'd heard that she and several Hollywood actresses had similar facial characteristics. Hadn't her wide grin been compared to Julia Roberts's smile? Even her ex-husband, Jeffrey Charles Lambert—oh, wait, just JC to his friends—had told her that her face had the same shape as Jennifer Garner's, which wasn't true at all. As for Shelly Bonaventure, the only real resemblance, as she saw it, was that their eyes were the same shape and color, that is, if Shelly hadn't worn tinted contacts.

"Okay, okay . . . I get it." Heather held up her hands in surrender as she backed out of the office. "Mrs. Whitaker is here already."

"Great." Constance Whitaker was a hypochondriac who had too much time on her hands and spent it investigating illnesses on the Internet, then freaking herself out because she was certain she was contracting the latest disease du jour. "What about Dr. Cortez?" Kacey asked, shrugging into her lab coat.

"He called around fifteen minutes ago. He's on his way from the hospital," Heather said as headlights flashed across the window and Dr. Martin Cortez's Range Rover wheeled into the lot. "Record time."

Kacey shook her head. "He's been faster. When he had the Porsche."

Heather sighed. "I remember."

The sporty car had lasted one winter, and then he'd traded it in for an upscale four-wheel drive that could deal with the mountainous terrain and harsh winter weather.

The phone started ringing, and Heather retreated to the front desk just as the back door opened and closed sharply. Dr. Martin Cortez had arrived.

Kacey glanced at the article about Shelly Bonaventure, and yeah, she had to admit to herself, there was a *slight* resemblance between them, but it was minimal.

She tossed the article into the trash just as Martin stuck his head into the room. Already wearing his lab coat and a warm smile, he started the conversation with, "You pick up a triple-shot caramel mocha with extra whip this morning?"

"In your dreams." It was their morning joke. Every once in a while Kacey did surprise him with some outrageous, over-the-top coffee drink, but not today.

"How will I get through another minute?" He splayed one hand over his chest and looked to the ceiling, as if for holy inspiration.

"It'll be tough, but you'll manage," she said. "Soldier on, okay?"

"I'll try." His smile, a quick slash of white against his tanned skin, was infectious. No wonder half the single women in the county were interested. Dropping the Oscar-worthy pose, he turned serious. All local GP again. "So did you take a look at Amelia Hornsby's chart?" Martin knew the names of the family members of nearly everyone who stepped into the clinic. Amelia was an eight-year-old who had been through several rounds of antibiotics to fight a throat infection that just wouldn't go away.

Randy Yates, a male nurse just out of school, stuck his head into the door. "Hey, Docs, time to rock 'n' roll," he said, flashing a quick grin. His brown hair was shaved nearly to his skull, leaving little more than stubble over the top of his head, but he made up for it with a neatly trimmed goatee. "I've got exam one, two, and four ready to go. Vitals taken."

"I'll take Mrs. Whitaker," Martin said.

Kacey checked the chart on exam room two. Elmer Grimes. "I'm in two," she said and opened the door to her first patient.

Detective Jonas Hayes of the LAPD wasn't buying the setup. He hadn't last night, when he'd responded to the call to Shelly Bonaventure's apartment, and he didn't today, as he sat at his desk and clicked through the images of the crime scene on his computer. This morning the department was buzzing, phones ringing, conversations drifting from one desk to the next, footsteps shuffling, computer keys clicking, and somewhere a printer was clunking out copies.

Hayes took a swallow of his coffee, a cup he'd picked up at the Starbucks a few streets down, as he worked his way through the statements collected the night before. Again. He had perused them all around four in the morning and now was reading them more slowly five hours later.

Last night, from the minute he'd stepped through Shelly Bonaventure's front door, he'd been hit by the sensation that everything wasn't as it was portrayed. He felt as if the crime scene had been staged à la Marilyn Monroe some fifty years earlier. Half a century later there were still conspiracy theories and the question of murder still hung over Marilyn's grave. He didn't want the same controversy to be a part of Shelly Bonaventure's death. Not on his watch.

And the crime scene just hadn't felt right last night.

Still didn't.

And that, in and of itself, was odd. A man of science, Hayes believed in cold, hard facts. He wasn't big into gut feelings or hunches. He believed that the truth of a crime was found in evidence.

But this case was different.

For one thing, he didn't believe that Shelly, no matter what her mental state, would call 9-1-1 while stark naked. If she'd had enough sense to make the call, then why not put on a robe at the very least? Was this a ploy for publicity? Did being nude ramp up the curiosity factor? Had she wanted to die sensationally?

Then where the hell was the suicide note?

Rubbing the back of his neck, he felt a craving for a smoke, but he'd given up cigarettes years before at Delilah's urging. God, he missed them. Almost as much as he missed her.

Scowling, he turned his thoughts back to the case. He expected, when the tox report came in, to find a concoction of pills and booze in her bloodstream. Xanax, if she'd taken her own meds. A bottle of the sedative had been right there on her nightstand, not in the medicine chest with the rest of her prescriptions. Only three pills were left in the vial, and according to the label, the prescription had been filled only last Saturday.

It was obvious she'd OD'd.

So, why was he not buying the pat suicide theory? She could have kept the pills at her bedside, he supposed, and she might have been naked because of a recent shower. The shower stall and curtain had been wet.

But her hair and skin had been bone dry; her makeup only

slightly smeared and faded. More like worn off rather than scrubbed away. The shower cap hanging on a hook near the stall had been damp, so maybe she'd stuffed her hair in it so well that not even the tiny hairs around her face had gotten wet . . . maybe.

And her cat wasn't inside, but out. Would she really kill herself and leave her usually pampered cat on the patio? He didn't think so, yet, of course, anything was possible. Maybe she thought it would be more humane than having kitty locked up with a rotting corpse.

Frowning, he tapped a pencil eraser on his desk as he pored over the crime scene photos. Shelly was sprawled on the bed, her right hand still holding her cell phone, as she'd used it to call 9-1-1 minutes before slipping into a drug-induced coma and dying.

Rotating the kinks from his neck, Jonas went over the past twelve hours in his mind. He had gotten the call around midnight and had driven to her apartment, where the responding officer had already started a crime scene log.

Hayes and Gail Harding, his junior partner, had waited for the crime scene guys from the scientific investigative division and the coroner's office.

Eventually Shelly's body had been sent to the morgue, the crime scene techs had come and gone, the next of kin had been notified, and a press release from the public information officer, already in sound bites for the morning news, had been issued. The tabloids had already been calling, as Ms. Bonaventure was much more fascinating in death than in life. Shelly's agent had given a short statement, lauding Shelly's talent, career, and good heart, then asking the public for privacy for the deceased's family.

Everyone he'd interviewed who knew her claimed she'd been full of life, a fighter, never too depressed. In a town where uppers and downers were tossed down like M&M's and rehab was a way of life, Shelly had seemed to stay relatively clean and out of trouble.

Hayes glanced down at the hard copies of the sworn statements they'd taken. According to the neighbor who lived above her, Shelly had been calling for her cat less than half an hour before the 9-1-1 call. He'd heard her front door open and close around eleven.

And within forty minutes she was dead.

The suicide theory just seemed too easy. Too pat.

And she'd died pretty quickly from the time she'd taken the pills, if she'd swallowed them all upon returning to her apartment. But maybe he was wrong; there were still phone records to check, friends and neighbors and old boyfriends to call. Leaning back in his desk chair, he eyed a five-by-seven of his daughter, Maren. Now in high school, she was blessed with her mother's good looks and wide smile. Her skin was a soft mocha, her eyes dark and vibrant, and she'd confided that she wanted to be an actress, that she saw herself as a new Angela Bassett or Halle Berry or Jada Pinkett Smith.

And she was good, too.

But, man oh man, Hollywood? For his kid?

He turned his gaze from the picture of Maren's smiling face to his computer monitor and the image of Shelly Bonaventure, her skin gray, her lips blue, death having claimed her. What, he wondered, had Hollywood had to do with her death?

Maybe nothing.

Maybe everything.

Hayes climbed to his feet and heard the soft, unfamiliar ruffle of the heating system, which was barely used. Even in winter the temperature in the police administration building, where the robbery-homicide division was housed, rarely needed a boost.

He heard the clip of Harding's footsteps before he saw her rounding the corner. She was frowning, her plucked eyebrows pulled into a thoughtful scowl.

"You got something?"

"Not much," she said. "Finally caught up with the bartender who was working the late shift at Lizards, the place Shelly was last seen. That would be Lizards as in Lounge Lizards, according to the cheap advertisement on the Internet."

"And?"

"She was pretty drunk," Harding told him. "The guy she was with kept buying her drinks to celebrate her birthday."

"A friend?"

"Some dude. Maybe a pickup. The bartender wasn't sure. He remembered the guy, though. Mid- to late thirties, good-looking, dark hair, medium length. Caucasian, but with dark skin. Couldn't remember the eye color or any distinguishing characteristics, other than he seemed pretty interested in Shelly, and the bartender was surprised they didn't leave together. A lot of flirting going on."

"I don't suppose this guy paid with a credit card."

She smiled, showing off the hint of teeth that weren't quite straight, as her incisors flared slightly. "We're not gonna get that lucky."

"Suppose not."

"Besides, we think it's a suicide, right?" Harding prodded.

"Yeah." He said it without a lot of conviction. He figured he would check into the last few days of Shelly Bonaventure's life and delve into all her relationships. He was also interested as to whom would benefit from her death. There was talk of her being up for a part in a new television series and a rumor of her nearly inking a deal for a tell-all book. First, though, he'd start with the last person to see her alive.

"So, you're buying the accidental overdose?" Harding asked, eyes narrowing, and when he didn't respond, she nodded, as if agreeing with herself and a foregone conclusion. "You're still thinking homicide."

"I don't know what to think. Not yet," he admitted. "I'm just not ruling anything out. Let's go talk to the bartender, face-to-face. Maybe we can jog his memory about our mystery man."

"You're the boss," she said, and there was just an edge of sarcasm to her voice.

"That's right," he teased her, grabbing his jacket off a hook near his desk. He slipped his Glock into its shoulder holster. "Just don't forget it."

"How could I when you remind me of it every day?"

"No reason to cop an attitude."

"Huh," she said. "Let's go."

His footsteps creaked on the old stairs as he slowly descended to the basement, located under the garage end of the house, which had been built before the turn of the century. The last century.

Cool and airtight, once used for stacked wood and a wood-burning furnace, now its purpose was primarily storage. Crates, old furniture, broken lamps, canning jars, and pictures from bygone eras collected dust.

No one ever ventured down here.

Except for him.

And only when he was alone.

Cobwebs dangled from the exposed beams of the floor above, where the old John Deere sat parked, as it had for the better part of a decade. He ignored the scrape of tiny claws against the bricks of the floor. Let the mice and rats and squirrels, or whatever rodents chose to live down here, be. A rattler or two wouldn't be bad, either. Anything to insure that he wasn't bothered.

He walked past bins of rusted tools to his private room, the old chamber once used for root vegetables and apples to winter over. His great-grandmother's old milk separator, a device that hadn't been used in fifty years, still stood guard at the heavy, padlocked door, and there was rust on the walls where pipes had once brought water to and from a wringer washer that had occupied a space in the corner. He had to duck to keep from hanging himself on the lines where once upon a time, long, long ago, sheets had been draped to dry in the winter.

Unlocking the padlock, he pulled open the old door his great-great-grandfather had built before refrigeration. The door was nearly a foot wide and filled with sawdust. When the door was sealed shut, any sounds from within were completely muted.

Once inside, he snapped on the fluorescent lights and locked the door behind him. The room was instantly awash in the unsteady bluish illumination, and it was as if he'd been propelled forward in time by a century and a half. Stainless-steel counters gleamed against three walls; a computer center complete with wireless modem, twenty-five-inch monitor, and all the technology to keep his private business safe and secure filled one corner.

An oversized map of North America stretched over a bulletin board that filled one long wall. It was a political map, showing state lines, cities, and roads. Scattered across its flat surface were red pushpins. Thirty-seven in all. Each indicating the spot where one of the pretenders lived. Like spatters of blood marring the smooth surface of the map, the pins reminded him of how much work he had to do and soon.

They were a worry, those pins, a serious worry.

There were far too many of them, he thought. There were a few other pins as well, ones with black heads, indicating death. Those pins affixed photographs to the map, though the pictures were turned facedown, showing only white squares of paper with dates of birth and death written in solid black letters. There were six of these in all, scattered across the United States.

But he was making progress—steady progress. It was slow going because he could rely on no one but himself; he'd learned that lesson the hard way.

Smiling to himself, he removed a red pin from the Southern California area, then walked to his printer, where a digital picture had already been printed. Shelly Bonaventure's frightened face stared back at him, and he grinned again, satisfied by the look of pure terror on her countenance. She'd known at that moment that she was about to die. He'd snapped the shot with his cell phone just before exiting the back door of her apartment, then sent it wirelessly here.

He'd taken too much time with her; he'd heard the sound of sirens fast approaching as he'd let himself out and dashed across the street.

But he'd managed to get away.

Again.

Using the scissors he kept in a drawer, he cut the small picture from the paper, trimming away the excess, then carefully placing her date of birth and death on the back of her picture before pinning it, facedown, with a black pushpin. No longer could he see the small Photoshopped head shot she'd used as her publicity picture.

Perfect.

He surveyed his work, noting the others that had died before Shelly, and the raft of faces of those still alive, those waiting to serve out their sentence. They were in their own ways striking, all between the ages of twenty-eight and thirty-six. Mostly brunettes, though there were a few bottle blondes in the group and a couple of redheads.

The pictures were clustered mainly in the Northwest. Two in British Columbia, both near Vancouver Island, one in Alberta, several in Washington State, a slew in Oregon, and some scattered in California. Three in Nevada, two in Arizona, and a handful in Montana. One lived as far away as Delaware, and there were six in the Midwest. Three in Chicago.

The ones who lived within the same district or state worried him as the deaths could be considered suspicious if he wasn't careful.

Shelly's "suicide" was a risk. The others, so far, appeared to have died in accidents, no questions asked.

All of which was perfect.

Meticulously orchestrated.

But there were so many more.

He glared at the cluster of pins that swarmed around Missoula and Grizzly Falls. Access to each of those pretenders would be easy as they were nearby.

But when so many people in their late twenties and early thirties ended up dead, the authorities would take note.

Unless there was a huge catastrophe and they all died together, along with others, of course, to throw off suspicion. And he'd have to either distance himself from the tragedy or, more likely, be a part of it and escape, not entirely unharmed.

That would be tricky; but it caused his blood to sizzle a bit as he thought how clever he was. He'd baffle the police and turn out a hero and be revered . . . but no! He had to blend into the woodwork, couldn't afford to have any kind of light shined upon him, couldn't allow some idiot member of the press to start digging. . . .

He walked to a file drawer and pulled it open. Inside were neat folders, information gathered over time on each of the pretenders. Some were thick, others slim, but it didn't matter.

He opened the first one, and his gut twisted as he glared at the picture tucked within his notes.

Dr. Acacia Lambert.

She was special. A small town girl from Montana with enough brains to send herself to college and medical school. Married briefly to Jeffrey Lambert, a heart surgeon who still worked and resided in Seattle, Washington.

Until the mistake.

When he'd gotten too bloodthirsty, too hungry, too eager to destroy the one person who could ruin everything.

And the job had been botched.

Kacey had lived.

Her marriage had fallen apart, though, and after the breakup Kacey decided to become a small-town doctor in the same town where her grandparents had resided all their lives.

Touching.

And perfect.

After escaping his original plan, she'd nearly fallen right into his waiting hands.

This time, there wouldn't be a mistake; this time he'd take care of her for good.

A slow-burning fury ran through his veins as he studied her picture. His jaw tightened as he noticed her thick red-brown hair, high cheekbones, full lips, and green eyes, which seemed to spark with intelligence, even in the small snapshot.

He'd watched her.

Followed her.

Learned her routine.

She lived in her grandparents' old home just outside of town. The house was hidden from the road, down a long, tree-lined lane, which would make things a lot easier. . . .

But she would have to wait.

Unfortunately, there were others he had to deal with first.

And when he dealt with Kacey, he intended to take his time, to make certain she realized her sins.

He flipped open a few more files and sorted them. None of the people he was surveilling realized that he was watching them, collecting all the ones that were in close proximity to Kacey.

He wondered if any of them had run across each other.

If so, they hadn't guessed the one thing they had in common.

Each was born to die long before her time.

And it was his mission to make it happen.

CHAPTER 2

"Your son or daughter did not attend one or more classes today. . . ."

Detective Regan Pescoli felt her blood boil as she listened to the dreaded prerecorded message from the high school where Bianca was supposed to have attended class. "Well, why the hell not?" she whispered aloud and clicked off her cell. She'd dropped her kid off at school herself, and Bianca was too young to drive.

Dialing Bianca's cell, Regan was put through to voice mail. Of course. Neither of her kids ever picked up. She texted: **Where are you? The school called and said you were a no-show. Call me!**

"Great," she muttered, sliding her chair away from her desk at the Pinewood County Sheriff's Department. She glanced at her watch as she walked to Selena Alvarez's cubicle, where her partner was huddled over her desk, her telephone cradled between her ear and shoulder as she sorted through neat stacks of paper on the desk. Alvarez's black hair was scraped into a thick knot at the base of her skull and shining blue under the overhead lights.

Glancing up, she held up a finger as Pescoli approached.

"Yeah, I know, but we've been waiting for those test results for a couple of weeks now," she said, her voice tight, her lips twisted into a frown. If there was one thing Alvarez couldn't stand, it was incompetence. "Uh-huh . . . yeah, well, we're all shorthanded. I get it. . . . What? If that's the best you can do . . . okay . . . Tomorrow's fine." She hung up, fuming. "What do you bet that tomorrow comes and I still don't know what was in Donna McKinley's bloodstream?" She leaned back in her desk chair and scowled at her computer monitor, where the picture of the woman in question was visible. "I'd just like to get this off my desk, y'know."

Pescoli did know. They both wanted to be assured that Donna McKinley's death was a stupid accident, that she'd fallen asleep at the wheel and run off the road. That her death was not the result of something nefarious by her ex-con of a boyfriend, Barclay Simms, who just happened to take out a hundred-thousand-dollar life insurance policy on Donna three weeks earlier. This while he was collecting unemployment.

Alvarez sighed loudly. "Sorry."

"No problem. Just letting you know that I'm outta here. Gotta track down my kid."

"She skip school?"

"Looks like," Pescoli said with a shake of her head. Until a year ago, Bianca had been an A student, always on the honor roll, proud of being "the good one," as she'd referred to herself often enough, until her grades had started slipping the year before, in junior high. She'd promised to work harder again in high school, "when it really counted." So far, she wasn't keeping to her word.

"I've got things covered here," Alvarez said, which was true enough. A serious workaholic, she rarely clocked in during normal work hours. Alvarez was single and dedicated, and it appeared to Pescoli as if the younger woman had no social life whatsoever, which was a shame. But today she didn't have time to think about it.

"I owe ya one."

Alvarez snorted. "I'll remember that."

Along with about a hundred other times, Pescoli thought as she found her jacket, scarf, and hat, then hurried out the back and past the lunchroom, where Joelle Fischer was opening boxes filled with all kinds of holiday decorations. Silver stars, glittering tinsel, fake candy canes, and strings of lights, even a slightly salacious-looking Santa, which had, year after year, given Pescoli a case of the creeps, were being placed on empty tabletops as Joelle plotted where to put up her "little bit of Christmas" around the department. Why Sheriff Dan Grayson put up with her nonsense, Pescoli had no idea. But Joelle, forever bubbly with her short blond hair, oversized earrings, and three-inch heels, never seemed to notice that the rest of the de-

partment didn't get into the spirit of the holidays with the same fervor and sense of enthusiasm as she did.

"Regan! Hey!" Joelle called, clipping after her to stand in the doorway to the hall. She was already wearing a Rudolph broach with a blinking red nose. "You know we're having the drawing for the Secret Santa on Monday morning?"

"And you know that it's not Christmas for nearly six weeks."

"It sneaks up on you," she said solemnly. "Next Thursday is Thanksgiving, and why not celebrate the season for as long as possible?"

"Count me out for Christmas in July."

"Don't be such a crank!" She pretended to frown, but the edges of her Kewpie-doll lips twitched. "You'll be here at eight, then? Monday?"

"With frickin' bells on," Pescoli muttered. She couldn't really get into the spirit when she didn't know where her daughter was.

"Make sure they're jingle bells!" Joelle tittered at her own joke and gratefully returned to the lunchroom and her decorating.

Insane, Pescoli thought as she pushed open the doors and strode along a path that intersected the brittle grass. If the clumps of snow didn't remind her that it was already winter in western Montana, the icy wind that rattled the chain on the flagpole certainly did.

She found her Jeep, slid inside, and didn't search for the pack of "emergency" Marlboro Lights she kept in her glove box. She'd officially given up the habit last January, after a homicidal maniac had nearly killed her, but once in a while, when things got too hard to deal with, she'd sneak a cigarette. And she told herself she wasn't going to feel guilty about it.

She didn't think her kid cutting class was enough of an emergency to break down, but the day wasn't over yet. Maybe Bianca had gotten herself into more trouble. Closing her mind to the horror she often saw in her work, victims of horrendous accidents, furious husbands, or out-and-out psychos, she threw the rig into reverse and somehow avoided Cort Brewster, the undersheriff, as he wheeled in. Brewster and she weren't exactly cool with each other, never had been, and when their kids had been hanging out, her son, Jeremy, had been blamed for every bit of trouble that Brewster's perfect little princess, Heidi, had gotten into.

"Perfect, my ass," Pescoli said under her breath, not giving Brewster so much as a nod as she pulled out of the lot. In Pescoli's opinion the guy was a supercilious hypocrite, and she prayed under her breath that she didn't pull his name out of the hat when Joelle hosted her ridiculous Secret Santa drawing in the morning. No way could Pescoli stomach buying him little gifts and hiding them around his desk or in his vehicle.

What was that tired Valley Girl saying? Gag me with a spoon? Well, in this case, she thought, it was gag me with a damned shovel.

Deciding she was being petty, she turned her attention to the traffic and, using her Bluetooth, tried to call her daughter again. Sure enough, voice mail picked up. "Come on, Bianca, answer," she muttered.

Night was falling fast.

She called the house, as they still had a landline. It rang four times before being answered. "Hullo?" her son said without a drip of emotion, and Pescoli, slowing for a red light, felt a moment's relief. Although why Jeremy, who'd moved out over the summer, was at the house was a bit of a question, one for which she didn't have time. Not yet.

"It's Mom. Is Bianca there?"

"Yeah."

Thank God! "She okay?"

"Uh . . . yeah, I guess."

"Put her on the phone."

"She's sleeping."

"I don't care."

"Jesus! You don't have to yell."

"And you don't have to curse."

"Fine."

As the traffic light turned green and she drove along Boxer Bluff, where the uppermost part of Grizzly Falls was sprawled, she heard a series of muffled voices and finally her daughter's sleepy "Yeah?"

"What's up?" Pescoli demanded.

"Me, now," Bianca grumbled.

"The school called and said you missed class."

"I didn't feel good."

"Well," Pescoli automatically corrected as she turned onto the street winding out of the town. "You didn't feel *well.*"

"Whatever."

"How'd you get home?"

"Chris."

The on-again, off-again boyfriend. "He doesn't have a license."

"We were with his brother, Gene."

The seventeen-year-old who already had been involved in a wreck. Pescoli knew all about that one, she'd seen what was left of the 1990 Honda Accord after it had hit a mailbox, then a tree. It was a wonder the kid had survived, let alone got away with only a broken collarbone and a few scratches. "Look, I'm on my way home. We'll talk then." Checking her mirrors, she changed lanes to avoid a work crew that had dug up the street.

"I already 'talked' with Dad."

More good news. "And what did your father say?" she asked through gritted teeth. Luke "Lucky" Pescoli was hardly the epitome of parenthood.

"To get some rest."

Perfect. "I'll be there in fifteen. Now put your brother on the phone."

"Your turn." Bianca's voice was a singsong reprimand as she obviously gladly turned the receiver back to Jeremy.

Again, Pescoli considered lighting up but thought better of it as the storefronts lining the street gave way to homes.

"Uh-huh?" Jeremy said as his way of greeting.

"Just wondering, what are you doing at the house?" When he'd moved out of her small place, little more than a cabin in the woods and the only home he'd ever known, this past summer, his leaving had been a blessing as well as a curse.

"Uh . . . 'cuz it's home."

"You moved out. I didn't want you to, but you insisted last summer," she reminded him. "I thought you'd be at work."

"They turned off the gas at my place. There's no heat. Guess they, um, didn't get the check in time. But that's bogus, 'cuz I mailed it yesterday. It's not my fault that one of my roommates didn't get the money to me."

"And your job?" she asked with extreme patience.

Hesitation. "Lou didn't need me at the station today."

"Is that right?" Jeremy had been pumping gas at Corky's Gas and Go for nearly nine months, while he "decided" if he wanted to go to school. "Jer?" she said when he didn't immediately answer. "Just tell me you didn't lose your job."

"Okay. I won't." He was defensive. Short.

Damn it all to hell. If only Joe were still alive. Jeremy's father, another cop, had been great in a crisis. That is, until he was killed in the line of duty when his son was too young to really remember his father. So Pescoli had become mother and father to her boy, until she'd made the mistake of marrying Luke, who had tried to step in and had only made a worse mess of things.

"Wait for me. I'll be home soon. And before I get there, would you please make sure Cisco's had his dinner?"

"We're outta dog food."

"Then get some."

"I, uh, don't have any money."

"Fabulous."

"I gotta go. Heidi's texting me."

"Jeremy! Wait—" But the phone was suddenly dead in her hand. She hadn't even had a chance to warn him off Heidi Brewster again. God, she'd hoped *that* teen romance had died a quick death last year.

Looked like her prayers hadn't been answered.

But then, that wasn't a big surprise.

Maybe she'd made a mistake by not moving in with her boyfriend, but she hadn't thought it would be wise. Just because a man could turn her inside out in the bedroom was no reason to bring him home and slap the name tag STEPFATHER on him. As much as she thought she was in love with him, she'd decided not to go to that next level. Yet.

There was a good chance she was a commitment-o-phobe, or whatever you wanted to call it, but she'd been married twice and that might just be enough.

For a while.

Until her kids were raised.

Or until she was more comfortable with the situation.

You might lose him, that nagging inner voice warned, and she scoffed. Then it wasn't meant to be.

She stopped at a small convenience store at the next crossroads, bought a small bag of dog food, a gallon of milk, and two Snickers candy bars to stuff into her glove box, along with the pack of Marlboros.

Just in case.

Then she hit the road again.

Twenty minutes later she was walking through the door from the garage of her little cottage. Cisco, her terrier of undeterminable lineage, shot off the couch, sped across the living room floor, and yapping excitedly, began doing pirouettes at her feet.

"Hey, I'm glad to see you, too." After placing her groceries on the counter, she leaned over, patted Cisco's scruffy head, scratched his ears, then straightened and walked through the dining area to the living room, where all six feet two inches of her son were sprawled, his feet hanging over the end of her couch. "I'm not so sure I can say the same about you."

"Nice, Mom," he said, not bothering to glance up as he stared at the television, where some reality show was playing out.

"Tell me about work."

"Nothin' much to tell."

God, he looked like his father. Dark hair, intense eyes, sharp cheekbones, and two days' worth of beard stubble darkening a hard, masculine jaw, a darker spot on his chin, where he'd managed to grow a soul patch. "Did you get fired?"

He finally looked up, glaring at her as if she were an idiot. "Just got my hours cut back, that's all."

"That'll make it tough paying the rent or the gas bill."

He lifted a shoulder. She wanted to spell it all out to him, about the consequences of his slacker lifestyle, but Jeremy had always been a kid who learned by experience rather than example. The cutting off of the gas and the cost of reconnecting would be a good object lesson.

She patted him on the shoulder. "I *am* glad to see you, you know. I just wish it was that you came over to see me, rather than because you were freezing your butt off at your apartment."

"Yeah," he said finally. "I know."

"I'm going to check on your sister." Another pat. "Could you please feed Cisco? There's dog food in the grocery sack."

"Yeah." He didn't move.

"I'm talking about in this century."

"Very funny," he said. But he did manage a slow grin, and it was a heart-stopper. Again, just like his father. No wonder Heidi Brewster hadn't shaken loose.

Jeremy actually climbed to his feet and said, "Come on, runt," to the dog as Pescoli made her way down the short hallway and rapped on Bianca's door before stepping inside the mess. Whereas Jeremy's old bedroom downstairs had posters of basketball players and rock bands, Bianca's room was a study in all things girl, from a canopy bed that she'd decorated with Christmas lights to a makeup desk and lighted mirror, where at least ten brushes of varying sizes stood in a jar next to baskets of lipstick, eye shadow, and God only knew what else. The walls were a shocking pink, a color she loved.

Bianca was curled on the bed, a silvery duvet tucked around her, a Pepsi One bottle on her nightstand, next to a pile of teen and fashion magazines that had spilled onto the bed beside her. While her laptop was playing some movie, she was texting on her cell phone.

"So what happened?" Pescoli asked as her daughter glanced up from her cell phone to offer a quick, aren't-I-just-so-cute smile. Red-blond curls framed a face where freckles were barely visible across the bridge of her small nose and large hazel eyes. While her brother was the spitting image of Joe Strand, Bianca resembled her own father, Luke Pescoli. Fortunately—well, at least up until recently—Bianca seemed a lot smarter than her father.

Time would tell on that one.

"What do you mean?" Bianca asked innocently.

"Don't play dumb. You know what I'm talking about. Why did you cut class? If you were sick, you could have gone to the office and they would have called me."

Bianca rolled her eyes. "You can't always come, because of your job. And Chris said he'd give me a ride."

"You mean his brother, Gene, did."

"Does it matter?"

"Yeah. Big-time. Chris doesn't have a license, and it's a miracle that his brother still does." Her eyes narrowed. "Maybe he doesn't."

Bianca avoided her gaze. Not answering. Which was telling.

"Come on, Bianca, be smarter than this. If Gene Schultz had gotten into another accident or—"

"He didn't, okay?" Bianca snapped.

Pescoli pushed some of the magazines to one side and sat near the foot of her bed. "You can't cut class."

"Jer did it all the time."

"Case in point." She shook her head. "His options now are limited. Don't make that mistake." Seeing that this was getting her nowhere, she said, "So, why did you come home?"

Bianca sighed. "I was just tired."

"That's not an excuse to—"

"And I felt weird. I don't know. Like maybe I was getting the flu. Kara White and Shannon Anderssen both have it, and I think Monty Elvstead, and they're all in my Spanish class. So I came home. Big deal." She glared at her mother. "I couldn't call you. You're always working, and I wasn't going to, like, sit in that outer room and have weird Mrs. Compton, the vice principal, look at me all day."

"Isn't there a health room?"

"That's worse. It's . . . gross! I just wanted to come home. Geez. It's not as if it's against the law or anything."

"Have you taken your temp?"

"No. And I'm not going to!"

"So what is it? Stomachache? Cramps? Sore throat?"

"All of the above, okay!" She burrowed deeper into her duvet, and the rest of the magazines slid to the floor. "Can't you just leave me alone?"

"Not for a few more years. You're kinda my job."

"Seriously? That's what I am? Geez, Mom, you're so . . ." The rest of the diatribe was thankfully muffled as Bianca flung an edge of the blanket over her head. One slim arm snaked from beneath the covers; her hand patted the bed, but before her fingers connected with her phone, Pescoli grabbed the cell.

"You won't need this," she said, pocketing the cell as she reached down to pick up the slick tabloids that had scattered onto the worn shag carpet.

The top magazine caught her attention with the headline SHELLY BONAVENTURE'S DEATH RULED SUICIDE. Beneath the bold letters was a picture of a pretty woman with a wide smile and eyes that glinted mischievously. Her skin was clear; her hair a tangled mass of auburn curls. As if she had the world by the damned tail.

Instead, Shelly Bonaventure, an actress Pescoli now remembered as having been on that vampire series Bianca had been hooked on a few years back, had become another statistic, yet one more senseless death in Hollywood.

Looked like things were bad all over.

Tucking the magazine under her arm, she walked out of the room and left her daughter sulking under her covers.

CHAPTER 3

Jocelyn Wallis felt like crap as she eyed the dark sky through her window. It wasn't snowing . . . yet, but a storm had been predicted, and there were patches of ice and snow on the roads and parking lot of her apartment complex. The temperature was below freezing, and it was only expected to drop.

If she didn't take her run now, she decided, peering through the blinds, she might not get a chance in the next couple of days.

And Thanksgiving was next week; she was certain to pig out at her aunt's house, so she should exercise in anticipation of the feast.

Besides, it wasn't going to stay light for long; already the street-lamps outside the apartment building that she called home were starting to glow.

As a schoolteacher, she didn't have a lot of daylight in the dead of winter, so she was confined to the treadmill during the week and jog-ging outside on the weekend, when the weather allowed.

Maybe she should forget it. She'd just felt so crummy the past few days. Not quite the flu, but her energy was low, and she found herself kind of zonking out.

Finishing a cup of leftover coffee from her morning batch, she threw the last swallow down the sink, checked her watch, frowned, then gave herself a quick mental kick and nearly knocked over the cat's water dish in the process. That cat, her pet, was a stray that had shown up four weeks ago and had been MIA for the past two days. Jocelyn had looked for her, worried, and had called the local shel-ters, to no avail. When she got back from her run, she'd find Kitty, come hell or high water. Maybe she'd even come up with a name for her.

Pushing thoughts of her missing cat aside, Jocelyn walked quickly to the second bedroom, which basically collected the overflow from the rest of the living area. Books and discarded clothes were piled on her ironing board, an old television set was propped on the dresser she'd had since she was ten, bags of clothes that no longer fit were piled in one corner, ready to be donated to the church thrift store, and even a few Christmas presents that she'd bought at a school bazaar had been labeled and tossed onto the twin bed she used for guests.

And who are those guests?

The truth was, ever since she'd moved back to Grizzly Falls two years earlier, after her second divorce, no one had stayed with her.

"Pathetic," she told herself.

In one corner was her "office," where her computer and printer were tucked on an old desk, and where she kept her personal files. The closet was filled with clothes she hoped to wear again, once she slimmed down, and paperwork for art, science, and math projects for the coming school year.

Quickly, before she changed her mind, or the storm broke and changed it for her, Jocelyn slipped out of her jeans and sweater and into jogging pants, shirt, and fleece jacket. She scraped her hair into a ponytail, snapped it into a rubber band, pulled on a baseball cap, and tucked her feet into her favorite pair of Nikes. She took another cursory glance around the apartment for her cell phone but didn't see it; the damned thing had been missing since last night.

She hated to leave without it but didn't have much of a choice. Not if she was going to get in the exercise she'd promised herself.

"Tough," she muttered under her breath.

Then she was out the front door, where she took a few minutes to stretch on her small porch and push the earbuds of her iPod into her ears and select a playlist of dance songs.

Now or never!

She took off, the bottoms of her shoes slapping time to "Bad Romance" by Lady Gaga, her arms pumping as she accelerated to a comfortable speed as the first flakes of snow began to fall.

At the entrance to the apartment complex, she turned south,

starting along the same route she usually jogged. She could make her course either two miles or three, depending upon where she turned back. Today, she vowed to herself, she'd go the entire three-point-one miles. Maybe if she got her blood moving fast enough, she could shake the feeling that she might be coming down with the damned flu, which was making the rounds at Evergreen Elementary, where she worked.

She was getting into her rhythm, the music pounding in her ears, her breathing regular as she jogged through the puddles of slush and avoided the few cars and trucks that were moving along the roadway. A dark blue pickup trailed after her for a few blocks, not passing, and she glanced over at the driver as he finally pulled around her. They didn't make eye contact; he was too busy fiddling with his CD player or phone or something that kept his attention away from the road.

Idiot, she thought as he finally passed her, taking a corner three blocks down, his taillights glowing red until they disappeared.

Adjusting the volume of her iPod, she concentrated on the course. She still felt low. Maybe it was the flu. It was certainly that time of year, and a grade school was a great breeding ground for all things contagious.

Or her malaise could be the result of overindulging in her favorite junk foods. She had been on a real bender this weekend and had devoured nachos, pizza, and two pints of ice cream, one of mint chocolate chip, and one of jingle-berry ribbon, in honor of the holidays.

Stupid.

She was thirty-five and had put on ten pounds in the past four years, ever since transferring to Evergreen Elementary, where the fourth graders she taught were difficult and the parents . . . Well, she didn't want to think about them. Talk about overbearing! Half of them acted like she didn't know her job; the other 50 percent didn't seem to care what their kid did in school. Their attitude was they didn't want to be bothered.

Sometimes she wondered why she stuck with it.

Because you love the kids.

Because you feel like you're making a difference.

Because you like the paycheck and benefits.

And because you really like having most of the summer and two weeks at Christmas off!

Then why did she have to keep reminding herself? she wondered as she passed a laurel hedge in serious need of trimming. She looked over her shoulder before crossing the street.

She thought she saw the same dark pickup creeping up behind her, and she went instantly on alert as she was completely alone and the apartments and houses had dwindled a little as she'd reached the outskirts of town.

But the truck turned down a side street, and she breathed a sigh of relief.

Don't let your imagination get the better of you.

Still, she couldn't help but feel a little anxious, her nerves strung more tightly than normal. Darkness was settling more quickly than she'd expected, the winter air stark and cold, trees shivering, their naked branches rattling over the steady beat of a Black Eyed Peas song.

Concentrate on your breathing.

She glanced over her shoulder again. The truck was nowhere in sight, and the snow was really coming down.

Good!

She was already breathing hard and blamed her lack of breath on cigarettes. She had quit twice before but had taken up the habit again after the breakup with Trace O'Halleran a little over six months ago. Her blood still boiled when she thought of the sexy cowboy and how she'd pinned her hopes on him, even though they'd dated such a short period. Tall and rangy, with wide shoulders and a slow smile that showed off just the hint of a dimple when he was really amused, the rancher had gotten to her. In a big way. He was a single father of one of her students last year, and she'd zeroed in on him on Back-to-School Night.

And it had been a mistake. Of course. She should never have gotten involved with him. When it came to men, she always jumped in feet first, without really thinking. Didn't she have the divorce papers to prove it?

Another stab at romance with Trace not long ago had ended up badly, and she still blushed when she remembered her attempts at seduction and his rebuke. God, if she thought about it, she could feel his big hands over her wrists as he pushed her against the wall and, instead of kissing her, said, "Enough. It's over. This was a really bad idea," before releasing her abruptly and walking out her door.

She had slammed it behind him and could still hear the hollow thud reverberate in her mind.

Live and learn, she thought sourly before checking the street and turning up the hill that was the toughest part of her route. It was worth it, she told herself, because at the crest she was able to run along the cliff that overlooked the river and the falls, the most picturesque point of her run, though her mind was still on Trace. She wondered, now that she wasn't Eli's teacher any longer, if there was a chance she could rekindle the relationship.

Maybe she could take him over something she'd baked for Christmas. Cookies? No, that was too corny. A bottle of wine with a Christmas label? Again, he'd see right through it.

Hadn't she tried the "let's be friends" routine and had it blow up in her face? How many times had she called him since they broke up? Three times? Four? Eight? *Stupid, stupid, stupid!* And really, they hadn't exactly broken up, just like they hadn't exactly ever been in a relationship, no matter what she'd ridiculously put up on Facebook after two dates. That was what too much wine and listening to friends who were even drunker than you were got you.

Havoc.

Trace, when he'd learned of it through his son, no less, hadn't been happy, and that had been the beginning of the end. She should never have called him and now winced when she realized she'd dialed his number the night before, then hung up just as his voice mail had answered.

Just be smart and get over him. There are other men out there, even in Grizzly Falls.

She checked the street and crossed to the other side so that she could run along the bluff overlooking the river before the trail opened up to a park where she could take a U-turn and start back.

Three cars passed, beams from their headlights shimmering on the wet road, tires splashing up dirty water. Gritting her teeth, she kept at it, breathing with more difficulty as she veered into the park with its series of hiking trails. *Just a little farther,* she told herself. She was really breathing hard now, and her calves were beginning to cramp.

Finally, the ground leveled off, and she ran along an asphalt trail along the bluff that overlooked the river's chasm. A short stone rail, less than two feet tall, had been built over a hundred-some years earlier and allowed a view of the ravine where the river swept over the falls of the town nearly two hundred feet below. The older section of Grizzly Falls was strung along the river's banks just below the falls, streetlights glowing like iridescent jewels in the gathering gloom.

Dragging her eyes back to the path before her, Jocelyn followed the bluff until the path forked, and she veered toward the interior of the park, away from the street. Sweating despite the wintry air, she headed toward the lone hemlock that she always circled before returning on the same path.

Her breath was fogging the air now; her blood pumping crazily.

Almost there!

She was alone; no one else was nutty or obsessive enough to be out in this weather. God, it was cold. Despite her gloves, her fingers were numb.

Around a final bend, she spied a massive tree rising darkly to the stygian heavens.

She slowed a bit, gasping from the exertion and removing her earbuds for a second. Leaning forward, she braced her hands on her knees. She usually didn't stop midway, but tonight she needed a quick breather.

Over the sound of her labored breathing and the rapid tattoo of her heart, she heard the sound of the river and the moan of the wind. She was fiddling with her iPod when she heard another noise . . . footsteps? Was someone else out jogging?

Her head snapped up.

Not a big deal, and yet she was wary. Careful.

Probably just another dedicated runner.

Maybe you aren't the only idiot out tonight.

She plugged in one earbud and took off again, listening to a Beyoncé number with one ear and the sounds of the coming night with the other.

Just to be certain she was okay.

The wind was chasing down the river's canyon, cold as ever, and she thought she heard an owl hoot, welcoming the gloaming, then, again, the regular smack of feet on pavement behind her.

Yep, another jogger.

And a fast one, from the sounds of it.

She glanced over her shoulder, saw no one, and picked up her pace. It was time to go home, stand under a warm shower, and try to feel better. There were still three more days of school before the holiday—

The footsteps were closer now.

Clipping along. Rapidly.

Again, she turned her head.

The path behind her was empty.

The hairs on the back of her neck prickled.

It's just your imagination, Jocelyn. Nothing sinister.

Ignoring the burning in her lungs and the cramping in her calves, she kicked into a sprint, running quickly through the trees. It was dark now, only a few lamps offering any kind of illumination, the trees with their black trunks stark as they rose from the winter-bleached grass, a blur.

Don't freak out. There's no reason to freak out. Even though you don't have your phone with you, it's nothing to worry about.

She was really sweating now.

The main road rimming the bluff was close, just around the next corner—

"Oh!"

She caught a glimpse of the other jogger, a tall, athletic man dressed head to toe in black running gear and a ski mask.

Her heart clutched.

Nothing to worry about. Let him pass.

Adrenaline sped through her bloodstream. She kicked her pace up a notch, to a full-blown run, her feet slapping the path faster and faster, her breath hard.

It's all right. It's all right. It's all right. . . .

But was it?

He was closing quickly.

Panic swept through her.

He was close enough that she could hear his breathing. Strong. Steady—

The toe of her running shoe caught, and she stumbled forward, arms flying. She managed to catch herself before she went down and somehow kept her balance, though her stride was off.

"Careful," a deep voice said from behind.

Oh, God! He was only two steps away.

She set her jaw. Told herself to be calm.

Did his voice sound familiar?

Her heart raced crazily.

Out of the park she ran. Onto the path edging the bluff. She'd hoped that he would turn the opposite direction, but he was just a step behind her, heading for the downhill run. Maybe she should just stop and let him breeze by.

If only she had her damned phone.

Or the canister of pepper spray she kept in her purse.

"On your right," he said, catching up with her, matching her pace stride for stride. Now was the time to pull back. "Enjoying yourself, Josie?" he asked.

Josie? She nearly tripped again. He knew her? Oh, God, why was his voice familiar?

"You should be careful, y'know." His shoulder bumped against hers.

She lost her footing and was starting to go down when he suddenly caught her, the fingers of one strong hand circling her upper arm.

"I *told* you to be careful!" he declared, his grip tight, painful.

"Let go of me! Who are you?" she demanded as they both stopped. Behind his ski mask he was breathing loudly.

"Don't you know?" His fingers grew punishing.

"Who you are? No! I said, let go of . . . Hey!" He jerked hard on her arm. "What're you doing?" But she knew. In one heart-stopping second, she realized he meant to kill her! "Let go of me!" Her feet slipped out from under her as he pushed, and before she realized what was happening, he propelled her to the side of the cliff and the short stone railing. "Don't! Oh, God, Help me! *Help!*" She was scrambling now, certain of the son of a bitch's intent.

Oh, God, no! No!

Frantic, she flailed, trying to keep her balance as he shoved her sharply against the stone rail, cracking her shins.

Pain screamed up her legs.

"No!" She fought, but it was no use. He pushed hard, and her weight forced her over the guardrail. To her horror, arms windmilling, she went sailing into the growing darkness. Screaming, she tumbled through the air to land hard against the frozen hillside.

Crack!

Her head banged against a rock, and the world spun as she slid and bounced, twisting and rolling, trying to grab on to anything, her fingers scraping over dirt, roots, and rocks as she slid down the cliff face.

Please, God, help me—

Pain ricocheted up her spine, and somewhere in the distance she heard the roar of rushing water. Closer as she rolled, faster and faster, out of control, her skin bleeding, the world spinning.

But far above she caught a glimpse of him standing high above her, a black figure in the night, looking down.

Waiting.

For her to die.

CHAPTER 4

Trace O'Halleran was pissed.

In fact, he was pissed as hell as he drove ten miles over the speed limit from Evergreen Elementary School, where he'd picked up his kid. Now they were on their way to the clinic for X-rays as Eli had been hurt on the playground.

Someone hadn't been watching his boy, and once Trace was assured that Eli was all right, that *someone* had some serious explaining to do!

"Hang in there, buddy," he said to his son, who was seated beside him in his battered old pickup.

Eli nodded and sniffed, either fighting tears or a nasty cold that had been hanging on for about a week.

Squinting through the windshield as the first flakes of snow swirled to the ground, Trace followed the steady stream of traffic that drove down the hillside known as Boxer Bluff to the section of town spread upon the banks of the Grizzly River.

Eli, all of seven, cradled his left arm, which was already in a splint and a sling compliments of an overworked school nurse, whose advice was, "He needs to see a doctor. I've already called the clinic on A Street, so you shouldn't have to wait, like you might at Pinewood Community or St. Bartholomew's. Have the arm x-rayed. I don't think it's broken, but there could be a hairline fracture. The clinic has a lab. While you're there, you might have the doctor check his ears and throat. I ran his temp, and he's got a bit of a fever—a hundred and one."

Trace hadn't argued against driving to the hospital. Once, he'd sat in the emergency room at St. Bart's for five hours before anyone could look at his mangled hand, the result of his wedding ring getting caught on a cog of his combine machine when he'd been harvesting wheat. The combination harvester and thresher had nearly torn his arm off before he'd been able to shut it down. Even after saving his arm, he'd almost had to have his ring finger amputated. In the end his finger had been saved, but the nerve damage had been severe enough that he'd lost any feeling in that finger. He'd decided then and there he'd never wear the wedding band again. It hadn't really mattered, anyway. Leanna, Eli's mother, had already had one foot out the door.

No, Trace didn't want his kid to sit on the uncomfortable plastic chairs of the waiting room at St. Bartholomew Hospital, if he could avoid it. They'd start with the clinic, the same damned low-slung building that had been servicing patients for nearly seventy years. Of course, over its life span, the building housing the clinic had been remodeled several times.

Trace's own father had taken him to the place nearly thirty years earlier, after he'd been bucked off Rocky, the spirited bay gelding that his father had taken in trade for three head of cattle. Rocky had once been a rodeo bronc, and when Trace, at nine, had tried to ride him, some of the gelding's old fire had resurfaced and he'd sent Trace flying. The result was a concussion and old Doc Mallory's advice after a quick examination. "For the love of Mike, boy, use the brain God gave you and stay off wild horses!"

Now Trace glanced over at his son, who, cradling his injured arm, was staring out the window.

Eli's small jaw was set; his eyes were red from the tears he wasn't about to shed. His breath fogged against the passenger window, which was already smudged with nose prints from their dog, Sarge, a mottled stray who'd shown up half starved the year before. Part Australian shepherd, part who knew what, the dog had become part of their little family. Today, when Trace received the call from the principal of the school and took off for his truck, Sarge had galloped after him, then had stood at the gate, disappointed, when Trace told the dog, "Next time." Despite the cold, and the fact that the shepherd could get into the warmth of the barn, Sarge would probably be waiting at the gate when they got home.

As if he felt his father's gaze upon him, Eli muttered, "I hate Cory Deter! He's a jerk."

"Cory do this to you?"

Eli lifted a little shoulder.

"Come on, bud. You can tell me."

Doodling in the foggy glass with the index finger of his good hand, Eli coughed, winced, then said, "He pushed me. We was on the jungle gym, way up top, and he just hauled off and pushed me."

"And you fell."

"Yeah."

"Where were the teachers?"

"Under the covered area." He slid a glance over his shoulder. "Miss Wallis wasn't there."

"I didn't ask about her," Trace said with more bite than he'd meant. He flipped on the wipers.

"I know." Again the shrug.

Trace felt like an idiot. What had he been thinking, going out with his kid's teacher last year? It had been a mistake, and he'd known it from the second she invited him to dinner. He'd told himself that it was because of Eli, that she wanted to discuss his son and the trouble Eli was having in school, but Trace had known better, sensed it.

And yet he'd gone out with her four times. Well, five, if he included that last night of their final argument after trying to rekindle something that had never really sparked.

He'd only ended up disappointing everyone involved, himself included.

He sighed. Jocelyn Wallis had thought she could be the woman to heal the scar left by Eli's mother walking out on them. She hadn't believed Trace when he'd told her he wasn't interested in a relationship, that he was okay raising his kid alone.

She wasn't the only one. Eli couldn't seem to forget the few times that his father had been with his teacher.

Yep, he'd made a royal mess of things.

Now his son said, "She wasn't at school today."

"Miss Wallis? Doesn't matter. Someone was. Someone had playground duty."

"Mr. Beene was on duty 'cuz Miss Wallis wasn't there. He's a substitute."

"I need to talk to him."

"It wasn't his fault," Eli assured him. "It was that stupid butt Cory Deter!"

"I know you're mad, but no name calling, okay?"

"But he is." Eli swiped at his nose with the sleeve of his jacket and set his jaw again. "He's a stupid butt."

"C'mon, Eli. It's not nice to talk about someone like—"

"He pushed me!"

"And that was wrong," Trace agreed equably.

"Yeah, it was!" Eli glared at him, offended his father didn't seem to grasp the gravity of Cory Deter's actions.

"Okay, so maybe he is a stupid butt."

Eli relaxed a bit.

"Just keep it between us, okay?" Trace pointed a finger at Eli, then swung it back toward himself, repeating the motion several times. "Our secret."

"Everybody already knows he's a butt."

"Okay, whatever. You don't have to say it again."

"But Becky Tremont and her friend Tonia, they laughed at me." Eli's face was suddenly flushed with color. Embarrassment. Even at seven, what girls thought mattered.

"Don't worry about them," Trace said. "Hang in, okay? We're almost there." They reached the bottom of the hill just as the railroad crossing signs flashed and the alarms clanged, and Trace gritted his teeth as a train with graffiti-decorated boxcars and empty flatbeds sped past. Traffic backed up behind the crossing bars.

Come on, come on, he thought, frustrated with anything that slowed them down. He was worried about his son, wondered how badly he was hurt. "We're almost there," he said again and patted a hand on Eli's small shoulder.

Eventually the train passed, and they, along with a snake of other vehicles, were allowed to pass. One more stoplight and they'd be at the clinic.

"Got an emergency," Heather said as she poked her head into Kacey's office. "Eli O'Halleran. Seven years old. Hurt on the playground. The school called his father and sent him here."

"He's a patient?" The name didn't ring any bells with Kacey.

Seated at her desk, she'd just opened a container of blueberry yogurt for lunch. She hadn't had a chance to catch her breath since the minute she'd walked through the door to exam room two. Elmer Grimes, her first patient of the day, had taken up more than his allotted time with her. She'd been running late ever since.

"Eli O'Halleran hasn't been in before. The boy's pediatrician was Dr. Levoy over in Middleton."

"And he retired last year." Kacey nodded, already pushing the yogurt container aside. She'd received several referrals from patients who hadn't been happy with Levoy's replacement, and though she was a GP, rather than a pediatrician, she'd spent a lot of time in pediatrics in medical school. She liked kids and had considered going back and specializing in pediatrics, but then all hell had broken loose in her personal life and she'd decided to return to Grizzly Falls.

"The school sent him here rather than over to St. Bart's as we're closer," Heather said, mentioning the nearest hospital. "They came in about five minutes ago, and I've already taken all his insurance and personal information. I've also got a call into Levoy's office, requesting the boy's files." She offered a knowing grin. "I figured we could squeeze him in before the afternoon patients. That you wouldn't turn him away."

"All right, let's take a look at him." Kacey pushed her chair away from the desk.

"He and his dad are in exam three. I've set up his preliminary info on the computer."

"Good." Kacey was already slipping her arms through the sleeves of the lab coat she'd just shed. She'd gotten used to having her life interrupted at the most inopportune of moments. All part of the job of country doctor. "You said you talked to someone at the school?"

"The nurse, Eloise Phelps." Heather peeled off toward the front desk as Kacey made her way to the examination room, tapped lightly on the door, and pushed it open.

She found a slim boy sitting on the examination table. With a shock of unruly dishwater blond hair, he was white faced, blinking hard against tears and sniffling as he cradled his left arm, which was supported by a sling.

His father, expression grim, stood next to the exam table.

Dressed in battered jeans, plaid shirt, and worn boots, which were a staple around this part of Montana, he was tall, maybe six-two, with a rangy build and wide shoulders. A day or two's worth of dark hair covered a square jaw, and he stared at her with deep-set, angry eyes. His arms were crossed over his chest, and he looked about to spit nails.

"I'm Dr. Lambert," she told the boy and, glancing at the chart on the laptop Heather had left, added, "You must be Eli."

The kid nodded and pressed his lips together. He was trying to be brave and, she guessed, might be more scared than hurt.

"Trace O'Halleran." The cowboy introduced himself, extending his hand, his gaze focused on the name tag on her lab coat, which read: DR. ACACIA LAMBERT. His hand was big. Calloused and strong. His face was tanned, weathered from the sun, his brown hair showing streaks of blond, again, she assumed, from hours outside. His eyes were a startling shade of blue, his jaw hard, his nose appearing to have been broken at least once, probably twice, and he couldn't scare up the ghost of a smile. "I'm Eli's dad."

She shook his hand, then let it fall. "So, what happened?"

"Playground accident," Trace said. "Tell her," he said, prodding the boy gently.

"I got pushed off the jungle gym." Anger flared in the boy's brown eyes.

"Why don't you tell me about it while I look at your arm? That's okay, right?"

Eli glanced at his dad, who nodded. "I guess."

After quickly washing her hands at the small sink located in the room, she dried them with a paper towel, then pulled on a pair of latex gloves as she stepped closer to the boy. Gently, she removed the sling and splint, some cotton padding, and a small ice pack, all the while watching as he blanched even further. "Hurts, huh?"

Eli couldn't speak but nodded, his eyes filling with tears, which seemed to embarrass him further.

"So how did the accident happen?"

"Cory Deter pushed me off the jungle gym." Eli was blinking rapidly now, and his jaw tightened. "He's a jerk!"

"Well, I guess so, if he did this," she agreed. "So, then what happened?"

"I fell! And . . . and I put my hands out like this . . ." He extended his arms, winced, and sucked in his breath. His left arm fell back to his side as he turned ashen again.

"Okay, so you broke your fall by stretching out your arms." She was nodding. "When?" She glanced at the dad.

"Don't know exactly," Eli's father said. He was staring at her hard, as if trying to figure her out. "I got the call about forty minutes ago, so I assume it was right after it happened."

"Okay." She said gently to Eli, "Now, I'm gonna need to take a look at your arm a little more closely. Okay?"

From beneath his beetled eyebrows, the boy glared up at her suspiciously.

"It's okay," his father said, placing a big hand over the kid's, but his expression was as concerned as his son's.

" 'Kay," Eli finally said.

Gently she examined the boy. Testing his movements, running her fingers along the muscles and joints, watching his reaction. All the while, Trace hovered.

"I don't think it's broken," she said finally, "but we can't be sure without X-rays. There's always the chance of a stress fracture."

A muscle in Trace's jaw worked. "That's what the nurse at the school said, and she also said he was running a fever. He's had a cold he hasn't been able to shake."

"Since you're here," she said to Eli, "let's double-check that temp, then take a look at your throat and maybe your ears."

Reluctantly, Eli agreed. His temperature was 100.1, his lymph nodes were slightly swollen, his eardrums were red, and his throat was so inflamed, she swabbed it to check for strep. "Looks like you probably need some antibiotics," she said. "I'm betting your throat is pretty sore."

"Really sore." Eli bobbed his head emphatically.

Trace frowned. "You didn't say anything."

"Didn't hurt before," his son said.

"It can come on fast. Looks like a double ear infection, and I'm betting on strep throat," Kacey said to Trace before moving her gaze to his son. "But you, Eli, should feel better in a couple of days," she promised. "So, now, let's get an X-ray of that arm, okay? The lab is in the next building." She turned to her laptop and made a note, then said to Trace, "You can take him over there and have the X-rays taken. They'll send them over, and I'll look at them. It won't take long. We'll meet up here again, after I check them. If I think you should see an orthopedist, I'll let you know and set up an appointment with Dr. Belding in Missoula. Or whomever you want." She offered a reassuring smile, which wasn't returned. "I've worked with Dr. Belding. She's good."

Trace nodded curtly. "Thanks." To his son, he said, "Let's go, bud."

Heather appeared with the request forms for the lab just as Trace was helping Eli from the examination table. "Do you need anything else?" she asked Kacey.

"I think we're okay. Thanks."

As Heather returned to her desk, Kacey handed Trace the request forms, then, to make the boy feel more at ease, said to Eli, "Look, I know a shortcut, so I'll walk you over. Is that okay?" She smiled at Eli. "Just in case your dad gets lost."

"He won't! He was an Army Ranger."

Trace snorted and held the door open. "That was a few years back."

"But you were!" Eli insisted.

"Back in the Dark Ages," he admitted as they headed through a series of short hallways and out a back door, where the wind knifed through her lab coat and snow was collecting in the planters.

"Right here," she said, holding her coat closed with one hand while hurrying down the short walkway. Before she could reach the door, Trace pulled it open and waited for her and his son to walk inside.

The heat was blasting, of course, Christmas music drifting down the hallways.

"Okay, from here on in, you're on your own," she said as she dropped them off with one of the lab technicians. "I'll see you in about an hour, after we get the X-rays back."

"Got it," he said, and when his eyes met hers, she saw something dark and undefinable in his gaze.

Just your imagination.

Maybe Trace was just worried about his boy, but there was something more to the guy's reaction, an undercurrent of distrust that seemed out of line with the situation, almost as if he didn't trust her. Or maybe it was doctors or the medical profession in general. Not that she had time to worry about his hang-ups, whatever they were.

She and Randy, her nurse, spent nearly an hour with other patients: Cathy Singer was dealing with adult acne; two kids came in with flu symptoms; Kevin Thomas's mother was certain he had head lice as there had been a case at school; and even Helen Ingles, having apparently found a replacement babysitter for her nephew, returned to have her own health and diabetes monitored.

An hour after being sent to the lab, the O'Hallerans were back in exam room three with the X-rays, which proved there was a small fracture in Eli's left ulna. "Looks like we're going to need a cast," she told father and son as she showed them both the tiny hairline fracture in the bone. "So you can have your pick of colors. Pink or blue."

"Pink?" Eli looked stricken. His nose wrinkled in disgust. "No way!"

"Blue it is," she said with a grin as Randy found the appropriate colored kit from a supply closet and helped her apply the cast. For his part, Eli was a trooper, didn't flinch too much, tried to be as stoic as his father.

Once the cast was in place, and Randy was cleaning up the extra packaging, Kacey gave them instructions. "The main thing is that you don't reinjure it. So you"—she eyed the boy—"have to take it easy for a while. No more climbing on the jungle gym, or being pushed by Cory Whoever." She leaned down so that she was eyeball-to-eyeball with him. "Can you do that?"

Eli nodded, then looked down at his cast. "Maybe you tell him that? He's a butt head."

Trace was long-suffering. "I thought that was our secret. Remember?"

"Everybody knows," Eli said.

"I guess the secret's out," Kacey said with a grin, then told Eli, "But I wouldn't worry about Cory . . . uh . . ."

"Deter," Trace supplied.

"Right. I think your dad will handle any trouble you have from him. I heard that he was an Army Ranger. From what I understand, those guys are pretty tough."

"They are!" Eli declared, and Trace looked as if he wanted to fall through the floor.

"I think that's enough," he said, reaching for his son's jacket when the boy blurted, "You look like Miss Wallis."

Kacey glanced up at the father, who visibly winced. "Is that a good thing?"

"Yeah. I guess." Trace nodded without a lot of conviction.

"Great." First Shelly Bonaventure, now the unknown Miss Wallis. It seemed to be her week for resembling someone else.

Eli announced, "She's my dad's girlfriend."

Every muscle in Trace's body appeared to stiffen. "Eli, I told you that Miss Wallis and I—we're not dating. She's *not* my girlfriend." Totally abashed, he said, "Sorry. Miss Wallis was Eli's teacher last year, when he was in first grade."

"And you went out on dates!" Eli glared up at his father.

He gazed apologetically at Kacey. "She and I did go out a couple of times, and yes, you *do* look a little like her."

"I must have a face that looks familiar."

He closed his eyes for half a second and shook his head, the overhead light catching in the blonder strands of his hair. "So, now that I'm completely embarrassed, can you tell me how to slow an active seven-year-old down?"

"It's probably impossible, but you, Eli, remember to take it easy. No roughhousing. Got that?" She leaned down to meet the boy's gaze, eye-to-eye once more.

He nodded solemnly.

"Promise? Scout's honor?"

"I'm not a Cub Scout."

"Okay, I'll believe you," she said, raising her eyebrows as if she really didn't trust him, not quite.

"I will!" Eli was completely earnest.

"Good. 'Cuz your dad'll be reporting to me." She smiled at Trace, who started to smile back, then thought better of it when she told him that if the pain in his son's arm was so great that over-the-counter pain medication didn't help, he should call her. He nodded grimly.

As she wrote out the prescription, she added, "I'll call about the throat culture. I'll want to see you again"—she pointed her pen at Eli—"in about ten days. Can you do that?" The boy was nodding vigorously. "Good." She ripped off the prescription and handed it to his father. "He's going to be okay, though I think he should stay home from school for a couple of days."

"Yessss!" Eli said and pumped his good arm, which suggested to Kacey that he was feeling better.

"Anyway," she said to Trace, "call me if he's in a lot of pain or something looks wrong to you. You'll know. My service can reach me twenty-four-seven, and either Dr. Cortez or I will call you back ASAP."

Trace tucked the prescription into his pocket and seemed a little less uptight than when she'd first examined his son a couple of hours earlier. He dropped Eli's jacket over the boy's shoulders.

"Now, Eli, you be good, okay? Do as your father says, and don't give him any trouble. And, oh, stay away from bullies," Kacey advised.

"Thanks." Trace's intense blue eyes were sincere, and when he shook her hand again, she thought the clasp lasted a bit longer than normal. Then again, maybe she was imagining things.

She exited the room as Randy made notes on the computer and followed her into exam room two. Attempting to push all thoughts of the rangy cowboy from her mind, she turned her attention to Delores Sweeney, a mother of four who was always battling a cold, the flu, or a yeast infection . . . or something. . . .

CHAPTER 5

"The drawing for Secret Santas was this morning!" Joelle scolded as Pescoli walked into the lunchroom to fill her coffee cup in the early afternoon. The entire cafeteria area was what Pescoli had termed "Joelled." Christmas lights winked around every surface, the tables all had little snowmen centerpieces, fir boughs festooned with ribbons had been swagged over the doorway, and the regular white napkins in the coffee station had been replaced with red and green.

Even so, Pescoli suspected, the decorating wasn't yet finished; it would soon spill into the hallways, offices, and reception area, where already a ten-foot, yet-to-be-adorned tree stood near the bulletproof glass that had been installed over the counter this past spring.

"I was here at seven, then had work out of the office," Pescoli said, then gave herself a swift mental kick. She didn't need to explain her whereabouts to the receptionist.

"Well, you're not the only one who missed out." Joelle's eyes twinkled, and Pescoli inwardly groaned, knowing she hadn't escaped. "So here . . ." She picked up a basket decorated with candy canes and held it high over her head, as if she truly expected Pescoli to cheat and look at the names she'd scribbled on the scraps of paper.

"Seriously? Everyone's doing this?" Pescoli asked suspiciously.

"Of course!"

"Including the sheriff?"

"Absolutely."

"What about Rule?" Pescoli asked, mentioning Kayan Rule, a strapping African American man who had no use for any kind of silliness.

One of the more independent of the road deputies, Rule was as unlikely as anyone to be involved in Joelle's stupid games.

"Already drew his name this morning, as did Selena."

Great, Pescoli thought but, deciding she had been accused too many times of not being a team player, lifted her arm and reached into the basket, where she plucked one of the few remaining scraps of paper with her fingertips.

"Wonderful!" Joelle was pleased with herself. "Now, don't forget to leave him or her little gifts at least one a week, until Christmas!"

Pescoli unfolded the piece of paper, and her stomach dropped as she read the name scrawled across the small scrap:

Cort Brewster.

"I have to draw again!" she blurted.

Joelle snatched back the basket and raised a condescending, if perfectly tweezed eyebrow. "There are no do-overs, detective. That's what happens when you come late to the party."

Pescoli wanted to argue the point but decided she couldn't stoop to groveling over something so trivial. She nearly forgot her cup of coffee as she left the lunchroom, with its festive snowmen and sparkling lights, and made her way to Alvarez's cubicle.

Her partner, as usual, was bent over paperwork. "Trade with me," Pescoli said.

"What?" Alvarez glanced up.

"For the Secret Santa thing. Trade with me."

For once, Alvarez actually laughed. "No way."

"I'm serious."

"So am I."

"The whole thing is ridiculous," Pescoli grumbled.

"So don't worry about it. Just buy some candy or a DVD or something, leave it on Brewster's desk, and call it good."

"You know?"

"I *am* a detective. No one else's name would get you so agitated." Her smile was knowing. "You could have some fun with this, you know."

"It's not that easy," Pescoli said, thinking of how the undersheriff and she hadn't gotten along since the debacle last year, when Jeremy had been arrested. At the time he'd been with Heidi Brewster, and her father had intervened. Pescoli hadn't, and her son hadn't really ever forgiven her. Nor had Cort. He seemed to blame Pescoli for her son's and *his* daughter's bad behavior.

"Sure it is. Or opt out."

"Joelle said—"

"That it was mandatory? Seriously? The Secret Santa thing? I don't think so, but I'll double-check the personnel policy manual."

"Do that," Pescoli said, annoyed.

Alvarez's grin widened, and she slowly shook her head. "Since when do you listen to Joelle?"

"Since I don't want to appear to always be bucking the system."

"Then quit bitching, okay?" Alvarez turned her attention back to the stack of papers in front of her. "I hate it when you start whining like a baby."

"I can't believe *you* bought into it," Pescoli declared, then noticed her partner's expression turn more serious, her eyes darken a bit. "Is this a sheriff's department or a damned bridge club?"

"Maybe we could all use a little Christmas spirit," Alvarez said, adding, "Don't you have something more important to worry about?"

"Only about a million things." Not only her work, but there was that meeting at the school later today to discuss Bianca's waning interest in anything to do with Grizzly Falls High School. Then there was Jeremy . . . always Jeremy.

"So forget Secret Santa. Who cares?"

She was right, Pescoli supposed, sipping her cooling coffee on her way to her office. It was nothing and yet she was bothered. Working with Cort Brewster and having him as her boss were bad enough; sucking up to him by buying inane little Christmas gifts turned her stomach.

"It could get worse," Alvarez said.

"I don't see how."

"Joelle could have your name."

Pescoli closed her eyes and shuddered, envisioning myriads of plastic elves, cards that sang Christmas carols, windup nutcrackers with their grouchy faces, and chocolate reindeer, which Joelle, no doubt, had already squirreled away. Soon some of those items could litter her desk, every day a new and even more ridiculous cutesy Christmas gift hidden between the gory images in her homicide files.

"Pray that isn't so," she muttered under her breath and found her way to her desk, where so far, thankfully, no tiny surprises from her Secret Santa lay in wait.

"You gotta let it go." Gail Harding had sneaked up on Hayes, approaching his desk without him knowing. The department was buzzing, voices filtering over the half walls, telephones jangling. Jonas Hayes had barely noticed. He'd been lost in thought.

Shelly Bonaventure's file lay open on his desk, her death certificate on the top of the stack of papers, her picture, a head shot taken just last year, staring up at him.

"I'm not letting anything go. Not yet."

"Her death was ruled a suicide." Harding pointed to the appropriate line on the certificate. "See here? Cause of death. Probable suicide."

"*Probable* being the operative word."

"Case closed. It's over."

Hayes shook his head and shoved back his chair. "It doesn't hurt for me to work on this, on my own time." He stood and, in so doing, towered over her by nearly a foot. They were an odd pair, he knew. He was an ex-jock, a black man who still kept his body honed with ratball and weights, and she was a petite white girl with spiky red hair and huge eyes.

"I'm on my way over to an 'accident' on Sepulveda, a few blocks from the airport. A motorcycle pulled into oncoming traffic. First reports are that there was no reason for it. It looked intentional. The Honda, with a rider on the back, got hit by an SUV going the other way. You coming?"

He grimaced. "Wouldn't miss it."

Glancing at the file one more time, he gave it a cursory scan before shutting it and following Harding to the elevators. She was probably right. It was time to let the Shelly Bonaventure suicide go, but he just couldn't.

They'd interviewed most of her friends and family, none of whom had seen the suicide coming. Yes, there had been a little talk of depression, and yes, her career wasn't on the upswing, and her love life had been nonexistent for the past year, but suicide still seemed unlikely.

The bartender at Lizards had mentioned that she'd been flirting with a man who hadn't paid with a credit card and whose image hadn't been clear on any of the security tapes of the building. But he had left after Shelly and, according to the one camera near the front door, had headed in the opposite direction that Shelly had taken twenty minutes earlier.

Just a chance meeting at the bar?

Or something more?

"Hey!" Harding said as they pushed open the doors and stepped into the warm winter sunshine. Seventy-five degrees, and already the local stores were decorated to the max with wintry Christmas images, festooned with fake fir trees and even faker snow. Santas, reindeer, elves, and gingerbread houses were on display, and it wasn't quite Thanksgiving.

Strings of colored lights had been wound over the trunks of the royal palms, their fronds billowing in a balmy breeze blowing in off the Pacific.

Christmas in L.A.

He slid into Harding's car. The interior of her hatchback was sweltering, and he rolled down the window. "Okay, so tell me, why do you think someone murdered Shelly Bonaventure?" she asked.

"Not sure."

"She had no enemies, no angry boyfriends, no life insurance, no will, and less than three hundred dollars in the bank. Her biggest assets were a ninety-five Toyota and her cat. Who would want her dead?"

"I don't know," he reiterated as she tore out of the lot, her lead foot pressing hard on the accelerator.

"Yet," Harding added as she sped toward Sepulveda. "You didn't finish your sentence. You don't know *yet*. You're not letting go of this."

"I'd just like to personally talk to the guy at the bar. He's the last one to have seen her alive. He might remember something more."

"Good luck with that. You've heard about needles and haystacks, right?"

"Right."

She slashed him a knowing grin as she took a corner a little too fast. "That might not ever happen."

For once, he couldn't argue.

But he still wanted to have a chat with the mystery man at the bar.

Trace grabbed his cell phone by the third ring. As he did, he noticed that it was nearly four and caller ID listed Evergreen Elem. as the caller. Eli's school. "Hello?" he said into the phone.

"Mr. O'Halleran? This is Barbara Killingsworth, the principal here at Evergreen Elementary. I was just calling to check on Eli." In his mind's eye, he pictured the woman: midforties, impossibly thin, with pinched features and a wide mouth that was forever in a tight, forced smile.

"He's doing all right," Trace said, glancing over at his son, who was sleeping on the couch, his arm in the cast, the television turned to some movie he wasn't watching, the dog curled at his feet. "But I want to know who was supposed to be watching him." He walked into the kitchen of the old farmhouse and pulled the swinging door to the family room shut so that he wouldn't disturb Eli.

"We had several teachers on playground duty."

"And none of them saw the potential danger in . . . ?" He let his question fade away and forced his anger at bay. What was the point? He knew accidents happened. No one at Evergreen Elementary was malicious or even inattentive. The kids were just messing around, and his boy got hurt. End of story. He didn't want to come off like some overprotective jerk, and yet when it came to Eli . . .

"I'm very sorry."

"I know. Look, he's got a double ear infection and possibly strep throat, so I'm going to keep him home for at least a couple of days."

"I'll have his teacher e-mail you, and tell Eli that we're all thinking of him."

"I will," he said and hung up just as he heard a rumble outside. He glanced out the window and saw Ed Zukov's truck as it rolled down the twin ruts of the long drive.

Sarge, who had been sleeping seconds earlier, lifted his scruffy head and gave a low bark.

"Shh!" Trace headed for the back door.

Ed and his wife, Tilly, were the neighbors a quarter of a mile down the road and had been friends of his father. Trace had known the couple, now in their seventies, all his life. He walked through the kitchen and back porch with Sarge at his heels.

The wind was picking up, causing the old windmill's blades to creak as they turned and the naked branches of the trees in the orchard to rattle. Snow was falling steadily now, big white flakes swirling and beginning to cover the ground, as the old truck slowed to a stop near the pump house.

Spry as a thirty-year-old, Tilly hopped down from the cab of the ancient truck the minute her husband cut the engine. "We heard about Eli," she said, a baseball cap covering her head as she marched around the front of the old Dodge. She was carrying a hamper, which wasn't unusual. In the face of any crisis, Tilly Zukov turned to her pantry and stove.

"He'll be fine." Since Tilly was a world-class worrier, he decided not to mention the ear infections. "How'd you know?"

"I have a niece who works in the kitchen at Evergreen."

"Small town." Ed, a solid man with a wide girth and arms as big as sapling trunks, slammed the door of his truck behind him and followed his wife up the two stairs of the screened-in back porch. "Jesus, it's cold!"

"Ed! Do *not* take our Lord's name in vain," Tilly reprimanded as they stopped just inside the kitchen door. In her plaid jacket and faded jeans, she was tiny, half her husband's size, but she obviously ruled the roost. Her hair was steel gray and tightly permed, and rimless glasses were perched on the bridge of her tiny nose. From behind the lenses, dark eyes snapped with intelligence. To Trace, she said, "I brought over some stew and fresh baked corn bread, and some ranger cookies, 'cuz they're Eli's favorite."

"She also brought a pie," Ed added. He took off his trucker cap, showing off a bald spot in his snow-white hair, then unzipped his down jacket, beneath which were bib overalls and a flannel shirt.

"I had to!" Tilly insisted. "I wanted to try out this new recipe I found in the *Better Homes and Gardens,* last year's holiday edition. It's pumpkin custard with sour cream."

Trace eyed the pie. "Sounds great. But, really, it wasn't necessary."

"Course it wasn't." Tilly was already stuffing the pie into his bare refrigerator. "But I wanted to give it a whirl before I served it on

Thanksgiving. Ed's sister, Cara, she's pretty picky, so you and Eli are my guinea pigs."

"Nothin' wrong with the old recipe," Ed grumbled.

"The one on the pumpkin can?" she demanded. "We've had that every year for the past forty-five years! Time to try something new."

"It's a tradition." Ed was unmoved.

Tilly rolled her eyes. "Oh, show some originality, would ya, Ed?"

"Cara likes it," Ed pointed out.

"What does she know?"

"You're the one trying to impress her."

"And I don't know why," Tilly admitted. "Ever taste her banana cream? Soggy crust. Overripe bananas. Horrible! Just . . . horrible!"

"Then quit tryin' to impress her, and make the damned recipe that comes with the fillin'." Her husband sighed broadly, his teeth stained slightly yellow from years of chewing tobacco. "I always say, if it ain't broke, then don't fix it."

"You always say a lot of things, and I don't listen to too many of 'em! Now, let's quit bickering and I'll heat up the stew."

"She's a bossy one, ain't she?" Ed said to Trace.

"And you love it!" Despite the bite to her words, she sent him a fond glance, the kind they'd shared since high school, some fifty-odd years earlier.

"Seems to have worked out between you two," Trace observed.

"That's because he usually does what I ask."

She began fiddling with the stove as her husband said, "I thought I'd help you with the livestock. Tilly, here, was frettin' and fussin' over at the house, worried you wouldn't be able to get the chores done with Eli laid up."

Tilly's features pulled into a knot as she turned to Trace. "It's just that I didn't see how you'd leave the boy and take care of the cattle all at the same time."

"Dad?" Eli called from the living room.

"Right there, bud!" Trace slipped through the swinging door and found his son in his stocking feet, looking groggy. "You okay?"

"Yeah. Who's here?"

"The Zukovs. Come on into the kitchen."

"Is that my boy?" Tilly called loudly, and for the first time all day, Eli smiled.

He was already tossing the blankets aside when Trace said, "I think she brought you something."

"I heard that, and I sure did!" Tilly raised her voice and added, "Eli, you come on in here and sit up to the table. We'll have ourselves some cookies and milk and a quick game of checkers. That is, if you don't mind being beat."

"I'm pretty good!" Eli was already through the swinging door and finding the box of checkers on the shelf in the dining cove.

"We'll see how good you are. . . . Oooh weee, take a look at that cast, would ya, Ed?" Tilly had placed a plate of cookies on the table and had poured Eli a glass of milk as she spied the boy's arm. "Blue as a summer sky!"

"That it is," her husband agreed.

Beaming, Eli scrambled onto his chair and began pulling the checkerboard out of its battered, taped-together box.

Ed, who had snatched a cookie, was at the back door. "Let's go deal with the cattle."

Trace snagged his jean jacket from a hook near the back door, then stepped into his boots and followed Ed along a cement path that petered into a trampled dirt trail on the other side of the gate that separated the yard from the barnyard.

Snow was still falling steadily, covering the ground in a fine layer that allowed patches of grass to poke through. Most of the cattle were already inside the barn, and when Trace pushed open the wide doors, rolling them aside, the smells of hay, dust, and dung reached his nostrils.

He climbed to the hayloft, his boots ringing on the metal rungs as the cattle mooed and shuffled. Once in the loft, he pushed bales through the opening in the old floorboards. They landed with soft thuds, and Ed took over, slicing through the string and breaking the bales before strewing them in the manger where part of the herd of Hereford and Angus mingled.

Once the bales were scattered inside the barn, they carried several outside the doors to a covered area, where the roof was supported by poles, and mangers and a water trough filled the inner area.

Cattle shifted and lowed, their black and red hides wet where snow had melted upon them, their breaths fogging in the cold air.

After the herd was cared for, Trace and Ed walked to the stable, and the whole process started over again, though Trace owned only four horses, so the job was quicker. They added grain to the mangers, and Trace rubbed the palomino's muzzle and scratched the ears of the dun, who tossed his head, his dark eyes gleaming with fire.

By the time they returned to the kitchen, the scents of garlic and rosemary filled the room. Tilly's stew was simmering on the stove, and it looked like Eli was beating his mentor at their game of checkers.

"You're sure you didn't cheat?" Tilly teased him.

"No way!" Eli insisted. Half his milk had disappeared, and the crumbs on the table in front of him indicated he'd had at least one of Tilly's cookies.

Trace had just taken off his boots when his cell phone jangled.

"Second time that's happened since you went out to feed the cattle," Tilly observed as her final checker was captured by a beaming Eli.

"Better see who it is." Trace gave his son a high five, then scooped up the phone as it jangled for the fourth time. "Hello?"

"Trace? This is Mia Calloway. I'm the school secretary at Evergreen and . . . well, how's your boy? Eli?"

"Doing better. I already talked to the principal." He was walking out of the kitchen and into the living area, where he could have a little more privacy.

"Yes, yes, I know. . . . This isn't really about Eli," she admitted and seemed a little nervous. "It's about Jocelyn Wallis."

His stomach tightened, but he didn't say a word, just let her ramble on.

"She didn't come to school today and didn't phone in, didn't leave a lesson plan for a sub or . . . anything. No one here heard from her, but I know . . . Well, she said you two had been going out, and I thought you might know . . ." Her worried voice faded away.

"I have no idea why she didn't show up," he said.

"Oh . . . well . . . I'm just concerned, that's all. We're friends, and I drove to her house, but all the windows were closed. I couldn't see in. There were lights on, but that doesn't really mean anything. I know she wasn't feeling well, but I tried to call and voice mail answered after one ring. I mean . . . I don't know what to think. Did she leave town? Is she just too sick to answer the phone?" She let the suggestion hang in the air and, when Trace didn't answer, added, "As I said, I'm just trying to find out what happened to her."

"If I hear from her, I'll let you know."

"Oh . . . okay. Uh, you don't have a key to her place, do you? I mean, before anyone calls the police, or whatever it is you do, maybe it would be a good idea to go inside?"

"I don't have a key," he said. "I haven't seen Jocelyn for months."

"Oh! I thought she said she called you yesterday. . . ."

"She didn't."

"Then . . . well, I'm sorry to have bothered you. If you hear from her, would you have her call Mia?"

"I won't. But, yeah, sure. At the school?"

"That, too, but if she could call my cell?" Mia sounded seriously worried. "This is just not her usual style. Jocelyn is the most focused, dedicated teacher I know. She just wouldn't not show up and leave her students high and dry. . . . It just doesn't make any sense. Well, thanks."

He hung up and turned to find Tilly standing in the doorway, not even trying to hide the fact that she'd been eavesdropping. "That was the school again, right? About Jocelyn Wallis?"

"A friend of hers," he admitted.

Tilly's expression was dark. "I heard from my niece that she didn't show up today. It was odd."

"The niece again," Ed clarified.

"Her friend said she called me yesterday, but I didn't get a message." Trace saw Eli slide farther down in his chair. "Or did I?"

The boy shook his head, but Trace walked to the ancient wall phone that was an answering machine as well. No light was blinking, no message waiting, but when he pressed the button to see who'd called, WALLIS, J. showed on the screen.

"Did you hear a message from Miss Wallis?" he asked his son, but Eli was already shaking his head.

"Uh-uh . . . there wasn't any message." The boy looked stricken, but Trace believed him. He poked a few buttons, heard nothing, and a cold feeling crawled slowly up his spine. He hung up and found Tilly staring at him.

"Maybe you'd better go check it out," she suggested. "We'll stay here with Eli."

"But I want to go, too," his son protested.

"What?" Tilly said with mock horror. "And get out of a rematch? No way, *Jose!* This is my chance to dominate!" She sent Trace a quick glance, and he got the message.

"I'll be back soon," he said and headed out the door, leaving the Zukovs in charge as he strode to his pickup with Sarge at his feet. "Fine. You can come this time." He opened the driver's door of the cab, and the dog hopped inside, settling into his favorite spot in the passenger seat.

Trace climbed behind the wheel, started the old Chevy, and wondered what the hell he'd find at Jocelyn Wallis's apartment.

"Probably nothing," he told himself, ramming the truck into gear and flipping on the wipers. But the sensation that he was about to step into something bad hung with him as he stared through the windshield to a dusk that promised a darkness he couldn't comprehend.

CHAPTER 6

Once again, Pescoli's daughter was a no-show.

"I assumed you knew that Bianca wasn't in school today." The counselor, Miss Unsel, sat behind a massive desk piled with folders and surrounded by bound copies of college catalogs and directories. The only natural light came from windows mounted high overhead, and the room had a slightly musty smell to it.

"I dropped her off right before the first bell." Pescoli was terse.

Miss Unsel, with a thick black braid that fell over one shoulder, turned her palms upward. "She wasn't in her homeroom for attendance. Mr. Cohn marked her absent, as did every other teacher in her block."

"She hasn't been here all day. That's what you're telling me."

"Yes." Peony Unsel was nodding her head in agreement, the end of her braid moving against the bright stripes of the serape she was wearing. "Can you tell me what's going on?"

"That's why I'm here. I was hoping you could tell me, well, us, because she was supposed to be here."

The counselor picked up a pair of heavy-rimmed glasses and studied her computer screen, then typed in another command or two and said, "She's failing two classes, Spanish and algebra, and just getting by in the others." Miss Unsel regarded Pescoli over the rims of her glasses. "But she missed two major tests today, one in U.S. history, the other in English."

Pescoli's heart sank. "She can make them up?"

The counselor was nodding. "If she has a valid excuse and her teachers agree, I don't see why not. It's our mission to help our students become successful adults." She offered Pescoli a beatific, "Kumbaya" type smile that Pescoli couldn't help thinking had to be fake.

"Just one more question. Out of curiosity. Was Chris Schultz in school today?" Pescoli asked.

"Let's see . . . This is confidential information, you know."

"Chris is my daughter's boyfriend."

"I know. But—"

"I am a cop."

"I know that, too. But we have rules about the privacy of our students. . . ." Miss Unsel turned back to her computer, typed on the keyboard, and sighed. She looked up at Pescoli but didn't say a word. She didn't have to.

"Thanks," Pescoli said, worried sick.

By the time she left the counseling area and walked through the hallways lined with lockers and benches, Pescoli remembered how much she, herself, had hated high school, how often she'd cut class. But she had never let her grades drop, had never jeopardized her future.

And that was what Bianca was doing.

Throwing it all away.

Just like her older brother.

Outside, Pescoli turned her collar to the brittle wind and watched a few kids scurrying to their cars or carrying athletic bags, hurrying toward the gym. Daylight was fading fast. A thick layer of snow had already covered the tracks she'd made when she'd wheeled into the parking lot, and more of the white powder continued to fall.

Climbing behind the wheel, she turned on the engine, and as the wipers pushed a thick white film off her windshield, she tried texting her daughter.

Where R U?

She hit SEND and waited.

Nothing.

"Damn it, Bianca!" she burst out as the phone suddenly rang in her hand. "Pescoli," she snapped, expecting her daughter's apologetic voice on the other end.

"Santana," Nate said, mimicking her tough, no-nonsense tone.

"Oh. Hi. Thought you might be my kid." But her voice softened a bit.

He chuckled, and she imagined his face, all bladed planes and taut dark skin, evidence of a Native American ancestor somewhere in his family history. And then there were his eyes, deep set and so sharply focused, she sometimes wondered if he could see straight into her soul. Except, she reminded herself, she didn't believe in any of that romantic garbage.

"I'm not disappointed," she said. "Just worried. She ditched school again."

"With the boyfriend."

"Seems so."

"Sounds like she needs a father figure."

"Sounds like she needs a *better* father figure. She's got Lucky, remember?"

"He know about this?"

"I haven't talked to him," Pescoli admitted as the windshield, now cleared of snow, began to fog.

"You could move in with me," he said. "All of you."

Something deep inside of her melted, and she was tempted. "Look, you know how I feel about this. Until the kids are set—"

"Some people might think you're putting your own life on hold for your kids."

"That's what you do if you're a responsible parent."

"Is it?"

"Look, I'm not in the mood for any psychological mind games, okay? I just left the counselor's office, and let's just say it wasn't a great experience. Now I have to run down my kid."

He didn't say anything, and she closed her eyes for a second. "Santana, don't do this. Okay? Not now. I'll call you later." She hung up before he could argue, even though she knew he wouldn't. As she drove out of the parking lot, she felt empty inside, as if she were intentionally undermining her one chance at happiness.

Maybe Nate Santana was right.

Maybe she should do what she damned well pleased and let her kids just deal with it.

Then again, maybe not.

* * *

Knowing nothing good would come of this, Trace pulled into the lot of Jocelyn Wallis's apartment building and parked his truck in one of the few vacant visitors' spaces.

He'd called her twice on the way from the house, but there had been no answer. He caught a glimpse of his reflection in the rearview mirror and noticed how haggard he looked. He didn't like being here; this was a mistake. He knew it deep in his gut. Just as he'd known he should never have gotten involved with her, not in the least. Not only had it been a bad idea for him, but getting hooked up with Jocelyn had been a disaster for Eli, who, though he'd never said it, had to have noticed Jocelyn Wallis's slight resemblance to his mother. . . . What was that called? Transference? Close enough.

He glanced around the snow-covered grounds as his windows began to fog with the chill. Lamplight glowed from Jocelyn's apartment, one in the living area, another in her bedroom, but the shades were drawn.

He walked to the front door and knocked, then waited.

Nothing.

No sound of a television or music coming from her unit. He probably should just call the manager, or Jocelyn's sister, but decided that since he was here, he'd check her place out himself. She kept a spare key hidden in the beam that supported the roof of her porch, so he used the bench near the front door and hoisted himself upward to a spot where he could see the key hanging on a small nail.

Without a second's thought Trace snagged the key, hopped down, and after one more try at knocking, let himself in.

A blast of heat hit him full force, but he knew the minute he stepped through the door that he was alone in the apartment. It was just that still.

"Jocelyn!" he called loudly. "Hello?" But he sensed it was useless as he slowly walked from room to room, noting that her purse was on the kitchen counter, her schoolbag, filled with papers and books, on the seat of one of the two bar stools.

The bed was unmade; a half-drunk glass of water and some crumpled wrapper of over-the-counter flu medication were on the night table, next to a paperback novel and her cell phone charger. Clothes were tumbling out of a laundry basket on the open bedroom floor, and the remote control for a small television had been left on the mussed coverlet.

Suddenly music erupted.

He nearly jumped out of his skin, turning quickly. For a second he thought someone was inside; then he realized it was probably her cell phone's ring tone. He followed the sound to the living room and a small recliner. The music stopped abruptly, but he dug through the cushions and finally found the phone under the chair.

He checked the list of incoming call numbers on the display and saw that the most recent was unknown; prior to that, his name was listed twice, then Evergreen Elementary, interspersed with names, some of which he recognized, others that he didn't. He checked the texts and saw that all the messages asked her to text or call back.

"Where the hell are you?" he wondered aloud, the small apartment almost echoing his voice. There was no sign of a break-in; nothing seemed out of place. Her laptop, television, and even some change left on the kitchen counter hadn't been disturbed. Wet cat food was turning dry in one of the small bowls on the floor near the garbage can.

He walked back to the living room hall, where he saw that her car and house keys had been left in a small dish by the front door.

Odd.

She left and locked herself out?

Unlikely as the dead bolt had been latched.

Nothing more to do than call her friend back and tell her what he'd found: nothing. From there, he supposed, the next step was to alert her family or maybe the police.

Locking the front door behind him, he replaced the key where he'd found it, then returned to his car and hoped to high heaven that Jocelyn was all right.

He had a very bad feeling she wasn't.

It was after seven when Kacey turned her Ford Edge off the main road to her house. She'd been fighting a bit of a headache for the last couple of hours, and her stomach was rumbling.

She checked her rearview mirror, and the car that had been following her sped past, a minivan with a Christmas tree strapped to its roof, as it turned out. Nothing sinister. Unless you thought cutting a Christmas tree *before* Thanksgiving was a sin, and Kacey was on the fence about that.

The minivan was followed by a dark pickup, the primary mode of transportation in these parts, and a light-colored sedan, none of which appeared malevolent as they all continued on the county road leading into the hills. Most of the time she was fine, but she wondered if she would ever feel completely safe. Whenever she was alone, old memories and doubts crept in.

All your imagination. Again. Get over it! The attack was nearly seven years ago. Are you planning to live your life by always looking over your shoulder? You're here. In Grizzly Falls, not Seattle. You're safe.

Kacey clenched her teeth and counted to ten. Her headlights cast warm beams over the two inches of snow that covered the ground and reflected in the millions of swirling flakes that fell from the dark sky.

The old farmhouse where she lived came into view, and she almost smiled at how, under the blue bath of the security lamp, the little cottage appeared quaint and welcoming. Built of clapboard nearly a hundred years earlier, the house had a steeply pitched roof, two dormers, and a wide porch that skirted the entire first floor. Two lights were burning, one in the living room, the other in the den, both on timers so that she wouldn't have to walk into a dark house.

She hit the garage door opener, then, as the door yawned wide, drove inside. She made certain to close the garage door before climbing out of her SUV. She was cautious, much more careful than she'd been growing up here as a child, or as a student who had let nothing get in her way in her quest for success. With stellar grades and an athletic scholarship to a small junior college, she'd been fearless.

Which had proven to be her downfall.

Now, grabbing her laptop case, she let herself out of the garage. After locking the door quickly, she hurried along a short walkway to the back porch, where a welcoming light burned by the door. Her boots broke a path in the snow, then were muffled a bit as she climbed the few steps. Unlocking the door as she stamped off the snow, she then slipped inside and twisted the dead bolt.

She thought about getting another dog but couldn't face the thought of leaving it for the length of time she would have to be at work every weekday. Sometimes she left the house before six in the morning and didn't return until nearly eight in the evening. Since she lived alone, it just didn't seem fair or right to leave a dog alone that long, and though she could adjust her schedule, and she could hire people to walk the dog, or she could bring it to the office or to the doggy day care in town, so far she'd resisted the idea. But maybe it was time to rethink that?

She glanced around this kitchen that had been a part of her life for as long as she could remember. As a child, she'd visited here often, this little house on the farm her grandparents had owned. And with the house had come a succession of strays and herding dogs, sometimes three at a time, which she remembered from her long summers and winter vacations when she'd visited. The dogs had been a part of the landscape and the house.

Later, while she was married, working opposite shifts as her husband, they'd owned an aging Boston terrier he'd inherited from his mother when she'd moved into a condo that prohibited pets. The black and white dog had lasted another two years, but when Black-Jack had finally died, their marriage had been eroding and they'd never made the effort or commitment to find another dog.

Or to save the marriage.

Peeling off her coat and scarf, she hung both in a closet near the back door, then kicked off her boots and lost two inches in the process.

After filling a cup with water and placing it in the microwave, she scrounged in her refrigerator, where she found two pieces of a pizza she'd picked up three nights earlier and an unopened salad in a bag.

"Perfect," she muttered under her breath and reminded herself that she *had* to stop at the store tomorrow. Her toilet paper, dish detergent, and coffee levels were getting dangerously low.

The microwave dinged and she quickly made a cup of tea, which she carried upstairs to her bedroom tucked under the eaves. Between sips of the hot brew, she stripped out of the slacks and sweater she'd worn all day. As she reached for her flannel pajama bottoms, she eyed her workout gear, black sweats, and an old Huskies long-sleeved T-shirt.

Could she do it?

Really?

With this headache?

The last thing she wanted to do was lift weights in front of the television, even though there was bound to be a *Real Housewives* of somewhere on and she could indulge in her own personal guilty pleasure. She'd rationalized that the mindless TV helped her unwind, and if she could exercise while watching it, all the better.

"Damn it," she muttered under her breath, but she was already pulling her sweatpants from the hook where she'd hung them.

Back downstairs she finished her tea, ate half a banana, then turned on the television in the den, a cozy room separated from the front foyer with French doors, a spot where, if she closed her eyes and imagined, she could still smell her grandfather's blend of pipe tobacco and her grandmother's potpourri—a mixture of cinnamon, vanilla, and fruit, which she'd hoped would mask that very same tobacco.

Of course those scents, like the memories, were all in her mind. After a quick perusal of the news and finding it too depressing, she switched channels and began an exercise routine she could do by rote. While the housewives spent their normal days deep in high drama, four-inch heels, and glittering jewelry, Kacey worked out with the hand weights she kept in the long cabinet under her flat screen, while balancing on a large ball she kept tucked in the closet.

She thought longingly of the treadmill she'd left in Seattle as part of the divorce decree. At the time of the split, when she'd been an emotional wreck, Jeffrey had insisted that he needed all the exercise equipment they kept in their personal gym, and she'd been too tired to fight him for something so trivial. She had just wanted to move on, had been desperate to start a new life.

And now, with snow falling, running the country roads was out, and she wished she had the damned treadmill instead of a cardio workout tape from the nineties.

She finished her routine, somehow managing to work up a sweat. The housewives were over, and she had the remote in her hand to click off the television when the lead story for one of those entertainment "news" shows flashed on the screen and she found herself staring at Shelly Bonaventure's smiling face while the announcer, in a cheery voice, said, "And now the latest news on Shelly Bonaventure's suicide." A slide show of Shelly's life, from the time she was a toddler until her most recent red carpet appearance, rolled over the screen. Kacey hated to admit it, but Heather was right: she and Shelly Bonaventure did look a little alike. During the quick biography, the announcer mentioned that Shelly had spent the first five years of her life in Helena, Montana, before the family moved to Southern California.

"Huh." So the B-level actress was born in the same city as Kacey and had Montana roots. Not exactly an earth-shattering coincidence. Just because they looked alike and came from the same area, there was no reason to make anything of it. The situation was a little odd, maybe, and even possibly a bit disturbing, but really, it was just coincidence.

"And though the case has been ruled a suicide, there is still one Los Angeles detective who isn't quite convinced," the announcer said. The screen flashed to a handsome black man in a crisp suit and sunglasses. He was standing outside, palm trees visible in the background. The announcer's voice continued, "Veteran detective Jonas Hayes has been with the LAPD for over fifteen years."

A reporter appeared on the screen with the policeman. "Detective Hayes, could you comment on the ruling that Shelly Bonaventure's death was a suicide?"

Hayes's face turned into a scowl. "No."

"A reliable source quoted you as saying you weren't convinced that she took her own life."

"No comment."

"But, Detective Hayes," the reporter insisted, chasing after the much taller man as he strode toward a parking lot of cars. "Is it possible that her death was a homicide?"

Hayes's broad shoulders, under the expensive weave of his jacket, visibly stiffened. He turned slowly, pinning the reporter beneath his shaded glare. Very slowly he said, "As with all investigations, Shelly Bonaventure's case will remain open until all the facts are in."

"So there's a chance of foul play?" the reporter replied, pushing.

Unlocking his car door remotely, Hayes shrugged. "Isn't there always 'a chance'?" he asked rhetorically, then slid behind the wheel of his vehicle.

The final frame was of taillights as his SUV blended into the thick Southern California traffic, and the screen returned to the hosts of the show.

"So I guess nothing's conclusive," the blond anchor said. "You know, Shelly was found much like Marilyn Monroe was half a century ago. The similarities in their deaths are really bizarre." With that the camera panned to a large black-and-white head shot of Marilyn Monroe, which morphed into a montage of pictures of the iconic blonde and ended with an interior black-and-white shot of the death scene, her bedroom within her Brentwood bungalow.

"Trash TV," Kacey muttered because of the exploitive edge to the segment.

And yet, possibly because of the morbidity of the report, she experienced a chill crawling up her spine, and she glanced to the window and the darkness outside.

She remembered the depths of her own despair, the fear in those frightening moments when her own life had been threatened, when she was certain she would die, when she stared into the face of evil.

For a split second, she remembered those horrid last words spoken by the man who had meant to run a knife through her heart. She shuddered, his last words, which had been snarled as he staggered away, reverberating through her mind. *It's not over. . . . You're one of them.*

His vile prediction had meant nothing, the ramblings of a deranged man whose psychosis and deadly intentions had somehow been trained on her. *Don't go there. . . . It's over!*

Shaking off the memory, she forced her attention to the television screen.

The hostess of the show, a blonde who appeared to be a human version of a Barbie doll, mentioned Shelly's acting credits, rumored lovers, and reiterated the fact that though her death was ruled a suicide, detectives at the LAPD "hadn't ruled out the possibility of foul play."

Wide-eyed, glossy lipstick perfect, the hostess went on to the possibility of a conspiracy with her cohost, a younger, hipper man in a dark suit, with spiked hair.

Kacey clicked off the television.

On her way to the bathroom for a quick shower, she started peeling off her workout clothes and was naked once she reached the small room. Inside, she turned on the water and hit the play button on her radio before stepping into the old claw-foot tub and drawing the curtain closed.

Hot water pulsed against her skin, and she felt the tension of the day start to ease from her muscles. Lathering, she washed, humming to a song by Katy Perry and forcing her mind away from Trace O'Halleran, where it had wandered whenever she had a free minute to herself, which, today, in the midst of flu season and appointments all day, hadn't happened often.

In those few minutes, though, she'd found herself wondering about him, about Eli's mother, and the unknown Miss Wallis, his "girlfriend" according to his son.

"Forget it," she said aloud, twisting off the tap. He wasn't even her type. She'd never been one to go for the backwoods, rugged alpha male in battered jeans, a beat-up jacket, who lacked a razor.

Yeah? And what good did that do you? Remember polished, sophisticated Jeffrey Charles Lambert, the heart surgeon whom you fell for? Was he your type? That didn't turn out so well, now, did it? Face it, Acacia, your track record when it comes to men is pretty dismal.

"Oh, stop!" she muttered under her breath, disgusted with the turn of her thoughts. Maybe she spent too many hours with her own thoughts when she was alone. It could just be time to rethink the issue of owning a dog.

So O'Halleran was the most handsome cowboy she'd met. So he seemed dedicated to his child. So her own biological clock was ticking like crazy, so loudly that she avoided the maternity wing in the hospital. So what?

The old pipes groaned. She heard over the DJ's chatter on the radio a noise that didn't seem to belong in the house. Grabbing a towel, she wrapped it around her as she stepped out of the tub, listening hard.

Nothing.

Was someone in the house?

Or was the sound only her imagination?

Still dripping, her heart pounding a little, she toweled off quickly and snagged her robe from its hook on the back of the bathroom door. Shoving her arms down the thick terry sleeves, she strained her ears, hearing nothing. Cinching the robe around her waist, she moved cautiously into the hallway.

Nothing looked or sounded out of the ordinary.

Scraaaape!

Her heart flew to her throat, and she walked stealthily along the hallway toward the noise. *It's nothing. . . .* But she felt the skin on the back of her neck prickle in warning. Peeking around the corner, she saw that everything was just as she had left it. The exercise ball still in the middle of the den, the remote for the television on the carpet nearby.

She rounded the corner and was starting for the kitchen when the sound, a deep grating noise, erupted nearby. She spun around, her eyes wildly searching the darkened dining room, her heart a drum.

Scraaape! Against the glass of the old window. She nearly shrieked when she saw a skeletal hand rake along the pane.

"Oh, God!" She staggered back, a scream rising in her throat just as she recognized the blackened hand for what it was—a weathered, leafless branch of the shrubbery on the east side of the house.

She sank down hard on a kitchen chair, drained, her vivid imagination and her deep-seated fears getting the best of her. She was a doctor, a professional, trained to be calm in emergencies, and yet a stupid tree branch had nearly sent her running for her grandfather's shotgun. "Get a grip," she told herself, feeling like a fool. "This is ridiculous."

Pulling her wits about her, she heated the slices of pizza in the microwave, threw the salad into a bowl, poured herself a glass of red wine from the bottle she'd opened three days earlier, and carried it all to the den, where she clicked on the television again and told herself this was the life she'd always wanted after she'd divorced Jeffrey.

She glanced out the window to the darkness beyond.

There was no one lurking in the shadows, just beyond the veil.

She was safe here. Home at last.

Or so she tried to convince herself as she shuttered all the blinds and refused to look beyond the frosty glass.

But in her heart, deep in the darkest of places only she recalled, she knew that she'd run away. Not only from a cheating husband, a doctor with a God complex, but also from the past, and the one night she tried never to remember.

The problem was, she couldn't run away.

Wherever she went, the memory of that night chased her down, nipping and snarling at her heels, the pain and terror never quite leaving her alone.

From the knoll, he trained his long-distance binoculars on the cottage, but even with the high magnification, he saw little through the curtain of snow. Yes, there were images of her in her den and kitchen, and the bathroom light came on for a few minutes, but her figure was indistinct, her face completely blurred, and when she finally pulled the shades, he could watch no longer.

He had the audio, of course, tiny microphones hidden in her house, in spots she would never find, but he'd never been able to install a remote camera, and that bothered him for he would have enjoyed watching her surreptitiously, from a distance, learning more about her, about her routine, about what really made her tick.

His fascination was obsessive, he knew, as he stood shivering in the thicket of aspen and spruce that grew at the edge of a field near her house, but he couldn't help himself.

She was the special one; of all the pretenders, she was the most dangerous. Smart and beautiful, Acacia Collins Lambert, a doctor no less.

Sliding his binoculars into their case, he took off the way he'd come, through the surrounding forest to a back road that he'd taken after following her home from the clinic where she practiced. Telling himself he had to be patient, he broke a trail through the snow.

It wouldn't be much longer.

CHAPTER 7

"You're sooo grounded." Pescoli glared at her daughter as Bianca slunk through the front door.

"Why?" Bianca asked as she headed to her room and Cisco, who had been sleeping on a pillow on the couch, jumped down and began wagging his tail frantically.

"Are you serious?" Pescoli had had it with her kid. "You skipped school."

"I told you I didn't feel good."

"Well."

"Whatever." Yanking off her gloves with her teeth, Bianca deigned to pat the dog on his head, then headed straight for the refrigerator. She tossed her gloves onto the table with the mail and opened the refrigerator, only to stare inside. "Isn't there anything to drink?"

Pescoli followed after her and slammed the refrigerator door shut with the flat of her hand.

"Hey! Watch out!" Bianca said, stepping back quickly and facing her mother. She was pale, dark circles showing under her eyes as she pulled off her stocking cap and tossed it onto the table next to the gloves. "What's your problem?"

"Exactly what I was going to ask you."

"I said I'm sick. Duh!" She glared at her mother as if Pescoli were as dense as tar and certainly not as interesting.

"You didn't call me, and you didn't come home."

"I hung out at Chris's."

"Instead of going to school?" Pescoli stepped back, allowing Bianca access to the refrigerator again.

"I was *sick*." She pulled out a can of Diet Coke and pulled the tab. *Pop. Ssst.*

"And when you are sick, the protocol is to phone me and let me know that you need to A"—she held up a finger—"come home, or B . . ." She held up a second finger. "Go to the doctor. There are no other options."

"I could call Dad." Bianca took a swig from her can.

"Did you?"

"No."

"Why not?"

" 'Cuz it wasn't an option, I guess." Another swallow of cola.

"Nor was going over to your boyfriend's house. Were Chris's parents home?"

"No. Duh. They work."

"Precisely."

"It's not like I need a babysitter."

"I'm not sure," Pescoli said. "So what did you do?"

Her daughter's eyebrows drew together. "Hung out. What did you think? Oh, God, I know. You think we were having sex or something."

Pescoli's insides curdled. "Yeah, I think that when you're alone with your boyfriend for hours, lying to everyone about where you are, that you could be getting yourself into some serious trouble!" She heard the accusations in her voice and dialed it back a bit. "Okay . . . listen . . . tell me, what were you doing? I know, I know, about the 'hanging out' part, but let's get a little more specific."

"We watched TV, played video games, rented a movie. . . . It was no big deal."

"Except that you were supposed to be in school," Pescoli said, keeping her voice low and serious. "It was a big deal, Bianca. A very big deal. I don't know what's going on between you and Chris, but I do know that whatever it is, it's not worth cutting school and getting behind in your classes."

"You're so ridiculous! I just watched some movies!" She started huffing her way out of the kitchen, trying to act like she was affronted. Pescoli caught her elbow as she passed and spun her around.

Nose-to-nose with the fifteen-year-old, she said, "We're not talking about me, Bianca. Don't try to deflect. This is about you, your behavior, consequences, and yeah, the rest of your life. Because you seem intent on messing it up."

"Just get off my case!"

"Nuh-uh. Not for a few more years."

Bianca yanked her arm back. "I could call child services on you! You can't touch me."

"Is that what Chris told you?"

"You can't touch me!"

Pescoli reached for the phone, grabbed the receiver, and held it close to her daughter's face. "Take it. Call. See what happens. If they believe you, they'll remove you from this home, and where will you go? To your dad's? To a foster family? Is that what you want?"

"Maybe!"

Despite the pain in her heart, Pescoli said, "Fine. Make the call." Bianca eyed the phone, and for half a second Pescoli thought her daughter would call her bluff. For another half a second she didn't care. No fifteen-year-old was going to bully her or try that stupid-ass emotional blackmail on her. She slapped the receiver into her daughter's free hand.

Bianca sputtered, "They—they won't believe me. You're a cop! You'll twist things around!" She slammed the phone onto the counter, and this time she marched off to her room.

"Slam that door and I'll take it off its hinges! Bianca, I'm not kidding!"

Slam! The entire house shook. Cisco let out a startled yip.

"Son of a bitch," she muttered under her breath and left the phone on the counter, then made her way to the garage, where she found Joe's twenty-plus-year-old toolbox and carried it back inside.

The front door burst open, and all six feet and then some of her son walked inside. A gust of cold wind followed him, and Cisco went nuts again. The little dog yapped and spun in elated circles.

"Hey, Cis," Jeremy said, bending down and scooping up the wiggling dog in his big, gloved hands. At eleven, Cisco still thought he was a puppy and washed Jeremy's unshaven face with his eager tongue. "What's for dinner?"

"I haven't gotten that far, yet," Pescoli answered.

"So, what's going on with Dad's tools?"

"I was just about to wrestle your sister's door off its hinges."

"Oh, Mom, don't do that." He set the dog down and pulled off his gloves, then stuffed them in the pockets of his down vest.

"Why not?"

"It's lame."

"So is slamming the door so hard, it nearly breaks the jamb."

He yanked off his stocking cap, and his hair, still filled with static electricity, stood on end, giving him a few more inches and a shocked look.

"You can help," she suggested.

"No way . . . uh-uh, I'm staying out of that catfight."

"What're you doing here? Aren't you supposed to be at work?"

He looked suddenly uncomfortable and worked hard at smoothing his hair while avoiding her eyes.

"What happened?"

He hesitated. "Okay, I got laid off."

Her heart took a nosedive. "Because?"

He shrugged his big shoulders. "Dunno. The economy, I guess."

"You guess?" *Not now.* She didn't need this now.

Jeremy heaved a loud sigh, then fell onto the couch. The old springs groaned. Cisco leaped up to his lap, and he absently petted the wriggling dog's head. "I got fired," he admitted.

"Fired," she repeated in a careful voice.

"Lou claims I stole from the station, that the receipts didn't add up." Head lowered, he looked up at her from the tops of his eyes. "Swear to God, Mom, I didn't do it." His Adam's apple bobbed, and his big hands clamped over his jean-clad knees.

"You told Lou that?"

"About a hundred times! You know what? I think it's either Manuel or Lou himself, like maybe he's covering his ass. Manuel's a good guy. Really honest. But I thought Lou was, too. Shit!" He gritted his teeth. "How could this happen?"

Her heart was pounding, and a mixture of anger and fear slid through her blood. "I don't know, Jer, but you have to fix it. Figure it out. If you didn't do it—"

"*If?* Really? You don't believe me?" He was shocked and offended, his lips flattening. "Come on, Mom!" Slamming a fist onto the arm of the couch, he declared vehemently, "I'm *not* a thief! Someone set me up!"

"You didn't let me finish, Jer. I was saying that if you didn't do it, then you have to find out who did. Prove it. It couldn't be that tough. The station has cameras and records of all the transactions."

"Are you crazy? You think they're going to let me see any of them?"

"They'll have to if you sue them and they fight it. Your attorney will—"

"I don't have an attorney, and I can't afford one. Get real!" He was starting for the back stairs.

"Where are you going?"

"My room."

"You moved out, remember?"

"It's still my room." Big feet began clomping down the steps.

"I was going to turn it into a sewing room."

"You don't even sew!" he yelled up the stairwell.

His door slammed shut, though not with the same righteous, passionate thud as Bianca's had.

"I'm a failure as a mother," Pescoli confided to the dog. "A complete and utter failure." Opening the toolbox, she searched for a screwdriver with which to pry the pins out of Bianca's door hinges. After digging through the rarely used wire cutters, pliers, and wrenches, she found a large screwdriver with paint drips on it, proof she'd used it to force open stubborn paint cans, and was about to attack the door in question when her cell phone rang.

"Pescoli," she said as she pressed the talk button.

"Alvarez," her partner answered her. "I think you should come up to the bluff over Grizzly Falls. Looks like a jogger slipped and fell over the railing up around the park. No ID on her."

"Dead?"

"Nearly. EMTs are working with her. Probably an accident. It's slippery as hell out here."

"Don't you have enough to do with the cases we've already got?" Pescoli asked. "This isn't even a death yet, much less a homicide."

"Hmmm . . . yeah."

"Well, it beats what's going on here," Pescoli decided. "I'm on my way," Pescoli said, tossing the screwdriver back into the open toolbox. Clicking off, she yelled loudly toward her daughter's closed bedroom door, "This is a reprieve, Bianca, but only a short reprieve. I'll be back." For once she didn't change her voice into her pathetic Arnold Schwarzenegger impression.

Today, she figured, it wouldn't be appreciated.

Cisco trotted after her as she headed for the back door. "Not this time," she told the dog as she zipped up her insulated jacket and stepped into her boots. She patted him on his furry little head. "Today you're in charge." His tail began moving so quickly, his whole rear end nearly gyrated. Then she slipped out the back door to the garage, where her Jeep was still dripping melting snow.

She opened the garage door, slid behind the wheel, and backed out. Jeremy had parked in his usual spot, as if he'd never taken a stab at moving out. There was a part of her that wanted him back home, but that was a purely emotional mother response. She knew better, had witnessed some of her friends allowing their kids to yo-yo in and out of the house.

That wasn't for her.

The kid had to start making some serious choices.

She threw her Jeep into gear, hit the remote on the visor, and saw the garage door begin to close.

How had it come to this, where she and her kids were forever testing each other, and they determined to make the wrong choices? Last year, when she'd been in the clutches of a madman, thinking she would never see either of her children again, she'd vowed to make it up to them, to either turn in her badge or change her ways, work only a forty-hour week, put her family above all else. And her kids, too, had promised to change their self-involved habits, to walk the straight and narrow, get good grades, make the right choices, never give her a minute's grief.

All those New Year's Eve vows had been broken by Valentine's Day, and they'd slipped into their same old dysfunctional routines.

Maybe she'd made a mistake by not moving in with Santana. Maybe a strong male role model was just what Jeremy and Bianca needed.

"It's never too late," she told herself.

Obviously what she was doing alone wasn't working.

On the outskirts of town, where the neon lights began to glow, she told herself to close her mind, for the moment, to her kids and their problems and turn her attention to whatever lay ahead.

By the time she reached the crest of Boxer Bluff, she saw police and rescue vehicles, their lights strobing in the night, flashing red and blue on the surrounding snow. Firemen, rescue workers, and several cops were working the scene of the accident. Alvarez, dressed in department-issued jacket and hat, was standing near a short, crumbling wall overlooking the falls and talking with one of the town cops.

Pescoli nosed her Jeep into an empty parking slot near the park as two medics loaded a woman on a stretcher into the back of a waiting ambulance. A crowd of about fifteen people had gathered, all craning their necks and talking amongst themselves beyond a police perimeter. A news van and camera crew were following the EMTs' every move as they transported the injured woman.

Pescoli flashed her badge at the town cop, who seemed to be in charge of keeping the bystanders at bay.

"What gives?" she asked Alvarez.

"She's alive, but barely. Looks like she was jogging and either tripped or slid and fell over the rail." Alvarez indicated a spot where the snow was disturbed on the top of the crumbling guardrail, an old rock wall that had been built over a hundred years earlier and was barely two feet high.

She shone her flashlight over the broken snow and path where the woman had fallen over the cliff face. "She hit on that ledge down there and somehow didn't slide farther, into the river. It's a miracle that she's alive." The beam of her flashlight played upon the broken ground below.

"Is she conscious?"

"No. Don't know how long she was out here or how serious her injuries are, or if she'll make it." Frowning, Alvarez shined the light back on the path. "Too many footprints and too much snow to see if anyone was with her."

"And no ID, no car?"

"Her run didn't start here, just ended here."

"But you think it's more than an accident."

"Unknown." But Alvarez was clearly puzzled, eyeing the snow-covered path where dozens of footprints had been left. "The crime scene guys are doing what they can, separating out her prints, the ones that match her shoes, and they're looking for anything that might help, other prints."

"Nothing on her to ID her?"

"Just a key. No cell, no iPod, or anything else."

"She could have just tripped."

"Yeah." Alvarez's breath fogged in the air.

"No witnesses?"

Alvarez shook her head.

"Who found her? And please don't tell me it was Ivor Hicks or Grace Perchant," she said, mentioning a couple of the locals who had a history of being in the middle of trouble. Ivor thought he'd been abducted by aliens years earlier, and Grace Perchant claimed to talk to ghosts. Pescoli didn't think either of them was all that reliable.

"No," Alvarez said. "Iris Fenton was out taking a walk." She motioned to a woman bundled in a heavy down coat, gloves, and a red stocking cap, from which silvery curls protruded. "She lives on the other side of the park with an invalid husband. Already checked her out."

Pescoli was nodding.

Alvarez glanced to the departing ambulance. "Hopefully she'll wake up and tell us she's just a klutz." She then eyed the embankment, the steep ravine, and the river, tumbling over the falls, the water roiling wildly far, far below. "Helluva place to slip so hard that you vault over the rail and land just where the cliff drops off, four feet from the wall, right here at the very top of the bluff. A few years ago this part of the hill fell away." She ran her light over the outside of the rail, to make her point. In either direction the drop-off beyond the guardrail wasn't as sheer, the vegetation more viable, but the spot where the accident occurred was the most steep. "Real bad luck."

"That why the crime scene people are here?"

She nodded. "I've already called Missing Persons. We'll see if we can find out who she is. In the meantime, I want to go to the hospital and talk to the docs who examine her, find out if her injuries are consistent with her accident."

"Which you're not buying."

"The jury's still out," Alvarez said as she reached into her pocket and withdrew her keys. "You coming?"

"Meet you there."

CHAPTER 8

Early the next morning, Trace looked out the window and saw snow falling steadily only to pile up around the fence posts and drift onto the front porch.

Eli was still asleep, though he'd had a bad night, the pain in his arm and his cough waking him every few hours. In the end, around three this morning, Trace had carried the kid downstairs, and together, with Sarge curled up near the banked fire, they'd bunked on the oversized sectional. At five thirty Trace had woken, let the dog out; then, once Sarge had taken care of business and Trace had started the coffee, he'd turned on the television to catch the weather report.

The first thing he'd seen was a woman reporter on the screen, snow covering her blue hooded jacket, a microphone clutched in her gloved hands as she stood near the entrance to the park on the crest of Boxer Bluff. Rescue and police vehicles were visible behind her, lights flashing in the dark as snow continued to fall. She was speaking to the camera, but her voice was too soft to hear.

Trace scooped up his remote and upped the volume.

". . . where an unidentified female jogger was discovered just an hour ago on a rocky ledge that juts out over the river nearly a hundred feet below street level."

The camera panned behind the reporter, to the steep grade and an area below. A narrow shelf protruded over the roiling water, and upon it was one rescue worker in a harness, a coil of rope in his hands. The snow on the ledge had been disturbed by boot prints and what Trace assumed was the area where the jogger's body had lain before the rescue.

"You can see how lucky this unknown jogger was," the reporter was saying. "Had she slid off the ledge, she would have fallen into the river." The camera panned to Grizzly Falls, where white water sprayed and churned before a swift current sliced beneath a hundred-year-old bridge and past the glittering lights of the town.

The camera's eye returned to the reporter. "This is Nia Del Ray," and she signed off to the two anchors sitting behind a joined desk. The blond female anchor clarified, "That footage was shot last night, and the latest report from the hospital is that the woman is in critical condition, but the identity of the jogger has not yet been confirmed."

Trace stared at the set and felt that same sense of doom that had been with him when he'd visited Jocelyn's apartment. Without a thought to the time, he picked up the phone and dialed Ed Zukov's number. He'd need his neighbor's help; someone would have to look after his boy for a couple of hours. Though he didn't want to believe that Jocelyn Wallis was the unidentified jogger who'd lost her footing and nearly her life at the crest of Boxer Bluff, he had to find out.

Pescoli's cell phone rang sharply near her ear.

She groaned and rolled over to the side of the bed, scrabbled for the damned thing where it was charging on her night table and knocked her reading glasses onto the floor.

"Great," she muttered as she flipped on the lamp, then said into the phone, "Pescoli."

"I think you'd better come down here," Alvarez said as Pescoli eyed the clock near her bed. The digital readout shone a bright red 5:57.

"And 'here' is where? The station? Geez, Alvarez, it's not even six. What the hell time do you get up in the morning?" How could anyone be so alert at this god-awful time of day?

"Yeah, the station. I think we might get an ID on the Jane Doe."

"Give me half an hour." Pescoli rolled out of bed and stumbled into the main bath, where she yanked off her University of Montana

Grizzlies football jersey and panties, then stepped under a much too cold shower spray.

Twenty-eight minutes later she was walking toward the back door of the sheriff's department. Ignoring the rumbling in her stomach and Joelle's winking snowflakes in the windows, she clomped the snow from her boots and walked inside, down a series of short hallways to Alvarez's desk, where her partner was busy talking to a tall man in an unzipped fleece jacket, faded jeans, work shirt, and sporting a dark beard stubble. He was sitting in the visitor's chair but got to his feet as she approached.

Alvarez glanced up. "This is my partner, Detective Pescoli, and he"—she hitched her chin to indicate the visitor—"is Trace O'Halleran. He thinks he knows who our Jane Doe is."

O'Halleran's lips pinched at the corners a bit. He shook Pescoli's hand. "I just think it's an odd coincidence that a woman I know is missing about the same time. She jogs, too, and I dropped by her house yesterday because I heard she hadn't shown up for work."

As Alvarez waved him back into his chair, she listened to O'Halleran while he explained that he and Jocelyn Wallis, a schoolteacher whom he'd met through his kid at Evergreen Elementary, had dated a few times and that the relationship had stopped before really getting started. Then, yesterday, he had gotten a call from a friend who worked at the school and was informed that the Wallis woman hadn't shown up for work. He'd noticed she had phoned him but hadn't left a message, so he'd gone to her apartment, investigated on his own by letting himself in with a hidden key he knew where to find, and subsequently discovered her missing. Her purse and car had still been at her home. As had been her phone. He'd found it odd, as it was out of character for her; to his knowledge Jocelyn Wallis had never missed a day of work.

"Then I saw this morning's news," he said, wrapping up. "That woman was pulled from an area of the park . . . one of the trails Jocelyn runs. So, I came to you."

Pescoli watched him closely all through the recitation. He seemed earnest, intense, and worried. His hands were clasped between his knees, the thumb of his right hand working nervously. He hadn't called her family, hadn't wanted to worry them, thought maybe the school would start contacting friends and relatives, and hoped that she would show up.

He was emphatic that he and she weren't dating. There had been no big blowup; they'd just quit seeing each other. It had been O'Halleran who had cut things off.

Pescoli wanted to trust the rancher. Handsome in that rugged way she'd always found sexy, he was used to working outside and had the winter tan to prove it. His thick hair brushed the collar of his fleece jacket, and his hands were big, calloused, and had a few tiny white scars. A single father whose wife, he'd admitted, had left him, O'Halleran seemed sincere, and he had come in of his own accord, but that didn't mean a whole helluva lot.

She'd seen the most pious, timid of men turn out to be cold-blooded killers.

"So, is this Jocelyn Wallis?" Alvarez asked as she slid a couple of pictures of the battered woman to him.

O'Halleran swept in a breath. "God, I hope not," he said fervently but studied each of the two shots. "I—I don't know. Maybe. Jesus."

"I've got a few pictures of Jocelyn Wallis," Alvarez said.

"From the school's Web site?" Pescoli guessed.

"Motor vehicle division." Alvarez clicked on her keyboard, and a driver's license appeared on the screen. The woman in the picture was somewhere in her early thirties with a bright smile and long reddish-brown hair.

"Could be." Pescoli looked at O'Halleran. "Any identifying marks? Tattoos? Scars? Birthmarks?"

He lifted a shoulder. "Don't know."

"You didn't see her naked?" Pescoli questioned. "She didn't talk about any surgeries or injuries as a kid? Or getting a tattoo?"

"We didn't get that far."

"You didn't sleep with her?" Pescoli asked.

He hesitated and looked down at his hands before meeting her eyes again. "Once. At her place. I didn't see anything. She didn't tell me about anything like that, but she did wear earrings. Three in one ear, I think, and two in the other."

"That's something," Pescoli said. "So why don't you come down and see if you know her?"

"The hospital will allow it?" he asked.

"We've got friends in high places."

He was already climbing to his full six feet two inches, and Alvarez was reaching for her jacket, purse, and sidearm. "I'll drive," Pescoli said. She wanted to see his reaction to the injured woman, and then she'd double-check his story.

And if the woman turned out to be someone other than Jocelyn Wallis, there was still the problem that the schoolteacher was missing.

If what O'Halleran had told them was true.

"Oh, thank God, Doctor Lambert! I was so afraid. . . . Oh, sweet Jesus!" Rosie Alsgaard said, the fingers of one hand theatrically splayed over her chest as she hurried along the hallway of the second floor of the small hospital. Dressed in scrubs, the ear tips of the coiled stethoscope peeking out of her pocket like the tiny twin faces of a double-headed snake, the ER nurse jogged over the shiny linoleum as she met Kacey. "Oh, man, I was worried. We all were."

"Worried? What're you talking about?"

"Because of the patient who was admitted last night, before my shift! She's a dead ringer for you, and Cleo, she was certain it was you! The Jane Doe."

"Cleo?"

"The nurse's aide who was working ER last night. And not just her. Me, too. I saw the patient and . . . and it's freaky!" Rosie was breathing hard, her words tumbling out of her mouth in no sensible order. "I mean, of course her face is swollen and bruised, her nose broken, but her hair . . . and she looks like you. I was sure when I saw her this morning . . . I mean, I was worried sick that you had fallen and—"

"Rosie! Slow down," Kacey ordered, one hand up. "Let's start over."

An aide pushing a medication cart passed by, while another nurse whipped past them and hurried toward the bank of elevators located at this end of the small building housing the newly reopened St. Bart's Hospital.

"Okay, okay!" Some of Rosie's color was coming back, and she took a long, deep breath. "Last night a patient came into the ER by ambulance. Apparently she was out jogging and fell down the ravine by the river. She didn't have any ID on her, and she was—is—in bad shape. Head trauma, broken pelvis, fractured tibia in two places, sprained wrist, two cracked ribs, ruptured spleen, and cuts and contusions. I mean, she's a mess, must've rolled down that hill, hitting rocks and roots and God knows what else. But the thing is, she does resemble you. She's got the same build, and we all know that you jog, sometimes up in the park. . . . We all were hoping that it wasn't you, but we were worried just the same."

"Someone could have called."

"Too busy last night. The police were here, too. And there were two multiple-car accidents with the snow, so there wasn't any time. Cleo and I, we figured if you didn't show up for rounds today, that we'd call the clinic."

"Where's the Jane Doe now?"

"In ICU, but she might have to be sent to Missoula or Spokane, depending. Right now, no one wants to move her."

"I'll check on her when my rounds are finished."

Rosie offered a tentative smile. "I'm just glad you're okay."

As Kacey went about her rounds, she wondered just how "okay" she was. For the second time in a week she'd heard that someone who looked like her was either dead or fighting for her life. Weird. But until she saw the woman in the ICU, she couldn't be certain that Rosie's imagination wasn't working overtime.

An hour later, after she'd finished checking on the few patients who were under her care in the hospital, she made her way to the ICU.

Anita Bellows was the nurse on duty. Barely five feet, Anita, at forty, was as lithe and agile as a woman half her age. A gymnast in college, she now ran marathons and trained year-round to keep in shape. With short brown hair, a quick smile, and large eyes surrounded by lashes caked in mascara, she had moved from Missoula when St. Bart's opened this past year, giving the aging Pinewood Community Hospital a run for its money.

Today, like Rosie Alsgaard, Anita, spying Kacey push open the door to the ICU, was visibly relieved. Anita was situated at the large circular desk from which private, curtained "rooms" radiated, much like the petals of a sunflower. "Oh, thank God," she whispered, making a quick sign of the cross over her thin chest, where a tiny gold cross was suspended on a fragile chain. "I thought . . . I mean, I was worried that . . ." She sighed and hitched her chin toward a woman lying in one of the two occupied beds. "I'm just glad she's not you."

"She's the Jane Doe?"

"Uh-huh. Brought in last night."

Kacey approached the private, curtained area for the patient.

The muscles in her torso tensed as she stared down at the patient's swollen face. Kacey saw the resemblance despite the contusions and probable broken nose. High cheekbones, deep-set eyes, which were now closed, a heart-shaped face, a few freckles still visible were like her own. The patient's hair was a deep auburn hue, and it fell in unruly waves to her shoulders, just as Kacey's did, even though a part of Jane's head had been shaved to allow an intracerebral pressure catheter to be inserted into her skull. The ICP monitored pressure inside the skull and drained off excess fluid.

Not a good sign. Heart monitor, ICP, IVs, urinary catheter were just a start. Jane Doe's body was draped beneath a sheet, one leg splinted, but Kacey already knew from Rosie and Anita the patient was a similar size and body type.

She touched the woman's hand. *Who are you?*

An eerie whisper swept over the back of her neck, and she told herself she was being foolish and unprofessional. Just because Rosie, who wasn't known for being rock steady, thought there was a resemblance, so what? Yet, as she looked at the comatose woman, just for a second she imagined her own self in this woman's place. In her mind's eye she saw herself helpless, comatose, on the cusp of death, while nurses and doctors scurried around to try and save her life.

"See what I mean?" Anita asked.

Kacey lifted a shoulder. "Maybe she does look a little like me."

"Try 'she looks a lot like you.'" Anita straightened the sheet, but her gaze was focused on her patient. "Pretty compromised. Just when we think we've got her stabilized, she starts to crash." She bit at her lower lip as she concentrated. "Some of her symptoms aren't consistent with her injuries, and Dr. Henner is still trying to figure out what's going on internally. X-rays, MRIs, CAT scans, but . . ." She glanced at the laptop computer that was also hooked to all the monitors. "Since she's comatose, we can't ask her what happened, and no one was with her or has come forward. She can't give us any information on her pain or if she was on some kind of drug or had a seizure . . . lots of unanswered questions, but the lab work should come back this morning. Then we'll know a little more. A couple of detectives were here last night and said they'd be back in the morning."

"Detectives?" Again, that tiniest of shivers.

"Yeah, two women who were checking out the accident." She glanced at the clock mounted on one wall. Frowning, her eyebrows drawing together, she added, "They'll probably show up soon, so I'll double-check with the lab. Maybe they'll know something more. You'd think someone should be missing her. She came in wearing top-end jogging clothes, jewelry, and had an iPod in her pocket. It's not like she was destitute. Trust me, someone's missing Jane."

Kacey, too, saw the time. "I've got to get going. Tell anyone who might still think I'm lying in that hospital bed that I'm alive and kicking and I'm definitely *not* the Jane Doe."

"Will do," Anita said. She was just walking back to her station when the ICU buzzer announced a visitor.

Anita hit a button that unlocked the doors, and they were immediately pushed open as Trace O'Halleran, his face a grim mask, strode into the unit. Unshaven, hair mussed, wearing work clothes under a heavy jacket, he looked shaken and none too happy about being at the hospital. Two women were with him, just a step behind. The taller of the two was a redhead, mid- to late thirties, who introduced herself as Detective Pescoli. Her partner was shorter, Hispanic, and said her name was Alvarez. Both wore the no-nonsense attitude of cops on duty.

Anita wasn't impressed with their credentials. "We can't have more than one visitor at a time in ICU. What's he doing here?" She pointed at the rancher.

O'Halleran's gaze met Kacey's, and she noticed a spark of recognition in those deep-set eyes. What was it his son had said? That she looked like his girlfriend? A little drip of trepidation slid through her bloodstream.

"This is Trace O'Halleran," Pescoli said. "He thinks he might be able to identify the woman who was brought in last night."

Anita wasn't persuaded. "Only one at a time." She held up a hand as if to physically halt the two officers. "There are several patients here, and we're not going to disturb them." As if to enforce her authority, she glanced toward Kacey. "This is Doctor Lambert. She can take Mr. O'Halleran to the patient's bed, and you two can wait here, by the door."

The officers looked as if they wanted to argue but held back, and Kacey managed a smile she didn't feel. She was suddenly cold as ice inside. O'Halleran and the Jane Doe? "Over here," she said and led the way, slowly drawing back the curtain so that he could view the patient.

He visibly flinched at the sight of her, his jaw tightening, his eyes closing for the briefest of seconds before he opened them again and took a long look.

"Jesus," he whispered under his breath. Then more loudly he said, "It's Jocelyn," turning away from the bed to face Kacey. "Jocelyn Wallis. The teacher Eli was talking about." He didn't explain any further to the detectives, and Kacey figured they'd already covered that ground. He looked once more at the battered woman lying, unmoving, in the hospital bed. The corners of his mouth twisted downward. "How the hell did she fall?"

"That's what we want to find out," Pescoli said. "We'll need you to tell us everything you know about her." The taller detective was moving toward the newly identified patient, but Anita stepped between them.

"Uh-uh. You can handle this interview outside the room." The smallest person in the area, she was still very much in command as she faced off with the cops. "I mean it. Out. But . . . I'll need to get some information, too." She glanced at O'Halleran. "Medical. Family."

"I don't . . . I don't know her that well." He rubbed a hand behind his neck, and Kacey wondered how much he was covering up. How involved was he with Jocelyn Wallis? "I think she has a sister somewhere in California."

"California's a pretty big state," Alvarez pointed out.

"That's all I ever heard. California. I told you I don't . . . didn't really know her." But he was thinking now. "Her maiden name was Black, she said, and her parents are from somewhere in Idaho. Around Pocatello?" he said as if asking himself a question. "She mentioned her dad a couple of times. . . . What the hell was his name? Cedric? No . . . *Cecil*." He snapped his fingers. "That's right. Cecil Black, but I don't remember her mother's name. The school would have a lot more information. You can probably get it from the principal. Her name is Barbara Killingsworth."

Anita was nodding and shepherding them out. O'Halleran glanced back at Kacey just as one of the monitors started to give off an alarm.

Anita spun on her heel. "Oh, hell! She's crashing!" To the detectives, she said, "All of you, get out of here! Now!" She was already reaching for the alarm button on her desk to alert the rest of the staff. Kacey had moved to Jane Doe's—now, presumably, Jocelyn's—side, ready to administer CPR and hoping to high heaven that the crash cart and doctor arrived soon.

She started CPR on the woman . . . two breaths, then chest compressions. *Come on, come on, Jocelyn. Stay with me,* she thought as she counted aloud.

"One, two, three, four, five—"

For a second, the woman's eyes opened, and Kacey nearly gasped as the resemblance to herself was almost uncanny.

"Doctor!"

Anita's voice pierced her brain, and she realized she'd stumbled on the count.

"That's fifteen, sixteen, seventeen," Anita prompted, and Kacey caught up just as the doors to the ICU flew open again, three nurses and two doctors streaming in, the crash cart rolling toward the bed.

"Get these people out of here!" a strong male voice ordered, and from the corner of her eye Kacey watched as Anita shooed the detectives and Trace O'Halleran through the doors. "I'll take over now," the same voice said, and she glanced up to see Dr. Wes Lewis walk quickly to the bed, waiting for her to hit thirty before stepping in as she withdrew her hands and a nurse sidled the crash cart to the patient. Lewis began giving orders to the staff as easily as he had as a quarterback in college. Big, black, and usually affable, he was all business today, but Kacey felt it was too late. She'd sensed it, that recognition that a patient was slipping away. Whether it was conscious or not, there came a point where the body was done.

"It's when St. Peter comes a-callin'," her grandmother, Ada, had whispered into her ear as she, crying miserably, watched as her favorite old horse, lying in the straw of his stall, shuddered his last breath.

Her grandfather had glanced at his wife, as if to disagree, but the look she'd sent him had silenced whatever he'd wanted to say.

"St. Peter needs horses?" Kacey, at nine, had asked. Her throat had been so thick, she'd barely been able to get the words out.

"Course he does," Grannie had insisted, hugging her so close that the smells of the barn—the acrid odor of urine, the dust in the hay, and the warm, heavy scent of horses—had faded to the background. All Kacey had been able to smell was the sweet scent of the wild roses in her grandmother's favorite perfume. "Course he does."

And now, Kacey thought, as the patient was being treated, the defibrillator standing at the ready, St. Peter seemed to be needing and "callin' for" Jocelyn Wallis.

CHAPTER 9

Dr. Lambert's expression said it all, Trace thought.

Her jaw was set, her lips were thin, her eyes somber as she walked down the short hallway to the area where he and the two cops were waiting. It had been only half an hour since they'd been banished from the ICU, but obviously things hadn't gone well.

"Jocelyn Wallis didn't make it," she informed both of the cops, who had been in and out of the waiting area, talking on cell phones, checking their watches, speaking in low tones, and sipping the weak, free coffee from paper cups. They'd questioned him further about his relationship with the teacher, and he'd told them about the last time they'd gotten together, that Jocelyn had wanted him to spend the night.

Going over to her place had been a mistake.

One that he hadn't made again.

He'd been taken in by her good looks, quick smile and, if truth be told, a sexual need that hadn't been fulfilled in a long while. But he hadn't allowed himself to be seduced more than once, if that counted for anything.

Chivalrous, he wasn't. And he'd seen that unspoken accusation in the shorter detective's, Alvarez's, eyes as she'd taken notes.

Now he shoved his hands through his hair as Kacey went on.

"She was just too compromised, too many internal injuries and head trauma. Dr. Lewis, who was the admitting doctor, will be out in a few minutes. He can answer any questions for you." She glanced at Trace, then walked quickly toward the elevators.

"Stick around," Pescoli advised him, as if she sensed he was about to try and leave. "We've got some more questions."

"About Jocelyn?" he asked but sensed there was something deeper.

Pescoli nodded as Alvarez eyed him with more than a grain of suspicion.

Trace got the message. "You think that this wasn't an accident?" he asked, feeling a new rising sense of anger. "And you think I know something about it?"

Pescoli shook her head. "We didn't say that."

"But you implied it."

Alvarez stepped in. "We're just looking into all the possible scenarios. For all we know, she slipped and fell over the railing. That's certainly likely. But we're trying to be thorough." She offered him a smile that didn't exactly light up her face, a smile that said without words, "Don't worry. This is just a formality," but his innate sense of self-preservation counteracted her forced affability. There was something more going on here; these women were part of the homicide investigation team.

Trace said, "I've got a sick kid and a ranch to look after. I've told you just about everything I know about Jocelyn Wallis, but if you have more questions, you can call me."

He thought they might try to stop him, but at that time a big black man in a lab coat swept out of the ICU and caught the cops' attention.

Good.

Trace made his way to the bank of elevators and felt a jab of disappointment that Kacey was already gone. Not that it mattered, he told himself as he stepped into the next car, where a male attendant was holding on to the handgrips of a wheelchair where a woman in a cast was seated. Trace sidestepped the outstretched, casted leg and waited as the doors whispered shut.

It was weird to think that Jocelyn was dead. He'd seen her less than three months ago, when she'd asked him over and they'd made another stab at it, or at least she had. He hadn't been interested but had wanted to smooth things over. The evening had ended with her asking him to spend the night. He had been tempted but had known that going to bed with her would be a bad idea. At that point, when he'd said he'd better leave, that getting involved wouldn't be a good idea, primarily because of Eli, she'd become instantly furious. White hot and pissed as hell.

The elevator stopped with a jolt, and the doors swept open in the main lobby. Trace waited for the patient in the wheelchair to be pushed out of the car, then headed toward the lobby doors at the front of the hospital.

Outside, it was snowing again, the wind bitter and harsh, the promise of December heavy on its breath. Turning his collar against the cold, he dashed across the emergency lane to his truck. He was yanking open the door when he caught a glimpse of a gray coat from the corner of his eye.

"Mr. O'Halleran?"

He recognized the doctor's voice before he turned and caught sight of her avoiding iced-over puddles, flakes of snow catching in the wisps of auburn hair that had escaped the hood of her coat.

"Trace," he said.

Already her face was red with the cold. "I just wanted to ask how Eli's doing."

"Better, I think," he said, leaning on the open door to his truck. "I indulged him with movies and soda last night."

She managed a smile. "Just what I prescribed." She shifted from one booted foot to the other and cocked her head toward the hospital. "I'm . . . I'm sorry about Jocelyn." She seemed sincere, her green eyes clouded. "That was rough."

He felt the muscles in the back of his neck tighten, and he nodded. "Eli's gonna take it hard."

"Will you call the sister you mentioned?"

"I'll let the cops find her. Jocelyn and I weren't even really friends. The only reason I'm involved in this is that someone from the school called me and asked if I knew where she was. I got curious. Since I knew where she kept the extra key, I went to her place. Her car was parked in its regular spot. Her purse was inside the apartment. When I heard about an unidentified woman jogger being injured up at the park on Boxer Bluff, I contacted the police." He glanced back at the hospital, three floors rising toward the gray heavens, snow covering the grounds and piling on the cars parked in the lot.

"So, they asked you to ID her."

"Yeah."

"They were homicide detectives."

"I know. I don't get it," he admitted. "She was still alive when we got here, and I thought it was just an accident."

"So did I." Her eyebrows knitted for the briefest of seconds before she forced a smile again. "Well, tell Eli I said hello."

"I will."

She was off then, black boots walking quickly across the lot to a spot where a silver Ford Edge was parked. She opened the SUV's door and turned, waving to him, before sliding inside. Less than a minute later she'd reversed out of the space, then cranked the wheel and driven out of the lot, her taillights twin red dots as she melded into a stream of traffic.

Trace hadn't even realized he'd been standing and watching her until her car had disappeared. Then he finally climbed inside and fired up his Chevy.

Funny how he found Eli's doctor attractive.

At that thought, he scowled and reminded himself she was off-limits. Besides, there was something about her that reminded him of Leanna, Eli's mother, and that was enough to convince him to re-main single. His marriage to her had been thankfully brief, and he'd ended up with a son out of the deal, even if the boy wasn't biologi-cally his.

Didn't matter.

He ground the gears of the old truck, flipped on the wipers, and watched as they shoved an inch of snow off the windshield. Easing the Chevy out of the lot, he glanced back at the hospital and thought of Jocelyn Wallis, his kid's teacher, a woman with whom he'd made love. Now dead. His jaw slid to one side. Didn't seem fair. Had she tripped and fallen in a freak accident? Or, he wondered, had she been helped over that short wall with the hope that she would end up in the river?

Why else would *homicide* cops show up at the hospital?

Had someone jostled her, knocked her over the ledge, and then, panicking, taken off? Or had she been intentionally pushed? A ran-dom victim? Or a target?

Snow was really coming down now, big, fat flakes that covered the streets and flocked the surrounding shrubbery. Rather than driving directly back to the ranch as he'd planned, he turned onto the road that wound around the edge of the bluff to the park. The road was steep; the old engine ground as his tires slipped a bit. At the crest, he nosed into a parking spot and climbed out to walk along the jogging path to the area where Jocelyn's body had been discovered.

Hands plunged deep into the pockets of his jacket, he stared across the short, crumbling, ice-encrusted wall. Far below, the river rushed by, its angry roar echoing in his ears. Above the swift, icy current a ledge protruded, and Trace saw that the snow upon that rocky shelf had been disturbed, big ruts and divots cut into the blanket, now slowly being recovered by new flakes.

"What the hell happened?" he whispered, his breath fogging, his words inaudible over the sound of the surging river. He couldn't help feeling a little stab of undeserved guilt. What if he'd been around to take her call? What if he'd met with her? What if something he'd done, one little seemingly innocuous thing, could have changed the course of history? Could a bit of timing have saved her?

"I'm sorry," he said aloud but wasn't even sure he understood why he'd murmured the words. Her death seemed such a waste.

Preventable?

Who knew?

He turned his gaze away from the river, to the park, where spruce, pine, and hemlock showed frigid, frosted needles and the aspens stood with naked branches. Two groups of women in stocking caps and gloves walked briskly by, a man jogged, and a couple, their baby wrapped close to the husband in some kind of sling, strolled past.

Seemingly serene.

A winter wonderland.

Aside from the snow disturbed on the ledge far below, where Jocelyn Wallis had tumbled to her death.

With no answers about a woman he barely knew, he returned to his vehicle and backed into the street, then guided his truck to the road that wound out of the town to the surrounding farmland. He needed to see about his kid and relieve Ed and Tilly. They did have a ranch of their own to run.

All the way home, he thought of Jocelyn and Leanna and, now, Acacia Lambert, the doctor who reminded him of two women who had been a part of his life, but the foremost thought on his mind was how he was going to tell his young son that his teacher, Miss Wallis, was gone.

*   *   *

"I can't tell you much about Jocelyn except that she was an excellent teacher," Barbara Killingsworth said from the far side of a wide desk in an office decorated with framed, matted artwork created presumably by the students of Evergreen Elementary. Rudimentary houses drawn in crayon were mounted beside detailed representations of buildings and still lifes brushed in shades of watercolor or etched in pencil.

Pescoli and Alvarez were seated in the two visitors' chairs, while the principal, a slim woman with slightly pinched features and pale skin, folded her hands over the desk. She sat as straight as if she had a metal rod up her spine; her blouse was crisply ironed; her brown sweater without a speck of lint or bit of fuzz. Not one strand of highlighted hair dared be out of place.

The terms *neat as a pin* and *perfectionist* and *a little OCD* flitted through Pescoli's mind.

The wall behind Killingsworth's desk was a bookcase filled with tomes on child psychology, education, and school administration. The top of her desk was neat as a pin, with only a bud vase holding a sprig of holly, a picture of her and some friends in a tropical paradise, a sun-spangled blue ocean glittering behind three women holding up drinks with parasols in the cups, and a thick manila folder marked WALLIS, JOCELYN.

"I know she was married a couple of times, no children, and her parents live in Twin Falls, Idaho, and, I think, a sister who lives in San Francisco. She visited there last summer." Principal Killingsworth's neatly plucked brows drew together to show a small line in her forehead.

"I believe her sister's name is . . . Jacqueline. I remember because it was a lot like her name. But . . . I'm sure she referred to her as a stepsister. Maybe ten years older? I think Jocelyn said her father had been married once before, but I'm not sure of that." Sadness darkened her eyes, and her hand trembled slightly as she touched the tips of polished nails to her lips. "This is a very difficult day for all of us at Evergreen."

"We're sorry for your loss," Alvarez said.

Killingsworth nodded, and her gaze focused a little more tightly on Alvarez. "You said you were detectives. Do you think there was more to her death than an accident?"

"Just covering all our bases." Pescoli gave the stock answer, but the principal didn't look as if her worries were allayed. She set up appointments with Mia Calloway, the school secretary and a friend of Jocelyn Wallis's, and two other first grade teachers, part of the "team" who worked together, offering to step into the classes as the teachers spoke to the detectives.

They didn't learn much more about Jocelyn Wallis, only that she had definitely been married twice, she had no kids, the exes were out of the picture, and other than a little on-line dating, the only man she'd seen since moving to Grizzly Falls was Trace O'Halleran.

Eventually, they left Evergreen Elementary, where the bell had just rung for recess and the kids were walking in long, snaking lines toward the covered playground area.

They slid into Pescoli's Jeep, and Alvarez said, "Let's get coffee," just as her cell phone rang. Answering with one hand, she clicked on her seat belt with the other as Pescoli drove around the teachers' vehicles and out of the once-plowed lot.

Half a mile closer to the town, Pescoli found one of those coffee-shack buildings that seemed to be sprouting up on every street corner. Alvarez finished talking to the manager of her apartment building about a number of outdoor lights that weren't working as Pescoli pulled into the open lane of the drive-through and rolled down her window just a crack. She waited for the barista to finish taking the order from a car on the other side of the building. Silver tinsel had been strung around the window; snowflakes stenciled onto the glass. A big red sign with a winking Santa offered coffee gift cards at a discount.

The window slid open, and the barista, a girl of about eighteen who was wearing braids and a pilgrim bonnet, called out, "What can I get for you? We've got pumpkin lattes, a dollar off, just this week." She offered a wide, toothy smile.

"Just a coffee, black," Pescoli said.

"Skinny latte, no foam," Alvarez said, angling her face so that she could meet the barista's gaze. "Plain."

"But the pumpkin is on sale."

"Plain," Alvarez repeated and dug into her wallet for a five-dollar bill.

The barista looked disappointed, as if she got brownie points for selling the special of the week. Pescoli rolled up her window as the espresso machine started whistling shrilly.

Digging into the Jeep's console, Pescoli pulled out enough quarters to pay for her drink. "So tell me," she said, turning to her partner before Alvarez could make another call. "Why are you so hell-bent to prove that Jocelyn Wallis was murdered?"

Alvarez readjusted the small hoop in her left ear. "Just a feeling I have. Something's off about it."

"Maybe."

"Worth checking out."

A red Dodge Dart, circa somewhere in the mid-seventies, rolled in behind her Jeep just as there was a sharp tap on the driver's window. The pilgrim barista was holding two paper cups with plastic lids.

Pescoli rolled down the window, collected the two cups and, after snagging Alvarez's fiver, paid for the drinks and left a bit of a tip.

"Wow, that's hot," Alvarez whispered after taking an experimental sip.

"Just what you need on this cold day."

Alvarez settled deeper into the seat as she cradled her cup. "What I need are answers. Lots of answers."

"About life's most important questions."

One side of her mouth lifted. "I'd be satisfied for the answer to why Jocelyn Wallis, a young woman, experienced jogger, and, from all reports, athletically fit and sane, ended up on a ledge jutting over a river." Her eyes narrowed as Pescoli braked for a red light. "Seems as if she might just have been helped over that rail."

"Maybe."

Alvarez was nodding as she lifted the lid from her latte and blew across the hot surface.

"And maybe not."

She took a long sip. "I guess we'll find out. Maybe the answer's at her place."

"We should be so lucky," Pescoli said but was already driving to Jocelyn Wallis's apartment complex.

They found the key where O'Halleran said it would be, unlocked the door, and stepped into the one-bedroom unit the schoolteacher had called home.

To Pescoli, nothing in the dead woman's apartment seemed out of place. Jocelyn Wallis had no home phone, but Alvarez found her cell on a table near her recliner; her house key and car key had been left in a dish on a table in the foyer, by the front door. They discovered her purse on the counter and schoolbag on the seat of one of two bar stools, near a small desk where her laptop was plugged into the wall. Over-the-counter flu medication and a few tissues in the trash near her bed indicated she hadn't been feeling well, yet she'd still gone out jogging. That was a little odd, but then the flu felt like it had settled in for winter, and sometimes serious joggers and exercise enthusiasts got tired of waiting to get completely well.

Her ten-year-old Jetta was parked in its spot in the long carport that housed the vehicles for this building, one of four in the complex. But an animal was missing—a cat, if the tins of food in the pantry didn't lie. Pet bowls half filled with water and food were on the floor, and a litter box had been tucked near the toilet in the bathroom. It was clean, no evidence of the feline.

"Where's the cat?" Pescoli asked.

"Apparently missing," Alvarez answered, looking around. "Nothing here indicates anyone broke in or that there was a struggle of any kind. It looks like Jocelyn just decided to get some exercise. If someone jumped her, it wasn't here. Probably on the trail."

Pescoli followed Alvarez's gaze. The apartment appeared to be just as someone going out for a jog would leave it.

Still, Alvarez wasn't satisfied that Jocelyn Wallis had just taken a fateful misstep that had ultimately ended her life. "It just doesn't feel right," she said again as they stood in the living room, where the scent of some plug-in air freshener was nearly overpowering.

"Since when did you start paying attention to feelings and hunches?" Pescoli asked. In all their years as partners, Pescoli had known Alvarez to be single-minded and scientific, one who never relied on anything other than cold, hard facts.

"Since Jocelyn Wallis's death doesn't add up," her partner said. Alvarez was already gathering the dead woman's laptop, cell phone, and bills from the desk. "Let's just take a little time and check it out. Don't you think it might be interesting to find out just who would benefit if she died?"

"Actually, that might be real interesting."

"Good," Alvarez said. "Let's do it."

CHAPTER 10

For Pescoli, Thanksgiving was the usual nightmare. This year the kids were supposed to spend the day with Luke and his Barbie doll of a wife, Michelle. Not quite thirty, the woman wore her long blond hair straight so that it brushed the middle of her back, and she preferred clothes that accentuated her hourglass figure. Michelle was as "girlie" as they came and pretended to be much more naive than humanly possible. Pescoli figured beneath the pale lips, thick black mascara, and perpetually surprised, sexy expression was a smart woman who for some unknown reason had set her sights on Lucky, who was handsome and, if not strongly educated, smart enough, just lacking in any kind of ambition. He drove his truck when he wanted to, and when he didn't and the weather allowed, he either fished or golfed. Otherwise he planted himself in front of his big screen.

"Made for each other," she said beneath her breath as her children dragged themselves out of their rooms. Pescoli had insisted they spend the holiday with their father, even though Bianca feigned sickness again and Jeremy grouched that Luke wasn't his "real" dad.

"Too bad," had been her unsympathetic response.

For the sake of the children and because she'd nearly died last year, Pescoli and Luke had made a stab at burying the hatchet. Their divorce had been less than amicable, and now, in retrospect Pescoli realized their animosity had been a mistake. However, old habits died hard, especially with all their past history. Trying to be civil was difficult, and trying to become friends had proved impossible, considering the circumstances. However, Pescoli was a firm believer in the old grin-and-bear-it motto, the reason being that she also trusted in the what-goes-around-comes-around adage. Luke Pescoli was handsome, charming, and a smooth talker. He was also a womanizer, gambler, and was pretty damned convinced that he was the center of the universe.

Michelle had gotten herself no prize.

She pushed open the door of her daughter's room just as Bianca, miffed, swept into the hallway. "You're doing this 'cuz you're mad at me," Bianca accused, her lower lip protruding, her eyes dark with accusation.

"I'm doing it because I have an agreement with your father."

"No one asked me," Bianca said as she stomped into the living room.

"With that attitude, you're just lucky you still have a door."

Jeremy, just coming up the stairs from his basement room, said, "Nobody asked me, either."

"So you two can bond over the injustice all the way over to your dad's. Oh, wait, I said I'd contribute to the festivities." She reached into the pantry, found an old can of cranberry sauce, the kind Luke detested. She slapped the can into Jeremy's outstretched hand and imagined the congealed sauce slithering onto a serving plate, still showing the ribs of the can. "Here it is."

Jeremy caught her gaze. "You're wicked, Mom."

"Just doing what I said I would."

Jeremy tucked the can into his backpack.

"We could just stay here," Bianca complained, though she was looking at the screen of her phone, reading a text.

"No. I've gotta work. This way I'll get the time off at Christmas so I can torture you both then."

"Funny," Bianca said, then, moping, put on her down jacket and wool hat, smashing down her curly hair, the tie strings dangling past her pointed chin. "But four days . . ." She was really whining now. "I'll die."

"Three nights. You come back Sunday morning. Think of it as a vacation from me."

Bianca managed to roll her eyes for what had to be the twentieth time since dragging herself out of bed. She let out a disgusted puff of air that caused her newly cut bangs to float up and down.

"Drive carefully," she advised her son.

Jeremy said, "I always do!"

"That's what I love to hear." Pescoli didn't believe it for a second and, spying Cisco dancing near the front door, ready to go anywhere Jeremy would take him, scooped up the feisty little dog. She was rewarded with a slopping doggy kiss, Cisco's tongue washing her cheek while his tail thumped against her side and he wriggled in her arms. "Tell your dad and Michelle, 'Happy Thanksgiving.'"

"Yeah, like you mean it," Jeremy grumbled.

"I do. I hope you have a great time." Holding the squirming dog, she stood at the door and watched as the two of them made their way along the snowy path to Jeremy's truck. In her mind's eyes she saw them as they once had been, Jer, the older, lanky brother with missing teeth and socks that never stayed up, Bianca, all springy reddish curls, chubby legs, and rosy cheeks, tagging after her adored older sibling.

Where had the time gone? Her heart twisted a little as she saw Jeremy help Bianca into the cab, slam the door, then trot around the front of his truck to climb behind the wheel.

Within seconds the pickup rumbled to life, a steady throb of bass reverberating from inside the cab as Jeremy pulled away. She stood for a while, watching the truck rumble through the trees guarding the lane, then slammed the front door shut.

"What do you think of that?" she asked, setting Cisco on the floor. "Alone at last, just you and me. Think of all the trouble we can get into."

As if he understood, the little dog went crazy at her feet, wiggling and prancing toward the cupboard where she kept his leash and a few doggy treats. "Okay, okay, it *is* Thanksgiving." She tossed him a bacon-flavored biscuit. "But we are *not* making a habit of this."

She did need to run into the office; that wasn't a lie. Alvarez seemed hell-bent to prove that Jocelyn Wallis's death was a homicide. They planned to go over the autopsy, as it should have come in late last night.

Afterward, Pescoli was going over to Santana's place. A small smile played upon her lips at that thought. If there was one thing about the man, it was that he was always interesting.

And that wasn't a bad thing.

Definitely not bad at all.

*   *   *

Trace was halfway down the stairs when he called over his shoulder to his son, "Hey, Eli, let's get a move on!"

No response.

He paused on the landing. "Eli?"

Trace drew a breath and headed up the stairs to the second floor of his farmhouse. Eli had been exceptionally quiet after Trace, trying his hardest not to stumble and pause and struggle for words, had told him that Miss Wallis had met with a terrible accident and was now in heaven. Eli hadn't said anything in response, so Trace had asked if he knew what heaven was. Then Eli answered promptly, "That's where you go when you're dead. If you're good."

"Uh . . . yeah," Trace responded, uncertain where to go after that. Eli had taken matters into his own hands by saying he wanted to watch TV. The subject had been dropped ever since.

Now Trace wondered if he was about to get into a deeper discussion about death with his seven-year-old. He mentally cursed Leanna for running out on them. He might not miss her, but he could've really used some help raising their son about now.

"Hey, bud," Trace said, entering Eli's room. "We gotta get over to the Zukovs for Turkey Day. Gobble, gobble. Let's get a move on." Eli's room was one of two that faced the front of the house, and as Trace moved into the room, he saw that his son was seated on the floor, some of his Lego blocks scattered around him, cradling his blue cast. "Are you in pain?"

"Do we have to go?" Eli asked, looking up. Trace saw the shimmer of tears in his son's eyes.

"Hey, what's wrong?" As Trace crouched to comfort him, Eli shook his head. His little chin trembled, and he swiped at his eyes with the sleeve of his good arm. "Is this about your teacher? Miss Wallis is in good hands, son."

Swallowing hard, Eli stared at Trace with serious, worried eyes. "Where's Mommy?"

Trace tried hard not to react. It felt as if his heart were being ripped from his chest. What a fool he'd been to think that Leanna's leaving had been forgotten. He totally got it that Eli losing his teacher had brought these feelings to the surface, but it still threw him for a loop. "I, uh, I don't really know where she is right now," Trace admitted.

"She should be here. I want to talk to her."

Of course he did. "I don't know how we can do that." Reaching for the down jacket tossed on the foot of the unmade bed, Trace tried to reassure his boy. "At least not today. But I can try to find her if you want."

"You don't know where she is?"

"Not at this exact moment." His guts twisted. Truth be known, he hoped Leanna never showed her face around here again. He prayed she'd leave her son to grow up without her intervention, because she was certain to screw the boy up.

Or was that his own selfishness talking? Maybe the boy would be better off knowing his mother, despite the fact that she was a liar and had left him without a word.

"Sometimes, I'd like to talk to her, too," Trace said to Eli, still crouching, though it was a bald-faced lie.

"I want to talk to her now."

"I'll try to find her. That's the best I can do. C'mon, now. Tilly and Ed are waiting for us."

"Promise?" Eli demanded. He wasn't going to let Trace off the hook.

"Promise." Knowing this would lead to no good, he agreed nonetheless and tried to help the boy struggle into his damned jacket. The bulky sleeve fit over his good arm; the other side had to flop over his cast. Since Eli was already wearing a thermal undershirt, a long-sleeved sweatshirt, and a down vest, he'd be warm enough for the short span of time he was outside. Trace tried to force the zipper of the jacket, then gave up fighting with the stubborn tab. The Zukovs were right next door. Usually, on Thanksgiving, Trace spent the day alone with Eli. They played games, watched sports or cartoons, and ate a turkey dinner he bought as takeout from Wild Will's, his favorite restaurant, but this year he'd decided to take the Zukovs up on their invitation. He'd figured Eli was probably tired of being cooped up and needed a change of scenery, and there was also the sadness and shock over losing Miss Wallis.

Now, as he and Eli clambered down the stairs, he wondered if he'd made a mistake. He shook his head. Today wasn't the first time his son had asked about his mother, nor would it be the last, but every time the subject of Leanna came up, the questions were always unexpected and difficult to answer truthfully.

Get used to it. They're not going to get any easier as time goes on.

They walked through the kitchen, where Sarge had taken up his favorite spot under the kitchen table. He thumped his tail as they grabbed gloves and hats from the hooks near the back door.

"She should call." Eli's little face was drawn into a frown of concentration. "She should call me."

"Yeah, that she should." Trace had tried to be honest with his boy from the get-go, but it hadn't always been easy, especially with the trickier queries.

"Can you call her? Right now?"

That one stopped him cold. He snagged his jacket from a hook and shoved his arms down its sleeves. "I don't know," he said, holding his son's gaze. "I think it would be best if she found us. She knows where we are."

"You need to call her. Maybe she's hurt! Maybe she's dead like Miss Wallis!"

"She's not dead," Trace assured him.

"How do you know!"

"If anything happened to your mom, someone would phone us." He jammed his Stetson onto his head.

"Not if they don't know our number!"

Trace placed his hands on his son's shoulders. Even with the padding of his quilted vest and down jacket, Eli's body felt thin and small. "After Thanksgiving, I'll call her."

"Tell her to come back."

"I'll talk to her."

"Tell her to come back!"

"Eli, it's not that simple."

"Why not?"

Trace sighed. "Because . . . grown-ups always make things complicated."

Eli's jaw jutted out. "Then they should stop."

"Probably." He opened the door to the porch and felt the chill of winter seep into the house.

"She should be here."

"She should be here, but she's not." He managed a thin smile. "But you and I, we're solid." With a gloved finger, he forced Eli to look into his eyes. "Right?"

"Yeah," his son said without a lot of conviction, and one more time Trace found himself mentally berating his ex-wife for how callously she'd left her son.

"Are you gonna be okay?" he asked, knowing damned well the boy wasn't.

Eli lifted one shoulder.

Trace took his kid's hand and helped Eli down the back steps. "Okay, let's go see Tilly and Ed." They trudged through the broken path of snow to the truck. "I think Tilly mentioned something about taking you on at checkers again."

"She'll lose," Eli predicted.

"Big talk."

"I'll show you." For the first time that day, Eli almost flashed his smile.

"Don't show me. Show her." Feeling that this latest emotional storm had been weathered, Trace bustled his kid into the truck. The boy really did need a mother, but he'd be damned if he'd go out looking for some woman for the sole purpose of helping him raise his son.

No reason for that.

For a second he thought of Eli's doctor, Acacia Lambert. She, like Leanna, had auburn hair and a wide mouth, but that was where the resemblance faded. Where Leanna had blue eyes, the doc's were closer to green and sparked with intelligence.

He wondered about her, what she was doing on Thanksgiving and, as he drove the quarter mile to the Zukovs' place, had the unlikely pang that he wanted to spend more time with her.

"Ridiculous," he muttered, turning off the plowed road and onto the rutted lane, where several cars had already parked around the Zukovs' garage and pump house.

"What?" Eli asked.

"Oh, I was just thinking," he covered up, nosing the truck into a space beneath a winter apple tree where clusters of red fruit were visible as they dangled on leafless, snow-covered branches.

"About what?"

"About what you're gonna want for Christmas this year."

"You said 'Ridiculous,' " his son charged.

Trace cut the engine. "That I did, because I imagined you wanted a mountain bike."

"Sweet!" Eli said, then paused and skewered his father with his concerned gaze. "Why would that be ridiculous?"

"Because you're wearing a cast, kiddo!" He rumpled his son's already unruly hair. "How dumb would that be to put you on a bike when you already have a broken arm?"

"I'll be fixed by then!" Eli said, unbuckling his seat belt and reaching for the handle of the door. He hopped down to the snowy ground and was racing to the front porch before Trace could climb out of the truck.

The boy's exuberance was infectious, and Trace felt only a smidgen of guilt for lying to his son. But he didn't want to admit the cold, hard truth to Eli. Nor did he really want to think it himself.

But the fact was, he'd been having trouble pushing Acacia Lambert out of his mind.

And that spelled trouble, plain and simple.

The kind of trouble he didn't need.

CHAPTER II

Kacey didn't like the place.

No matter how many "stars" or "diamonds," or whatever the ranking was as far as retirement homes went, Rolling Hills just wasn't her idea of "independent" living. But it didn't matter. Her mother loved it here in this lavish, hundred-year-old hotel that had been converted into individual apartments. Her mother's place, a two-bedroom unit on the uppermost floor, had an incredible view of the rooftops of Helena and, farther away, on the horizon, the mountains.

There was a pool and spa, exercise room, and car service, if one preferred not to drive their own vehicle, though each unit came with one parking spot in an underground garage.

The building was spacious, the amenities top-notch, and still, when Kacey walked through the broad double doors and signed in at the reception desk, she felt a pang of sadness for the home she'd once shared with her parents, a little bungalow with a big yard.

That's what it is, she decided. There was nothing wrong with Rolling Hills other than it wasn't the place she'd grown up and this was the place where her father, after suffering a stroke, had died.

"She'll be right down," the receptionist, a petite woman with narrow reading glasses and lips the color of cranberries, advised Kacey. "If you want to take a seat . . ." She waved a hand toward a grouping of oversized chairs and a love seat near a stone fireplace that rose two full stories. Kacey crossed the broad foyer and stood before the glass-covered grate, where warmth radiated to the back of her legs.

For the past three years, ever since her divorce, Kacey had spent her Thanksgivings here, and she couldn't help feeling a bit of nostalgia. *Don't go romanticizing your childhood. You know better.* . . .

Maribelle, her mother, when invited to Kacey's, had steadfastly refused, insisting Kacey make the trip to Helena instead.

"You must come here," she'd intoned. "Chef Mitchell is a god when it comes to the menu, and neither one of us will have to spend hours cooking and cleaning. Besides, it's just too much for me to get away."

That had been a bald-faced lie. Why her mother wanted to play the age card when she was on the south side of seventy was beyond Kacey. Maribelle Collins had more energy than a lot of women half her age, and, for the most part, she was sharp as a tack. Kacey believed her mother was a bit of a queen bee at Rolling Hills Senior Estates and didn't want to leave her position for a second.

But Kacey had decided making the trip would be simpler than insisting Maribelle come her direction.

"There you are, darling!" Her mother's voice rang out across the grand foyer. Kacey snapped out of her reverie to spy her mother, shimmering in a silver dress and high heels, hurrying toward her.

Tall, thin, and striking, Maribelle smiled widely and clasped both her daughter's hands as they met, which surprised Kacey as the last time she'd seen her, all she did was frown and complain. At sixty-five, she was spry and youthful, dressed as if she were going shopping on Fifth Avenue in New York City. Her hair was white, thick, and cut in a soft pageboy; her eyes were a sparkling blue behind fashionable glasses; her chin as strong as it ever was. "I've been so looking forward to this. Come, come!" She was already leading Kacey to the dining room near the back of the building. Garlands of pine boughs had been draped around the windows. White lights winked from beneath the long needles, while another fire burned brightly and the tables had been covered in white cloths and decorated with small poinsettias in red and white. A few other residents were scattered around the room, seated at tables, some as couples, a trio of friends, and a couple singles.

"Isn't it festive?" Maribelle enthused. "They get a little jump on Christmas here, but why not? Oh, this is my table over here." She motioned toward the windows, and as she did, she glanced around the seating area, her gaze skating over the few other diners.

"A lot of people are missing today. Off to see their children or siblings or whatever. So we have the table to ourselves!" For the first time in a long while she seemed excited and bubbly. "Sit, sit." She waved Kacey into one of the cushy chairs as she took her own seat and unrolled a napkin that had been placed in her wineglass.

"So tell me," she said, smoothing the linen carefully over her dress. "How's work going?"

"Hectic," Kacey said, trying to understand the change in this woman who was her mother. Gone was the dour, stubborn, glass-is-half-empty person, replaced by a smiling, happy woman who seemed to embrace life. Someone who was interested in her daughter. "Just the other day a woman was rushed into the ER. She'd been out jogging and had fallen over that short little guard fence up on Boxer Bluff, by the park, you know the one I mean. Just at the crest, near the falls, from what I understand."

"Oh, what a shame. I hope you fixed her back up again." Maribelle flashed a quick smile and effectively changed the subject. "Now, honey, check out the menu," she said, pointing with a cranberry-glossed nail to the list of offerings on the menu left on Kacey's plate. So much for her interest in her daughter's work or the patient's well-being. "Look. You can have roast turkey *or* baron of beef. Can you believe it, an actual choice? It's because of the new chef. Mitch." She rotated her hands upward, as if to praise the heavens. "He's just what this place needed after that miserable Crystal. How she ever got the job here in the first place is beyond me. . . . Let's see, well, I don't know why I even care. I'm having the turkey, of course. Tradition, you know!"

Who was this woman? Kacey wondered as her mother flagged down the waitress, Loni, and they ordered. Maribelle took another scan of the room, then welcomed the glasses of Chardonnay that Loni poured.

As the meal was served, they sipped and chatted, making small talk and working their way through a squash soup, green salad garnished with hazelnuts, feta cheese, and cranberries, and eventually sliced, moist turkey served with buttered sweet potatoes, sautéed green beans, and a delicate oyster stuffing with gravy. The meal wasn't as homey as the corn-bread stuffing, Campbell's soup green bean casserole, and yams with a marshmallow topping that Ada Collins,

Kacey's grannie, had served every year, but it was a close second best.

Better yet, her mother was in a cheerful, almost festive mood, so unlike the times she'd either sulked or just "gotten through the day" at her in-laws' farm, the very spot Kacey now called home.

Tonight her mother smiled and kept up the conversation, regaling her with humorous little anecdotes of "senior living." As long as they talked about Maribelle, everything seemed fine.

Little did Kacey know that she was being set up, though she should have seen it coming.

After the main course was finished, Maribelle asked the question that had probably been on her mind all evening, or quite possibly the last three years. "So," she said pleasantly as she stared across the table at her daughter, "what have you heard from Jeffrey?"

Ahhh, Kacey thought. *The ambush.* "Nothing."

Maribelle's eyebrows pulled together in concern. "Maybe you should give him a call."

"Why would I do that?"

"To be friendly," Maribelle said, lifting her shoulders innocently. "It's the holidays."

"We're divorced, Mom. Have been for three years."

"Oh, darling, don't you think I know that, but . . . sometimes a couple can get past whatever it was that kept them apart." Maribelle's smile disappeared slowly, and she set her fork on her plate. "I always liked him, you know."

Oh, yeah. She knew. "It didn't work out."

"You didn't give it enough time. Three years? My God, that's barely a sneeze in life. I was married to your father for over thirty-five years! And trust me, not all of those times were rosy."

Kacey did believe her.

"You should just contact him."

"Not gonna happen, Mom," Kacey said and pushed her plate aside.

Her mother let out a long-suffering sigh as the waitress came with offers of dessert and coffee.

"I'll try the pumpkin cheesecake with the caramel sauce and decaf, Loni," Maribelle said familiarly.

Kacey said, "Just regular coffee with cream."

"You have to try some dessert. It comes with the meal, no extra expense, and it's . . . out. Of. This. World!" her mother insisted, then turned to the waitress again. "By any chance did Mitch make crème brûlée today?"

"Espresso flavored," the waitress said with a knowing smile.

Maribelle's eyes brightened. "My favorite, but I think I really should sample his cheesecake." To Kacey she added, "Order the brûlée and we'll swap bites. I'm not kidding you when I say it's scrumptious. If I weren't so stuck on tradition with the pumpkin, I'd order it myself."

"I don't think—"

"Oh, come on, Acacia! It's Thanksgiving, for God's sake!" To Loni, she said, "Please bring us a bit of each. It's a holiday, and we're not to-gether that often." She placed a thin, cool hand over Kacey's, as if sharing dessert would actually be a bonding experience.

"Okay," Kacey said, surrendering.

"You won't be disappointed." Her mother actually patted her hand. What was this? Maribelle wasn't known for any public displays of affection.

The waitress disappeared through double doors leading to the kitchen.

"I wish you'd give Jeffrey another chance." Maribelle was nothing if not single-minded.

"I'm not interested, and I think he's engaged."

"Seriously?" Maribelle's dark eyebrows shot skyward.

"I don't know it for certain, and really, I don't care, but one of my friends in Seattle, Joanna . . . You met her, I think, once or twice. Any-way, she called the other day and mentioned that Jeffrey was going to get married next year sometime."

"Well . . ." She played with the napkin in her lap, and the shadows from the candle on the table played against her face, aging her a bit. "It's just that I . . . I would so love a grandchild."

"Really?" Kacey was surprised. She had been an only child and had been told often enough that she hadn't been planned. Though she was certain her mother loved her, Maribelle had never been one to fawn over children or even show an interest in becoming a grand-mother. Until today.

"Are you seeing anyone?" her mother asked hopefully.

Kacey's wayward mind flitted to Trace O'Halleran before she brought herself back to reality. "No."

"No one at the hospital? Another doctor?"

"I said—"

"What about on-line dating? I see all sorts of sites advertised on the television, and Judy Keller's daughter found the love of her life on some Christian matchmaking Web site. I'm sure there's one for professionals. In fact, I checked."

"I really don't have time."

"Of course you do. It's a matter of priorities, that's all! And if I were you, I wouldn't give up on Jeffrey so soon. He's a well-respected surgeon, and he's even written a book and has speaking engagements all over the country."

"And you know this . . . how?" Kacey asked.

Maribelle didn't bat an eye. "I have the Internet, darling. It's a wonderful tool. And nowhere on Jeffrey's Web site did he mention a fiancée."

The desserts and coffee appeared at that second, but Kacey caught the look of disappointment in her mother's eyes. Maribelle had loved Jeffrey Lambert from the second she'd met him. "A heart surgeon," she'd whispered to her daughter, her eyes alight. "And handsome, too."

Never mind that Kacey herself would soon be a doctor in her own right. Or that Jeffrey had an ego that would rival Napoleon's.

The bottom line with her mother was Jeffrey Lambert, MD, was one helluva catch and her daughter had let him slip away. Now, as she bit into the crème brûlée, Kacey wondered what her mother would think if she admitted that the man she found most interesting these days was a hardscrabble rancher with a seven-year-old son.

Finally, as her mother was in her own private heaven, sampling her cheesecake and moaning softly in ecstasy, Kacey brought up the subject that had been weighing on her mind. "So, Mom, did Aunt Helen have any kids?"

"Of course not." Maribelle glanced up quickly. "She and Bill couldn't. You know that."

"What about on Dad's side?"

"No. Neither of his brothers married. Again, you already know this."

"Maybe not married . . . but had some kids they didn't talk about? Or maybe know about?"

Her mother was shaking her head as if the idea were impossible. "As far as I recall, they never dated much."

"So, you're saying I don't have any . . . cousins that I was never told about? Since you and Helen have been estranged, I thought—"

"What? That I lied? Why would I do that?" Her mother looked perturbed again and straightened her napkin. "I'm telling you, no cousins. You know that. I don't understand why you're asking now."

"Okay, okay. I know it sounds a little crazy, but remember that patient I was telling you about, the one who fell while jogging and ended up in the ER?"

"Yes. At Boxer Bluff." So Maribelle had been listening.

"Unfortunately, she didn't make it. Her name was Jocelyn Wallis, and she was a schoolteacher, who, as it turns out, was born around here. And she looked a lot like me. Enough to freak out some of the nurses I work with."

Her mother grew deathly quiet for the first time since they'd sat down as Kacey explained the details. She refolded the napkin twice before Kacey launched into her resemblance to Shelly Bonaventure, another woman who looked like her and was born in the area.

"I saw that she'd died. Not much of an actress, if you ask me," Maribelle said. "And I suppose she might look a little like you, but so what?" She was shaking her head. "What are you suggesting? That those women were fathered by your uncles?" She rolled her eyes. "And then what? Adopted to other families and we never heard about it?"

"Or maybe Dad, before he met you . . ."

"Oh, Acacia, stop it! Right now! If Stanley had any other children, don't you think I'd know about it?" she demanded.

"Maybe he didn't know."

"We're talking about your father! Remember him?" She shot her daughter a withering glance. "He would be mortified if he were here, Acacia! As it is, he's probably rolling over in his damned grave!" She shuddered theatrically. "Your friends have overactive imaginations, or some need to put some drama into their lives." Leaning back in her chair, she glared at Kacey and shook her head. "Come on, Acacia! How many long-lost cousins do you think the family's hidden from you?"

"Maybe none. I don't know. I'm just saying it's strange."

"So many things in life are 'strange' or 'odd' or 'coincidence.' " After making air quotes, she waved her hand as if to dismiss the en-

tire topic, as if it were inconsequential claptrap. But her cavalier attitude didn't quite match the sliver of concern that Kacey noticed in
her mother's eyes as she added, "You know, people see resem-
blances with each other all the time. People make entire careers out
of being celebrity lookalikes. Now, that's the end of this inane conversation!" She turned her attention back to her pumpkin cheesecake. "Mitch really outdid himself with this. Try a little, and don't
forget to get a bit of the whipped cream."

"Nice dodge, Mother," she said.

"Taste it, and drop this ridiculous inquisition—"

"It's not an inquisition. I'm just asking about the family."

"And I've answered, so that's that."

Her mother transformed into the Maribelle Collins Kacey recognized best: the set, jutted jaw; the pursed lips; the narrowed eyes.
Her neck was nearly bowed, and Kacey knew she would learn nothing else. Tonight. Not from her mother.

What Maribelle didn't realize was that, rather than turn Kacey's attention away, she'd practically insured her daughter was going to
keep digging. There were other ways to check birth records, and she
had access as a doctor. For now, she couldn't nudge her mother any
further and there was no reason to antagonize her, but she was not
giving up.

She'd learned while growing up that she could push her mother
only so far. So now, Kacey didn't argue. It wouldn't make any difference, anyway. If Maribelle didn't want to talk about something, she
just didn't.

So, it was time to feign the peace, if not make it. "Okay," Kacey
said, lifting her spoon. "Let's see if Mitch's cheesecake is all that it's
cracked up to be." Reaching across the small table, she plunged her
spoon into the dessert and noticed her mother's shoulder muscles,
beneath the shimmering silver silk, relax a bit.

"Mmmm, that is good," Kacey said, as if savoring the sweet taste of
caramel. But the words were rote as she wondered why her mother
was determined to change the subject away from her father or uncles
or cousins or anyone associated with the family. If she hadn't felt so
before, Kacey was pretty certain now that there were more than a
few skeletons in the family closet.

CHAPTER 12

"What're you still doing here?"

The sheriff's voice almost echoed down the empty hallway.

Seated at her desk, her gaze drawn to the computer monitor, Alvarez glanced over her shoulder just as Dan Grayson actually stepped into her office area.

Her insides tensed slightly, just as they always did whenever she was alone with him. The weird thing was that it wasn't because he was her boss; she had worked for different overseers since she was fifteen and had never experienced this reaction, but there was something about Grayson that put her just a little on edge. And she didn't like it. "I was just catching up on some things." Rolling the chair around, she found him looming above her.

He filled the doorway, a tall man with broad shoulders and a mustache going gray. Sturgis, his dog, a black Lab who was a washout with the K-9 unit, was right behind him.

"You do know it's a holiday."

"Thanksgiving. I heard."

He chuckled deep in his throat, and she hated that she found the sound pleasing, that she, too, wanted to smile. Good Lord, what was wrong with her?

"I haven't authorized any overtime."

"And I haven't asked for any, have I?"

"Or comp time."

She nodded. "As I said, just tying up some loose ends."

"Go home. It's a holiday," he repeated.

She lifted a shoulder. The truth was that she never made a big deal of holidays. Most of her family was in Woodburn, Oregon, and her studio apartment was really just a place to crash, not exactly homey or a place she'd want to invite the few friends she felt close enough to have over. Besides, they all had families and, holiday traditions. Pescoli had dropped by earlier and, upon learning that Alvarez had no plans for the day, had offered a halfhearted invitation for Alvarez to join her. Though she had declined, Alvarez had felt a stupid pang of regret that she was entirely alone, especially when Pescoli had hurried out the back door on her way to meet Santana. Alvarez, glancing out the window and watching Pescoli's Jeep drive off through the falling snow, had sighed. She could imagine Pescoli and Nate Santana enjoying a quiet meal alone, in front of a crackling fire, a turkey roasting in the oven of Santana's rustic cabin, making love until long into the night.

The thought had jolted her.

Time to get a pet, she'd told herself and gone back to work, here at her desk in the department offices.

Now, with Grayson watching her, she said, "It's quiet here. I get a lot done when no one's around. No distractions."

"What about later? What're you doing?"

"I was thinking Chinese takeout."

He actually smiled, his lips twitching beneath the mustache. "Great as that sounds, and, y'know, it does, why don't you stop by my place?" Her stupid heart nearly skipped a beat. "Got a few friends comin' by. Around six. Real casual."

So they wouldn't be alone. Good. "Maybe I will."

He chuckled again. "That sounds like a thinly disguised 'No, thanks.'"

"A bona fide, dyed-in-the-wool maybe."

"I'll hold you to it." His eyes, as brown as her own, pinned her and silently accused her of trying to placate him. "And get the hell outta here." With a nod, as if he were agreeing with himself, he whistled to the dog, then made his way toward the back door, the sound of his boot heels and the click of claws fading away.

She leaned back in her chair and reminded herself that Grayson was her boss. Yeah, she found him attractive in that grizzled ranch-hand way. With his long legs, slim hips, and broad shoulders, he was built like a cowboy, tough as leather, and, as far as she knew, had lived all of his life in the area. He'd been married once, and she didn't really know all the details there; Grayson kept a lot of his personal life close to the vest, which was another reason she admired him. She did the same.

Today, though, she hadn't been lying. The offices, for once, were nearly silent, aside from the hum of the furnace as it forced warm air through the vents. She was able to get a lot of work done without coworkers, ringing phones, fax machines, and e-mail blasting at her every ten seconds. But she wasn't playing catch-up, as she'd told Grayson.

Instead she was reviewing Jocelyn Wallis's autopsy and tox screen.

The autopsy indicated that the victim had heart disease, more advanced than she might have known. According to the ME, Jocelyn's arteries were partially blocked and could have been from a woman twice her age, the result probably of bad genes and a hard lifestyle. She probably would have suffered a heart attack if her condition was left untreated and might have died young. There was no sign of recent sexual activity, but along with evidence of the over-the-counter meds she'd been taking, there were traces of arsenic in her blood.

She looked through the report that listed the contents of the victim's stomach and found nothing out of the ordinary. It looked like chicken vegetable soup and coffee and little else.

Odd. Rather than the evidence absolving her of her suspicions, just the opposite had proved true. Glancing at a photo of the victim, she said, "So what happened to you?"

And more importantly, who did it?

Jocelyn had two ex-husbands, one living outside of Laramie, Wyoming, the other in Edmonton, Alberta, in Canada. Both had iron-clad alibis and, it seemed, had had little contact with their ex-wife. Without children or custody issues or jointly held businesses, there had been no reason for them to keep in contact with her.

Also, Jocelyn had next to no life insurance, just enough to bury her. The beneficiaries listed were her parents. Nothing out of the ordinary there. She still owed on her car, so no one would end up with a vehicle. However, her phone records were more interesting. Aside from her girlfriends, she had called Trace O'Halleran a couple of times, though it seemed as if she'd just left messages; the calls were short.

Something? Alvarez wondered. He had gone into Jocelyn's place, admitted to doing so; his fingerprints would probably match several latents they'd collected. He was one of the only persons they'd found who knew where she hid her spare key, though anyone could have found it.

Still . . . Trace O'Halleran was the last man she'd dated with any kind of interest. And he was the one person someone at the school had called when they were worried about her.

He seemed normal enough, but even calm, even-keeled people could be pushed into violence given the right situation.

He was worth checking out.

Clicking off her computer, she decided it was time for a little more investigation. Even though it was Thanksgiving, a skeleton crew was working in the crime lab, so she made a quick call and asked Mikhail Slatkin, the investigator on duty, to meet her at Jocelyn Wallis's apartment. Now that she had proof that Ms. Wallis didn't just die of a misstep, she needed to take another, deeper look at her home, life, and job.

He dressed in dark slacks, a crisp shirt, and a casual sweater, then checked his hair in the mirror and decided his look for the command performance on Thanksgiving Day was perfect. Impeccable.

Truth be known, he detested the holidays, all of them, but he put on a good front, pinning on a smile and driving through the snow to his sister's home, a lakeside manor always in some phase of reconstruction.

His large family collected here each and every third Thursday in November, at his sister's home, and he was expected to show, which he always did. He feigned interest in all their petty little problems, even played with his nieces and nephews, deflected any questions about his personal life and the women he dated.

Because he knew they didn't care. In fact, they didn't trust him. He was, and always would be, the outsider. No matter how hard he tried to fit into their close-knit group.

He brushed his lips across his sister's cheek as he handed her a bottle of expensive wine that both she and her husband fawned over. He swung his niece off her chubby legs and heard her giggle in delight. He, after all, was the "fun" uncle. He even went to the trouble of going outside and trudging through the snow to view his nephew's snowman and snow fort, from which the niece, of course, was forbidden.

Inside he was charming, even suffering through one of his sister's guided tours of what they were "doing" to the house this year—a complete gutting and remodeling of the guest bathroom in the south wing.

"God help us that it gets done before Christmas. Lord, is that only five weeks away?" his sister said, looking around at the gaping holes where sinks and a toilet had once stood. Tile and grout had been displaced; the mirror, still hanging, was cracked in one corner. She sighed heavily. "I guess I'll have to get on that builder!"

"It's going to be great," he answered, forcing enthusiasm.

"I hope so. Then you can stay with us! You'll have your own suite, and the kids would love it." Her eyes darkened just a shade with the lie. "I'd love it, too." Her hand touched his arm then, lingering just a bit too long. She retracted it quickly when her husband walked in, his voice booming, "Welcome to our nightmare. The continuing nightmare."

They made their way downstairs, and shaking off his sister and her oaf of a husband, he saw that the music continued to play, the wineglasses were always refilled, that his father was never out of the conversation. Of course, he was in charge of carving the turkey, even deigning to wear one of his brother-in-law's stupid man aprons.

Throughout the meal at the seemingly mile-long table, he smiled and laughed, dodging the most pointed of their prying questions. Over the top of his wineglass he winked at his cousin, and she quickly averted her gaze, one that had been drawn to him throughout the evening, and blushed.

His sister, of course, had seen the exchange, and her lips had pursed in abject disapproval.

All of his family had speculated about his love life, and he'd given them just enough information to keep them satisfied, but it was a game, really, watching them offer help to set him up with different women.

As if he needed their charity.

This year the banter had started when his sister announced that her best friend was going through a messy divorce. The woman's attributes were pretty, good figure, decent job, *no* kids. Might even end up with several hundred thou, if her husband, the snake, didn't screw her over.

Then there was one of his brothers' old high-school girlfriends, rumored to be back in town and newly single. His mother had made note. However, his father had pointed out, the woman they were all so sure was "the one" did have three girls, the oldest already in her teens.

But what about that woman he used to work with, oh, what's-her-name? You know the one. A lawyer, wasn't she? And good-looking, too. Smart as a whip.

Such a shame his job took him so far away so often.

He needed to settle down, his father reminded him. Was the old man afraid? Did he suspect?

Maybe next year his schedule would slow down, and he could spend more time here. . . .

He let the conversation swirl around him, smiling affably, talking about the upcoming holidays and how they would all spend Christmas together, though it was getting more and more difficult.

His sister pulled him aside when he helped clear the plates, and she worried aloud about their father's health. Who knew if the old man would make it to next Thanksgiving? Every day he was still alive and ambulatory was a blessing, didn't he know?

Next year, well, she couldn't think that far ahead.

Of course not. Who knew what new construction project would come between then and now?

But five to one the old man, hearty and hale, would outlive all his progeny. And that was saying something.

He stayed to watch his father finish a last scotch, then load himself and his wife into their waiting SUV, a Cadillac complete with driver. He shook his father's hand and found the old man's handshake as firm as ever.

"Say something to Mother," his sister insisted, and lying through his teeth, he told the old bat that she looked "radiant," and that he couldn't wait until they all got together again at Christmas.

The second they were driving away, through a falling screen of snow, his thoughts turned toward the future. He managed a round of quick good-byes, and then, saying he had to get home because he had an early flight in the morning, he half jogged to his car.

Only when the rambling lake house disappeared from his rearview mirror did he let down his mask and unhinge his jaw from the insipid smile he'd pinned there for the past five hours. He rubbed at the scar hidden beneath his sideburn and let his thoughts darken.

He didn't have time for holidays or nonsense.

The radio was playing some insipid Christmas carol, and he snapped it off, his eyes trained on the road ahead and the twin beams of his headlights cutting through the storm. The miles rolled too slowly under his tires.

He couldn't waste any time.

He had too much to do.

The ingrates that were his family just didn't know it. Couldn't. Not ever.

CHAPTER 13

"So that's it," Alvarez said as she and Slatkin and an assistant, Ashley Tang, packed up the contents from Jocelyn Wallis's apartment and carried the bags to the waiting van from the state crime lab. The evidence had been photographed, bagged and tagged, then initialed before they hauled the bags along the path broken in the snow to the crime lab van.

Mikhail Slatkin, not yet thirty, was tall and rawboned, with a keen intelligence and guarded demeanor, and was physically the diametric opposite of the woman who worked with him. Petite and Asian, Tang was a woman who, Alvarez guessed, barely tipped the scales at a hundred pounds even in boots and insulated ski suit. Rumored to have graduated from Stanford before she was twenty-one, Tang, at twenty-eight, was sharp and intense, qualities Alvarez understood only too well.

Together they'd gone through the unit, gathering evidence that might have been overlooked before anyone realized that the victim had been poisoned, most likely, in Alvarez's opinion, murdered, though she didn't quite understand how the homicide had taken place.

True, there were traces of poison in the woman's system, but she'd died from the result of wounds from her fall. Had she been delirious and taken a fateful misstep, or had the killer been nearby and, rather than wait for the poison levels in her body to become deadly, given her a little push?

Slatkin unlocked the white van with its shadow of grime where someone had scrawled "WASH ME."

"I'll need this ASAP," Alvarez said as Slatkin arranged the evidence bags to his liking in the back of the van.

Slatkin slammed the back door closed. "Big surprise."

Tang, her breath fogging in the frigid air as she climbed into the passenger side of the van, assured Alvarez, "We'll be on it."

Alvarez made her way to her Jeep just as a blue older model Plymouth rolled into a covered spot and a woman, somewhere in her upper seventies, climbed out. She was bundled in an oversized coat. The second her booted feet hit the cement under her covered parking area, a wildly enthusiastic dachshund in a ridiculous red sweater that matched his owner's scarf and hat hopped from the car to twirl on his leash. Barking madly, wrapping the leash around his owner's legs, the dog took one look at Alvarez and stopped dead in its tracks. Dark eyes assessed the newcomer with undisguised suspicion. "That's a good boy, Kaiser," the woman cooed as she opened the trunk and hoisted a sack of groceries from within.

Kaiser growled at Alvarez, and his owner, looking over the tops of her glasses, chuckled. "Don't mind him," she said. "He's all bark and no bite." Slamming the trunk closed, she whistled softly. "Come along, Kaiser."

"Excuse me, do you live here?"

"Yes. One-C." She nodded toward her unit, right next door to Jocelyn Wallis's apartment.

"You're neighbors with Jocelyn Wallis."

Her lips drew into a sad frown, and her eyebrows slammed together above the dark rims of her lenses. "Yes. Poor thing. I heard about what happened to her, on the news. I was out of town, you know, visiting Frannie. God, she's an awful cook. She's my sister and I love her, but do you think she ever cracks a cookbook or looks up a recipe on-line? No. Just roasts a turkey the same old way she always does and cooks it until it's dry as the Sahara, but not her stuffing. Lord, how do you cook a dry turkey and still end up with wet, slimy dressing?" Then, as if she realized she'd been rambling, she said, "It's too bad about Jocelyn, really. She was a nice enough girl, well, woman, just a little . . ." As if she thought better of what she had intended to say, she lifted her shoulders, tugged on the leash, and half dragged Kaiser toward her front door.

"Excuse me, ma'am." Alvarez pulled out her badge and introduced herself. "If you don't mind, I'd like to talk to you about Ms. Wallis." The truth was that few of her neighbors had been interviewed as her death had been deemed an accident.

"Surely," the woman said after studying Alvarez's badge. "I'm Lois Emmerson. . . . But, please come inside, where it's warm." Shifting her groceries to her other arm, she walked to the front door of the unit abutting Jocelyn Wallis's and let Alvarez into an apartment that was neat and tidy.

After setting the sack on a counter that separated the kitchen from the living area, she unsnapped Kaiser's leash, hung it up, and took off her coat, gloves, scarf, and hat. Beneath the outer layer was a red sweater with white dots . . . just like the dog's.

"You knit," Alvarez observed.

"Voraciously! Never met a skein of mohair that I didn't love!" The dog's nose was at the crack of the pantry door, so she gave him half a doggy biscuit and said, "I'll put on some tea."

Alvarez tried to decline, but it was of no use. Lois Emmerson declared they both needed to be "warmed up," and it became increasingly evident that the older woman, as she heated water in the microwave, was lonely. Single. No children. Just Kaiser for company and the poor excuse of a cook, Frannie, as family. It appeared as if she wanted to talk, so Alvarez took off her coat and tossed it on an empty bar stool.

"You were saying that there was something about Jocelyn Wallis that bothered you."

"No, I don't think so." The microwave dinged, and Lois was on it like a flea on a dog, quickly sliding the glass pitcher out of the microwave. Deftly, as if she'd done it a million times, she began pouring steaming water from the pitcher into twin porcelain cups that bore the stains of countless uses. She plopped a used tea bag into her cup, then asked, "Orange pekoe or English breakfast?"

"Pekoe," Alvarez said, just to keep the conversation flowing. She was standing in the dining area, the kitchen counter separating them, and watched as Lois found some loose tea and dropped a spoonful into the second cup.

Once the tea was steeping, Lois slid that cup across the Formica.

Alvarez reminded, "You said, 'She was a nice enough girl, or woman, really, just a little . . . ,' and then you didn't finish. What were you going to say?"

"Oh. Well." As if she were suddenly lost in thought, Lois dunked her tea bag several times, then let it steep. "Jocelyn was complicated, not that I knew her all that well." She pinched the last drops of tea out of the tiny wet bag, then tossed it into the trash. Immediately Kaiser stuck his long nose into the open container. "Out of there, mister! You know better!"

Tail between his legs, the doxie scurried out of the kitchen. A step behind him, Lois walked into the dining area and waved Alvarez into one of the antique chairs.

"What do you mean, 'complicated'?"

"Maybe that's the wrong word." Blowing across her cup, Lois settled onto a well-worn cushion in one of the chairs. She rested her elbows on the table. "Jocelyn was young and . . . not really wild, more like enthusiastic and so anxious to fall in love. She'd already been married, y'know. Not once, but twice, and what was she? Thirty-four?" Disapproval etched the lines near the corners of Lois's mouth.

"Thirty-five," Alvarez said. "It's not uncommon these days to be married several times by that age."

"Oh, I know. I know, and I'm not judging her." Shaking her head emphatically, she added, "But it seemed to me that she was looking for a man. Really looking hard. Had dated on-line, I think, and then there was the father of one of her students, and she just was getting a little desperate." She tasted her tea. "Again, in my opinion."

"A lot of men visit her?"

Lois was sipping, but she lifted her free hand and waggled it, as if she didn't really know the answer. *Maybe yes. Maybe no.*

"There were some that I saw around here. But I'm not a snoop, so I wouldn't really know. There was the rancher who was a father to one of her students. I think I mentioned him. Trask or Trevor or . . . Tall. Good-looking."

"Trace O'Halleran."

"That's the one. But that relationship was a while ago." She pursed her lips as she remembered. "I think she was very disappointed about that one. Her biological clock was really ticking."

"Had she been dating anyone recently?"

"No one I could name. But there were a couple, I think. One man, tall and looked kind of like a bodybuilder, carried himself that way, you know, erect, stiff shouldered. Drove a dark truck, I think. I only remember because Kaiser, the little stinker, lifted his leg on the truck's front tire. A Michelin. I remember."

"Local plates?"

"Oh . . . I have no idea." She was shaking her head. "The second Kaiser did his thing, I hurried into the house."

"Do you remember what kind of truck?" Alvarez asked. This was probably nothing, but they didn't have a lot to go on.

"No . . . but it was large, not one of those smaller ones."

"Domestic?"

She shrugged. "All I remember is that it was dark. Black or blue or gray and was fairly new, I think, no dents, and had really nice tires." She smothered a little bit of a smile, as if her dog were such a naughty, but clever little beast.

"But you didn't get a look at the man's face."

"No."

"What about his ethnic background or race? White? Black? Hispanic?"

"White . . . I think. Can't be sure."

So much for identifying the mystery man.

"He was here often?"

"Oh, I don't know. I just noticed his truck a couple of times. Only saw him once, walking up to the door, and I was behind him, with Kaiser." Offering a feeble smile, she said, "Sorry."

"You said there was a second one?"

"Oh . . . maybe. Maybe not." Lois thought it over. "Might've been just the one with the dark truck."

Alvarez asked a few more questions but got no more information. Ms. Emmerson knew little about Jocelyn's friends, though she thought most of her social life was through people she worked with at Evergreen Elementary. She had heard of a sister living somewhere out of state and parents maybe; the two women had essentially met at the mailbox or the common area or the parking lot when Jocelyn was jogging and Lois was walking Kaiser. The information Lois had gleaned had been in bits and pieces.

Alvarez learned what she could, which wasn't much more, then drained the remaining tea from her cup. She was standing, intent on ending the impromptu visit, when Lois looked up at her expectantly.

"Mind if I read the leaves?"

"Pardon?"

"The tea leaves in your cup. That's why I gave you loose leaves, so I could read them."

"You do that?" Alvarez couldn't believe it. Since moving to Grizzly Falls, she'd met Ivor Hicks, who swore he'd been abducted and probed by aliens, and Grace Perchant, the woman who believed she spoke to ghosts and saw the future, and now this . . . woman, who looked like an ex-librarian, was going to read the dregs of her hot beverage?

"Of course I can."

"Have at," she offered, but Lois had already stood and rounded the table so that she could peer into the cup. She turned it upside down on a napkin so that the final drips of tea were removed from the cup; then she righted the porcelain again and studied what remained inside.

"Oh, my . . . hmmm . . ."

Alvarez wasn't going to rise to the so obvious bait.

"This is interesting," Lois went on and, when Alvarez didn't respond, said, "It looks like you're in for a change . . . work related, maybe? Or . . . maybe not. Certainly a love interest. There's a heart in your near future, but . . ." She frowned.

Don't ask! However, the words tumbled out of her mouth. "But what?"

"There's danger, too . . . evil." She pointed to a squiggle of small leaves on the rim of the cup. "This is the present, and here, the heart, a little further into the future . . ." One of her graying eyebrows lifted. "A new boyfriend?"

"I doubt it." Alvarez pulled her coat from the bar stool.

"I take it you're a nonbeliever."

"Depends upon what you're asking me to believe in." She was just shrugging into the coat's sleeves when Kaiser, who had been lying beneath the table, scrambled to his feet. Barking madly, he raced to the sliding door, where he stood on his hind legs and began clawing at the glass while growling and barking and working himself into a frenzy.

"Hush! Kaiser! You stop that!" Lois yelled as she scooted her chair back. "What in the Sam Hill?" She was on her feet and heading to the back door. "Oh . . . my." Her hand flew over her chest as she looked through the glass.

Alvarez followed her gaze and spied a bedraggled cat seated on the back patio's covered table, its luminous eyes unblinking as it stared into the apartment through the slider.

"Dear God in heaven, that poor thing is Jocelyn's. Oh, for the love of . . . I can't let her in because of Kaiser. He'd tear her limb from limb . . . but she's freezing."

"I'll take her."

"Oh, no! I won't let you take her to a shelter! We'll find her a home." Lois was horrified as she bent down and picked up her quivering, anxious dog.

"I meant I'd take her home."

"Oh, well . . . good!"

Still barking as if he'd seen the face of Satan, Kaiser wiggled and scrambled as Lois carried him out of the living room. "His kennel is in my bedroom," she called over her shoulder, then reprimanded the dog. "You know better, Mr. Kaiser. . . ." Her voice became muffled, and the cat, frost in its whiskers, looked up at Alvarez.

Alvarez unlocked the door and slid it open. Without a second's hesitation the cat, black with white toes and a spot under her throat, strolled inside to rub up against Alvarez's jean-clad leg. "Hey." She leaned down, petted the cat's arched back, and melted when the animal started doing figure eights between her ankles.

Somewhere a door shut.

"I swear he *hates* cats!" Lois said, returning to the living area. "Oh, I see you've already made friends. Poor little thing! She must be starving."

"I'll feed her."

"Good! Good!" Lois tried to pet the cat, but it ran and hid beneath the sofa. "Uh-oh. So now she's shy. You know, I've got an extra pet carrier. I used it when Kaiser was a puppy. We could put her in that."

"If we can catch her."

"You try and I'll find the crate."

To Alvarez's surprise, the cat didn't put up much of a fight. Within ten minutes, she was in the car, driving back to her own apartment, the animal yowling piteously from its carrier in the backseat.

She wondered, as she hauled Jane Doe, the name she'd settled on for the moment, toward her front door, if she would have the heart to take the cat to the shelter, or if as of now Jocelyn Wallis's cat was hers. In her mind's eye she saw Lois Emmerson and her dog in matching sweaters and couldn't help but fast-forward to her own life. Would she suffer the same fate as the older lady? End up living alone with an animal who was a surrogate child, a cat with her own set of clothes?

"Never," she breathed, unlocking her door and stepping into the sterile studio she called home. She fed the cat from a can she'd gone back and swiped from Jocelyn Wallis's apartment, folded a towel for a kitty bed, and let the cat explore. While Jane Doe was nosing around, Alvarez poured some of the kitty litter she'd also taken from the dead woman's home into a box with short sides. She placed the cat into the box. "Remember this, okay, Jane?" she asked, and the cat promptly ran out of the bathroom. "Great."

Alvarez hurried through the shower, toweled off quickly, and changed into black slacks and a rust-colored turtleneck. She added big hoop earrings, and for once, let her long black hair fall free.

Back in her small kitchen area, she found a dusty bottle of Cabernet in the pantry and swiped it clean while the cat dared jump onto the counters. "You're pushing it," she warned, and Jane responded by yawning and showing off needle-sharp teeth. "Be good."

Not on your life, she imagined the cat saying as she grabbed her coat and scarf, threw them on, and, before she could talk herself out of it, snagged the bottle and her purse and walked out the door.

Snow was softly falling, millions of tiny flakes glistening in the lamplight.

Telling herself she was six kinds of a fool, she made her way through the coming blizzard to her Jeep, where, once inside, she paused.

Was she really going to do this?

Take up Dan Grayson on his offer?

With a stray cat locked in her apartment?

Keys poised over the lock, she closed her eyes and counted to ten. "Oh, hell," she muttered. What was the worst that could happen? She'd embarrass herself? She'd find him alone with some other woman? He'd be home alone, not expecting anyone and surprised to find her outside his door?

Who knew?

Nothing ventured, nothing gained. Or *Nada aventurado, nada adquirido,* as she used to say as a teen, an expression that made her grandmother shake her head at her.

Jabbing the key into the lock, she twisted on the ignition. Seconds later, she was driving out of the lot, through the falling snow, and wondering what the hell she would say to her boss once she landed on his doorstep.

CHAPTER 14

"We've been over this before." In Santana's large bed, with fire-light flickering through the open doorway to the living area of the cabin, Pescoli levered up on one elbow. Sighing, exasperated with her own conflicted emotions, she stared down at the man she hated to admit she loved. God, she was a fool. Especially for him.

The lingering scent of chili—*turkey* chili, he'd informed her—mingled with the smell of burning wood. Their Thanksgiving dinner had been less than traditional, and she loved him for it. Most of the hours together had been spent right here, in his massive bed, his dog, a husky named Nikita, curled on the floor near the door. Outside the windows, snow fell softly, and for a few peaceful hours it was as if they were totally alone in the world.

Santana, too, was naked, his skin tanned against the white sheets, his black hair mussed and falling over his forehead, his eyes still dark with passion, and she found him incredibly sexy. Still. After over a year of being together.

The bastard had the audacity to grin, his teeth a slash of white in the shadowy room. "And I have the feeling we'll go over it again and again and again before you can face the fact that you need me."

"*Need* you?"

"Yep. That's what it is. Deal with it."

"I don't need—"

"Anyone," he finished for her. "Yeah, I know. I've heard it enough."

"So why are you pressuring me?" He'd asked her to move in with him. Again. A year ago, while she'd been recovering from the mental and physical wounds from dealing with a madman, she'd agreed that living together would be a good idea. It had sounded safe. Smart. Been so tempting. But now . . .

"Come on, Regan. Would it be so bad?" He was reaching up, his warm, calloused hands scaling her ribs. Her skin tingled where he touched her, her blood warming. "We could have a lot of fun." He raised himself upward and touched the tip of one of her nipples with his tongue. His breath was warm against her wet skin. "Think about it. Making love every day, late at night, and in the morning . . ."

She felt that familiar yearning deep within. As if he sensed her response, he reached lower and fanned his fingers between her legs, fingertips skimming the most sensitive of areas. "Think about it," he whispered against her breast.

"You know, cowboy, you can be a real bastard when you want to be."

"Years of practice." Again with the tongue. A quick little flick that caused her insides to melt.

Her damned nipple tightened and she moaned.

She wanted him. Damn, but she wanted him. It was as if she couldn't get enough of the man.

As if he could read her mind, Santana laughed, white teeth a slash of irreverent mirth.

"I'm being serious."

"So am I." Quick as a cat, he rolled atop her, pinning her to the mattress, his eyes gleaming a dark, intense fire. "We've talked about moving in together for a long time now."

"I know, but I still have kids at home—"

"Who could use a strong father figure."

"Oh . . . ," she said, but just his weight, pressing against her in all the right places, was making it difficult to think straight. What the hell was wrong with her? All of a sudden, when she was pushing forty, she was as randy as a teenager. At least she was with damned Santana, and the worst thing was, the son of a bitch knew it!

"We have a good thing going just as it is," she said.

"But it might be better."

"Or worse," she argued.

"Come on, Regan, take a chance." His eyes were dark with the night. He captured her mouth with his, kissed her hard, then nipped at her lower lip.

"If you think you can convince me by . . . oooh." His hand was between her legs again, and she couldn't help but arch upward, her blood racing, her heart beating a wild tattoo. Her fingers curled in the sheets, and finally, she let go, closed her eyes, and groaned as he entered her, feeling that familiar, yet exciting flush that started in the small of her back and worked its way upward as he moved, his breathing suddenly out of control, his skin dewy with sweat.

Would it be so bad to think of the future?

To spend the rest of her life with him?

Right now, she couldn't think about it, didn't want to try. For the moment, she would just let the night bring what it may.

Kacey glanced out the broad back windows of Rolling Hills and decided she was long past her pull date on this Thanksgiving meal with her mother. The snow was coming down, fluffy flakes being caught in the beams of outdoor lighting strategically placed around the grounds. A gazebo, decorated with strings of white lights, glowed in the distance, and one of the conifers had been decorated as well.

Several of the other patrons had finished their meals and, on their way out of the dining area, waved to Maribelle or stopped by to wish her a Happy Thanksgiving. Maribelle introduced them to Kacey and wished them a wonderful holiday season.

Kacey was about to stand up when a tall, stately man with a shaved head, military bearing, and easy smile paused by their table.

"Is this your daughter?" he asked, and Maribelle quickly introduced Kacey to David Spencer, who pronounced that he was "charmed." As if they were on the set of some movie out of the 1950s. "You're as beautiful as your mother," he said with a wink at Maribelle, who actually blushed. "Best bridge partner in the place, well, probably the whole damned town. Nice to meet you, Acacia." Fondly he patted her mother's shoulder before striding out the double doors to the grand foyer.

"See why I like it here?" her mother said, her gaze following Spencer's stiff back.

"I do. And I see why you were so dead set that I come here. You wanted me to meet him, didn't you?"

Her mother started to deny it, then shrugged. "You found me out."

"Are you and he serious?"

"Oh, no!" Maribelle laughed then, a tinkling happy sound that Kacey hadn't heard in years. "I call him the Commander," she confided, almost giddy.

"But you're in love?"

"Well, I don't know about that."

"Mom. Don't lie to me. I can see it plain as day. Why haven't I heard a word about him before now?"

"There was really nothing to tell." But the sparkle in her eyes belied her words. "What do you think?"

"About him? Or you?"

"About us."

"I just want you to be happy," Kacey heard herself saying, but beneath her good wishes there were questions, one of which was, why, in all the years she had been married, had her mother never once showed this youthful, giddily happy side to her daughter or husband? Why had Kacey felt the strain of her parents' marriage for almost as long as she could remember? She'd come to think that her mother had never loved her father, that she'd thought she'd married beneath herself, becoming the wife of a laborer when she had an education, a career . . . and, probably, aspirations to something more, something she saw now in David Spencer.

Kacey wondered how well she knew her mother. How well she'd ever known her. Maribelle was full of secrets and obfuscation. The truth was a thing to hide.

"How about that? You actually showed up."

Dan Grayson's smile stretched across his face as he stood in the doorway and swung the door open to allow Alvarez to step inside.

She'd almost turned around when she'd spied the unfamiliar car parked near the garage, snow piled four inches over it, so that it was impossible to tell what make or model it was. A small compact, it looked like.

"Hey, Hattie! We've got company," he called over his shoulder, and Alvarez's stomach dropped an inch or two. "Come in, come in. Cold as the devil out there!" Stepping out of the doorway, he waved her inside, and she forced a smile she didn't feel.

What a mistake! He'd suggested she come over just to be polite, that was all. But now there was no turning back; she'd just have to make her excuses early and leave. She stepped into the entryway of the cabin and heard the thunder of footsteps.

Two girls who looked to be around seven, identical twins, rounded the corner. One was dressed in pink, and her hair was pinned back behind her ears with a matching headband. The other, in green, wore a ponytail that was slipping out of its band, and when she smiled, she showed a missing front tooth.

"Girls, this is Detective, er, Ms. Alvarez." Then to Alvarez, "Selena, meet McKenzie and Mallory."

"Hi," the girl in pink, McKenzie, said. Her sister's eyebrows pulled together, and she glared at Alvarez as steady footsteps clipped from behind and a woman who could have been a twin for June Cleaver appeared. Tall, slim, in heels and a sheath, she smiled brightly as she spied Alvarez.

"I'm Hattie," she said with a warm smile. She was actually wearing a strand of pearls and one of those flimsy, useless aprons that wrapped around her wasp-thin waist. Her hair was pulled to the back and pinned with a fancy comb of some sort. She looked as if she'd just stepped off of a 1950s television soundstage.

"Selena," Alvarez said, feeling awkward as she handed the woman, obviously the hostess, the bottle of wine.

"So glad you could make it. And just in time!" To Grayson, she said, "You *could* offer to take her coat. Geez, Dan, sometimes I wonder!" She glanced at the wine. "Cabernet! My favorite!"

Save me, Alvarez thought and mentally kicked her way into the dining area, where the old beat-up table had been covered with a pressed cloth, and fresh greens and a sprig of cranberry surrounded fat white candles as a centerpiece. Four place settings, chipped china on faded place mats, screamed that she hadn't been expected.

"Dan, can you open this?" Hattie asked and actually winked at him as she handed him the bottle, then hurried through a doorway to what was obviously the kitchen.

"You got it." To Alvarez he said, "Hattie is . . . was . . . my sister-in-law. The girls are my nieces."

"Oh."

That didn't explain a lot, and as if he could read the confusion in her eyes, he added, "Hattie's my ex-wife's sister."

Oh, God, this was getting more and more complicated.

They walked into the kitchen, where Hattie was pulling another plate from a cupboard and a turkey, roasted to perfection, was cooling, waiting to be carved, an open bottle of Chablis standing next to two mismatched wineglasses.

Inwardly, Alvarez groaned as Hattie rattled in the cutlery drawer and came up with a place setting.

Make the best of it, she told herself. *Just get through the next couple of hours and smile. Even though this is your own private nightmare, you can handle it. How difficult is small talk compared to searching for clues to Jocelyn Wallis's death or studying the crime scene left by a sadistic, brutal killer? It's only a meal, for God's sake!*

"Dan, why don't you start carving?" Hattie asked as Grayson uncorked the bottle of red.

"Good idea."

Alvarez buried her nose in the glass he offered her. This was a side of Grayson she'd never seen. The relaxed family guy. Dear God, what had she been thinking?

Hattie glazed the sweet potatoes to perfection, then whipped up gravy for the white potatoes as well. There was cranberry sauce and a pumpkin pie cooling on the counter . . . just too damned Martha Stewart for Alvarez. Why the hell had she decided to come . . . no, make that intrude?

They were all crammed around the table, Alvarez seated opposite the twins, Grayson at one end of the table, Hattie at the other, and Alvarez thought of all kinds of ways to escape. Hattie insisted the girls say some kind of grace. Mallory clammed up, but McKenzie said a sweet prayer that Alvarez thought she'd memorized in anticipation of the request.

The meal was tasty, the turkey succulent, the sweet potatoes a concoction that melted in her mouth, and yet Alvarez couldn't enjoy it at all.

As Hattie served dessert and was literally beaming at Grayson, Alvarez found her cell phone and managed to hit a button that would make an alarm. When the phone beeped, she grabbed it and said, "Alvarez." She managed to appear concerned, held up a finger, and pushed her chair back. "Yeah? Okay, go . . ." She walked to the entry hall and made all the appropriate noises into the phone, then, after three minutes, clicked off and returned to the dining area. "Sorry, I've got to run," she said. "Don't get up. I'll find my coat."

"Trouble?" Grayson was already on his feet.

"Nothing serious." At least that wasn't a lie.

"Then, please, stay for pie and coffee." Hattie's perfectly arched eyebrows had drawn together in concern, little lines of worry evident between her brows. McKenzie imitated her mother's expression, while Mallory was dipping an experimental finger into the dollop of whipped cream that was melting on the pumpkin filling of her pie.

"Sorry, I can't. Thanks for the dinner. It was spectacular." Alvarez avoided Grayson's eyes because she hated trying to fabricate excuses and had always prided herself as a straight shooter. Lying didn't come easily.

Grayson followed her into the hallway and found her coat on a peg near the door. "Whatever it is can wait."

"Don't think so."

He grabbed the crook of her arm. "What's going on?"

"Just a mix-up with some lab requests and reports." He let go, and she almost sighed in relief. "As I said, nothing serious. I just want it straightened out ASAP." She slipped her arms into the wool sleeves and felt like a fool as he helped her shrug into the shoulders. Grabbing her scarf from one of the pegs with one hand, she reached for the door with her other. "Thanks so much for the meal. It was incredible," she said and hurried outside.

Reaching her car, she glanced back to see Grayson standing on the stoop, watching her slide behind the wheel of her Jeep.

"Dan?" Hattie's muffled voice sounded from the other room.

Alvarez rammed the keys into the ignition and, as the engine sparked to life, flipped on the wipers to brush off the accumulation of snow that had collected on the windshield. She backed around and hit the gas. In her rearview mirror she spied the door to Grayson's cabin close, all warmth and light shut away from the winter night.

Disappointment clutched her heart in its cold, bitter grasp, and she chided herself. What had she expected, huh? That she and the sheriff would eat an intimate dinner alone, that they would sip the wine she brought, maybe even share a kiss?

She could scarcely bear her own thoughts. She turned onto the main highway, only to be trapped by a snowplow steadfastly pushing snow to the side of the road, its huge blade scraping a layer of ice.

Alvarez slowed to fifteen miles an hour and advised herself never to be so foolish again.

She was still gone.

He knew it by the lack of ruts in her driveway and the fact that the lights glowing in Acacia's home were the same ones that were wired to timers, set to go off at specific hours. The den's desk lamp clicked on at 5:00 a.m. every morning, and the downstairs table lamp brightened the rooms at four-thirty in the afternoon without fail. Day in, day out.

But no other patches of light were visible through the bare-branched trees. In spring and summer her home was hidden from the road, but this time of year, with no foliage on the cottonwoods, aspens, and chokecherries that rimmed her house, the buildings could be observed. Yes, they were nearly a quarter of a mile off the main road, with fields and the sparse trees separating the house from traffic, but even on a wintry night like this, lamplight was visible.

He had been careful as he didn't know if she was returning tonight and he feared his footsteps would be visible in the snow. Though he knew that he should be cautious, that attacking her now could bring more attention to him than he wanted, he was also a believer in taking any opportunity that presented itself. The holidays provided cover as there was more traffic, and people were busy and distracted. Currently she had no alarm system, no guard dog, and no roommate, but any of those factors could change in a heartbeat. He had to act swiftly, while he could.

Driving slowly, he had passed by the lane leading to her house once, then once again, and convinced she hadn't shown up, decided to take the chance.

He'd parked a mile and a half away, behind a pile of boulders at an old rock quarry, then strapped on his cross-country skis for the trek. Fortunately, her family's farm abutted a national forest, and he had few fences to cross. There were trails that wound through the stands of pine, tamarack, and juniper, and he'd learned the closest routes.

Wearing night-vision goggles, he'd skied carefully through the quiet forest, scaring up a snowshoe hare, which had hopped quickly into a thicket of snowy pines.

His blood had been pumping; his ears were straining to listen; his eyes scanning the frigid landscape. He'd caught sight of a deer, which had stood frozen as he passed, and saw the back of a martin as it had slunk through the underbrush.

Jamming his poles into the snow, he'd pushed through the woods until he'd reached the far side of the Lambert property. He'd hesitated a minute, ears straining, eyes searching the surrounding acres for any sign of life. Now, satisfied that he was alone, he slid out of his skis and strapped on his snowshoes before crossing the fence separating private property from government land.

Once inside the fence line, he moved quickly and silently, as he had years before in the desert, when he'd been in the marines. Keeping near to the fence so as not to make his tracks too apparent, he noiselessly made his way to the outbuildings. Despite the freezing temperature, he was sweating, his nerves strung tight as guy wires, his muscles tight. Ready.

At the back of the nearest shed, he paused, drew a deep breath, then keeping close to the walls of the outbuildings, made his way ever closer to the house, where once again he saw a warm patch of light glowing from the den.

He couldn't help but smile.

Her attempt to make the house appear occupied was amateurish, even naive.

As he entered the back of the main yard, he paused, checking the house again, making sure no one was inside; then he stepped through the bushes to pause near the exterior wall of the garage.

The night was thick with falling snow; the silence broken only by his own breaths and heartbeat. No other sounds disturbed the stillness.

He was safe.

But he didn't know for how long.

Quickly he unstrapped the snowshoes from his boots, then eased across the rear of the garage and around the back corner. Carefully, he dared flick on his flashlight and peer through the window of the side door.

No vehicle was inside.

She hadn't returned.

Yet.

Patiently, planting his feet in the footsteps she'd made earlier, he made his way up the back porch to the door. From deep in the pocket of his ski jacket, he retrieved a ring of keys and found the one he'd had made earlier. He smiled as he remembered disabling the furnace, pretending to be a repairman, and "running out for a part" after he'd lifted the keys from the purse he'd found in her desk. He'd had the key made, returned, dropped her keys into the side pocket of her purse, then "fixed" the furnace by replacing the part he'd taken from it. So simple. So easy. And now, just as easily, he unlocked the door.

He took off his boots, hid them behind a stack of outdoor furniture, then, in stocking feet, stepped inside Acacia's home. Scents enveloped him—cold coffee lying darkly in the glass pot of the coffeemaker, warm spices because of the scented candles placed throughout the interior, and even the tiniest waft of her perfume, still lingering in the air.

He reached into his pocket, opened a vial, and poured the powder into the ground coffee sitting on a shelf near the coffeemaker. Then, as he'd learned during his tour of duty in Afghanistan, he set about placing bugs in her bedroom, living room, kitchen, and den. They were remote, could be accessed from a receiver a long distance away, conversations listened to or recorded.

Perfect.

As he set the last tiny microphone under her bed, he smiled to himself and wondered what he might hear.

Then, checking his watch, he made his way out of the house the same way he came in and felt confident the snowfall would cover his tracks. He locked the door behind him, pulled on his boots, and carefully stepped in the very footsteps she'd originally created. Unless she arrived home in the next half hour, the snow would cover any hint of his tracks. She wouldn't notice that her own boot prints were smaller than his.

Oh, she was a smart one, but Acacia Lambert had no idea what she was up against.

But then none of them did, and there were others who demanded his attention.

Grinning to himself, he adjusted his night goggles and found his snowshoes where he'd left them.

In his mind's eye, he saw the bitch making her first cup of coffee in the morning. She didn't stand a chance against him.

And soon she would realize it.

But by that time, it would be too late.

CHAPTER 15

As Kacey drove home, snow was falling in big, lacy flakes, which, had she been in a better mood, might have filled her with delight. As it was, she was bothered about her mother's interest in David Spencer. Not that she didn't want Maribelle to be happy, but for years the woman had been miserable, the dutiful if disinterested wife of a man she barely tolerated. When Kacey's dad had suffered his stroke and never fully recovered, they'd sold their house and moved here, to Rolling Hills. Maribelle, with the help of the staff, had grudgingly tended to him, and during that time she'd barely been able to scare up a smile.

He'd died within a couple of years, and only then did she show any emotion that she'd loved the man or missed him.

Even then, Kacey had suspected that Maribelle had been more interested in portraying herself as the martyred widow, rather than feeling any true loss at her sick husband's death.

"Stop it," she chastised herself while staring at the ribbon of plowed road ahead. Her mother was happy, and that was all that mattered, she told herself, grateful that she was nearly home. Just a few more miles. Kacey should be thankful that Maribelle had found someone.

And yet she felt a gnawing dissatisfaction and wondered why her mother had found a way of skirting the most difficult of subjects.

There was something off about how she'd handled the questions about her husband's infidelity or the possibility of any other children, something that bothered Kacey.

She's lying. She frowned, catching sight of her troubled expression in the rearview mirror just as headlights blazed in the reflection. *Your mother's lying to you, straight out.* "But why?" she wondered aloud.

Maybe it wasn't her father who had other children; maybe it was Maribelle herself. But was that even possible?

The headlights were blinding, the guy behind her having his beams on high, the light refracting crazily as it caught in all the falling snow and mirrors.

Her mother's reticence with the truth wasn't going to stop her. As a doctor, Kacey had access to information and medical records that might help her get to the truth, and if she couldn't dig it up herself, then she also had a patient who, while under anesthesia, once had claimed to have hacked into all kinds of government files. She decided that if she couldn't get the information she wanted on her own, there was no reason not to see if Tydeus Chilcoate was the real deal, or if he was only a computer hacker demigod in his own mind due to the effects of local anesthesia. She was willing to take the chance and enlist him if need be because her mother's reticence had really ticked her off.

What was it Maribelle had said? Oh, right, she'd suggested that Kacey's questions were an "inquisition." Yeah, right. Throw on the guilt, avoid the real issue. Deflect, deflect, deflect.

Irritated, she saw the bastard in the vehicle behind her pull into the oncoming lane and gun it. Engine roaring, tires spitting up snow, his light-colored van pulled up alongside hers. Was he out of his friggin' mind?

She slowed to let him pass. "Idiot!" she muttered and glanced over. Two people were in the front, a man and a woman, she thought. The woman, in the passenger seat, was smoking a cigarette. She looked over at Kacey and said something to the driver.

Suddenly, the guy lost control.

The van swerved into her lane.

"Damn!" Kacey stepped on her brakes and veered toward the shoulder, which sloped off to the deep ditch that ran alongside the road.

Her heart clutched.

Her tires skidded.

She gripped the steering wheel hard, her knuckles showing white as she tried to remain calm. "Come on, come on!" she said, nervous sweat dampening her brow. Her car began a slow, steady spin. The other car sped past, throwing up snow.

Drive with the spin. Don't fight it! She remembered the old axiom her grandfather had pounded into her head from the time she was old enough to get her learner's permit. But aiming toward the piles of plowed snow that had been swept to the edge of the road seemed wrong.

Don't panic!

Heart racing, fear spurting through her blood, she tried like hell to steer her careening car back into the lane, but as the Edge righted, her fender sheered through the packed snow, sending a spray of ice into the air.

"Crap!"

She overcorrected, and the car began to twist again, shuddering and sliding into the oncoming lane.

Headlights glared bright.

Oh. God.

A big truck was bearing down on her!

Frantically, she yanked on the wheel.

The car slid sideways, and she worked the brakes again. Desperately she tried to steer out of the truck's path.

A horn blasted, echoing in the night.

"Oh, Jesus!" Her heart nearly stopped.

The damned brakes locked.

Still the little SUV skidded sideways, the driver's side exposed to the massive grill of a pickup barreling down on her.

"Son of a bitch!" Frantic, Kacey stepped on the gas while forcing her steering wheel to turn. Her car lurched, tires spinning crazily. "Come on, come on!"

Sweat beaded on her brow.

The truck bore down on her, close enough that she could see the driver's face. Their eyes locked. For a split second she thought she recognized him, had seen his face somewhere before. Then she braced herself for the impact. The driver turned away and blasted his horn. The truck slid as the driver stood on his brakes.

She hit the gas.

Her Edge jolted suddenly, tires catching hold.

The little SUV leaped forward, straightening, but not before the corner of the pickup's front panel clipped her back bumper.

Bam!

The entire SUV shuddered! Kacey's seat belt cinched tight. Her vehicle was sent spinning crazily across both lanes, snow and ice flying, the inky night flashing through her frozen windshield.

"Come on, come on," she said, as if the damned vehicle could understand her. She worked the brakes and the steering wheel, fighting the spin, feeling sick.

The whirling, swirling darkness eased a bit.

Frozen, snow-covered trees that had been reeling monoliths careening past her windows now became distinct.

The road seemed to straighten.

Finally the Edge stopped.

Kacey's stomach settled. "Oh, damn," she whispered, her heart thudding wildly, her pulse jumping. She took a deep breath and felt nervous sweat begin to dry on her skin.

Her vehicle's nose was pointed in the opposite direction of her house, now facing oncoming traffic as she was in the wrong lane. Fortunately, there were no cars or trucks approaching from either direction. Farther ahead, the pickup had stopped, his taillights glowing a bright red and reflecting against the dirty snow packed onto the asphalt.

Her hands were shaking violently as she eased onto the gas and carefully drove forward, sliding into the correct lane behind the idling pickup. She was pointed in the wrong direction, away from her house, but now, at least, she was in the right lane as far as traffic was concerned, though thankfully there was still none.

Like it or not, she had to talk to the dark-haired guy in the pickup and explain what had happened as she exchanged insurance information with him, but as her headlights reached the tailgate of the snow-covered truck, the once-idling truck took off, snow and ice flying from beneath its tires.

"Hey!" she yelled. *What the hell?*

For a split second, she considered taking off after him. There was damage to her car, and potentially to the pickup. Technically, unless the driver of the car that had passed her and nearly sideswiped her was found, she was at fault. She stepped on the gas, but her tires spun and the truck was disappearing into the night, its license plate, from Idaho, smudged and dark, only the number eight—or was it three?—visible.

What was it about the driver that had seemed so familiar? His dark hair? The way he stared down at her? Something else?

Straining so hard to see the license plate of the retreating vehicle, at first she didn't notice the woman at the edge of the road. But a movement caught her eye, and she realized she wasn't alone. A tall, slim woman with graying blond hair peeking out of a white stocking cap was walking along a trail leading from the surrounding woods. Grace Perchant. The local woman who claimed to speak with ghosts and predict the future. At Grace's side was a huge dog, its bristly fur tan and gray, its eyes, those of a cunning predator. Part wolf, local gossip claimed, and Kacey believed it.

Grace approached her car as Kacey rolled down the window. "Did you see that?" she asked, and the other woman nodded. "I don't know why he took off."

"Don't worry about it."

The wolf dog growled low in his throat, eyes as pale as his master's fixed on the surrounding forest.

"Bane, hush!" Grace commanded, and the big animal became mute.

Kacey was still talking about the other driver. "But . . . his truck might be damaged and my car—"

"Your car is fine." Grace glanced toward the darkness into which the driver had guided his truck.

"I should speak with him."

"No." Grace's gaze returned to Kacey's. Pale green eyes were round with concern. "You should never speak to him."

"Why? You know him?"

Grace was shaking her head and again turned to face the stretch of icy road that disappeared into darkness. "I only know that he's evil," she said, her breath clouding in the air. "He means you harm."

"He took off! And I don't think he meant to hit me."

Grace turned back to her. "Be careful," she warned and, whistling to the dog, walked across the road to a spot where the ditch wasn't quite so deep and a path curved into the surrounding forest.

"Weird," Kacey said under her breath, still shaken up, then, with some effort, turned her car around and cautiously drove the last four miles to the house she now called home. The lane was piled thick with snow, but her car, dented though it was, churned through the white powder and drove easily to its spot in the garage.

It was nearly eleven by the time she let out her breath and listened to the engine tick as it began to cool. After climbing out of the car, she flipped on the interior lights to survey the damage to her car.

A crumpled bumper on one side, a few scratches, and a small dent were all that had happened. Easily fixed. And she was lucky to have survived. The accident could have been so much worse. Telling herself to deal with everything in the morning, she locked the garage behind her and started for the back door. The night was still, snow gently falling, the path she'd broken earlier already partially filled with new snow. Yet she had no trouble following it, her boots stepping in the large prints she'd left earlier. On the porch she paused and looked around the yard. Why, she didn't know, just an uneasy feeling that had been with her all night. The accident hadn't helped, nor had the other driver's quick exit.

What had Grace said? That the driver was "evil," that he meant Kacey harm?

That's ridiculous. Don't go there! He was just another driver in a hurry. And yet she felt a chill deep in her soul and remembered thinking fleetingly that she'd seen the driver somewhere before. "Now you're imagining things." She let herself inside and made certain the dead bolt was secure behind her.

Snapping on lights, she had the ludicrous sensation that someone had been inside. "Oh, for the love of God." Still, she eyed each room, stepping through the archways and doors as she unwound her scarf, then hung it and her coat on the hall tree near the front door.

No knife-wielding, masked boogeyman leaped out at her.

No dark shadow crossed her path.

No pairs of eyes glowed from behind the curtains.

Muttering beneath her breath, she headed up the stairs. One step down from the landing, she paused, certain she smelled something out of the ordinary lingering in the small alcove where a portrait of her grandparents was mounted on the faded wallpaper. Kacey had sworn she would take it down. She hadn't. The pale pink rose pattern had been Grannie's favorite, and Kacey had had neither the time nor the heart to strip it from the walls.

She touched her finger to her lips, then brushed it over her smiling grandparents' faces and wondered what they knew about the women who looked like her. Jocelyn Wallis and Shelly Bonaventure, "dead ringers" for her who had lived in the area.

She continued to climb the stairs. The third step from the top creaked as it always did, and Kacey smiled, remembering how she'd avoided stepping on that particular plank as a child, first considering it "bad luck" and later so as not to wake her snoring grandfather and light-sleeping grandmother as she snuck out of the house during those blissful, hot Montana summers, when the smell of cut hay and dust filled her nostrils and she rode her horse bareback through the moonlit fields.

It seemed an eternity ago, part of a childhood disconnected from the woman she'd become, the driven medical student who had been attacked by a madman and had nearly given up her career before it had gotten started.

Who was she kidding?

She'd never been the same since the maniac had leapt out at her in the parking garage.

Gone was any vestige of the girl who had raced her horse at midnight, or swung on a rope to drop into the river that cut through these mountains in summer, or hiked fearlessly through the surrounding hills. . . . No, between her mother's constant criticism and that horrific attack, Kacey's self-confidence had eroded.

She'd gotten some of it back over the years, even handling the failure of divorce with more spine than she would have expected, but still, deep inside, in a place she rarely acknowledged, there was a frightened shell of a woman, and right now she was rearing her scared, trembling head.

Don't let it happen. Don't let some weirdo derail you. Grace Perchant thinks she can talk to ghosts, for crying out loud!

Giving herself a silent pep talk and a hard mental shake, Kacey walked to the room she'd always occupied, never having moved into her grandparents' bedroom. That had seemed sacrilege somehow. Rather than turn on the light, she walked to the window in the dark and stared across the moonlit fields.

Again she felt an unlikely, malicious wind rush through her insides, though the room was perfectly still. She thought about the driver of the pickup that had hit her car, remembered seeing his fleeting face. Did she know him? Or had she, in that heart-stopping instant, been mistaken?

All in your mind, she told herself but didn't believe it for an instant.

CHAPTER 16

"Okay . . . no . . . wait . . ." Pescoli, seated across from Alvarez in a booth at Wild Will's held up both hands and cocked her head. It was the day after Thanksgiving, and they'd agreed to meet at the local restaurant and bar located in downtown Grizzly Falls. "You had your fortune read in a teacup by a woman who wears matching sweaters with her dog, and then you stole the victim's cat?"

"Adopted. Maybe temporarily."

Pescoli stared at her as if she'd just sprouted horns. "Who are you, and where's my partner?" she demanded, grabbing the ketchup bottle and pouring a huge glob on her plate. "The next thing I know, you'll be claiming to be beamed up into a spaceship to face Crytor, or whoever he was, the alien lizard general who Ivor Hicks thinks captured him years ago."

Alvarez played around with the remains of her tuna salad and decided she had to confess. If she didn't, Pescoli might hear it from someone else. So she admitted going to Dan Grayson's for Thanksgiving.

"For the love of God," Pescoli said, stunned. "You barged in on his family Thanksgiving and—"

"I was invited, okay?"

"Out of pity."

Alvarez glared at her partner. "It was a mistake, okay? I get that now. I only told you so that if the sheriff said anything, you wouldn't be blindsided." She jabbed her fork into a bit of lettuce. "So, what did you do?"

To her surprise, Pescoli actually blushed as she grabbed her Reuben and dredged it through the ketchup before taking a bite.

"Thought so." Alvarez tried not to sound envious.

"So, you find anything interesting at the neighbor's besides the cat?" she asked as she swallowed and washed the bite down with Diet Coke.

"Could be that we're on the lookout for a dark pickup."

Pescoli sent her a glance. "When *aren't* we on the lookout for one?"

Alvarez lifted a shoulder.

"So does this pickup have plates? Distinguishing marks? Maybe a camper or toolbox?"

"Possibly, but Lois didn't see or remember."

"Lois is the dachshund-walking, sweater-matching, tea-leaf-reading, charter-member-of-PETA neighbor?"

"Yes," Alvarez answered patiently.

"Huh. Not exactly the most credible witness." Pescoli drained her soda, and before she could decline, Sandi, the waitress and owner of the establishment, slid another drink in front of her. "Thanks. That's enough."

"Free refills." Sandi, tall and a little on the gaunt side, grinned widely. She never stopped selling. She'd ended up with the establishment in a bitter divorce from her husband, William Aldridge, for whom the restaurant had been named, and she'd poured her heart and soul into the restaurant, changing up the once-boring menu with local fare that included huckleberries, venison, and trout, then redecorating the place to look like a hunting lodge. The chandeliers were wagon wheels with lanterns affixed to their rims. Mounted on the rough plank walls, high overhead, the stuffed heads of bighorn sheep, antelope, deer, and even a moose stared through glassy eyes at those who occupied the tables and booths below. It was eerie, weird, and kind of macabre to Alvarez's way of thinking, but totally in step with the Grizzly Falls way of life.

With a wink of an overly shadowed eye, Sandi hurried off to a table where a couple were trying to deal with three loud kids who looked as if they ranged in age from two to six. Mom and Dad were obviously frazzled as they tried to sort out drinks, juggle their bags, and answer questions from the squirming trio of sons. Sandi whipped out tiny coloring books from her apron, found a glass filled with crayons on a nearby table, and, once the kiddies were into their new-found art, took the couple's order.

"So tell me again about the poison." Pescoli took another bite as Alvarez repeated what she'd discovered in Jocelyn Wallis's apartment and how it all added up to murder.

They discussed the case and, after paying the bill, put on their jackets and headed through the front doors and past Grizz, the stuffed grizzly bear that greeted customers as they entered Wild Will's. Grizz, frozen in time, his mouth a perpetual snarl that bared his long teeth, was usually dressed for the season. Today was no exception, as he wore a white bonnet and collar over his shaggy coat, as if he were a Pilgrim woman. Gourds, squash, and an overflowing cornucopia were situated at his long, clawed feet, and a stuffed turkey peeked around the dry stalks of corn that surrounded him.

"Cute," Pescoli muttered under her breath.

Alvarez shouldered open the glass doors, and a blast of winter air hit her full in the face. The sidewalk had been shoveled and salted, concrete peeking through, and the roar of the falls was audible over the traffic rolling along the street. The pedestrians were bundled in a variety of jackets and coats, most with scarves wound around their necks, boots covering their feet and stocking caps pulled over their ears. Some juggled packages, while others held tight on to the mitten-clad hands of their children. A few idled and smoked while huddled in doorways of the shops already decorated with cedar wreaths, red bows, and glittering lights, all heralding the Christmas season. The snow had quit for the day, but the cloud cover hung low, hugging the earth, blocking the sun.

They had arrived in this part of town in different vehicles. Alvarez had been at the department's offices before daylight. She'd called Pescoli, who had agreed to meet her. "You know this is supposed to be my day off," Pescoli said as they reached her Jeep.

"Just thought you'd want to be kept up to speed."

"Yeah, you're right. Lucky's got the kids, so it isn't a big deal. It's Black Friday, you know. Michelle's taking Bianca shopping."

"I thought you said she was fighting some bug."

"Did you not hear me? It's Black Friday, the sacred day of holy shopping. There'll be no stopping of the laying down of the credit cards." Pausing before she unlocked the Jeep's door, she said, "I suppose you're going to make a workday of it."

"Yeah."

"And probably a night."

"The holidays, always more domestic issues." That was a trend that seemed to have no end. Get a few relatives together, offer them food and drink, and pretty soon all the old wounds were opened again. Fueled by a little booze and a handy weapon, things could get out of control pretty fast. Hadn't she witnessed it often enough in her own family? "I've got plenty to keep me busy."

Pescoli opened the door, then hesitated. "Keep me in the loop."

"Will do."

As Pescoli pulled out of the parking spot and drove off, Alvarez walked to a side street near the river where her own vehicle was parked. Even in the cold, there were fishermen leaning against the railing, their lines disappearing into the dark, swirling water far below, while a few pedestrians bustled along the sidewalk. Moving away from the river, she turned a full one-eighty and stared upward, over the facades and rooftops of the storefronts, to the crest of Boxer Bluff. Without really understanding her motives, she forced her gaze along the darkened hillside and the railing to the park. Unwittingly she focused on the crumbling wall where Jocelyn Wallis had fallen to her death.

Or been pushed.

Was the killer so anxious for her to be dead that he couldn't wait for the poison he'd put in her coffee to work? There was a chance he might not have known about her heart condition. For that matter, even Jocelyn herself might not have realized her heart had been compromised. But the killer certainly understood that given enough time and having gone undetected, the toxins he'd laced her food with would eventually steal her life.

"Who the hell are you?" she thought aloud, her breath fogging in the air.

Drawing her gaze from the bluff, she unlocked her car. Maybe the bastard was afraid her symptoms would force her to the doctor before she died. If she'd acted quickly enough, her life might have been spared.

Was he just antsy, unwilling to wait for her death, or was there a reason he'd altered his original plan of letting her die slowly?

If Jocelyn had been pushed, Alvarez reminded herself. That important fact hadn't been established.

"Yet," she reminded herself as she climbed into her Jeep, flicked on the engine, and glanced once more at the crest of the ridge. She could almost picture Jocelyn Wallis tumbling over the edge, arms and legs flailing, fear and pain twisting her features. And all the while a shadowy figure had watched her fall. Gloating. Mentally praising himself for his slyness.

Her stomach turned sour.

"I'll get you, you son of a bitch," she vowed under her breath, even though she wasn't even sure that he'd been on the ridge.

But she'd find out.

One way or another.

"Your mother on line two," Heather told Kacey as she walked out of the examination room where the seventh flu case of the day had just been diagnosed. "Hey, are you okay?"

The answer was no because the truth was that she hadn't slept more than twenty minutes at a stretch the night before. After thinking someone had been in the house, she'd woken up at every moaning joist, or branch hitting a window, or rush of the wind. She'd had dreams of the attack and woken up sweating. Twice, chiding herself for being a ninny, she'd gone downstairs and checked to see that the doors and windows had been bolted and latched. She'd even double-checked to see that her grandfather's shotgun was where it was supposed to be, tucked in the attic space under the eaves, accessed by a short door in the hallway outside her bedroom.

The night had been fitful, and when the alarm had blared at 5:00 a.m., she'd had to drag herself from the bed.

Even the two cups of coffee she'd swilled before work hadn't given her the jolt she'd been looking for, and she'd been dragging all day. And it had been a bitch. Along with her regularly scheduled patients, there had been the seven extras squeezed into examination rooms. They'd all exhibited flu symptoms, one elderly lady sick enough that Kacey had sent her directly to the hospital.

The office had been a madhouse; the waiting room overflowing; tempers short. Added to the tension of the extra work, the computers had gone down for nearly two hours, and Martin had been held up at the hospital.

"I'm fine. Just tired," she lied, because her stomach had been slightly sour all day. "Tell Mom I'll call her back."

Heather pulled a face. "I tried that. You know, 'The doctor's just finishing up with patients and will call you in an hour or two,' but"—she shook her head, her straight blond hair catching in the light—"it didn't fly."

"I'll take it," Kacey said, wondering at the sudden interest from her mother. They'd seen each other just last night, and sometimes they didn't speak for a week or two.

Once in her office, she slid into her desk chair, pushed the button on the phone of her antiquated system, and said, "Hey, Mom. Happy Black Friday."

"As if I'd be in the malls with the rest of America today!" There wasn't so much as a chuckle from the other end of the line. "Acacia, I've been thinking . . . ," she said, and Kacey bit her tongue to keep from saying something snide about her mother's thinking process. She could tell Maribelle wasn't in the mood for a joke of any kind.

"About?"

"Our conversation last night."

Kacey leaned back in her chair and stared out the window, where the snow, which had stopped earlier, was beginning to fall again, adding another frosty layer to the bushes surrounding the clinic. "What about it?" She was willing to bet it wasn't about the Commander or, for once, Kacey's love life. Last night Kacey had hit a nerve.

"Well, it bothered me that you seemed to think your father could have . . . you know, fathered other children, or that some other relative had done something similar. I didn't get the impression that you understood how preposterous that idea was." She was dead serious. "I know you're all worked up about these women who died and resembled you, and so I wanted to make sure that you were all right."

Translation: That you aren't digging any further.

"Thanks, Mom. I'm fine."

"So . . . everything's back to normal?"

Nope. "As normal as it is around here."

"Good." An audible sigh. "I'm so glad."

Translation: I'm glad you're going to cease and desist.

Maribelle, who didn't seem to really believe her daughter but wasn't going to call her on the lie, added, "Well, it was wonderful seeing you last night. I'm off to dinner soon. The Commander and I have a date. Can you believe that? At my age?"

"I think it's great, Mom."

"Really?"

"Really." That much was true. If Maribelle could find a man to make her happy, all the better.

"Me, too. So I'd better run and put on my feminine armor."

Translation: Make-up and slimming, smoothing undergarments.

"You do that, Mom."

"I'll talk to you soon."

"Bye." Kacey hung up and stared out the window, feeling empty inside. Why, she wondered, when there were so many women who had close, loving relationships with their mothers, had she ended up at the very most coldly affectionate with hers? They were just such strangers, and it seemed wrong. Not that there weren't much worse, antagonistic, even violent relationships, but that knowledge didn't dull the ache that still lingered from her childhood. No siblings. A distant mother. A father who cared but was too busy. If it hadn't been for her grandparents . . .

Disgusted at the turn of her thoughts, she looked to the positive. Maybe being somewhat distant from her mother wasn't so bad. She could do all the investigating in her family's past that she wanted. She didn't have all those hang-ups about family name and honor, nor did she worry about tarnishing her mother's or father's reputation. "It is what it is," she said aloud and wondered about how easily she had lied to her mother. The truth was, she'd already started the ball rolling. Before the first case had walked through the door this morning, she'd e-mailed the appropriate state offices and hospitals. She intended to see how many of the women—so far, just women—born within three years of her birth date in Helena had come to unfortunate, possibly suspicious, ends. She glanced at the newer celebrity magazine she'd picked up in the grocery store, another one with Shelly Bonaventure on the cover. In the article, she'd found the name of the lead detective on the Bonaventure case, a man by the name of Jonas Hayes of the LAPD. Once she began connecting the dots, if there were indeed dots to be connected, she'd contact him. Even if Shelly Bonaventure's death had been ruled a suicide.

There was a big chance she was jumping to conclusions. Perhaps Shelly Bonaventure did decide to end her life, and maybe Jocelyn Wallis did just take a misstep that sent her reeling over the cliff face.

So far, no one had e-mailed her back with any information, and they probably wouldn't until after the holiday weekend, if then.

Drumming her fingers on her desktop, Kacey frowned. She wasn't about to let her nerves get the better of her, nor did she intend on suffering through another night like the one before. She needed a sense of security so that she could relax and sleep. She glanced at the wall clock. Five seventeen. The local animal shelter closed at six. She'd already checked. And she'd glanced quickly at a few of the dogs up for adoption while eating some string cheese and crackers during her fifteen-minute lunch. She had come 180 degrees in her way of thinking and had now decided she needed a dog, and out there somewhere was a dog who desperately needed her. She'd work out the details of her job versus time spent at home, but she needed the company and the security of an animal who would alert her if anyone did try to break into her home.

You're being paranoid, she silently accused, then nearly jumped out of her chair when she heard the clinic's back door slam. Her heart went into overdrive. For nothing.

"Get a grip," she muttered, her stomach still queasy. Through the window, she spied Randy Yates sliding behind the wheel of his ten-year-old Chevy Tahoe, his dented SUV, which was perpetually out-fitted with an empty ski rack. A few minutes later Heather yelled, "See ya next week," and again the door slammed.

So she was alone.

"Get used to it," she told herself. Then, after popping a couple of antacid tablets, she grabbed her coat, set the alarm, and snapped out the lights.

Next up: the local animal shelter. Despite all the reasons against it, she was going to get a dog.

Outside it was already dark, streetlamps glowing softly and creating a loose chain of illumination against the falling snow. In the storefronts of the surrounding businesses colored lights winked brightly, reflecting against the frosted panes.

Hurrying to her car, Kacey barely noticed. The chill of winter knifed through her coat, and by the time she was behind the steering wheel, she was shivering. Before backing out of a parking space, she cranked the heater to its highest setting and hit the button for her favorite radio station. "Silver Bells," sung by a country music duo she didn't recognize, wafted through the speakers while her teeth chattered. Even through her gloves, the steering wheel felt like ice, and the Christmas spirit eluded her.

Despite the sluggish traffic she reached the animal shelter in about fifteen minutes, just about the time the interior of the car had heated to someplace north of frigid.

The door was locked, so she rounded the corner to the attached veterinary clinic. A chorus of yips and barks greeted her as she walked inside the barnlike building, where the smell of urine wasn't quite masked by the scent of pine cleaner, and a bell mounted over the door tinkled. The canine cacophony came through an open doorway behind the reception area.

A girl, barely out of her teens, stood behind a long counter, where she was tallying the receipts for the day. "Can I help you?" she asked. With kinky brown hair and braces, she put her paperwork aside and her impish face pulled into an expression of confusion. "Are . . . are you here to pick up your pet?"

"No, no. I was hoping to see the dogs that are up for adoption."

"Oh, uh, sure." The girl glanced at the round clock mounted over the back doorway, a gesture intended to remind Kacey of the late hour. "Sure, uh, all the dogs are in the back. You'll need to fill out these forms." She found a packet of papers titled ADOPTION APPLICATION and slid the stapled pages and a pen across the counter, then continued with her work.

As Kacey was filling out the paperwork, a slim woman appeared in the open archway behind the reception area. Her long black hair was clipped at her nape, and her tawny skin and bladed cheekbones hinted at her Native American heritage. Kacey recognized her as the local vet, Jordan Eagle.

"Amber," she said, bustling into the reception area in her lab coat,

"I just got a call from Trace O'Halleran. He's bringing in his dog, an emergency of some kind, and he should be here within ten minutes."

O'Halleran was coming here? Ridiculously, Kacey's heart skipped a stupid beat as Amber, shoulders slumped, sighed and slid another look at the clock. She frowned. "But I have—"

"Please just stay until he gets here. Then I'll lock up." The vet was stern, and Amber gave an agonized, acquiescing shrug.

"Fine."

"Go ahead and finish up the receipts for the day, and you can leave as soon as the injured dog is brought in." Jordan Eagle's gaze moved to Kacey and the forms she'd begun completing. "You're looking to adopt?" Her face softened a tad.

Nodding, Kacey introduced herself, then explained, "I don't think I'm interested in a puppy, but I would like a medium-sized dog, one that's housebroken and good with kids and other animals." For just a second she remembered her fears that someone had been in her house and the reasons she'd decided, despite all her arguments against it, to find a dog. "I'm interested in a dog that seems a little more intimidating than he really is. One that will bark if there's an intruder, but not attack a neighbor kid on a bike or go out of his head barking at squirrels running along the roof."

The vet actually smiled. "Oh, you only want the perfect pet."

"That would be nice. Yeah."

As she closed the till, Amber rolled her eyes.

If her boss noticed, she ignored the girl's passive-aggressive attitude. Cocking her head toward the archway behind the desk, Jordan added, "Come on through the back way and let me introduce you to Bonzi."

Amber immediately perked up. "Oh . . . Bonzi! He's the best!"

"That he is. Buzz me when the O'Halleran dog gets here," she instructed, then said to Kacey, "This way." With quick, sharp footsteps she led the way, whisking Kacey through a labyrinth of rooms. "Unfortunately, we've got a lot of dogs right now," the vet said, frowning as she led Kacey past an examination room, then a surgery station and an area with deep sinks where the animals were bathed.

A few cats and dogs who were under the vet's care watched from their cages as Jordan swept into another hallway to another part of the connected buildings, where the animals for adoption were kept.

At the sound of the door opening, a cacophony of barks and yips echoed to the rafters. "An enthusiastic lot," the vet said. They walked into a large room with several rows of kennels. "This is where we keep the animals that aren't being foster-cared," Jordan explained. "After they're given a health exam and their vaccinations. This is meant to be a temporary spot. We always try to place all the adopt-able animals with foster families before they find their forever home, but right now we're on overload." She walked along a short aisle, touching a few wet noses pressed toward her. "I'd adopt them all if I could, but . . . we do what we can. Here we go. This is Bonzi, breed undetermined, a regular Heinz Fifty-seven though if I had to guess, I'd say, probably boxer, pit bull and, oh, maybe a ridgeback some-where back in his lineage. He's about three or four, and docile and sweet, though his bark is pretty scary. Hey, there, Bonz," she said, opening the cage and snapping a leash on him. "This way." She pat-ted the dog's broad head as she snapped on the lead, then walked to another area, an expansive room where the dogs were obviously ex-ercised.

Bonzi's short coat was the color of warm caramel, and each of his paws was splashed with white to give him the appearance of wearing four white stockings of differing sizes. But it was his eyes that she no-ticed most. Dark brown and wise and kind. He stood as tall as her knee.

"This is medium sized?" she asked.

"Well, on the large end of medium," the vet admitted. "Not quite eighty pounds."

Despite the fact that he was about forty more pounds of dog than she'd expected, Kacey was smitten. Bonzi was calm and friendly, with a whiplike tail that Kacey was sure could clear a coffee table.

"His owners had to give him up because of a divorce . . . and now separate apartments with restrictions on pets. It's a bad situation, and they hated to leave him, but they had no choice. The good news is that he spent the first couple of years of his life with another, smaller dog, two cats, and a little girl. Gentle with all. The family struggled giving him up but just couldn't keep him." A bell sounded,

Bonzi gave out a deep, sharp bark, and the doctor said, "That's my patient!"

Trace O'Halleran's injured dog. Without thinking, Kacey looked toward the door leading to the animal hospital.

"I'll leave you two to get acquainted. Amber will come and put Bonzi back before you leave, and if you want to adopt him, give me a call tomorrow."

"Oh, I want him," she said, but Jordan was already gone, her footsteps fading and a door opening and closing behind her. Kacey eyed the "medium-sized" dog and sat down on the cement floor. "Okay, Bonzi. So what's your story?"

In response the dog yawned, showing a mouthful of huge teeth, then sighing, circled, lay down beside her, and placed his head upon her crossed leg. She scratched his ears, and he sighed through his nose, his wise eyes staring up at her.

Guard dog? She doubted it, though his bark was definitely unsettling, and when she thought of an intruder stalking the halls of her house, she knew she'd feel a lot safer with the dog in her house. Anyway, the decision was already made. With his heavy jaw upon her thigh, Kacey knew she'd be with this *almost* eighty-pounder for the rest of his life.

CHAPTER 17

The last person Trace O'Halleran expected to emerge from the back rooms of the veterinary clinic where he waited with his boy for the diagnosis on his battered dog was Doctor Acacia Lambert. But there she was, big as life, her eyes as inquisitive as he remembered, her face just as beautiful.

And it pissed him off that he even noticed.

"Hi," she said, a bit of a smile teasing her full lips as she let her gaze stray from him to his son. "How're you, Eli? Taking care of that arm?" She had to have passed the vet on her way out, had to have seen his wounded dog, and her concerned face spoke volumes.

"Sarge is hurt!" Eli blurted, his small face pulled into a knot of worry, just the way it had been since the dog had stumbled into the house, one leg bleeding and slashed to the bone.

"I, uh, saw," she said softly, "but he's with Dr. Eagle, and she's a pretty darned good vet." She knelt down next to Eli but glanced up at Trace. "What happened?"

"Don't really know. Looks like Sarge was on the losing end of a fight with God knows what. Maybe a bear or raccoon, even a cougar, I suppose. He was with me when I did the afternoon chores and then went nosing around like he always does. I called for him and waited, went back to the house to relieve the woman who looks after Eli here, and just as I started out to look for him, he came dragging back." His jaw tightened as he remembered first seeing Sarge limping and bleeding on the snow-packed trail to the back door. He felt like hell for the dog and worse yet for his kid, who was blinking against a tide of unshed tears. Like he was grown up or something. It killed Trace. More than a little. "We called the vet."

" 'Cuz he's hurt real bad." Eli's face was red; his lower lip quivering. "He can't die!"

"Let's not go there," Trace said gently.

"Miss Wallis died!"

"I know." Boy, did he know. It had been one helluva devastating week for all of them. "But Sarge is a fighter."

"Dr. Eagle will do her best to fix him up," Kacey concurred.

"He won't die, will he?"

She squeezed his good hand. "I don't know. We have to just wait and see." Glancing up at Trace, she said, "Why don't I take Eli over to Dino's and get him a pizza or something? Then, when you're done here, you could come over."

Since Dino's Italian Pizzeria was just across the street, the doctor's idea made sense, he supposed. Until they knew the extent of Sarge's injuries, there was just no reason for Eli to wait and worry. And if it came down to actually having to euthanize the dog, Trace wanted to handle it his own way. Better for Eli not to witness that decision. "I guess that would be okay," he said, knowing that Eli liked the woman doctor. "What do you think?" he asked his son.

Eli looked up at Kacey, and she took his small hand in her own. "How about we pick out our ice cream even before we order the pizza?"

"Can we eat it first?" Eli asked.

"Well . . ." She looked at Trace.

"Knock yourself out. I'll be right there," Trace answered, and they headed out the door together.

A blast of wintry air swept into the room, and the tiny bell over the doorjamb jingled, announcing their departure.

Through the front windows Trace watched as Kacey bustled his son across the street. She glanced up and down the snowy street, then over her shoulder, her forehead wrinkling with concern.

About the nearly nonexistent traffic?

Or was there something more in her quick scan of the area?

Don't borrow trouble. She's just being cautious, for crying out loud.

What was important was the way she guided his boy gently onto the sidewalk. For a second Trace's stupid heart twisted as he realized his son's own mother had never seemed so concerned about Eli's welfare.

Then again, Leanna hadn't been a prize as far as mothers went.

Funny, he thought as he watched Kacey open the door to the restaurant, whose modern style was at odds with the overall Western theme of the town. The pizzeria's storefront was all windows, now decorated for the season with painted snowmen and snowwomen skating, hoisting pizzas on their shoulders across a sea of glass. It was eerie how much Kacey reminded him of Leanna. An odd, almost sinister sensation slithered down his spine and burrowed coldly in his gut at the comparison. Hadn't there been that same thought with Jocelyn Wallis?

Weird, he told himself, bugged at the turn of his own thoughts as the door to the back room opened and Jordan Eagle, her expression grave, returned to the reception area.

"It's bad," he said before she could open her mouth and say one word about Sarge's condition.

"Well, at least not good."

"Are we gonna lose him?"

"I don't think so, but I'm not sure about his leg. The tendons and muscles are pretty mangled." Her dark, honest gaze held his as she explained that she wanted to do surgery, to mend as much as she could.

"Do what you can," Trace said. He'd grown up on a farm, seen animals suffer, others die, knew his old man had "put down" more than his share on his own, with his rifle or pistol, depending. Death was just a part of life. Trace accepted it. But he was thankful Sarge was going to pull through. He didn't want Eli to face losing the dog. Not yet. Not when he'd already been abandoned by his mother and just learned about his teacher's death.

"Do what you can," he repeated to the veterinarian.

"It could get expensive."

His jaw tightened. "Just keep me posted."

"I will."

"Thanks." He squared his hat on his head and made his way out the door.

In his mind's eye he saw the dog, wrapped in a blanket, usually bright eyes dulled with pain as he lay beneath Eli's short legs on the floor of the pickup. Damn, he hoped the mutt pulled through. Hands buried in his pockets, Trace jaywalked across the street, then peered through the glass doors of the pizzeria, where a Friday night crowd of patrons sat on benches surrounding long tables littered with half-eaten pizza pies and near-empty pitchers of beer.

Kacey had lifted Eli off his feet so that he could get a better view of the ice cream in the display case. Nearby a couple of grade-school girls in skinny jeans and oversized sweatshirts were discussing the options.

He pushed the door open, and the niggling sensation that something wasn't quite right followed after him into the noisy restaurant. The air was thick with conversation and the scents of oregano and tomato sauce, warm bread and beer. A bevy of teenagers cleaned tables and waited at the counter, where a man in his seventies, sporting a thick gray mustache, striped shirt, and black pants, barked orders, manned the kegs and wine bottles, and kept an eagle eye on the cash register all at the same time.

As if by a sixth sense, Eli heard the door open. His head jerked up, and he twisted around, spying his father. Sliding out of Kacey's arms, the boy hit the floor running. "Is Sarge okay?" he asked anxiously, his small face tight with concern.

"So far, so good, but he needs surgery." Trace swung his son into his arms. "Dr. Eagle is doing her best."

"You left him." Tears puddled in his son's accusing eyes. Embarrassed, Eli tried to swipe them away with the fingers poking out of his blue cast.

"Just for the night. The doc said she'd give us a call tomorrow."

"But he'll be okay?"

"As far as I know."

"Can I see him?" Eli asked as a heavyset girl behind the pickup area spoke into a microphone. Her voice rang through the barnlike building. "Forty-seven. Brown party. Forty-seven."

"Can I see Sarge?" Eli repeated.

"Maybe tomorrow. We'll see."

Eli wanted to argue; Trace saw it in his boy's eyes, so he tried to derail the endless questions. "What do you say we get dinner?"

"She said I could have ice cream!" Eli swung his casted arm toward Kacey.

"That's right," she answered smartly. "And I think you wanted Christmas Cookie Swirl, right?"

"Yeah!"

"Sounds . . . interesting," Trace said.

"Delicious," Kacey proclaimed. "You just can't go wrong with Oreo cookies, peppermint flakes, and mint ice cream. Yumm-o!" Her green eyes glinted with humor. "I think I'll get a double scoop!"

"Me, too!" Eli shimmied from Trace's arms and raced back to the barrels of ice cream.

"Thirty-nine," a girl with a deep voice intoned. "Rosenberg party. Thirty-nine." An athletic-looking teenager pushed away from a table of friends and headed for the pickup area, her long blond ponytail bouncing behind her.

"How about you?" Kacey asked, looking up at him. "Double scoop? Triple?"

"Uh . . . maybe I'll settle for a beer."

Her smile widened as they reached the counter near the ice cream barrels. "With your cone, right?"

"How 'bout with a Meat Lovers' Special?" He hitched his chin toward the overhead menu, beneath which a skinny kid with bad skin, a shaved head, and thick glasses waited, ice cream scoop in hand, for them to order as the two girls in skinny jeans drifted off toward a round table.

Trace said, "I'll buy."

She was reading the menu. "Or we could order half a Meat Lovers' Special and half a Veggie Delite and split the bill."

"Only if you can eat half a pie yourself."

"Half a pie *and* a double scoop," she assured him.

He felt one corner of his mouth twitch. "Tell ya what. I'll arm wrestle ya for the bill."

"Don't," Eli warned her. "My dad's the strongest ever."

"Is he now?" She was smiling more broadly now. "Well, I guess we'll see about that." To Eli she confided, "I'm pretty strong, too."

"Nah!" Eli shook his head. "Not like my dad!"

"Uh-huh." She winked. "Only tougher."

The kid behind the counter was getting antsy. "Can I get you something?"

"We'll have two double scoops of Christmas Cookie Swirl in . . . waffle cones." She looked at Eli, who was nodding rapidly.

"And sprinkles!"

Kacey chuckled. "And sprinkles." She cast a glance at Trace. "And?" Her dark eyebrows arched, and he noticed how thick her eyelashes were, how the green of her eyes shifted in the light. "For you?"

"I'll stick with pizza."

He placed their order for pizza, along with two beers and a soda, then, for the better part of the next hour, as the pizzeria became busier still, he sat in an uncomfortable booth, getting to know this woman, a damned doctor, who talked to Eli so easily. She had lied, though, about her appetite, and managed to eat only two slices of the vegetarian side of the pizza, while he and Eli polished off all the meat-covered wedges. Actually, as he thought about it, he'd eaten most of the cheese- and pepperoni-slathered slices himself, as his boy was pretty full after the ice cream. Just what the doctor ordered after the week they'd all had.

"I never asked. What were you doing at the vet's clinic?" He hitched his chin toward the window and the building on the far side of the snowy street.

"I'm looking for a dog," she admitted.

"Any kind?"

"The one I hope to adopt is a mutt. Big dog. Boxer and pit bull probably. At least according to the vet."

"Guard dog?" he asked, remembering the way she glanced over her shoulder as she crossed the street with Eli an hour earlier.

"That's one criterion." Her eyes shifted away, toward the area where Eli and a group of kids were crowding around the arcade-type machines. "I, um, live alone." She picked up her glass. "Could use the company. You know."

"Yeah." He nodded, thinking of Sarge and silently praying the dog would pull through.

"So, you grew up around here?" she asked, changing the subject and pushing a bit of uneaten pizza crust to one side of her plate.

"Been here most of my life, except for college and a few years in the army. Inherited the place and decided ranching was a good life. What about you?"

"I was born and raised in Helena, but my grandparents lived here, so I spent my summers at their farm." She smiled thoughtfully, caught up in the nostalgia of the moment, seeming to study her near-empty glass, though he suspected her mind was miles and years away, conjuring images of her youth. Vaguely, he wondered if she'd known Leanna, who had spent the first years of her vagabond life in Montana's state capital as well.

"So you decided to settle down here?"

"Eventually." Her eyes shifted, and she looked up at him again. "I went to college in Missoula, medical school in Seattle, and stayed for a while. I got married, then divorced and, since I'd inherited the farm, decided to move back."

"No kids?"

She shook her head, her nose wrinkling in distaste. "He . . . wasn't 'ready.' " She made air quotes, then, as if she'd thought better of it, shook her head. "It's over, has been for three years, and I told myself I'd try never to be catty about it, even if he is an easy target." She lifted one slim shoulder, dismissing the man to whom she was once married. "So, how about you? What happened to Eli's mother?" She took a sip from her glass.

"She took a hike. Never hear from her."

She thought about that long and hard.

"We do fine," he stated firmly.

Her expression was neutral, but he bet she didn't believe him for a second. And the thing of it was, she was right. He remembered Eli's most recent crying jag, when he'd begged to find out where Leanna was. God, it tore his heart out, and he couldn't help wondering how scarred his boy was.

Before the conversation went any further, they were interrupted. "Hey! Doctor Lambert!"

Trace turned to see the receptionist for the clinic wending her way through the tables. She was balancing a glass of wine in one hand. The fingers of her other hand were laced with those of a twenty-something guy who sported a scruffy beard and wore a frayed stocking cap drawn down over his ears.

"Hi, Heather," Kacey said.

"This is Jimmy," she said quickly; then her gaze landed on Trace. "And you're Eli's dad, right?" She was nodding, agreeing with herself. "How's he doing . . . oh!"

At that moment Eli came barreling back to the table. "I need more money!"

"Hey, dude, don't we all?" Jimmy said.

Eli cast him a who-the-heck-are-you glance. "To play the games," he said to his father.

"I think maybe it's time to go." Trace scraped his chair back.

"Wow." Jimmy took a look at Kacey as she stood. "You kinda remind me of someone."

"Miss Wallis!" Eli said; then his expression clouded as he remembered that she was gone.

"Shelly Bonaventure," Heather said.

Jimmy snapped his fingers. "That's it. Man, you're like a dead ringer or something."

"Or something," Kacey said, and she, seeming to suddenly want to leave as quickly as Trace did, reached for the coat she'd tossed onto an empty chair.

But the kid was right. Trace was only vaguely aware of Shelly Bonaventure as an actress, but in the last week her picture had been splashed across the front of every magazine near the checkout stand of the store where he bought groceries. He'd also caught the end of an "in-depth" story on the woman when he'd been channel surfing the news for an update on the weather.

"She was from around here, wasn't she?" Jimmy asked.

"Helena, I think," Heather said.

"Helena," Trace repeated, his gaze meeting the doctor's. *Like Leanna. And Kacey.*

"I think I'd better get moving," Kacey said. "Thanks."

Heather's gaze swept from her boss to Trace and Eli, and she had trouble smothering a smile.

"Can we see Sarge?" Eli asked again as Trace helped him with his jacket.

"Tomorrow, bud."

"But I want to see him now." Eli's gaze traveled through the window and across the street to the veterinary clinic.

"We have to let Dr. Eagle work with him."

Eli's lower lip protruded, but he didn't offer up any further arguments. Kacey told Heather she'd "see her back at the office next week," before they all eventually worked their way out of the crowded restaurant and into the icy night, where a few tiny flakes of snow were falling and the temperature was hovering just below freezing.

He and Eli walked the doctor to her car. As she fumbled for her keys before unlocking the Ford, she smiled up at him. "Thanks for the pizza."

"No problem. Eli . . ." He nudged his boy. "Don't you have something to say to Dr. Lambert?" His kid looked up at him and blinked. "About the ice cream?" Trace reminded him.

"Oh. Yeah. Thanks," Eli said, remembering his manners.

"Anytime. Take care of that arm, okay?" With one last glance up at Trace, she said, "Dr. Lambert sounds a little too formal anymore, doesn't it? It's Kacey."

"Kacey," Trace repeated.

Then she opened the door of her Edge and slid behind the wheel.

Still holding Eli's hand, Trace watched as she nosed the Ford out of its space and drove away. He bustled his son to his own truck, parked nearby, and as he headed out of town, he thought about her and Leanna and Jocelyn Wallis and Shelly friggin' Bonaventure.

Two were dead.

One was missing.

And the fourth, Kacey, had glanced guardedly over her shoulder as she'd shepherded Eli across the street earlier.

Three of them had ties to Helena.

And they all resembled each other.

As he slowed for the stoplight near Shorty's Diner, he wondered what the hell, if anything, their connection was.

She was home!

He heard the key in her lock, the creak of the kitchen door, and the sound of her footsteps as she crossed the kitchen floor.

It was amazing how crisp the quality of the sound was, and he settled deeper into his chair to listen remotely as she snapped on the radio and ripped something that sounded like paper. Oh, of course. Her mail!

Though he had no camera equipment—he hadn't risked that yet—he could imagine Acacia walking through her house, kicking off her shoes . . . running the bathwater. . . .

That a girl . . .

In his mind's eye he watched as she pinned up her hair, then stripped off her clothes, tossing them into a corner in the bathroom. Then, naked, her nipples tight and hard with the cold air, she would settle herself into the steaming tub.

Would she add a stream of bubble bath and let the foam surround her? Perhaps light a candle or two and watch the flames flicker and gleam against the cold panes of the frosted window? Would she sink down low enough in the tub that the tendrils of hair on her nape would become damp? Would the water drops glisten on her long legs as she hooked her ankles over the rim of her old claw-footed tub?

He licked his lips and traced the tip of his finger along that narrow little scar at his temple, the spot where she, with his knife, had sliced his skin so neatly.

His heart was beating loudly in his ears as he heard a soft little splash over the headphones. He didn't really have time for this; there was so much to do and yet . . . He leaned back and closed his eyes. His heart was beating fast now; his breathing a little shallow; his cock coming to life.

Imagining the slim column of her throat, he envisioned the very knife with which she had forever scarred him, a shining blade that sliced neatly across her white skin. As her eyes widened in her surprise, drops of blood formed, glittering gemlike upon her skin before running in dark rivulets down her sternum and over her breasts to slide into the water and bloom a deep scarlet. White bubbles floated, dissipating, becoming stained, as she sank into the warm pool.

He let out a soft moan at the image, a ripple of pleasure moving through him.

Now!

"No." His own voice startled him, but he told himself to hold on to his patience, that he couldn't give in to primal urges. There were others who had to be dealt with first! "Wait," he told himself, but deep within him, in the darkest corners of his heart, he knew that he wouldn't be able to hold out much longer. With Acacia Collins Lambert, it was personal.

As he listened via the tiny hidden microphone to the gentle lap of water surrounding her, he imagined her lying in her own cooling blood. Soon, she would breathe her last.

Again he traced his scar, running his finger along the thin white slice, the cleaved hairline at his temple. Barely visible, but a reminder. His eyes narrowed, and he stood to look into a round mirror he'd placed on the wall over his desk.

For a moment, he thought he saw her behind him.

Acacia!

Staring into the mirror and laughing at him! As if she expected him!

Startled, he whipped around.

But no one was there. Of course not. What he'd seen was the coatrack and a sweatshirt with a hood dangling from one hook.

His breathing slightly erratic, he returned his gaze to the mirror again, and the scar that she had left.

Few people noticed the thin white line.

Fewer had asked about it.

But he knew.

And every day he remembered.

CHAPTER 18

"I'll be damned."

Leaning back in his desk chair, Trace stared at the computer monitor, where, after sifting through public records, he'd found that Jocelyn Wallis, too, had been born in Helena, Montana.

Four for four. What were the chances of that, especially considering the small size of the town?

And you've known three personally. Coincidence?

What the hell did it mean?

Nothing?

Of course not. As the pages stacked in the tray, he lifted off the first set and read through them again, trying to figure out a connection. Coming up with nothing, he lifted a hand high overhead, stretching out his shoulder muscles, then rotated his head. Yawning, he snapped off the computer and checked the clock. Midnight had come and gone, and Eli had fallen asleep on the couch in front of the television. Trace had tried to get him to bed earlier, but his son had protested that he couldn't be alone in his own room because he missed Sarge. Was worried about the mutt.

Trace left the small parlor that he used as a den and found his son sprawled over the crushed pillows of the couch. In sleep, his hair at odd angles, dark lashes lying against his cheeks, Eli looked nearly angelic. Except he'd traded his wings for a bright blue cast.

The boy had been a game changer for Trace.

Before becoming a father, Trace O'Halleran had been known for too much drinking and an interest in the wrong kind of women. He had sown more than his share of wild oats but had stopped the minute Eli had come into his world and rocked it. He'd always heard kids changed everything, but he'd never really thought about it. Until he became a father.

Now he leaned down to pick up his boy from the couch. Eli didn't so much as crack one eyelid as Trace carried him up the old staircase to his bedroom on the second floor.

The room was a mess. Toys and books scattered everywhere, clothes near, but not in the hamper, his twin bed unmade. Light from the window, that eerie gray/white of a snowy-crusted night, spilled over the rumpled quilt.

Gently, Trace lowered him onto the bed, then tucked the quilt around him. Sighing in his sleep, Eli rolled onto one side.

His son.

Trace's jaw tightened at the secrets he'd kept from Eli. Someday he'd have to come clean, he supposed. It was Eli's right to know that Trace wasn't his biological father. But when Eli learned that unforeseen bit of information, the questions would start, and they would be as difficult as the ones fielded the other night, when Eli had been upset and demanded to find his mother.

And Trace wouldn't have answers.

The truth of the matter was that Leanna had never revealed Eli's biological father's identity. Trace had surmised she might not know, and even if she had, she certainly hadn't cared. Theirs had been a white-hot romance that had started in a bar with one too many drinks and ended with a brand-new pregnancy. Trace had done the right thing: he'd married Leanna and adopted Eli. He'd then eventually come to grips with the fact that she'd either miscarried or lied, because the baby she'd claimed to be carrying, Trace's child, never came to fruition.

Not that it had ever mattered.

The fights had begun, the accusations flung, and one night she'd just up and left. He'd woken up to an empty bed. Her car was gone; her clothes had been cleaned out of the closet; her phone, laptop, and make-up were missing.

All she'd left was her boy.

Which was just as well.

As he stared into the room where Eli lay sleeping, he couldn't imagine that he could love any child more. He didn't understand why she'd left, but when the divorce papers came, and she gave up all custodial rights to her son, Trace had signed quick and fast.

There had been a few phone calls and a handful of visits, but they had petered out over the years. He couldn't remember the last time he'd talked to Leanna. When Eli had called her six months ago, the phone had been disconnected.

You should have tracked her down.

He deserves to know his mother, no matter what kind of a heartless bitch she is.

For all you know, she could be dead.

Like Shelly Bonaventure.

Like Jocelyn Wallis.

He decided he would make a few calls about Leanna in the morning. He had a couple of ancient numbers he'd found on a scrap of paper in the desk drawer just last month, when he was searching for a new book of checks. One was a number in Phoenix—hadn't she had a girlfriend who'd relocated down there?—and the other number was for somewhere in Washington, which he didn't understand.

His thoughts turned to Acacia "Kacey" Lambert again, and he told himself to give it up for the night. Nothing sinister was going on. Strange things sometimes happened. Stripping off his shirt, then kicking off his jeans and socks, he fell onto the bed, closed his eyes, and let out a long sigh.

Kacey Lambert's face formed in his mind, and he told himself he was a damned fool.

From her cell phone, Alvarez left a message for Jonas Hayes at the LAPD. Though she didn't expect the detective to be working on a Saturday morning, she knew he'd hear his voice-mail message eventually and, she hoped, get back to her. She didn't really believe that the deaths of Shelly Bonaventure and Jocelyn Wallis were linked, but she believed in being thorough.

And the fact that the victims resembled each other troubled her.

She left some food out for the skittish Jane Doe, but the cat was hiding again. *Give it time,* she told herself as she downed a power shake of frozen blueberries, banana, yogurt, and some wheat germ blended into a froth. "Breakfast of champions," she said under her breath, then grabbed her gym bag and headed outside.

Of course the snow had iced over, glazing the walkways and gardens, but she eased her Jeep out of the slippery lot and onto the county road, which had been plowed sometime during the night.

Fortunately, traffic into the heart of Grizzly Falls was light as it was early, a weak sun just starting to brighten the eastern sky, a few pink streaks of dawn playing in the clouds. She turned on the radio, and as a weather report faded, the beginning notes of "Up on the Rooftop" popped through her speakers, but she barely noticed. She'd pushed aside all her mortification over the Thanksgiving debacle with the June Cleaver clone Hattie and her two kids at Grayson's house. What a mistake that had been.

Sister-in-law . . . oh, sure!

Ridiculously, she felt her cheeks turn hot. "Never again," she vowed, switching lanes around a slow-moving truck hauling a load of baled Christmas trees, and a chorus of children's voices blared from the radio:

"Ho, Ho, Ho!
Who wouldn't go?"

She found the exit for the gym, took the corner, and eased into the near-empty parking lot.

"Up on the rooftop,
Click, click, click!"

"Oh, stop already!" Alvarez snapped off the radio as she nosed into a parking space not far from the main doors of the massive building that housed an Olympic pool, saunas, weight rooms, and several basketball courts. She signed in and grabbed a towel, then made her way to the ladies' locker room, where she stashed her bag.

She hoped that she could exercise her muscles and relax her ever-spinning mind. Today her routine would be a cardio workout of forty-five minutes on the elliptical machine, then another half hour of weight lifting on different machines dedicated to toning and strengthening specific areas of her body.

Usually, somewhere in the middle of her routine, she would zone out, and whatever issues she was trying to work through on a case would start to unravel, but today, as she made her way through a series of arm, leg, and torso machines, no answers came on the Jocelyn Wallis murder. Alvarez had spent hours going over the woman's phone records and through her bills, even her garbage, but nothing had leapt out at her as odd or suspicious, no blinding lightning bolt of insight had illuminated her mind. The ex-boyfriends had alibis. The paperwork was benign.

No will had been located, at least not yet, nor had any life insurance beneficiary been uncovered.

Jocelyn Wallis was a schoolteacher who didn't have a lot of friends and had no known enemies, with no link to Shelly Bonaventure, aside from where she'd been born and her looks. The case was frustrating as hell.

Swiping her forehead with the towel, Alvarez settled into the seat of a leg press and upped the weight. Her muscles were loose now, and she was able to do three sets of fifteen reps, though she strained. When she was finished, sweat dripping from every pore in her body, she still knew no more than she had when she'd taken her first step into this two-storied, state-of-the-art gymnasium.

Heading for the showers, she told herself the truth would appear. She just had to dig a little deeper. Work a little harder.

Kacey rubbed the kinks from her neck as she glanced at the clock in her office. Two fifteen in the afternoon. The day had flown by with appointment after appointment, and, again, with a few extras squeezed in. The fact that it was a holiday weekend, *the* shopping weekend of the year, didn't deter flu viruses, chest colds, infections, or thumbs from being dislocated.

She'd looked down enough throats and into enough ears for a full day's worth of work. On Saturdays the clinic was scheduled to close at three, but rarely did that happen, not when so many working parents arranged doctors' visits around their job schedules.

Fortunately, Kacey worked only every other Saturday, while Martin took the other weekends. They also alternated on Fridays, so that they each had two consecutive days off each week, a plan that worked for the entire staff.

Now her stomach rumbled, reminding her that she hadn't eaten anything since a banana at six in the morning. The three subsequent cups of coffee hadn't been enough to sustain her. Reaching into her desk drawer, where she kept her stash of granola and candy bars, she found a Snickers and promised herself a healthy tuna salad with tons of vegetables for dinner.

Maybe.

Practice what you preach, she told herself, invoking one of her grandmother's, Ada's, timeworn bits of advice as she peeled off the wrapper. How often had she suggested her patients eat healthy, balanced meals, drink eight glasses of water a day, and avoid too much sugar? "Too often," she said aloud, then, ignoring the stacks of files on her desk, bit into the chocolate and caramel and sighed contentedly.

She'd felt a little off all day and attributed it to a restless night filled with worries about intruders and dark pickups, along with the more pleasant fantasies about Trace O'Halleran.

She reminded herself that he was her patient's father, strictly off-limits, but after running into him at the veterinary clinic yesterday and spending time with Eli and him, she'd had trouble pushing the rugged rancher from her mind.

She'd just taken the last bite of her Snickers when there was a tap on the door and Nadine, the weekend receptionist, poked her head inside. "Your next appointment called, a new patient, Mrs. Alexander. She's running fifteen minutes late, but Helen Ingles is here and asked if you would work her in."

Kacey nodded.

Nearing sixty, Nadine was trim, her jaw strong, and her eyebrows were plucked to a fine line. She wore little make-up, lavender-framed glasses, and let her gray hair feather around her face. Her pale lips were pursed into a knot of disapproval.

"Something else?" Kacey asked.

"This morning I was the first one in, and that damned circuit breaker had tripped again. Not a light on in this place!"

An ongoing issue. "Would you put in a call to the landlord?"

"I already left a message on his answering machine and shot him an e-mail," she stated primly. Once in the military, Nadine Kavenaugh was a stickler for detail and didn't like anyone who, as she put it, "couldn't get their act together." Routines were not to be changed.

"Good." Whirling her desk chair around, Kacey tossed the candy wrapper into her wastebasket, then grabbed her lab coat. As the chair stopped, she saw that Nadine's skinny eyebrows had dipped below the rims of her glasses. Obviously, she didn't approve of the changes in the schedule or much of anything else, for that matter.

"I'll put Mrs. Ingles in room two," she said with a bit of bite, "and when Mrs. Alexander gets here, in one."

"I'll be in as soon as Randy takes vitals."

Huffing her disdain through her nose, Nadine closed Kacey's door, but through the thin panels Kacey heard her sharp footsteps marching back to the main reception area.

Slipping on her lab coat, she checked her pocket for her stethoscope, then paused to take a look at her e-mail. She'd hoped for some word on the birth records she'd asked about, even though she knew no state offices had been open for the past three days. Her grandfather's warning, *Don't be gettin' the cart before the horse, there, Missy,* echoed in her ears, and as expected, there wasn't a response. Then again, maybe she was tilting at windmills. Just because a couple of women who resembled her had died, and her mother was a little weird about her family, weren't reasons to go off the deep end.

She clicked out of her account and headed down the short hallway to the examination rooms. Helen Ingles complained about being tired all the time. "Goddamned fatigue, it's killin' me," she admitted, though she swore she was monitoring her glucose levels religiously and eating right and exercising. "Then again, maybe it's because my daughter and her eight-year-old moved in. She's separating from her husband and doesn't have a job." Worry shadowed Helen's eyes.

"Let's talk about that," Kacey said and spent the next ten minutes listening. After determining that worry was as much a part of Helen's problem as her diabetes, Kacey ordered more lab work for the following week and suggested a consultation with a family psychologist.

"A shrink?" Helen said, horrified. "I'm not crazy."

"You've had a change of lifestyle. That's always hard. Here, take the doctor's card, and make an appointment, if you want to." When she saw her patient's hesitation, she added, "What would it hurt?"

"My pride, I guess. I've always thought I could handle all my problems."

"We all need someone to listen sometimes." Kacey left her to mull it over, then plucked the new patient's chart from the basket on the door of exam room one. Elle Alexander was thirty-five, fifteen pounds overweight, and complaining of a persistent cough that was keeping her up at night. Her previous physician was located in Coeur d'Alene, Idaho.

Knocking on the door, Kacey was still skimming the chart. "Mrs. Alexander? I'm Doctor Lambert."

The patient was seated on the examination table, her legs swinging over the edge. A little plump, with short red hair and rosy cheeks, she smiled broadly.

Kacey's heart nearly stopped because the woman resembled her enough to be noticeable. *Again?* she thought in disbelief.

"Hi," Elle greeted her.

Kacey tried to tell herself that she was imagining things, that she'd been too caught up in Heather's conviction that Shelly Bonaventure was her twin, or Nurse Rosie Alsgaard's fears that the Jane Doe patient lying near death in the hospital was Kacey, before Trace O'Halleran had identified her as Jocelyn Wallis. She might have blown it all off as coincidence, but now, staring at Elle Alexander and seeing Randy Yates's expression as he was removing the blood pressure cuff from her arm, she wasn't so sure.

"Are you two related?" Randy asked, and Elle laughed as she eyed the doctor.

"Oh, no," Elle dismissed. "I've just got one of those faces, you know. I remind everyone of someone." She shrugged her shoulders. "I guess it's just my curse." She grinned. "Besides, we really don't look that much alike. Way different body types, for one thing."

That much was true. Kacey was three inches taller and twenty pounds lighter, but the bone structure of Elle's face, the slope of her cheeks, point of her chin, and shape of her eyes, mirrored Kacey's. Elle's hair was lighter, redder, but that could be changed, and Elle's eyes were more blue than green, but there was just something . . . and she was around the right age.

For what?

"You know, though, I think I could start a look-alike club," she went on. "Since I've been in this town, I've met a couple of people who look a lot like me."

"Is that right?" Kacey asked carefully, her pulse elevating.

"Oh, yeah, well, take that poor teacher who died, and then there's a woman at the gym I go to. She's one of the trainers, I think. Her name is . . . Oh, what is it? Gloria, maybe." She puckered her face in annoyance. "Well, I just started at Fit Forever, so I'm not sure, but now there's you." She shrugged, as if it were all a normal occurrence.

As Randy made notes to Elle's chart on his laptop, Kacey tried to ignore the alarm bells jangling in her mind, alarms that said, *Something here is just not right,* and continued the examination, listening to the woman's lungs, hearing about how her cough had persisted for the past three months despite several rounds of antibiotics, swabbing her throat twice. "You were under a doctor's care in Coeur d'Alene?"

Elle offered up the physician's name, then searched in her purse and handed Kacey a business card for a doctor and clinic in Idaho. "I saw him before we moved here," she explained.

"Did you have any chest X-rays?"

Elle shook her head. "No."

"Let's start there, rule out strep and pneumonia, if we can."

"Pneumonia? Oh, I can't have . . ." She looked stricken. "I mean, I've never had pneumonia in my life! Bronchitis a time or two, but . . ."

"Let's wait to see what the X-rays show. Our lab isn't open on Saturdays, but I'll order it out and you can come by on Monday and they'll shoot the images over to me. We'll send the swabs to the lab for the strep test." To Randy, she said, "Please set up with the X-ray technician." She slipped the two swabs into individual plastic bags. While Elle was adjusting her gown and Randy's eyes were on the screen of his laptop, she slid one bag into the pocket of her lab coat. "And this needs to be checked for strep." That bag she set on the counter next to his computer.

Not looking up, Randy clicked the information into his keyboard. "You got it."

"Good." Kacey turned back to Elle as Randy swept up the bag and headed out. "Once I look over the films, and we get results back on your tests, I'll give you a call. In the meantime, I'm prescribing a stronger antibiotic. That should start things working." She wrote out a prescription, then asked Elle to return the next week. "You can make an appointment at the front desk."

"I will," Elle promised.

Feeling as if the extra swab were burning a hole in her pocket, Kacey nevertheless asked, "Did you grow up in Coeur d'Alene?"

"Boise. Why?" she asked.

"Just wondering." Kacey lifted a shoulder, as if she were only mildly curious, when her mind was spinning. *You're hypersensitive this week. She doesn't really even look that much like you. Not like the actress and Jocelyn Wallis.*

"I've lived in Idaho all my life," Elle said. "Born and raised there. That's what made the move so difficult, I guess. But Tom—that's my husband—he took a job over here and uprooted us all. The kids had just settled into the school year, and then we had to go." A trace of sadness colored her gaze. "It's the economy, you know. It even affects lawyers."

"I'm sure you'll make friends here fast, and the schools are great."

"I hope so. My son, he has no trouble fitting in, but my daughter . . . It's more difficult for her. She's thirteen, just kind of trying to figure out who she is, and, well, it's tough." She sighed.

"Grizzly Falls is a great town."

"I hope you're right." She didn't seem convinced.

"Just give it a little time."

"I guess I don't have any choice." She shrugged and started reaching for her clothes, and Kacey headed for her office. Then she waited until Elle Alexander, the last patient, had left, the exam rooms were cleaned, and both Nadine and Randy had gone home as well.

Telling herself she was making a mountain out of a molehill, she locked the door behind her. All her life she'd been fascinated with conspiracy theories, and they'd always landed her in verbal debates and lectures with her mother, in the beginning, or more recently, with her ex. JC thought she was out of her mind, but she was still half convinced that there was more than one shooter in the JFK assassination, that Princess Di was killed by her enemies or someone within the royal family, and that Kurt Cobain did not commit suicide.

Despite all her ex-husband's arguments.

Once she was certain she was alone, that everyone had left the clinic, she retrieved the bagged swab from her pocket. Though she realized that she was jumping at shadows, and despite the fact that she was going against everything she believed in, she sent the Baggie to the lab with a special request for Elle Alexander's DNA profile.

And there was that trainer at Fit Forever . . . Gloria somebody, who Elle thought looked like her. Kacey decided she would make a trip over there soon and see if she was "another one" of them.

"Bizarre," she said aloud as she turned out the lights.

CHAPTER 19

A s smart as he was, sometimes fate or God or whoever seemed against him, he thought as he hurried down the rickety old stairs. The scent of the basement, dust and dirt, filled his nostrils as he unlocked the door and stepped into his private office. Without thinking, he locked the door behind him and tried to calm himself.

"One." *Breathe.* "Two." *Take another, deeper breath.*

Agitated, he slowly counted to ten, then to twenty, but his fists were still clenched, his shoulders tight, his mind a blaze of red. A deep fury that burned bright. Opening a drawer in the desk, he saw the yellowed records that he had collected, soon intended to destroy. The ancient computer from which this information was taken was long gone, the floppy disks of that era already disintegrated into nothing, their files corrupted and irretrievable.

So all that remained were these papers he'd preserved with such care. And he would burn them, one by one, as soon as each of those he called "the Unknowings" was dead.

Of course, there was always a chance that one of them could still stumble upon the truth, and that thought twisted his guts. He couldn't, wouldn't, let it happen, he thought, anger rising again.

Wanting to kick something or someone, he made his way to the specialty bar he'd installed himself, slid out of his clothes, and stepped into his pair of gravity inversion boots.

After strapping himself in, he began doing abdominal pull-ups, curling himself toward the ceiling, feeling his spine decompress, forcing his muscles to work hard.

He needed the release and gritted his teeth as sweat began to run along his skin.

He'd plotted out his revenge neatly and spent years slowly taking care of the Unknowings. The pictures he had of them, all taken moments before their deaths, were proof enough of how patient and careful he'd been, the years he'd put into this project. But every once in a while, some of his best laid plans were undone.

The most recent case in point was Elle Alexander. How could he have predicted that her shyster of a husband would pull up stakes and join a law firm here? In *Grizzly Falls* of all places? It complicated things, and now that damned Elle was going to ruin everything. She'd already visited Acacia Lambert, and that spelled trouble.

But you can fix this. You know you can. Think!

His muscles strained as he pulled up, held the position, then slowly lowered himself to hang upside down for a second or two before repeating the process.

He couldn't afford any screwups now.

There's still time. Just concentrate!

Again he pulled upward.

This time his abs screamed.

Slowly he rolled downward, and while his muscles protested, he forced himself to do another set and unhooked his boots only when his abs and back felt as if they were on fire and sweat dripped down his body to pool on the floor.

Good. It's good.

Taking a deep breath, he flipped lithely to his feet. He was agile and strong, a high-school wrestler who'd gone to state and later, in college, a member of a competitive crew team. He'd rock climbed, explored caves, scuba dived, and snow skied.

And he'd never backed down from a challenge.

Even the biggest of his life.

So he couldn't allow anything to get in his way.

Not even that niggling sensation that caught him off guard once in a while. That someone *knew.*

"Stop!" he said aloud, to jar himself away from the unfounded fear that sometimes burrowed into his heart.

Already he'd had to accelerate his schedule. He'd planned on taking his time, to not arouse any suspicions, but now he felt a tightness in his chest, a sense of dire urgency. Time was running out.

At least he understood who would be next.

Finally, his thoughts were clear. He always had a plan B, which was always a little more dangerous, with more chance of being found out, but at this point, he had no choice. Elle had to be dealt with.

It would work out. Most of those far away had been dealt with, which left him a clear shot at those who were near.

He would have to tread carefully, as ever. One mistake now and he'd be exposed before his mission was finished, before he could be free. He couldn't allow himself the sense of ego to think that the cops were stupid; he'd just been lucky, as so far they had been in different jurisdictions. And the actress had brought national attention. Because of her fame, Shelly Bonaventure's untimely demise had caused a deeper scrutiny; because of her lifestyle, her death had been ruled an accident.

He'd gotten lucky; he knew it.

Now things were about to change.

Now that his work would be nearby.

The police here could possibly put two and two together.

Smiling, he thought of that answer: it was far more than four. He glanced at his stack of photos, proof that the Unknowings had died, and felt a buzz of excitement sizzle through his veins. He was about to add another.

Closer and closer to his ultimate goal.

Grabbing a clean towel from the neatly folded stack that he kept on the same shelves as his boots, he patted off the sweat that still sheened his body, then slid into a thick robe. Calmer now, in complete control again, he sat at his desk, where his computer screen was already glowing. He dragged up all the information he had on Elle, then stared at her photo. He'd have to follow her, but that wasn't a problem. She was a ditzy, scattered woman who could be dealt with fairly easily.

He'd make her a priority.

He was certain, with a little patience, the perfect opportunity would present itself.

He'd be ready.

* * *

All of Kacey's worries about adopting a dog had melted the second Kacey had picked up Bonzi on Saturday and driven him home. Calm by nature, he'd sniffed around the perimeter of the house, decided a near-dead rosebush near the garage was his favorite spot to relieve himself, and accepted the dog bed she'd purchased as his own. He followed after her everywhere she went, toenails clicking, ears cocked, eyes bright with curiosity, but she found out on Sunday that if she walked him for half a mile twice a day, he was content to sleep away most of the rest of the hours.

"Oh, right, a fine guard dog you turned out to be," she chastised as she made herself dinner and he yawned in response. She thought about calling Trace O'Halleran and checking on Eli and Sarge, but she realized it would sound too much like the excuse it was.

To her surprise she'd enjoyed herself on Friday night at Dino's. Since then, she'd found herself thinking, no, make that fantasizing, about him and his son. She had even picked up the phone a couple of times to call and ask about Sarge, then had thought better of it. But she hadn't put him out of her mind. At least not easily. And there were questions she had about him, and about his boy, about Eli's absent mother. Though it didn't seem as if Trace had a current girlfriend, he'd been recently involved, at some level, with Jocclyn Wallis, even ID'ing her when she lay in the hospital, clinging hopelessly to life.

How close had they been? she wondered now.

"None of your business," she told herself, but it didn't stop her thoughts from turning to him. She hadn't dated much since her marriage had crumbled, and after JC she'd sworn off men for a while. But, she sensed, Trace O'Halleran could change all that.

In a heartbeat.

Elle stepped on the gas. Her minivan was zooming along the dark road, but she wasn't worried, even though night had fallen hours earlier. She'd driven "hazardous" mountain roads since she was sixteen; they were no big deal. So, despite the crystals of ice that glittered on the asphalt in the beams of her headlights, and the light from a crescent moon rising high in the inky sky, she was confident.

She pushed the speed limit and stared straight ahead through the windshield at the landscape, truly a winter wonderland. The road was a black ribbon cutting through acres of snow-covered fields, then through thickets of aspen and pine, where heavy-laden branches glistened with snow.

Glancing at the dashboard clock, she realized it was nearly ten thirty, which meant she was a good two hours later than she'd expected to be. She'd spent longer than she'd planned in Spokane, at the mall, then even longer after stopping in Coeur d'Alene for a quick dinner on her way home for old time's sake. Big mistake. No doubt Tom would be starting to worry. She'd have to give him a call.

Before she could hit auto dial, a coughing attack erupted in her throat, and she gave up on the phone and quickly unwrapped a cherry-flavored lozenge, sucking on it with vigor. She was feeling a little feverish, too, but she wouldn't admit it to Tom and the kids.

Things just had to get done, and if she didn't do them, who would?

The holiday season was always super busy, and this year, with a new house and neighborhood, the pressure was on. She intended that her house on Aspen Circle would have the best Christmas display in the entire cul-de-sac.

Squinting against the sudden glare of headlights, she exhaled heavily. She'd met a few cars traveling the opposite direction, and though no one had sped fast enough to pass her, there were distant beams that occasionally reflected in the rearview mirror, from a vehicle far behind her. At least she wasn't totally alone on this lonely stretch of highway.

She needed to get back to Tom and the kids. He'd agreed to watch them while she made her hasty trip to Spokane for some major Christmas shopping. While at the mall, she'd found the cutest new addition to her grapevine reindeer herd, a new Rudolph that would knock the fading nose off her original once he was set up near the little fir tree in the front yard and plugged in.

Yep. Rudolph II was phenomenal, and he'd been on sale. Twenty percent off with the coupon she'd clipped from the local paper. She couldn't wait to display him in the frozen, snow-crusted grass, but she hoped the neighborhood would respect her display. Last year a couple of kids in the old neighborhood thought it would be funny to see Rudolph I mounting one of the female deer.

Elle hadn't found any humor in the situation. Not at all. Talk about bad taste. Then again, some of those hoodlums had been cretins. So maybe, in some ways, the move to Grizzly Falls was a godsend.

She coughed again and wished the damned antibiotics would kick in. Yeah, it had been only one day, but she'd been fighting this crud forever. And no bug was going to keep her from this weekend's price-busting sales. She'd missed Black Friday and Black Saturday, but damn, she'd scored big on Black Sunday, or whatever it was called.

Without slowing, she hooked up her iPhone to the console, then found her iTunes list and selected a special holiday mix she'd created herself. The music started to play, and within seconds she was singing along with Faith Hill as the wheels of her Dodge ate up the miles.

Her only problem, other than the nasty flu—pneumonia, really?— was that she wasn't all that familiar with the roads around these parts. As she'd told the doctor, she'd been an Idaho girl all of her thirty-five years, well, except for that one summer when she'd driven to L.A. and thought she'd bleach her hair blond, live near the beach, Venice or Malibu or somewhere that sounded exotic, and learn how to roller-skate in a bikini.

Big mistake.

Too hot. Too crowded. Too many other beautiful blondes.

She'd returned to Boise four months later, her proverbial tail between her legs, and decided being a "hick from the sticks," as she'd called herself, wasn't such a bad thing.

Besides, she'd met Tom Alexander, hadn't she? The love of her life. Or at least he had been when they had dated and were first married. Over a dozen years and two kids later, some of the passion had slipped out of their relationship. Lately, Tom had been distant.

Caught up in her worries about her husband, she sped past a road sign, just catching sight of it in the corner of her eye. "Crap!"

She realized she'd missed the turn and slowed at the next wide spot in the road and did a quick one-eighty. Some of the roads around here were so poorly marked and confusing! And it didn't help that it was dark, not a streetlight for miles. At the corner, she turned toward Grizzly Falls and noticed that the vehicle that had been following her at a distance was much closer now. It, too, turned toward town and followed the two-lane road that wound along the banks of the river.

Elle glanced at the dash clock again. She wouldn't get home until after eleven, and Tom would be worried sick. She probably should call.

In her rearview she noticed the car behind her was catching up to her, the harsh glare of its headlights reflecting right into her eyes. "Bastard," she grumbled, then turned on her Bluetooth, but, of course, it was dead.

Perfect.

She'd forgotten to charge the damned thing. That was the problem. There were just too many devices to keep alive, along with juggling the demands of a family, keeping the house, volunteering at the school and, of course, shaking this damned flu, or whatever it was.

Slipping her phone out of the console, she pressed the two key, her shortcut to home. After the third ring, Tom answered.

"Hey," he said, obviously recognizing her number. She heard the muted sound of the television in the background. "Where are you?"

"God, I wish I knew. On the right road, though. I think." The sign had said Grizzly Falls this way, hadn't it? The vehicle behind her was coming closer, right on her tail. "Shit, there's a guy behind me with his lights on bright. About to burn my eyes out."

"Slow down. Let him go by."

No way. Let the jerk ride her ass. She was tired and anxious to get home, didn't need the aggravation of the bastard's brights. Into the phone, she said, "Look, I'm probably still about twenty, maybe twenty-five minutes away. I couldn't resist the sales. So, how are the kids?"

"Unhappy that I made them go to bed at ten. They weren't quite in the back-to-school mode. I had to become the"—he lowered his voice—"dreaded Sleep Enforcer."

"Which they hate."

"Copy that."

She laughed as she took a sharp curve one-handed. The car behind her didn't slow for a second. In fact, he seemed even closer, right on her damned bumper! Her tires slid a bit, then caught, and her laughter gave way to another coughing fit. Lord, she was sick of being sick! "Oh . . . Tom . . . ," she managed, distracted by the car on her tail and her inability to catch her breath. "I . . . I have . . . to . . .

"Shit! . . . Tom!" She was coughing, her eyes were watering, and the car was slipping toward the narrow shoulder.

Bam!

Metal crunched and her car leapt forward. Her seat belt snapped tight.

"What the hell—?" She glanced in the rearview mirror and saw the huge truck behind her. He'd hit her? What kind of an idiot was he? She didn't have time to worry about it. The damned van was skidding. "You son of a bitch!" She dropped the phone and grabbed the wheel with both hands.

Too late!

The van was out of control! Sliding ever closer to the shoulder and the rushing, frigid river beyond.

"Damn it!"

She drove into the skid, then slowly turned the wheel as the front tire hit the shoulder. She was adding pressure to the brakes, trying to stay calm, though her pulse was jumping, her heart pounding, sweat instantly upon her hands.

"Elle?" She heard Tom's voice faintly from the phone, which was now on the floor.

"The bastard rear-ended me!" she screamed.

"What?"

"I said . . . oh, no!"

In the mirror, she saw the behemoth of a truck bearing down on her, bright lights glowing with evil fire. What was the matter with him? Oh, Lord, he was going to hit her again!

She slid from one side of the road into oncoming traffic, then, overcorrecting, skidded over the icy asphalt and onto the shoulder again.

And still the truck was behind her.

"Tom!" she screamed. "Call nine-one-one!!!! This guy's trying to . . . oh, Jesus . . ." The corner was only a hundred feet away, a sharp curve right before the bridge.

The truck's engine was deafening; its high beams were blinding in her side mirror. The idiot was going to pass her!

Good. Let him go by! Remember to get his damned license plate number. . . .

Oh, God, the grill of the truck was so close to her left rear panel! Too close! With a sick sensation she realized the driver had no intention of going around her. He was going to hit her again!

She had no choice. Though her Dodge was still sliding, she stepped on the accelerator to outmaneuver him.

Too late!

Bam!

Another shot to her bumper. Off center this time and hard enough to snap her neck.

Her van careened to the right. She stood on the brakes, but the tires kept moving, ever closer to the edge of the road and the river below.

The bridge . . . if she could just reach the bridge.

Bam! With the groan of twisting metal, she felt her vehicle take flight.

Over the edge of the road, above a strip of snowy bank, then the Caravan dived nose first into the swift, ice-cold river.

CHAPTER 20

Since Friday night with Kacey, it seemed to take forever to get through the rest of the long weekend. Between his chores, taking Eli to see Sarge the recovering dog both Saturday and Sunday. Trace had spent the rest of his time trying *not* to think about his son's new doctor. He'd told himself after Jocelyn that he was through with women for a while, at least until Eli was older, but now, here he was, in the damned barn, thinking about Dr. Acacia Lambert and wondering how he could see her again.

"Don't be stupid," he told himself as he finished feeding the cattle, who were housed during the coldest days of winter in the long barn.

He pushed aside all thoughts of her easy smile and the glint of humor he caught in her gaze. Starting something up with her would only spark trouble, and he'd seen more than his share.

He had even considered calling her again but had thought better of it. Besides, they hadn't really gone on a date so much as eaten together out of convenience, for the sake of Eli. He wondered about her interest in his son. It seemed more than professional, but then, he was probably reading more into the situation than there really was.

She was also attracted to Trace; he'd been with enough women to recognize the signs. But she'd been guarded as well. So it was best to just let it lie.

Besides, he had enough on his plate. Eli's arm seemed to be healing, but his persistent cough was deep and rattling and just wouldn't go away. His temperature was closing in on a hundred, or had been last night; he'd check again once the boy was awake for the day, but Trace was starting to worry.

For now, though, he had work to do. The smell of cattle, dung, and urine mingled with that of the dry hay in this hundred-year-old wooden structure that stored feed as well as provided shelter for the animals. The oldest part of the building, the middle section, where the cattle were now milling, was the original barn and was constructed of long-weathered cedar. It rose three stories high, and in the loft overhead, bales of hay were stacked to the ancient rafters. On either side of this central piece, additions had been built over the decades: a pole barn on one side, an enclosed shed that ran the length of the building on the other.

This morning the cattle, restless at being cooped up during the latest series of storms, bawled and pushed toward the trough he used for feeding in the winter. Their russet and black coats were thick and shaggy; their noses wet as they buried them into the hay he'd spread.

"Hold on. There's enough for everyone," he told one particularly pushy whiteface.

Then, satisfied that the cattle were cared for, he hung his pitchfork on a nail near the door and automatically whistled for the dog.

"Okay, that wasn't smart," he muttered. Sarge was still at the veterinary clinic and would remain there until Jordan Eagle said he was well enough to leave.

He left the lights on and stepped outside, where the sun hadn't yet risen and morning stars crowded the sky. Trudging to the stables, his boots crunching through the snow, he then fed and watered the horses, patting the youngest gelding's black nose. The horse had been named Jet for his coloring, but after Trace had bought him, Eli had decided to call the gelding Jetfire, who, he claimed, was a Transformer. "Hey, boy," he said, now scratching the horse behind the ears after he'd measured out the grain. "Maybe you'll all get out today."

Let's hope, he thought, as all the animals were getting antsy. He didn't blame them, as he hated to be cooped up as well.

"Later," he said to the small herd as he headed outside again, following his own path to the house, where the woodstove was already warming the kitchen and the coffee had brewed. He stomped the snow from his boots, wedged them off, one toe on the heel of the other, then carried them into the house. Once the boots were warming near the fire, he poured himself a cup of coffee and, though he knew it was way too early for any kind of response, checked his phone messages. Of course there were none. He'd hoped that someone who knew Leanna would call him, let him know where she was.

Now he examined the scrap of paper he'd taken from the desk with contact numbers for Leanna. Checking the time, he shrugged and dialed the Washington number, but it just rang and rang. No answering device. He then called the Phoenix number, also to no avail, but at least this time he could leave a message on voice mail after a computer voice said, "Please leave a message after the tone." He took the time to explain who he was, that he had been married to Leanna and would like to get in contact with her. Finally, he called the attorney with the firm Leanna had used when they'd divorced, one Kelvin Macadam of Bennett, Stowe, and Ellsworth in Boise, but, of course, their offices weren't open today. After that he was pretty much out of options.

So much for chasing down ghosts of ex-wives.

Sipping from his cup, he snapped on the small television he'd set on the butcher-block cart his mother had used as a baking station.

Hoping to hear the weather report, he pulled a carton of milk from the fridge and a box of Cheerios from the cupboard. While rattling around in the flatware drawer he heard about a local tree-lighting contest before the woman anchor said, "And on a more serious note, a woman lost her life in a one-car accident when her car plunged into the Grizzly River near the North Fork Bridge. Elle Alexander, a mother of two, was rushed to St. Bartholomew's Hospital, where she was pronounced dead on arrival."

Terrible, he thought. *More and more bad news.*

He poured the last of the cereal into a bowl and set it on the table for his son, then crushed the box and put it on the back porch with the rest of his recycling. When he returned to the kitchen, a different reporter was speaking, a woman standing at the crest of Boxer Bluff. Behind her, lit by bright lights, was the short stone guardrail, and around it had been placed bouquets of flowers, candles, and balloons, even stuffed animals all frozen solid, an icy memorial to Jocelyn Wallis.

Trace stared at the screen as the woman reporter gestured toward the display as her short near-black hair blew in the wind and she clutched her microphone in her gloved hands. Looking into the camera's eye, she said, "The Pinewood Sheriff's Department has released a statement saying that the death of Jocelyn Wallis, a schoolteacher at Evergreen Elementary School in Grizzly Falls, may have been foul play. The authorities are not ruling Jocelyn Wallis's death a homicide at this time, but they are continuing their investigation."

Trace, stunned, stood rooted to the kitchen floor as he saw Jocelyn Wallis's face appear on the screen. His guts twisted as he watched images of Jocelyn smiling into the camera, then a shot of the long brick building of his kid's school.

Once again the camera was on the reporter standing on the crest of Boxer Bluff, near the park. The camera's focus moved from her to pan over the raging falls and the snow-crusted ledge above the river, where Jocelyn's fate had been decided.

"The Pinewood County Sheriff's Department is asking for anyone who may have seen Jocelyn Wallis jogging in the park or anything the least bit suspicious on the day of her death to contact them. That number will be posted on our Web site." The screen split suddenly. The reporter out in the elements on one side, the two anchors sitting side by side behind a desk in the studio. "This is Nia Del Ray with KMJC News," the reporter said. "Back to you, Drake."

"Jesus," Trace whispered, disbelieving, as he stared at his small TV. What had the reporter said?

The authorities are not ruling Jocelyn Wallis's death a homicide at this time.

Homicide?

For the love of God, who would want to kill Jocelyn? And why?

The split screen returned to one image of the news set, and the story was quickly segued into another about a fire in a small town to the south.

Trace thought of his son and how he'd been close to Jocelyn. It had been bad enough to tell him that she'd died, but now to try and explain murder to a seven-year-old when he didn't understand it himself . . .

The weather report forgotten, he poured some milk over the Cheerios, then left the kitchen to climb the stairs to Eli's room.

Another thought struck him as he reached the top of the stairs. If

Jocelyn had truly been murdered, Trace's name would come up as a potential suspect. There was no way around that. He'd dated her. The damned school had called him when she hadn't shown up for work. He had been in her place, knew where she kept a spare key, had identified her in the hospital.

Yeah, he thought as he pushed open the door to Eli's room and found his son lying on his back, covers bunched, hair sticking out at all angles, casted arm resting on his chest while he slept soundly, as if he didn't have a care in the world, Trace O'Halleran's name would be on the suspect short list.

For a while.

He watched his boy's even breathing, as if he didn't have a care in the world.

Too bad that was all about to change.

By the time she left for work Monday morning, Kacey couldn't imagine not having adopted the dog. And she intended, at least at first, to drive home for her lunch and play with him for a half hour or so to break up her, and his, day.

As for Bonzi being a guard dog, that was yet to be seen, but he was company and she felt safer with him in the house. She had allowed his dog bed in her room and had found comfort in his soft snores throughout the night.

"A good decision," she told herself as she nosed her car through the drive-through coffee kiosk on the outside of town, then headed to the office.

The weekend hadn't passed without her thinking of Trace O'Halleran and his son. In fact, she'd caught herself daydreaming about him more than a couple times. She'd found him easy to talk to and sexy as the devil last Friday, but she'd attempted not to let her thoughts get ahead of her. She'd tried to keep herself busy with household chores, playing with the dog, and finding out everything she could about Shelly Bonaventure, Jocelyn Wallis, and, lastly, Elle Alexander.

Elle had claimed to have been born and raised in Boise. Kacey had checked and found no mention in any birth records of her being born in Helena, Montana, so maybe Elle's claim had been true and all Kacey's suspicions were for naught.

A couple of women who looked like her had died. And they'd been born near her. That was all it was. What had she expected? That they could all be related? Unlikely, and even if it were true, was that really so odd? She could have lots of shirttail relatives around these parts.

Ten minutes after picking up her latte, with the eastern sky just starting to lighten, she pulled into the parking lot of the clinic. She told herself to forget trying to find a link.

Holding her still-steaming cup with one hand and grabbing her laptop with the other, she did a juggling routine as she locked her car, then headed inside. Her first patient wasn't scheduled until eight, and she still had time to check her e-mail and get ready for the day.

But as she was stepping into her office, Heather sprinted down the hallway from the reception area. "Did you hear?" she asked, her eyes round.

"Hear what?"

"That one of our patients died over the weekend!"

"Oh, God, no." Kacey's heart nearly missed a beat.

"I never met her, but she came in on Saturday. I was just going to check with the lab about her schedule."

Kacey froze. "Who?" But she knew. Instantly.

"Elle Alexander. Remember?" she asked, clearly shaken.

Kacey felt as if she'd been hit by a shotgun blast. Elle? The woman had been so full of life. Married, a mother worried more about her children than her own health, even with her nagging cough, she had been so vibrant. "What happened?"

"She slid off the road. Up by the North Fork Bridge and into the river. Coming home from Spokane, where she'd been Christmas shopping, the news said. I saw a report this morning, while I was working out on my stair stepper!" Heather shuddered theatrically. "Can you imagine?"

"No," Kacey admitted, her heart squeezing. "Were her kids with her?"

"Don't think so. But there's a story in the newspaper. I put it on your desk."

"Thanks." Shaken, Kacey hurried into her office and sat in her desk chair. She read the article once, then again, all the while re-membering Elle's expressive face and quick smile.

As a physician, she dealt with death regularly. A person lived and died. It was all part of the circle of life. She knew it and accepted it, though she'd never become inured when a person passed from this life to the next. But with a woman so young, in the prime of her life, with two kids . . . it just wasn't right.

And something else bothered her. A vague intuition that skimmed along her body, just under her skin, and caused her a deep unease. Elle, like Shelly Bonaventure before her and Jocelyn Wallis just last week, resembled her.

She thought of the swab she'd taken of the woman's saliva and the fact that she was checking Elle's DNA. She was glad she'd done it. Maybe there wasn't a conspiracy going on, per se, but there was something there . . . something strange.

"You can listen to the nine-one-one tape yourself," Alvarez said as she walked with Pescoli into the lunchroom, which had been totally Joelle-ized from top to bottom. Christmas lights, garlands of fake pine boughs decorated with gold beads and red ribbons were draped around the room. Silver snowflakes dangled and twisted from the overhead lights like fishing lures on forgotten reels.

"For the love of God, is this even allowed in a public building?" Pescoli groused, noticing the coffeepot had a red bow tied to its plastic handle. "This is just too much."

Alvarez ripped off the bow and poured a long stream of coffee into a mug she'd pulled down from the shelf. She took a big gulp from her cup, then turned the conversation back to the single-car accident near the North Fork Bridge. "Tom Alexander thinks his wife was run off the road intentionally. Claims he was on the phone with her when her van was hit."

"Seriously?" Pescoli pulled her favorite cracked cup from the shelf. "So he's, what? Claiming that he heard her die?"

"Something like that."

"Dear God. Can you imagine?"

"No." Alvarez scowled. "So it's our case. Homicide."

"*Possible* homicide. Man oh man!"

Before they could discuss the case any further, the sound of footsteps reached their ears, and Joelle, dressed head to foot in Christmas red, appeared. "Happy Holidays!" she greeted them, her blond hair decorated with matching poinsettias tucked over her ears. She carried three pink boxes into the lunchroom and plunked them down.

Pescoli noticed that the same red flowers displayed in Joelle's blond locks were also pinned to the tops of her scarlet four-inch heels.

"I hope you all aren't sick of sweets!" Joelle chirped with a toothy smile.

"Never," Pescoli assured her.

Joelle picked up a little fake tree that, when she pressed a button, started to rotate, its lights glowing almost eerily, then set it back onto the table. She said, "My cousin Beth's kids came down with that nasty flu, so they weren't able to come to Thanksgiving dinner, and Uncle Bud and his wife, they're in their eighties, you know, and were snowed in, so they didn't show, either. Jennifer, my sister, she's on one of her wacko diets again, only eats fruit and honey, I think, so the upshot is, I had waaay too much food." Folding open each box, she exposed what appeared to be a pumpkin pie, some kind of berry torte, and a plastic container of sugar cookies cut into the shape of cornucopias, turkeys, and Pilgrim hats. Pescoli wasn't sure, but it looked like there was at least one Easter Bunny, which must've taken a wrong turn from the freezer six months earlier.

As Joelle leaned forward, Pescoli caught a glimpse of her gold hoop earrings. Dear God, a minuscule elf sat in each eighteen-karat loop.

Joelle quickly spread the cookies on a plate, then, hearing the phones start to jangle, froze for a second, her lips pursing. "Duty calls," she said with a shrug, then clicked quickly out of the lunchroom as a couple of road deputies walked in.

"She's something else," Pescoli muttered, but Alvarez wasn't listening, so she opted for a black hat cookie and bit off the crown, down to the gold-colored buckle.

Alvarez, deep in thought, ignored all the goodies and said, as Pescoli poured herself a cup of the strong-looking coffee, "The Alexanders' van is in the department's garage. I thought I'd swing by and take a look."

"I'm with you." Pescoli wondered about the single-car accident. Maybe the husband was frantic, grief-stricken, trying to blame anyone for his wife's single-car accident on an icy road. Or maybe it was to defer blame; maybe he knew something more than he was saying; maybe he expected the road crew to find evidence that the wife was run off the road.

You're too suspicious, been in the business too long.

She finished her cookie and said, "Before we head out, though, I'd like to hear the nine-one-one tape. Then we'll check the cell phone records, see where the pings come from." She took a sip from her cup and sucked in her breath through her teeth. "That's strong."

"Brewster made it earlier. He doesn't like, and I quote, 'namby-pamby weak-assed shit,' " Alvarez said.

"Strong words from a God-fearing man."

Alvarez shrugged. "Still a cop."

"And a deacon in the church."

"Your boss," Alvarez reminded.

"And a pain in the ass." She wanted to say more, but for once, Pescoli bit her tongue and wondered what kind of Secret Santa gift she'd get for the undersheriff. Rat poison or a one-way ticket to Mozambique or the South Pole came swiftly to mind, though she really didn't hate the guy. He was a decent enough cop, just overly protective when it came to his daughters, especially Heidi, who, in Pescoli's opinion, was two-faced and manipulative, and boy, did Heidi have Jeremy wrapped around her perfectly manicured fingers. God, Pescoli wished Jeremy would wise up and find someone else. Brewster probably wouldn't appreciate a box of condoms under the department Christmas tree, especially if they were earmarked for his precious little girl.

Alvarez started walking out of the lunchroom just as the back door opened and the sheriff, along with his ever-faithful dog, walked inside.

"Mornin'," he drawled with a smile that lifted the corners of his mustache.

"Morning," Pescoli said, and Alvarez smiled, though it seemed a bit stiff.

"I hear we've got a possible homicide." He pointed to his office, and Sturgis, tail wagging, hurried toward the sheriff's office.

"Looks that way," Alvarez said.

"Maybe." Pescoli wasn't convinced.

Alvarez added, "We're checking on it now."

"Good." The sheriff nodded. "Oh, and thanks for stopping by the other night. I hope my extended family didn't overwhelm you. The twins, even at seven they can be a handful. Imagine what they'll be at fifteen."

Pescoli didn't want to go there. She knew about fifteen . . . and sixteen and seventeen . . . twins to boot?

"No, they were adorable," Alvarez assured him, and Pescoli shot her a look. What the hell was this all about? Adorable? Alvarez thought some kids related to Grayson were *adorable?* This from the woman who never seemed to want children?

"Keep me posted about what happened out near the North Fork," Grayson said.

"Will do," Alvarez said as Grayson walked into his office and she and Pescoli headed down the hall.

Pescoli opened her mouth to speak, but Alvarez held up a hand and said, "I know." She cast a look down the hallway toward Grayson's office, and her face reflected no emotion. "I'll tell you more about it later. Okay? Right now I've got an investigation to work on, and I'm way ahead of you about Elle and Tom Alexander's cell phones. I've already made the request for the records for both of their numbers for the past two months. Just in case he called an insurance company or girlfriend."

"Or she called a boyfriend."

"Exactly. I should get the info today."

"Good girl," Pescoli said.

"Always."

CHAPTER 21

In the eighty-year-old sheep shed the next morning, he checked his truck. Parked near the old John Deere tractor that still dripped oil, the pickup was hidden away in this drafty, graying outbuilding that was nearly a hundred yards down the hill from the main house. As far as he could tell, there was no damage that looked new or out of place. Was there any transfer of paint that might link his vehicle to that stupid bitch's minivan? He didn't think so.

Quickly, he unscrewed the solid steel specialty bumper from the dark truck. He'd welded the bumper together himself, built it like a cattle guard, and made sure that when it was bolted to the Chevy, it partially hid the Idaho plates he'd stolen years before. He'd picked a truck with Idaho plates because those plates were common in this area. And he prided himself on finding a pickup that was the same make and model as the one from which he'd lifted the plates.

God, it was cold.

Inside this insulation-free shed, his breath fogged and his fingers felt a little numb. He worked quickly. As he had so often in the past, he replaced those old stolen license plates with the current Montana plates. He also removed the white sheepskin cover to his seats, exposing the black leather, just in case anyone caught a glimpse inside the window as he was doing his "work." The final step was to peel off the fake bumper stickers on the back of the truck. He'd made his own, though they were really magnets that he could remove at will. The truck, he knew, always needed to be disguised, even though during the day he drove his silver Lexus, bought at a dealer in Missoula, registered in his name, and sporting current Montana plates.

Once satisfied that the pickup, if ever found, would appear innocent enough, he carried the bumper to the other side of the shed, set up a drip cloth, and, after sanding off any traces of paint transfer, used a rattle can of dull black paint and restored the bumper to new. He'd have to let it dry for a while; then he could put it, along with the seat covers and metallic "stickers," in a hiding spot beneath the old manger, which still, if there wasn't any breeze, smelled of long-forgotten Suffolks and Targhees and other breeds popular half a century earlier.

He knew he was being overly cautious, but he didn't want to make the mistake of underestimating the police. He hadn't run his missions for over a decade without being careful; even so, he'd encountered a few problems along the way. Though he was a genius, his IQ scores had proved as much, and he was a damned sight smarter than his father, he still couldn't afford overconfidence.

So far, so good.

And then he felt it.

A crinkling of the skin on his nape—a warning.

That odd sensation that he was being observed by unseen eyes in this frigid shed.

His pulse skyrocketed and he turned quickly, looking over his shoulder, checking the cobwebby corners and shadowy doorways, but there was no one spying upon him. He squinted, glancing through the one dirty window to the snowy fields beyond.

There was nothing out of the ordinary.

He was just jumpy.

Because he was stepping things up.

His work was more dangerous than ever.

The moan of the wind in the rafters sounded like eerie laughter, mocking him.

Sweat suddenly dappled his hairline.

Don't let your imagination run away with you. He took in a deep breath. *You're the one in charge. You decide who dies. Do not forget that.*

He talked himself down, found his equilibrium once more.

Satisfied that his secret was safe, he locked the shed and jogged back to the house, where he intended to shower, shave, and face the day. There would be news of the "accident" near the bridge, and he wanted to catch what the reporters and sheriff's department were saying.

He lived for these moments when he'd neatly removed one of the Unknowings, and there was still some buzz about it. Soon enough the interest faded and the story slipped off the headlines.

A good thing, he reminded himself as he took the steps two at a time. The more disinterest, the better. Shelly Bonaventure had proved that. She'd gotten a helluva lot more press dead than she ever did during her lifetime. And yet he reveled in the recapping of the deaths, loved seeing the bafflement on the faces of the investigating officers, felt a sense of pride that he'd managed, once again, to outwit the authorities while working toward his ultimate goal.

But he had to be careful. Always. Time was of the essence. The problem was that most of the remaining Unknowings lived in and around this part of Montana, where they would be more likely linked. Oh, he'd taken care of some early on, years before, all deemed unfortunate accidents, but now, it seemed, most of his work would be here. He needed to be doubly careful as a cluster of deaths would now arouse more suspicion.

Again, he felt as if someone were surveying him, even seeing into his mind, but that was nuts. Crazy.

He closed his eyes and centered himself.

Pull yourself together! Do not fall victim to the paranoia. It's nothing. Nothing!

Finally, again, his pulse was normal.

Checking his watch, he realized it was too late to listen in on Acacia, the most troubling of the lot. Just thinking of her made his skin tingle in a way he found disturbing, yet slightly erotic.

Too risky, he reminded himself. She had been the reason, all those years ago, that he'd learned of the other Unknowings. Her existence had unwittingly brought them all to his attention and each's ultimate demise.

He should probably thank her.

He almost laughed aloud and wished that he could listen in on her and fantasize, but he knew it would be fruitless. There was no reason to try and listen now. She was already out of the house and probably at the clinic.

He smiled.

Maybe he should become her "patient."

Soon. He smiled to himself and felt his cock tweak just a bit. *Very, very soon.*

"So she has some vague, slight resemblance to the other women. So what?" Pescoli said two hours later, when she and Alvarez had reconnected and were driving to the department's garage. Today, it seemed, her partner was really grasping at straws. Her latest: Elle Alexander looked like Shelly Bonaventure and Jocelyn Wallis. That was just a leap of faith Pescoli wasn't about to take.

But she did have to agree with Alvarez that the 9-1-1 tape of Tom Alexander's frantic call to the emergency line sounded authentic, that he was out of his mind with fear, which was only reinforced when he showed up at the department earlier this morning. Upset, he'd stormed into the sheriff's department and demanded an investigation into his wife's death. But his anger had slipped as he'd talked to Pescoli.

Handsome and trim, he'd been the epitome of the grief-stricken husband who was still in shock.

"She was a good driver and was used to inclement weather. I'm telling you, she could navigate the worst roads in snow! And I heard it all! I was on the phone when he hit her. She was scared out of her mind and must've dropped the phone, because she wasn't answering, and I heard the sound of metal on metal. Oh, God it was . . . deafening. And then she was yelling and screaming, calling my name over and over, but she couldn't hear me!" At that point he dissolved onto one of the side chairs, burying his face in his hands, his shoulders shaking. "Then there was the screams and the rush of . . . water, I guess, and then . . . and then . . . nothing. The phone went dead. For the love of God, what am I going to do? Elle . . . oh, Jesus, Elle."

Pescoli hadn't been able to offer platitudes. She hadn't told him, "It'll be all right," or "I know it's tough, but you'll get through this." Not when she'd been where he was on the night that her first husband, Joe, had been shot.

It didn't matter that it was in the line of duty.

She didn't care that he was deemed a damned "hero."

All she knew was that he was dead, leaving her with a young son and a hole in her heart big enough that an army tank could have driven through it. She would never be able to talk to him again or hear his laugh or watch him haul Jeremy around on his broad shoulders, or make love to him long into the night. It had been over in an instant. Those first years after Joe's death had been hard. So hard that she'd mistaken lust for love and married Luke Pescoli, "Lucky," who had proved to be anything but.

So she didn't offer up bromides. Instead she said, "I'm sorry for your loss, Mr. Alexander," and slid the Kleenex box across her desk to him.

Somehow she'd managed to take his statement, and now she and Alvarez were heading to the department's garage. Alvarez was explaining that Detective Jonas Hayes of the LAPD wasn't convinced that Shelly Bonaventure committed suicide, though most of the evidence pointed that way.

"There were just some things that didn't add up to his satisfaction," she said as she pulled into the lot designated for official vehicles. She found a parking spot near one of the large metallic garage doors and switched off the engine.

"Just like the Jocelyn Wallis case," Pescoli guessed, still reluctant to accept any loose connection between two cases that were over a thousand miles apart.

So the two women resembled each other. So they'd both been born in Helena, at the same hospital. Their deaths weren't even the same, except, of course, they'd both been poisoned. But Shelly Bonaventure's death was from an apparent overdose, and Jocelyn Wallis had fallen over the cliff, which broke her back and crushed her internal organs, the reason she was no longer walking this earth. Neither was from the poisoning itself.

"I asked Detective Hayes to send me a DNA analysis on Shelly Bonaventure," Alvarez said.

"To compare to Jocelyn Wallis? Are you serious?"

"And Elle Alexander."

"Her death was entirely different," Pescoli reminded.

"I know. Could be our guy's getting desperate."

"Sounds like a wild-goose chase to me. And it'll take time. You think that's necessary?"

"Don't know," Alvarez admitted. "Could be that it's a dead end. But at least we'll know if these women have any genetic link." She opened the door to her Jeep and pocketed the keys. "I'm just ruling out all the possibilities."

"I think it's premature."

"Duly noted. Meanwhile, women are dying."

"Okay, okay. Point taken," Pescoli said and tried not to snap. Alvarez was, if nothing else, thorough, a good cop who relied on science and evidence and rarely on her gut instinct. This time it seemed she was trusting a little of each. Not a bad thing.

They walked inside the garage together and found the mechanics and forensic car team working on the minivan. Spread around the dented body of the Dodge was a mess of wet toys, clothes, and wrapping paper that had faded and started to disintegrate. Soggy, crumpled shopping bags had split, only those that were plastic having survived a trip into the icy river.

The back bumper looked as if it had been rammed, and the automotive forensic examiners were all over the vehicle, looking for any evidence they could find. Elle Alexander's cell phone and purse were located, and the dripping receipts in her wallet indicated she'd been shopping only hours before her vehicle was pulled from the icy river.

"Something hit the back end of the van with a lot of force," Bart, one of the examiners, said. A thin, wiry man with a bald pate and glasses that looked too big for his face, he was wiping his hands with a towel and staring at the wreck of a minivan. "Looks like another vehicle. There's no evidence that she hit something, like a deer or elk or anything, before the van plunged into the river. She might have swerved, but something hit her from behind. Something big and going fast, from the looks of the dents."

"The husband said the van was in pristine shape. They bought it less than six months ago."

Bart was nodding as if everything Pescoli said confirmed his findings. "Ahh, well, someone changed that, now, didn't they?"

"Yeah," Alvarez said on a sigh. "I guess we'd better find out who."

Bart smiled thinly. "Glad that's your job, not mine."

Tuesday passed uneventfully, and on Wednesday, her day off from working at the clinic, Kacey spent time playing with Bonzi, paying bills, and picking up the house.

After some debate, she called Trace O'Halleran and got his an-

BORN TO DIE   215

swering machine, so she left a message asking about Eli and leaving her cell phone number.

It hadn't really been a ruse; she was concerned about the boy, more about his flu symptoms than his arm. But she couldn't lie to herself. Of course she'd hoped to talk to Trace. She hadn't been able to get him off her mind.

In the late morning she decided to be proactive on the mystery of the look-alikes and made a quick trip to Fit Forever Gym in search of a trainer named Gloria. She talked to a cute girl of around eighteen behind the reception area and made up a story about thinking of joining the club. The receptionist, in white-blond pigtails, had the enthusiasm of youth and, Kacey guessed, the promise of a commission, as she quickly explained the benefits of becoming a Fit Forever member. When Kacey didn't immediately sign on the dotted line, she lost a bit of fire and just slid some brochures across the long counter, turning to a more promising customer, the next guy in line.

Quickly, Kacey went through the pamphlets. Sure enough, one of the trainers was Gloria Sanders-O'Malley, the woman Elle had said resembled her. Kacey walked down a hallway, as if she were already a member; she didn't want someone showing her around. At a large glass window that looked into a workout room, she saw the woman who had to be Gloria Sanders-O'Malley. It was just damned eerie as she watched the woman lead a spinning class. None of the members of the class looked a thing like her, thank you, God, but Gloria did have the same bone structure in her face as Kacey. Her hair was short, spiky, and a rich red-brown; her body toned to that of a true athlete.

When the class ended, Kacey entered and introduced herself as a potential number. Gloria was polite but didn't seem to notice the resemblance, and Kacey didn't bring it up.

Maybe she was chasing shadows.

Not sure what she thought about that, Kacey returned home and spent a few hours at her desk with her laptop. The e-mail from the state hadn't come through yet, so she decided to call a friend of hers from college whom she knew worked at the state offices in Helena, in the computer records no less. Years earlier, while attending the university, Riza had helped improve Kacey's computer skills in exchange for help in literature and Spanish.

It took three transfers and nearly seven minutes before Kacey was connected with Riza; apparently somewhere along the line she must've gotten divorced and taken back her last name.

"Hey, Riza. This is Kacey Collins . . . well, Lambert now."

"Well, hey. How've ya been?" Even as Riza spoke, the sound of her computer keys clicking reached Kacey's ears.

"Good, good." They caught up a bit, and yes, Riza was divorced from her high school boyfriend, whom she'd married right after college, and was now single, living with a new musician boyfriend. Kacey told her that she and JC had split and she was living in Grizzly Falls.

"About time you got rid of Mr. Know-It-All," Riza said. "I never liked him."

"Maybe you should have told me."

"You wouldn't have listened." And that was probably true, Kacey decided. "So what's this all about?" Riza asked. "You didn't just call me out of the blue. There must be a reason."

"Well . . . yeah . . ." Kacey got down to it. "Look, Riza, I need some help. Several women have died up here, and a couple of them were born in Helena, at Valley Hospital, which I think closed about twenty or twenty-five years ago. I wanted to find out if there were others. Women . . . well, I think only women, who were born between thirty-one and, oh, probably like thirty-eight years ago at the hospital who are now deceased."

"You know I only have access to Montana records."

"I'm willing to start there."

"It's all public record," Riza said, "but I can speed through the process for you. I shouldn't get into too much trouble, but you never know. People are touchy around here, and there are fees for everything."

"Does it help that I'm a doctor?"

"Yeah. It means you can probably afford all this." She chuckled to herself, then asked for Kacey's e-mail. "I'll have you know this is highly irregular. That's what my boss is gonna say if she gets wind of it. Nearly everything I do she considers irregular, so let's keep it between us. And don't worry about the fees. . . . I think I can bury them, too."

"No wonder the state's in trouble."

"Yeah, right." They talked a little more; then Riza promised to get her the information she needed, if she could.

"Step one," she told Bonzi, then leaned back in her desk chair, stretching her spine and neck. "Maybe we should go for a walk in the park," she said. "Go get your leash."

He had been lying on his dog bed, but at hearing the word *walk,* he was instantly on all four feet and trotting to the back door.

He sat glued to his desk chair, his earphones firmly over his head, his heart starting to beat out of control. Already Acacia was becoming suspicious, checking birth and death certificates. Though he could monitor her at home and at her clinic, he couldn't anticipate all her moves or what she might be thinking. It was only a matter of time before she had an idea of what he was doing.

She could ruin everything!

And there was still so much to do!

He'd heard that she'd gotten herself a dog, and that bothered him. Sneaking in and out of her place, though he'd done it only a couple of times, would now be much more difficult.

Just one more problem to be worked out. Nothing serious.

He could handle it.

He could, he reminded himself, handle anything.

But this . . . her linking the deaths. He couldn't allow it.

He ripped off the headset and stared at the death wall, the large area where he'd recently carefully pinned all those shots of the Unknowings. Some of them showed their surprise when they realized they'd been duped. Others displayed horror and fear as they caught on that they were taking their last breaths, and a few, like Elle Alexander, where the death had been from a distance, were only a blurry photo. He'd taken time to snap a quick shot on his cell phone before driving away and over the bridge, catching the minivan sinking into the water.

So many years of work.

So much time invested.

Almost finished . . . and now *she* was going to ruin it? No fucking way!

Furious, he kicked a trash can and sent it reeling, the plastic buckling as it bounced off a wall and spilled its contents of papers that he had intended to burn, empty cartons, and a burned-out lightbulb onto the slick tile floor.

He had to do something.

He had to stop her.

His cell phone jangled, and he gnashed his teeth, seeing on the screen that it was his damned sister. She called at the most inopportune moments. It was almost as if she could see him, read his frustration, and had to let him know it.

She's only trying to help you fit in. You should be thankful.

He wasn't. Because every single person in his family realized he would never be like the rest of them. He couldn't. From the beginning he was different, and they all knew it.

In the mirror he caught his reflection, handsome, but no longer calm, his face flushed, the white scar at his temple seeming to pulse with his frenzy.

So like the rest of them, but so different.

How could he have let this happen?

The phone rang again.

Calm down. Take the call. . . . Sister is an ally, though she may not know it.

He tried to force his blood pressure into the normal range.

"Hey," he said.

"Hi." She was breathless as usual, probably dealing with "that moron of a contractor," which was her usual excuse for being in a bad mood.

"Something up?" He didn't want to pressure her, but he didn't have time for idle chitchat.

"A lot, actually. It's Mom and Dad. . . . They . . . are resistant to change, and, well, you know that Dad's not as strong as he once was, and Mom isn't about to move or put him in an assisted-care place, but he needs more care than she can give. . . ." She went on and on, as she always did about this particular topic, one that made his blood run cold.

She was lamenting their parents' stubborn streak when he broke in. "So what do you want me to do about it?"

"Talk to Mom."

"I have."

"Again. Be firm. She listens to you, for whatever reason. You'd think since I'm the oldest, my opinion would carry some weight, but oh, no—"

"I will," he said, cutting off the next part of her no-one-values-my-opinion pity party. "I'll drive over . . . by this weekend."

"The sooner the better."

"I have a life, you know. A job. A highly stressful job."

"Okay, okay, just let me know."

"I will."

"Oh, and a final warning. Mom has someone picked out for you." He inwardly groaned. "And get this," his sister added, her voice elevating a fraction in excitement. "It's a nurse. Can you believe it? After all the things she's said about that particular profession? I guess she met this woman when she was taking Dad to his annual physical."

"It doesn't matter what she does." He wasn't in the mood for a potential romance, especially not someone his meddling mother had discovered. Not when there was just so much to do.

"Just be prepared. Her name is Karalee Rierson, a redhead."

He froze. The little worry that had been with him since he'd overheard Acacia's phone call was growing, squirming, wriggling through his brain. He glanced down at the pile of photographs he'd collected over the years, spreading them out until he saw the driver's license picture of Karalee Winters. No . . . it couldn't be! He swallowed hard, started searching through the old documents. He should remember this. Wasn't her maiden name Karalee Falcone . . . Yes, he found it. "What do you know about her?" he asked in a voice he didn't recognize as his own.

"I think she lived in Oregon when she was married, but I'm not sure. And then there was something about a brief, like ten-minute marriage, which Mom will gloss over."

Hence the surname of Winters.

"But she doesn't have any kids. I'm sure Mom will have all the details and will regale you with them when you see her."

His stomach seemed to drop to the cold tile floor. Everything was crumbling apart. "No doubt," he said. "Look, I've got to run."

"Okay, okay. Always busy, I get it. But after you see Mom and Dad and convince them to move, give me a call."

"I will," he promised and hung up. He stared at the photo of Karalee Falcone Winters Rierson. He'd messed up. Somehow missed that important tidbit of information. And now she knew his parents . . . so, so dangerous. He crushed the copy of her driver's license in his fist and told himself he had to up his game, move faster.

And he'd have to start with Acacia freakin' Lambert, then zero in on Karalee, with all her last names.

He didn't have a choice.

CHAPTER 22

Not only had Riza come through, but Kacey had gotten some information from the hospitals as well. Armed with her new, sketchy details, she drove to Helena. Riza, who also had a way to get into the DMV files, promised more information to come, birth and death notices, pictures, whatever she could find. "I could get fired," she warned Kacey.

"Or we might both end up looking for a good defense attorney."

She barked out a laugh. "Doesn't matter. I love this stuff. I watch *CSI* and *Bones* and all those crime shows. I'll see what I can come up with, but just keep everything on the down low."

"I will," Kacey promised but wondered how long she could keep that vow. She hung up and started to dial again, then replaced the receiver, figuring another phone call with her mother would be useless. Whether she liked it or not, she had to see Maribelle face-to-face.

It was nearly dusk when she cruised into Helena, down familiar streets where the asphalt was bare, the sidewalks shoveled, and new snow was falling softly. She guided her Ford past the Cathedral of St. Helena, its Gothic facade bathed in lamplight. Twin spires rose, seeming to pierce the darkening sky. This was the town in which she'd grown up, where she'd felt secure, and now, with twilight lurking, she felt somehow betrayed by it. Something wasn't right.

Glancing into her rearview mirror, she got a jolt when she saw a dark truck, one similar to the pickup that had hit her and sent her spinning a few days earlier.

The huge, weird grill was similar, but she couldn't catch a glimpse of the license plate, not even to note if it was from Montana or somewhere else. Her throat went dry as she watched the vehicle's reflection in the mirror, and then she let out a sigh of relief when it turned, heading off in the opposite direction.

Don't be so paranoid.

No one's following you.

Just because Elle Alexander was forced off the road according to the latest reports, you're not a target.

"Yet," she said, still nervous.

With a final glance telling her there was no truck with a massive grill tailing her, she relaxed a little. Before she headed out of town, she took one more side trip, slowing for a stoplight near Valley Hospital, a few blocks off Broadway. The sprawling glass and steel structure rose four stories, its windows reflecting the city lights as they winked on. As the light changed and she stepped on the gas, Kacey wondered what part Valley Hospital, where at least three women who resembled each other had been born, played in her own private mystery.

She would have to follow up on that later, however, she thought as she drove through the heart of the city and on toward Rolling Hills Senior Estates, where Maribelle and all her lies resided.

Trace had waited for Eli to get off the bus, then had driven him into town, where they picked up Sarge, complete with one of those cone things to keep him from licking his wound or tearing out his stitches. The dog was improving, thank God.

"He looks like an alien!" Eli said as he scared up a smile for the dog, and Sarge, running on three legs, nearly knocked the boy down in the reception area of the vet's office.

"Now you both have extra equipment on," Trace teased, lifting an eyebrow at Eli's blue cast. There were a few names scrawled on the surface and some grime near the edge that he hadn't been able to scrub off.

"I'd say it was a raccoon, maybe more than one," Jordan Eagle said as Trace paid the bill.

"I'm just glad he's going to be okay," Trace said. "Thank you."

Jordan patted Sarge's head and then Trace whistled for him and the dog raced after them in his ungainly way. Trace helped him into the truck, and they were on their way.

At the house, though his spirits had lifted upon retrieving Sarge, Eli crashed on the couch. He'd complained of feeling crummy from the minute he'd gotten off the bus, and though usually he was up for doing the afternoon chores, today he was spent. He fell asleep on the couch almost instantly, with Sarge curled up on the floor at his feet.

It was a bit of a worry as the boy was usually so active, but then he was still fighting the cold or flu or whatever it was, dealing with Jocelyn's death, and healing from the playground incident. At least he hadn't brought up Leanna for a few days.

Maybe the couch wasn't such a bad idea.

He let the kid sleep, but Sarge did deign to come with Trace for the afternoon rounds of feeding. He'd let the animals out during the day, but now, as the sky began to darken, he fed and locked them inside.

By the time he returned to the house and scrounged up a skillet dinner, Eli was awake. They ate in the kitchen, but Eli picked at his food and ignored the apple juice his father had poured and insisted he drink.

Afterward Trace stacked the dishes in the sink; then together he and Eli tackled a little bit of homework. They gave up when Eli, coughing and listless, just wanted to go back to the television. Trace took his son's temperature, which was still hovering around a hundred. He ran him through the shower, then allowed him a soda with no caffeine and put him to bed. The boy didn't protest, even though the digital clock on the bedside table read 7:15. Usually Eli would have protested loudly. Tonight he zonked.

It was definitely a worry.

And his son's health was just one issue, one of many.

It wasn't until he'd returned to the downstairs that he noticed the light flashing on the answering machine.

Listening to the one call, he heard Kacey's voice as she asked about Eli. "Nice," he thought aloud and played the message a second time, as much to hear her voice as to commit her number to memory. He thought about calling her just to talk, but as he picked up the phone, he stopped.

What are you going to talk about? The weather? Your kid's blue cast? The woman you dated, the one that looks like her? Jocelyn's death? Or are you going to admit to dreaming about her last night and waking up hard as hell?

He thought of Leanna. And Jocelyn.

Then put the receiver back.

"Acacia! What in the world are you doing here?" her mother asked, a hand flying to her chest.

Maribelle had opened the door to the hallway and, from her expression, clearly hadn't expected to find her daughter waiting for her on the other side.

"I thought we needed to talk."

"And the phone wasn't good enough?" Maribelle's voice was cautious as she stepped out of the entry. She allowed Kacey into the inner sanctum of her three-bedroom unit, but Kacey definitely felt the chill: she wasn't welcome.

Well, too bad, she thought, walking across thick white carpet toward a muted blue couch placed in front of a gas fireplace that burned softly. Few of the pieces of furniture were reminders of Kacey's youth. Most of the artwork, chairs, lamps, and tables were new, bought after her mother had sold the house where she'd grown up and had put what the new owners didn't want in the garage, where she had organized her own estate sale.

"I needed to see you face-to-face." Kacey's heart was knocking more than a little; she'd never been one to confront Maribelle, but then few had, and then there was the continuing problem of her slightly upset stomach, which felt like it had turned into a hard fist.

"Can I get you a cup of tea or a glass of wine? I've got a nice pinot breathing—"

"No, Mom. I just want to talk." She warmed the back of her legs before the fire as Maribelle, in jeans, gold sweater, and worried expression, settled into a corner of the couch, where a paperback book lay facedown and a half-drunk glass of wine sat neglected for the moment.

Kacey extracted an envelope from her purse, opened it, and slid the contents on the coffee table toward Maribelle. Pictures of Shelly Bonaventure, Jocelyn Wallis, and Elle Alexander stared up at her.

"What are these?"

"Notice anything, Mom? These women all look alike. They bear enough of a resemblance as to be sisters."

"So?"

"They're all dead. Died from accidents within the last week."

Her mother paled a bit. Reached for her wineglass.

"And they look like me, too, Mom. Don't tell me you can't see it. Then there's this woman." She pulled out the brochure from Fit Forever Gym, already folded open to a picture of Gloria Sanders-O'Malley, and placed it near the others. "She's a fitness instructor, still very much alive."

"What are you suggesting?"

Kacey stared at her mother. "I just don't think this is coincidence. I checked. Three of these women were born at Valley Hospital, here in Helena. Just like me. I'm not sure about Elle. Her background is a little murky, and unfortunately she's not around to tell us what she knows. She claimed she always lived in Idaho, but still . . ."

"I don't know what you're getting at. You think women who look like you are being killed?"

"Women who look like me and are from the *same damned hospital.*" Her insides were twisting, but she had to know, and Maribelle, if she wasn't specifically hiding something, was definitely worried.

"Lots of people look alike."

"I know. I was willing to dismiss it. But the hospital, Mom. If I go there, what will I find out?"

"I don't know. Nothing."

"What would I find out with a sample of my DNA? And a sample from some of the other women?"

"*What?*"

Kacey didn't answer; she didn't have to. She saw the change in her mother's eyes as she realized her daughter wasn't bluffing. Her thin shoulders slumped beneath her sweater. Suddenly Maribelle looked as old as her years.

"Oh, Lord." She twisted her hands and glanced away, toward the window and the night falling beyond.

"Tell me what I'm missing," Kacey demanded.

She shook her head slowly. "I was afraid this day would come."

"Why?"

Maribelle closed her eyes and let out a tremulous sigh. For theatrics? Or from her heart?

Oh, God, who could tell?

"I was hoping I'd never have to confide this," she said.

Kacey clamped her teeth together, waiting, wanting to scream while her mother slowly processed each word.

"Stanley isn't—wasn't—your real father. You seem to have figured that out."

"You mean, not my biological father," Kacey clarified, heart beating heavily.

"Yes." Maribelle was on her feet, the contents in her glass sloshing precariously. "No one knew, not even Stanley, at least not at first." She glared at her daughter, as if this were somehow Kacey's fault.

"Why didn't you tell me?"

"Because it would have killed Stanley," Maribelle said, as if Kacey were dense for not catching on. "When you were around seven and it . . . it was obvious that you didn't look like anyone in his family or mine, he began to get suspicious and we argued. He threatened to have a paternity test and so . . . so I told him. From that moment on, our marriage, what little there was left of it, was a sham."

There was a roar in her ears.

"We stayed together for you. He loved you," Maribelle said with a trace of regret. "It didn't matter that you weren't of his blood. You were his little girl." She had to clear her throat and look away. "We couldn't divorce . . . that was out of the question . . . or even separate." She shook her head. "Things were different then in a town this size. My parents . . ." She fluttered her fingers. "It was better."

Kacey wasn't so sure. She couldn't imagine herself remaining in a loveless marriage with Jeffrey. No way. But Maribelle's jaw was set. Defensive.

"Dad's gone," Kacey said, pointing out the obvious, the ache in her heart painful when she thought of the man she'd known as her father. "You . . . you could have told me."

"It was too late then."

"It's not too late now." Kacey's stomach ached. All the deception. All the lies. Her medical history compromised, her entire life a sham. And yet it all made a distorted kind of sense somehow. It explained so much, especially why she was close to her parents, even though they'd lost their bond to each other.

"Who's my biological father?" Kacey asked.

Her mother finished the wine and left the empty glass on the mantel. "Does it matter?"

"Of course it does. In so many ways I can't even begin to tell you. Women are being killed, *Mom*. Women I suspect might have my same DNA."

"That's the problem with all that . . . science!"

"You were a nurse, for God's sake," Kacey said, cutting her off abruptly. "You believe in science."

"Well, it's gone too far. Become too invasive. There is no privacy anymore. If you ask me, people should leave well enough alone!"

"This is my life, Mother!"

Maribelle rubbed her arms as if suddenly chilled to the bone. "I really don't want to talk about this."

"You've avoided it for thirty-five years!" Kacey couldn't believe what she was hearing. Her whole damned life had been a lie. "And now women are dying."

"In accidents!" Something flared in Maribelle's eyes. "Do you really think someone's out killing women who look like you because of some kind of DNA link? For the love of God, Kacey. Listen to yourself."

"Who is he?"

"There's no reason to bother your father with this."

Kacey practically sputtered, "He's *not* my father. You were married to my *father*. But . . . this other man? He's still alive?" Kacey was reeling.

"Yes."

"You still keep in contact with him?"

"No, of course not."

"Does he know about me?" she asked and, when her mother didn't answer, said, "And the others . . ." The faces of the women who had died ran through her brain, women with features so like her own. "Does he know of them? Are they . . ." She shook her head.

No, no, this was all wrong. Suddenly she doubted her convictions for coming here in the first place. But she couldn't, wouldn't, stop now. In a voice she didn't recognize as her own, she asked, "Are you telling me that this . . . this man went around impregnating women and just leaving them . . ."

But Maribelle had fallen silent.

"Mom . . . ?" There was something more, and Kacey braced herself. "What is it you're not telling me?"

The starch seemed to drain out of Maribelle, and she returned to her spot on the couch. Her eyes were focused on the fire, but Kacey knew that she wasn't seeing the golden flames licking the ceramic logs. No, her mind was far away, in a place that only she knew of, a spot that was in the distant past. "It wasn't like that. You have to understand. He's a fine, upstanding man. A pillar of the community, really. People look up to him. . . . Ours was an affair of the heart."

She'd elevated her relationship to something pure and special and unique. Still. After over a third of a century.

"Everyone thinks that. That's the reason people cheat on their spouses, because this new relationship is just so exciting and new."

"But ours . . ." A beatific smile tugged at the corners of her lips as she remembered. She still believed what she and this man had shared was unique to the universe. Swallowing hard, Maribelle shot Kacey a hard look. "You wouldn't understand. Couldn't."

"Don't patronize me, Mom!" Kacey hated that she was a part of this, an integral part of this. "Who is he?"

. A pause.

"Maribelle?"

"I promised myself that I would never say. And I've not broken that vow."

"I'll find out," Kacey insisted. "And it'll be worse if I have to go looking."

Maribelle stared at her hands. "David doesn't know."

David Spencer. Her mother's would-be boyfriend. "I won't tell him," Kacey stated flatly. "But if he finds out some other way, then there's nothing I can do about it. I'm not going to live this lie another second!"

Maribelle spoke in a voice that was little more than a whisper. "You're angry!"

"Angry and frustrated. You lied to me. All my damned life."

"I'm sorry for that. Truly." She blinked against tears. "It was different then. I was young. Impressionable . . ."

"Don't forget married."

Maribelle winced. "There were problems there, too. For one thing, I couldn't get pregnant, not that I planned this, of course, but your father, er, Stanley and I . . . Our marriage was pretty rocky at that time. I was taking classes and met a medical student who was . . ." She let her voice drift off before finishing. "Well, he was everything Stanley wasn't. We, um, became involved, and just when we decided to call things off, you were conceived." She looked up at Kacey with tears glistening in her eyes. "I was so happy. I'd thought maybe I was barren, but I'd never been tested, nor had Stanley, and then there you were, a miracle baby!" She smiled a bit through her tears, lifted her hands. "It was a blessing. At least for me. Look at you. I wanted a baby so badly, and you were conceived!"

Kacey thought of the hardworking father she'd grown up with, the grandparents whose home she'd inherited, and everything seemed off, just half a step out of sync. "Dad will always be—"

"I know." Maribelle snagged her glass and walked to her kitchen, where the bottle of pinot noir was breathing on the sleek granite counter she had installed just the year before. "Would you like a little?" she offered, rummaging in a cupboard for another glass.

Kacey shook her head. The last thing she needed was to think any less clearly than she already was. As Maribelle poured herself another drink, her hands trembling a bit, Kacey stood on the opposite side of the kitchen island. "So who is he, Mom?" Maribelle set the bottle aside. "I think I deserve to know."

Her mother twisted the stem and watched the dark liquid swirl, then sniffed it before taking a sip. "I suppose you do," she agreed finally. "I've often thought so, but I just couldn't tell you."

"You'd rather lie."

"Avoid the truth. It got easier over time, harder to find a way to . . . Oh, well, I finally decided it was best to let it all die."

"I need to meet him."

She was startled. "Oh, no! He's past all this now, and I don't want you bothering him or his wife."

"Wife?" Kacey repeated.

"Yes. Wife. Of what? Oh, I guess about forty-five years now," she said with more than a trace of bitterness.

"I'll find out who he is whether you tell me or not."

"Fine!" Maribelle was angry, but she saw that Kacey was dead serious. Taking a deep breath, she said, "His name is Gerald Johnson." She glanced up, as if the name would mean something to Kacey. When Kacey didn't react, she added, "He's a renowned heart surgeon who helped develop a special kind of stent, and no, he doesn't know about you. I decided it wouldn't do any good to tell him. Soon after he left his practice, he moved his family to Missoula." She shrugged. "It's common knowledge. You can find that out in seconds on the Internet, so I'm not divulging any secrets there, but please don't bother him. He wouldn't appreciate it, and neither would Noreen and her brood."

"Noreen being his wife, and his brood meaning his children?"

Half brothers and sisters. The missing piece. She, who had been raised an only child, had fantasized about a large family with enough siblings to play baseball or board games or cards, even another person for video games. . . . "How many does he have?"

"Children?" Maribelle looked up, met her daughter's gaze. "Five, I think. No, there were twins, so six. Or, was it seven? I can't remember!" She slid her gaze to the living room and the coffee table, where the pictures Kacey had brought were still strewn. "Well, I guess, maybe even more."

That was the understatement of the year. "Maybe a lot more," Kacey murmured, wondering.

Who was this guy? A doctor who didn't practice birth control, never used a condom, and had a string of affairs? The women in the pictures were all around her age, give or take a few years. What kind of Montana Lothario was he? No, something wasn't right.

And possibly women were being killed because of it?

"I need to meet him," she said again.

"No!" Maribelle fumbled with her glass. It fell from her hands and shattered against the granite of the counter, splashing red wine onto her sweater and sending shards of glass skittering to the floor. "Oh, look what you've done! This sweater cost me a fortune," she cried and raced off to the bedroom area. Kacey rotely began to clean up the mess.

A mess that was a whole lot deeper than the spilled wine and shattered crystal.

CHAPTER 23

He should have killed the mother.
That was where he'd made his mistake.

He knew it now as he sat in his truck just outside the gates of Rolling Hills Senior Estates. He'd trusted that Maribelle Collins would do anything to keep her secret locked away, but now, as he watched Acacia drive out through the gates, he wondered what she knew, what damage she could wreak.

Too much.

He should have expected this. Anticipated this move. Was it too late?

Probably.

But the old bat still needed to be silenced.

It shouldn't be too hard; from what he understood, she had a heart problem, took nitroglycerin tablets. . . .

He didn't have time to deal with her now.

He had to find out what her damned daughter had learned. If she had found out the truth, he had to stop her before she did anything that would ruin everything. With a final glance over his shoulder toward the still open gates of Rolling Hills, he silently vowed to return.

He felt his scar pulse as he grabbed his ski mask and pulled it over his head. Then he started his truck and eased out of his parking slot.

He caught sight of the taillights of Acacia's Ford far ahead, but he wasn't worried about losing her. The magnetic, splash-proof GPS device he'd installed in her rear wheel well wouldn't be discovered until she rotated her tires, and maybe not even then.

Which would be too late.

Switching on the tiny monitor, he saw that she'd turned onto the highway, heading west. Toward Grizzly Falls. As expected.

Relaxing slightly, he began to follow at a safe distance. Checking his rearview mirror, he noticed another vehicle pull out of an alley and turn on its headlights. A niggle of apprehension slithered through his brain.

It's nothing! Another car, another driver, no big deal.

And yet he watched as the headlights behind him, of some kind of sports car, he thought, were steady. Other cars came between them, but for every turn, the sports car behind slowly followed, never catching up, not even at the one stoplight.

Someone going the same direction as you. Nothing more.

But he thought of all the times he'd felt *he* was being watched, as if he were the prey rather than the hunter.

Even if the car follows onto the main road, heading west, it's just chance. Happenstance. Another driver going toward Missoula or beyond.

Relax!

But his fingers held the steering wheel in a death grip as he turned onto the highway and watched the traffic behind him. Yep, the gray sedan followed, but that wasn't the vehicle he was watching. . . . No, the car he was worried about, a black sports car, maybe a BMW . . . *didn't* turn onto the highway.

Good.

Exhaling a sigh of relief, he was instantly at ease again and, with one final glance to his rearview, turned his attention back to where it belonged. Hitting the gas, he homed in on Acacia. According to his nifty little device, she was less than two miles ahead.

He planned not only to catch her but to pass her as well.

Trace heard a moan and then a harsh round of rattling coughs from Eli's room.

Taking the stairs two at a time, he flipped on the lights at the second story and pushed open the door. Eli was on the bed, but his hair was sweaty, his face flushed, and his eyes looked sunken.

"Hey, buddy," he said, trying to rouse his son. "Eli?" Eli opened a bleary eye. "How ya feelin'?"

"My throat hurts. Bad." He blinked himself awake and started coughing deep and hard.

"I'm going to take your temp again," Trace said.

Eli wasn't very cooperative, but eventually Trace convinced him to slide the thermometer into his mouth. A few minutes later Trace discovered that his temperature had spiked, now showing 105 degrees, way too high for comfort.

Crushing a children's Tylenol into water, he insisted his son drink the whole glass, then, walking into the hallway, pulled the door to Eli's room nearly shut. Sliding a cell phone from his pocket, he dialed the number Kacey had left for him, peering through the crack into his son's room as he counted off the rings.

Answer, he silently thought. He was used to tending to injured or sick animals, had dealt with trying to save calves that were twisted in the birth canal, had fought blackleg and pneumonia, and had even had a favorite mare die of colic. Dogs and cats had lived and died, and he accepted that illness and death were part of life.

But now he was scared.

By the third ring, he was worried that she wouldn't answer, but then, just when he was certain he'd have to leave a message, she answered. "Hi. Trace?"

He got right down to business. "I got your call earlier. Look, Eli's temperature is up. A hundred and five and he's coughing, having trouble sleeping."

"Bring him down to the clinic," she said decisively. "I'm on the road and can be there in half an hour. Work for you?"

"It can."

"Good. I'll see you there."

She hung up and Trace wasted no time. He strode into his son's room and said quietly as he grabbed a jacket and sleeping bag to wrap around his boy, "Let's go, bud. I'm taking you to see Dr. Lambert."

Kacey had been lost in thought most of the drive back from Helena. It was dark now, long past the dinner hour, but she wasn't hungry. The radio had been playing, but she couldn't name one song that had been aired. She was too caught up in her own thoughts, replaying everything her mother had told her about Gerald Johnson and his family.

She dimmed her lights for an oncoming car. She hadn't been paying much attention to the other vehicles, driving by rote, her mind swimming in the waters of a murky past. Who the hell were Gerald Johnson and his wife? How had Maribelle played a part in their lives and marriage? Who were their children, her blood relatives, half siblings?

It was almost as if Maribelle was still half in love with Johnson, as if she'd elevated their affair to something that was more romantic, more tragic, as if there was some nostalgic reverence to it.

Maybe Maribelle was losing it.

And what about the man she still thought of as her father? Stanley Collins, a hardworking carpenter. She wondered about the day he'd learned the truth, though, of course, she couldn't remember it, couldn't even think of one action that indicated his love for his only child had shifted in the least little bit.

When she reeled back the years of her life, she remembered no incident that would indicate he'd found out the truth. The same held true for her grandparents. If Stanley Collins had ever confided in them, they certainly hadn't changed their attitude toward her in the slightest.

But she had the bad feeling that she'd just scratched at a hidden scab that was over a long-festering and maybe deadly wound.

She snapped off the radio as a rendition of "Hark! The Herald Angels Sing" was being warbled by some country star she'd never heard of. She needed the ride to be quiet so she could think and sort out what exactly she was going to do. Had Jocelyn Wallis or Shelly Bonaventure or Elle Alexander suspected they had been fathered by the same man? Had their mothers all hooked up with the same local Romeo?

What were the chances?

Bone weary, she tried to clear her head and concentrate on getting home.

Tonight traffic was light, the roads nearly clear of snow, though a few crystals shimmered as the moonlight pierced the thin cloud cover. Watching the play of lights, Kacey was thinking about the women who had recently died when she spied a still-open coffee kiosk less than ten miles from the outskirts of Grizzly Falls.

Pulling in, she rolled down her window and ordered a skinny decaffeinated latte from a woman who looked dead on her feet. The Christmas spirit was missing at the kiosk, despite the string of winking colored lights decorating the windows, stencils of snowflakes on the glass, and an advertisement for a Santa's Cinnamon Blend Latte.

Waiting in her darkened car, she hoped the steaming milk would coat her stomach, and she accepted the hot cup gratefully, leaving a tip. Showing the barest of smiles, the barista shut the window, then turned off the neon open sign.

Kacey tasted the hot drink, hoping to warm herself up from the inside out. No amount of adjusting the temperature in her little SUV had been able to ease the chill that had settled in her soul when she'd learned the truth.

As she was starting to pull out of the gravel, she saw fast-approaching headlights and, holding out her cup from her body, hit the brakes. Her SUV ground to a stop at the edge of the road as a big dark truck sped past. Her coffee slopped a little bit onto her lid.

For a split second she remembered the pickup with the big grill, the one that had put the dent in her back fender, and the driver Grace Perchant had referred to as "evil."

Kacey shook that off, still frozen in position. She brought her cup back and sucked up the overflow of coffee.

Grace wasn't reliable.

She thought she could talk to ghosts or something.

And this was Montana, where pickups reigned.

For a split second she thought about giving chase, checking to see if the big rig had out-of-state plates with a three or an eight in the lettering. Then Trace called about Eli. All her thoughts turned to the boy.

She made it into town in a little over twenty minutes and pulled into the empty parking lot of the clinic. This side of the building was shadowed and dark, only weak light from the streetlight at the front of the clinic offering any kind of illumination.

She left her finished coffee in the cup holder, locked her car and walked to the back door, where she let herself in with her key and reached for the light switch.

Click!

But nothing happened.

She hit it again, but the rooms remained dark, not even the few security lamps glowing. And it was colder than usual in the offices.

The damned circuit breaker!

She'd like to wring her lowlife, tightwad of a landlord's neck! How many times had she complained, even ordering out an electrician once herself?

"Great," she muttered.

She knew the layout of the offices, of course, and she had a flashlight in her desk drawer, so she worked her way through the back hallway and past the examination rooms, which somehow appeared dangerous and slightly sinister, the odd shapes of the equipment looming like robotic monsters and sending her already vivid imagination into overdrive.

It's just the damned lights.

Fingers running along one wall, she eased past the exam rooms and around the corner. She stubbed her toe on the edge of the freestanding scales, then bit her tongue to keep from letting out a yowl.

She did, however, curse under her breath.

All the electronic equipment, the phones and fax machines and computers, usually gave off a bit of light from the buttons, which reminded the users that they were plugged in and waiting, but no little green or blue lights glowed. The rabbit warren of rooms was completely and utterly dark, save for those rooms with windows, where the faint light from the streetlamps slid through the slats of the windows and striped the floors and opposing walls with thin, watery illumination.

The place was creepier than she expected, but with only a little trouble, she found the door to her office and pushed it open. Her eyes had adjusted to the semidark, and she made her way to her desk and opened the second of a stack of drawers to her right, her fingers delving into the dark space where she kept extra supplies.

The tips of her fingers touched the ridged handle of the flashlight, and she only prayed that the batteries weren't dead. With a click, she turned on the weak beam, which was just enough to help guide her to the mechanical closet, where the main switch had flipped.

Weird.

Usually the switch to the outlets in the front office would snap off, but the rest of the rooms were unaffected. Then again, this old wiring probably hadn't been up to code since the Kennedy administration.

Throwing the main switch, along with the security lights, she heard the furnace rumble to life.

Bam! Bam! Bam!

A loud pounding echoed through the rooms.

She slammed the door to the closet shut, realizing Trace O'Halleran and Eli were already here. Sure enough, she heard Trace's voice boom through the walls. "Dr. Lambert? Kacey?"

"Coming!" She was already hurrying along the hallway and through the front reception area, snapping on banks of fluorescents, which flickered before offering up any real illumination. "Sorry," she said quickly. "I'm having trouble with the electricity here. The circuit breaker is always flipping. A real pain in the behind." Then, as he walked inside, she said to the boy, "Hey, Eli. How are you feeling?"

He didn't answer, and she could see as the lights began to fill the offices with illumination that he was feverish. He coughed loudly, and he winced. "Complains of a sore throat," Trace said.

"Let's take a look." She twisted the dead bolt behind them and said, "Come on, Eli." The boy was wearing pajamas, a jacket, and was wrapped in a sleeping bag. Once in the examination room, she took his temperature and other vitals, looked down his throat and ears, and listened to his lungs. All the while Trace stood leaning against the counter, his fingers gripping its edge.

She forced a smile. "I think we need to get you into the hospital," she said, trying to sound encouraging.

"Hospital?" Trace repeated.

"Noooo!" Eli, taking a cue from his father, began to protest but ended up only with another coughing fit that made him cringe and his eyes water.

"I think yes." She glanced toward Trace, silently suggesting he support her on this. "It's just to make sure you're going to get better as fast as possible."

"Sounds like a plan," Trace said.

Eli's face crumpled as he had another coughing fit.

"Hurts, doesn't it?" she said to the boy. "I know. You'll feel better."

"You'll come with me?" Eli asked.

"Of course," Kacey assured him. "I wouldn't miss it for the world."

"I don't have to stay there."

"For a while," she said, "but let's figure that part out once we get there, okay?" To Trace, she added, "I'll meet you at the ER at St. Bart's, and we'll get him admitted."

"You got it."

Two hours later Eli was in a hospital bed, hooked up to an IV, pronounced "stable," and sleeping soundly. The nursing staff was taking care of his boy and had promised to call Trace in the morning and keep Kacey in the loop. From what Trace got out of it, his son still had bronchitis, along with strep throat and possible pneumonia. Kacey had insisted the boy stay overnight where he could be monitored, his fever tended, and Trace was a little relieved, though he wanted to camp out in his son's room on the one uncomfortable chair.

"I'll look in on him before I go to the clinic tomorrow," Kacey promised as they walked out of the main lobby of the hospital and into the parking lot, where several cars were scattered around and the sky was thick with clouds. A cold breeze skated down the canyon where the river, far below, cut through the shimmering lights of the town.

"He won't like being here."

"Who does?" She glanced back at the building, lights glowing upward for three stories, a garland of fresh cedar bows draped over the portico. "But he should be out tomorrow, I'd think."

He walked her to her car, and as she opened the door, Trace grabbed her by the crook of the arm, holding her back a second. "Thanks, Kacey," he said.

"No problem."

"I mean it."

She looked up at him expectantly, turning her face so that as the first flakes of snow fell from the sky, they caught in her eyelashes and melted against her cheeks.

In the bluish lights from the security lamps, she appeared a little ghostlike, her skin pale, her eyes a shade darker than they were in daylight. For half a heartbeat, he was reminded of Leanna.

Or was it Jocelyn?

A chill settled in his guts. "You're more than welcome, Trace," she said and smiled. "I'm glad you called. Eli needed to be here."

"You could have just advised me to bring him to the hospital. You went a step further."

"Yeah, well, maybe I wanted to see him," she said with a smile that touched his heart. In that second, he experienced an urge to kiss her. While the snowfall increased, fat flakes dancing around them, he wanted to wrap her in his arms and press his lips to hers and just see what happened.

She felt it, too. Her gaze held his, and his breath seemed to stop in his lungs.

Don't do this—kissing this woman will only complicate things.

And yet there it was. Between them.

"I'll give you a call after I see him in the morning." Then, before he could react, she stood on her tiptoes, hugged him, and even brushed a kiss along his cheek, her lips running across the stubble of his beard.

As she attempted to slide her arm from his grasp and climb into the open door of her car, he said, "No. Wait." His fingers tightened again, and she paused, looking over her shoulder expectantly.

"What?"

"I have something I want to show you."

"Now?"

"Yes, but at my house."

"You want me to drive over to your place?"

He saw the doubts in her eyes. She might have boldly hugged him and laid a kiss across his cheek, but he suspected her motive was to offer support and comfort. He was making her wonder with his request.

"I've got a new dog, and I've already left him too long," Kacey demurred.

"Then I'll come to yours. I just have to pick up something at home." He saw that she might protest and added, "I don't think it can wait." When she hesitated, he added, "I'll be there in about forty minutes. And it won't take long. But, really, I think it's something you should see."

"Can't you just tell me?"

He felt one side of his mouth lift. "No."

"Do you know where I live?"

He shook his head. "I did a little research. I'll tell you all about that, too. Trust me."

Her eyes narrowed in suspicion, but she gave him a nod. "Okay."

"Good." As she closed her Ford's door and started the engine, he heard the distinct notes of "Carol of the Bells" through the glass before she backed out of the parking spot.

Lifting a hand in good-bye, she drove off, and he jogged quickly to his truck. He didn't question why, suddenly, he felt the need to confide in her. Maybe it was the way she looked into his eyes, or the manner in which she tended to his son, or just because he thought she should know the truth. He didn't second-guess his motivations, just waited until she was out of sight, then slid behind the wheel of his pickup and turned on the ignition just as he heard the sound of a siren screaming through the night.

Red lights flashed as an ambulance pulled into the parking lot of the hospital and slid to a stop near the emergency room doors. An EMT hopped out of the back, and a stretcher with an elderly man hooked up to an IV and oxygen was quickly rolled through the sliding doors.

He thought once more of his boy up on the third floor and, with the knowledge that Eli was in safe, caring hands, drove with controlled urgency through the coming snow and home. Letting the truck idle, he hurried up the back steps and into the house, where he double-checked on Sarge. The dog, cone in place, was sleeping on his dog bed in the living room and glanced toward Trace, even thumping his tail. "Hang in there," Trace told the shepherd, then scooped up the information he'd gathered on his desk, grabbed his laptop, and headed out the door again. The truck was warm, and he slammed it into reverse, not allowing himself to ask himself what in the hell he was doing.

CHAPTER 24

Kacey glanced at the clock over the kitchen counter. She had been home half an hour and, while waiting for Trace to show up, had fed and walked Bonzi, had turned on the radio for company, and had already accomplished several searches on-line, looking for information on Gerald Johnson, who had resided in Helena, Montana, for most of his life, before moving to Missoula.

He hadn't been hard to find, and in a short amount of time she'd learned he'd been a heart surgeon of some prominence before, as her mother had told her, he'd started his own company to help develop stents for heart disease patients. As far as she could tell, he still worked there, along with several of his children.

As he was a prominent citizen in Helena, it hadn't been hard to find pictures of his family. His wife, Noreen, and six children, two daughters and four sons, though one of the girls had died ten years earlier. Kacey had printed out the obituary of Kathleen Enid Johnson, the victim of a skiing accident only months before her marriage. She'd been a beautiful girl, twenty-two, and she had the same jawline, cheekbones, and eyes as Gerald Johnson. In fact, most of his legitimate children took after him, she thought as she stared at a photograph from the past.

As did she, and those living and dead who resembled her. . . . Dear God, was it really possible?

It had to be.

Didn't it?

She stared at one particularly good shot of Gerald and Noreen, husband and wife, standing side by side at a charity function several years back. Both were dressed to the nines, he in a tux and white tie, she wearing a shimmering silver gown. Both of them had silver hair and lots of it; he showed no sign of fat; his skin was tanned, crow's-feet fanning from his eyes.

A golfer, maybe. Hours in the sun.

His wife was paler, her make-up subdued, her features sharp and defined. Tall and thin, Noreen Johnson was beautiful in her own right, though her genetic contribution to her children was more difficult to discern, perhaps the curly hair of her daughter Clarissa and one son, Thane, third in line.

Gerald Johnson had certainly fathered a flock of children.

Even more than he might know about, if her theory was right.

She saw the wash of Trace's headlights, heard the rumble of his truck, and as Bonzi put up a loud, deep-throated ruckus, she stepped onto the front porch. "Hush!" she commanded the dog, and he gave off one final, quiet bark just as Trace cut the engine.

She felt a little uptick in her pulse, which was just plain ludicrous. Bonzi stood beside her, his wagging tail a whip of friendly excitement, once again dispelling any of her hopes that he might just be a guard dog.

Companion? Yes. Final line of defense? Very unlikely.

He was already lowering his head, ready to be petted, as Trace, bundled in a heavy jacket, crossed the snowy lawn in that athletic/cowboy way she'd never found all that attractive.

Until now.

Swinging from one of Trace's gloved hands was a laptop computer, which changed his image just a bit.

"Is that what you want to show me?" she asked as he climbed up the few steps and walked into the pool of light cast by the porch lamp.

"Something on it. Yeah." He paused to pet the dog before they both followed her inside and down the short hall to the kitchen. Trace flipped open his computer. "You got a wireless setup here?"

"Uh-huh."

"Security code?"

When she shook her head, he said, "Let's put one on." He offered her a bit of a smile as he kicked out one of the café chairs. "Just to be on the safe side."

She wasn't going to argue. Not with everything else that was happening. "You want something? I've got coffee and tea and"—she peered in her refrigerator as he connected to the Internet—"Diet Coke, oh, or a light beer?"

"Sure, the beer," he said but didn't even glance up. "Okay, so here we go. Take a look."

She opened two bottles, twisting the tops off, and handed him one as she sat next to him. On the computer screen were several pictures, and at first she thought they were of the same woman, but as he clicked through them, she saw the differences. Her fingers tightened over her longnecked bottle, and she felt her stomach knot. "What is this?" But she knew.

"Pictures of women I know who resemble each other. Here you are," he said, and she recognized the photograph as one she had uploaded to the clinic's Web site. Next up was the school class picture of Jocelyn Wallis.

The third was of a woman Kacey couldn't name. It was a photograph taken at a distance and obviously scanned into the computer. "That's Leanna," he explained, his lips barely moving. "Eli's mother." He zoomed in so that her face, though blurry, was a little more visible.

Kacey's blood ran cold as she stared at features so like her own. "You were married to her and involved with Jocelyn. . . ." She looked up at him, heart in her throat.

"You're thinking just what the cops will, but I had nothing to do with any of this," he said, shaking his head in confusion. "I'm apparently attracted to a certain type of woman, but that's as far as it goes."

"So where is she? Leanna?" Kacey asked carefully.

"I don't know."

Kacey heard something in his tone. "You think she might be dead," she whispered and then was inordinately aware of the clock ticking off the seconds, of Bonzi snoring softly in the living room, of Trace's rock-hard jaw, the tension evident on his features.

He raked stiff fingers through his already tousled hair. "To tell you the truth, I don't know what to think, but I'm pretty certain that since I was the last guy Jocelyn dated, and I went to her house when the school called, I'm already on the police's radar. If they see pictures of Leanna, who could be missing . . . they might make a connection." He leaned back in his chair. "Then again, they could find Leanna, see that she's okay, which would be good. I can't seem to reach her. Eli misses her."

Stunned to think he'd been married to someone so much like her, Kacey stared at the image on the screen. This was all too freaky, and a part of her said she was going out of her mind, letting paranoia get the better of her, but she wasn't the only one who'd noticed her uncanny resemblance to the other women, including Trace's ex-wife. "Do you miss her?" she asked.

"Leanna?" He made a huffing sound. "Not hardly. Not that I would deny my kid a mother, but just not Leanna. She walked out and made it very clear she didn't want anything to do with either of us." A muscle worked in his jaw. "I took her at her word."

"You have to find her," she said suddenly. Maybe Leanna O'Halleran was the missing link, the person who knew what was going on. She could be the key.

"*If* she can be found. Trust me, I've been giving it my best shot." He took a long swallow from his beer, and Kacey decided it was time to give him some more bad news.

"Leanna and Jocelyn, they're not the only women missing, or possibly killed, who look like me."

"We don't know that Leanna's dead," he reminded. "She's . . . too mean to die." Kacey tried to keep her expression neutral, but he must have seen something in her expression, because he asked, "There were others?"

Could she trust him? Confide in him her half-baked theory? He was right; he was involved with one missing woman and one who was murdered, but in her heart of hearts she couldn't believe that he was dangerous. Not to her. Not when she'd seen how he cared for his son.

Decision time.

Trace was staring at her intently, and she decided to make a leap of faith. "Let me get my purse." She hurried from the kitchen, located her bag, and dragged out the pictures she'd shown her mother only hours before. Carefully, she placed each image on the table where her grandmother had served so many meals.

"This is Shelly Bonaventure," she said.

"That actress who died recently. I know she looks a little like Joce-lyn, and you. Suicide, wasn't it?"

"That's the official version."

"You think *she's* part of this? Seriously?" he asked, obviously skep-tical. "Other than her looks, what kind of connection is there to the others?"

"She was born in Helena, Montana, as were Jocelyn Wallis and my-self." Kacey pointed to the picture she'd printed off of Elle's Face-book page. "This is Elle Alexander—"

"The woman in the one-car accident last night."

"Yes, and this woman is still alive and works at a local gym." She slid the brochure from Fit Forever. "A trainer named Gloria Sanders-O'Malley."

"She from Helena, too?" He picked up the brochure, squinting as he studied her features.

"Don't know," Kacey admitted. "But I'm going to talk to her or check one of her social network sites. Lots of people list their home-town or where they've lived on Facebook or the like. If she's not there, I'll just talk to her."

"And say what?"

"I haven't completely figured that out yet," Kacey admitted.

"Huh. Yeah. How do you tell someone you think she's next on the list of some psychopath, especially when there's no real link estab-lished yet?"

"I'm working on that, along with finding out if Elle gave me false information or really didn't know where she was born."

"I don't know about this," Trace said after a long, silent moment.

"You came here," she reminded him. "With pictures of Jocelyn and Leanna. Don't you think it's damned odd that so many women who look so much alike, who are in their early thirties, are dying?"

"Yes . . . I do . . . but what are you really saying? You think a serial killer is searching for a type? And that the victims aren't random tar-gets? That he stalks them? That maybe he knew these people while they were in Helena?"

"That's probably unlikely," she admitted, as frustrated as ever. "Shelly left Helena when she was really young, and if Elle was there, she didn't know it. Her birth certificate's from Idaho."

He slid the picture away from the others that were clustered together. "So she's different."

"In that respect. But she's in the region. I don't know." Again she looked at the picture of the woman to whom Trace had once been married. "What about Leanna?"

He made a face. "She said she'd once lived around Helena, but she didn't remember any of it, either. I think her parents split, but the truth is, I don't know much about her. She liked it that way. Didn't want to talk about her childhood."

"You don't know where she went to school? Or her friends?"

He shifted in the chair. "I met her in a bar, it went down hot and heavy, and she ended up pregnant. We got married a few weeks later. Then she lost the baby and split."

"Leaving Eli?"

"That's the kind of woman she is. Not that I want it any other way. If she tried to take Eli from me, I'd fight her till the end. The marriage was one of those six-week wonders." Another swig from his bottle. Kacey watched his Adam's apple move, then turned her attention to the images.

Another woman near her age, who looked like her, who'd lived around Montana's state capital, possibly born there, and who was now missing.

"Here's something else," she added. "I just found out that the man who I thought was my father wasn't. My mother had an affair with a doctor in Helena, and even when my dad found out, he kept raising me as his own."

"So?"

"These women don't just look alike. Some of us are dead ringers for the other. For a while the staff at St. Bart's thought I was the woman in ICU when Jocelyn was brought in."

"You think you're *related* to these victims, these women? That this one guy fathered all of you, and now he's . . . what? Knocking you off?" He looked at her as if she'd lost her mind.

"I know it sounds crazy, but there's a connection there. I'm not making it up. Come into the den. . . ." She scraped her chair back and led him to her computer, where she pulled up the information she'd gotten from Riza and printed it out.

He read the reports, looked through the pages, checked pictures on driver's licenses, scanned obituaries, and scowled thoughtfully. "Where'd you get these?"

"A friend. It's mostly public record."

He examined the pages a second time. "If you're right . . . and I don't think you are . . . but this is pretty sick. It could all still be coincidence. These deaths . . ." He held up a stack of death certificates. "They were all ruled accidents."

"A lot of 'em. A librarian in Detroit, a ski instructor in Vail, a single mother and stay-at-home mom in San Francisco. Two others in Seattle and three . . . in Boise."

"All women."

"That we know of. But . . . I think we've just tapped the surface."

"We don't know anything yet. Some of these people died over ten years ago." He shook his head, denying the evidence, even while his eyes kept coming back to the pages. "Let me get this straight. You think one person is behind these deaths and is just incredibly patient. Taking time, over a long period of years. And now a rash of murders?"

"He's escalating," she said. "It happens."

"You don't know that."

"We don't know a lot, like you said, but something's really off here, and now the deaths, the 'accidents,' are happening closer together."

When he didn't seem convinced, she reminded him, "You came over here. You recognized that the women you were involved with are a type. I'm just taking it one step further. I think we might all be genetically linked. In fact, I'm running some DNA tests to prove it, but unfortunately, that takes time."

"Seriously?" He appeared skeptical.

"Yes. Elle Alexander was a patient of mine." She pointed to the picture of the woman. "I'm having tests run comparing her DNA to mine. I know already that we both have B-negative blood, and that's not common, so it's a start. Not real proof, but a start."

His eyes searched hers. "And if you find out something concrete?"

"Then I, or we, go to the police. Right now it's too early. They would blow me off as a nutcase. Kinda like you want to do."

"I'm keeping an open mind here," he said, though he didn't seem convinced as he finished his beer while going over again every scrap of information that Kacey, with Riza's help, had amassed.

As he did, he turned on the news, and they both learned that another car might have been involved in Elle Alexander's accident. The sheriff's department had issued a statement, then had asked for the public's help in letting the department know if anyone had witnessed the minivan going into the river.

"They think it's a hit-and-run," Kacey said as the news segued into the weather.

"It still could be an accident."

"Could be," she allowed.

"I'm just saying that her car could have been hit, her tires spun out on the ice, and the driver of the other vehicle freaked and left the scene."

"That makes him a criminal."

"But not necessarily tied to the other deaths."

"So you believe this is all coincidence?"

"Just playing devil's advocate here."

"Don't you think I've done the same thing?" she demanded. "Tried to talk myself out of this . . . bizarre situation. I wish I were wrong, I really do, but I don't think I am."

They turned off the news; then Trace, declining another beer, went to work setting up a security code for her computer and Wi-Fi. "The least I can do," he told her when she protested that she was taking up too much of his time. "For everything you've done for Eli."

She didn't argue, and if she admitted it to herself, she was grateful for his help. During school Riza and some other techie-type friends had helped her, and during her marriage to JC, who considered himself brilliant in all aspects of his life, had set up all their computer equipment. But since moving to Grizzly Falls and dealing with a house that was ill equipped with outlets, much less anything remotely electronic, she'd had to do the work herself or once in a while hire it out, which was what she'd done with the broken furnace, plumbing leak she'd had in the bathroom upstairs and the new exterior lights she'd had installed on the garage.

As Trace pulled out the desk and began examining her wiring, she watched him work and gave herself a swift mental shake for noting how his jeans stretched over his hips and butt as he reached over the desk. His sweater rode up a bit, showing off a quick glimpse of his back, skin stretched taut over smooth muscles.

Dragging her gaze away, she told herself she was acting like a teen.

"That should do it," he said as he straightened. "All set. I'll show you how to use the security code." Then he took hold of her wrist and, to her shock, pulled her tight against him. His hand found the back of her neck, and he whispered into her ear. "I think you've been bugged."

"Wha—" she started to say, but he held her fast, her body crushed against his.

"It's not that hard," he said loudly. "Just a matter of making a few changes!" But he didn't release her. In a voice barely audible, added, "We need to talk as if we have no idea about what's going on, okay? Just follow my lead." Pulling his head back, he stared into her eyes, and she nodded slowly.

"What should I use for the code?" she asked as he released her.

"Something that you'll remember. Here. But only you, just to keep it secure. Let me show you where the password needs to be entered. . . ."

CHAPTER 25

"Son of a bitch!" He ripped the listening device from his head and nearly threw it against the wall. He had been recording any noise in the house for hours and had determined that she was working fast. Somehow in the few hours since that withered hag Maribelle had spilled her guts, Acacia had found an ally, one in whom she'd confided that she'd connected the deaths of the women . . . but what was the remark about the man being "involved" with the women?

Whom had she meant? Jocelyn Wallis?

Someone else?

The conversation had been hard to hear, but he'd pieced two and two together. The male on the tape, the one providing her with security precautions, was Trace O'Halleran, Leanna's ex and the father of a kid who was her patient.

But he didn't understand why the guy was at her house so late at night and fucking up her computer! Why had she confided in him, told him about what that old hag Maribelle had told her, showed him whatever documentation she had?

He silently cursed himself for fucking up. He should have killed her back in the parking garage years ago! What a mistake to allow Acacia to live. And that bitch of a mother of hers.

He should have bugged Acacia's entire house, not just a few key rooms. He'd not been able to decipher the first part of her conversation with O'Halleran due to the radio playing too loudly, distorting his clarity.

Everything was unraveling.

Far too fast.

She was ruining things, would tell others, including the police, and everything he'd worked so hard to accomplish would be destroyed.

He couldn't let it happen. Not after his years of patient, hard work; he'd have to up his game even further. Who was *she* to force him to take more risks, to abandon his sense of caution?

Despite all his planning and his own desire to make her the last, to drag it out for her, to let her feel the terror, as payback for all her sins, he had to change things up. She had to be next.

He was quivering inside, rage storming through his body. He opened a drawer in his desk, then pulled out a narrow locked case with a combination lock. Turning the dial, he snapped open the lid and withdrew the knife. Holding the blade upward so that it glinted in the night, he remembered seeing her face-to-face as she turned, felt again the surge of power as he leapt at her, heard her surprised shout as their bodies collided.

God, what a rush!

He twisted the knife in his hand. Thin. Razor sharp. Perfect for skinning or boning or killing. One jab to her heart or lungs, or a quick slice across her throat, and she would die while she looked into his eyes, knowing he had drained the life from her.

But it hadn't happened seven years earlier.

She'd been stronger than he'd expected, and they'd been interrupted.

So she'd escaped. And he'd decided to wait. A mistake, it seemed now. He felt his blood pressure rising, his fury burning through his veins, images in his head turning red.

"Calm yourself," he ordered quietly. He paced to the door, grabbed the handle, then let it go. Closing his eyes for a second, he recaptured some of his fleeing composure. Finally he walked back to his desk. This wouldn't do. He prided himself on being in control. Somehow he had to regain his equilibrium.

This was a situation that had to be dealt with, that was all. A problem that needed fixing, and fast. His mind spun ideas for an "accident," not just for one, but two. The rancher would have to be killed, too. . . . Together, they had to die together.

Lovers in a passionate but deadly quarrel?

Murder/suicide?

A robbery gone bad?

Another car wreck, where neither one survived? The winter weather and coming storms would provide believability. He balled his fists and held them tight over his eyes.

Think!

You've worked too hard to give up now!

Again he wondered if the Fates were against him.

Of course not!

But he couldn't shake that same old feeling that something or *someone* was watching him. Like a deadly snake deceptively wound around a twisted branch, an unseen enemy lying in wait, ready to strike. His skin crawled, and he slowly let out his breath. This was insane; he couldn't let his fears undermine him.

He was in charge.

He was the protector.

And none of the Unknowings were going to outwit him.

With a glance at his inversion boots, he dismissed thoughts of sweating out his frustrations. For the moment. He had too much to think about, too much to plan. Grimacing, he slid the headphones over his ears and listened with the sole intent of righting a very old wrong.

Trace turned up the radio in the kitchen and the television in the living room. With the Christmas carols filtering from the back of the house and the news blaring from the front, he felt that he and Kacey could talk. He showed her the tiny microphones he'd located, including the ones in her bathroom and bedroom, which, when he pointed them out, drained the color from her face.

"Who?" she said in a low voice. "Why?"

"Someone who wants to know what you're doing."

"I should go to the police."

He nodded.

She started to shake. "He's been in my house!"

He drew her near and whispered in her ear, "You asked who. . . . Can you answer that question?"

"No . . . I don't think so. I'm usually here alone, and until Bonzi moved in, I didn't talk to anyone except on the phone, but those are pretty one-sided conversations."

They were practically in an embrace, and now Trace made it official, talking to her like a lover to keep their voices from being overheard. "What about disgruntled boyfriends or your ex-husband?"

"Not JC. He's over me and he wouldn't stoop to this. The divorce is long over. And there hasn't been an ex-boyfriend since my freshman year in college, maybe."

"An unhappy business partner, or someone who didn't like the medical treatment, or a girlfriend that thinks you put her down?"

"I'm telling you I don't have any enemies."

"Maybe someone you're making nervous."

"I just got this information. I haven't . . . done anything." She was shaking her head, but the images of the women who looked like her, some alive and some dead, slid through her brain. "But it has to be him. It has to do with this whole doppelgänger thing," she said, reluctantly releasing him to sink onto the couch.

"Has anyone ever tried to harm you?"

Her inner eye flashed on the attacker, a man in black, ski mask covering his face, leaping from the shadowy staircase of the parking structure. Terror sizzled through her, as it had that night.

"Kacey?" Trace prodded.

She let out her breath, and sensing she had a story to tell, he took her out to the front porch, where she whispered, "There was one time. But it was around seven years ago, when I lived in Seattle, still going to medical school." She shuddered, remembering that day. She had been fighting a cold and was dead on her feet. It was late, and she'd spent hours in the library, on the computer, as hers had been ravaged by the latest virus.

Just before the library closed, she'd left, crossed to the parking garage where she'd parked her car, and taken the elevator to the sixth floor.

She hadn't seen him hiding near the stairwell, had been too busy fumbling with her keys and wishing she were already in bed with the covers pulled up to her chin and a cup of hot lemon water with a teaspoon of clover honey, her grandmother's cure-all for everything, at her bedside.

As she walked to her car, she noticed that the lights in the garage seemed dim. Then she'd seen that two bulbs were smashed, the glass having rained onto the concrete floor.

All she'd been concerned with at that moment was that shards of glass might become embedded in her tires.

And then she'd heard something out of place—a quiet cough? Or the scrape of shoe leather? She'd started to turn. A glimpse out of the corner of her eye. A man leaping from the shadows near the stairwell. Dressed in black, some kind of body-fitting suit, a ski mask pulled over his head, he raised a hand as he jumped at her.

In his gloved fingers, a knife blade glinted.

She screamed, hit him with her purse, and tried to run. Too late. His weight came down on her. *Bam,* her forehead cracked against the concrete. Blood poured from her face as they wrestled. Adrenaline fired her blood, and she fought wildly, yelling and swearing, grabbing his wrist, forcing the blade away from her throat.

"Bitch!" he snarled, but there was another sound, that of a car's engine starting a floor or two above.

His attention wavered, and she shifted beneath him, twisting his wrist, turning the knife upward, so that when he looked down, she sliced open the mask near his eye, a thin line of blood showing near his temple.

"Help! Help me!" she screamed and heard the car above heading down.

He heard it, too. Swearing viciously, he threw her away from him, leapt to his feet, and ran off just as the car, a white Volkswagen, turned the far corner and headed directly toward her.

She lifted an arm, and the driver, a woman about her age, stood on the brakes, then flew out of her car, leaving it idling as she cried, "Are you okay? What happened?" She recoiled at seeing Kacey's bloody face but was already dialing 9-1-1.

Now Kacey relived the attack, feeling again that stone-cold fear that brought color to her cheeks and sweat to the back of her neck.

She told Trace about what had happened, how she'd escaped with her life, how the assault had seemed random, a crazy who was just waiting for his chance. He'd shown no interest in robbing her; he'd left her purse. Rape? Maybe. But she'd seen his eyes through the slits in his mask, and they, a steely blue, pupils dilated, were cold and deadly. Whether he first had planned to kidnap her, then sexually assault her or torture her, she didn't know, but she was certain in those few desperate minutes that he intended to kill her.

"The police never found him?" Trace asked soberly.

"No. I know I cut him, but they collected no blood except my own. And so he's out there, somewhere."

"Bugging you?" Trace asked, inclining his head toward the closed door, behind which the mics were still in place.

"Why?" she whispered aloud.

Trace didn't immediately answer, and she said, "Shelly Bonaventure's death was well planned, made to appear a suicide. Jocelyn Wallis fell into the river. Elle Alexander's minivan slid off the road. . . . Those attacks took time and thought."

"If they were attacks," he reminded, but Kacey was on her own track.

"When I was fighting off the psycho in the parking garage, I thought he was a wack job, completely off the rails. Not the kind of person who would meticulously plan someone's death."

"Do you have security here?"

"No alarm system, except for Bonzi."

"Weapons?"

"My grandfather's shotgun."

"Do you want to go to the police?"

"No," she answered immediately. "Not yet."

"Then I'll stay here till morning. You take the dog upstairs, and I'll camp out on the couch with the gun." He opened the front door, and they headed back inside, which was just as well because Kacey had started to shiver.

She wasn't sure what she thought about him spending the night. What did she know about Trace O'Halleran? He seemed like a nice enough guy, a good father, but that wasn't enough to hand him a gun and go off upstairs to sleep soundly. Not after what had been happening.

"How about you keep the dog and I'll take the gun?" she whispered.

He almost smiled. "Smart," he said, already reaching for the blanket that was always folded at the end of the couch. "Tell ya what. You take 'em both."

*   *   *

Snow was falling in big, wet flakes to pile on the ground at the edge of the night-darkened river. Shivering, Kacey stood on the icy bank, where the wind shrieked down the canyon and billowed her nightgown. Barefoot, she stared down at the rushing water and shivered with the cold.

"Kacey!" She heard her name over the screaming wind and saw Grace Perchant with Bane, her wolf dog. "Evil," she said, her voice a whisper over the keening wind. "Evil."

"Who?" Kacey tried to say, but her voice was lost and the thick falling snow became a shroud, Grace and the dog disappearing into the gloom.

Fear coiled around her heart, and when she glanced down to the water again, she saw faces beneath the surface. Distorted and pale, they stared up at her in horror. Shelly Bonaventure, her make-up smeared; Jocelyn Wallis, crying; Elle Alexander, her eyes round with accusations; and then her own face, floating up to the surface, as if disembodied, her features twisted and ever-changing, but hers nonetheless. And Leanna O'Halleran, she was there, too, with Trace's face, his mouth twisted into an evil grin, between Jocelyn and Leanna. . . . He stared up at her through a watery veil, and Jocelyn's naked body drifted past him. Her breasts were flaccid, the dark nipples pinched, and a jagged, raw, Y-shaped autopsy scar marred her pale skin.

Kacey tried to scream but no sound came. She tried to back up, but her feet seemed rooted on the bank, and the snow, as it continued to fall over the river, turned pink, then red, before dropping in thick scarlet drips of blood.

Sweet Jesus!

A dog growled and barked, and she looked across the river again, where she made out Grace, now no more than a skeleton, her pale hair whipping frantically in the wind, her jawbone opening to expose a dark hole as she whispered, "Stay away. . . . He's evil." The now emaciated animal beside her growled low in his throat as the bloody snowflakes caught on what was left of his coat.

"Who?" she cried again as the dog's voice startled her. A low, gruff growl . . .

Kacey sat bolt upright in her own bed.

The room was dark; her bedcovers were mussed. Bonzi stood at the window, staring out to the backyard. The hackles on the back of his thick neck were raised, hair stiff, tail unmoving, while his nose was pressed to the glass, fogging the pane in two tiny spots.

Her heart froze. "Bonz . . . ?" she said softly as she eased out of the bed. She stood next to him at the window, near the curtains, next to the shotgun she'd loaded and propped against the casing. Through the glass, she saw nothing out of the ordinary. The yard and surrounding shrubbery were covered in white, shivering in the wind that moaned through the rafters of this old farmhouse.

It was almost morning, but the outbuildings stood in dark relief, black against the blanketing snow, illumination pooling from the twin garage lanterns.

Was there something or someone out there? Just around the corner of the old barn? Or farther still, in the dark row of saplings and scrub pine that edged the fields her grandfather had plowed? A light snow was falling. Gentle and soft.

Nothing. It's nothing. Maybe a stray cat or a hare . . .

But her heart was knocking irregularly, her nerves strung tight as bowstrings. The edges of her dream clawed at her brain, disturbing images of dead women and bloody snow and Grace's ominous warning.

Evil . . .

She saw her own pale reflection in the window, an ashen image that reminded her of the women in her dream. Was it true? Could Gerald Johnson possibly have fathered all the women she'd found and who were now being killed one by one?

She heard a noise coming from the lower floor. Her heart jolted at the same moment she realized it was Trace.

"Kacey?" he called softly up the stairs, the sound of bare feet slapping the steps as he climbed upward. "I thought I heard—" He appeared, filling up the doorway, his bare shoulders, silhouetted by the night-light in the hallway, nearly touching the jamb, his battered jeans hanging low on his hips. "The dog." He glanced around the darkened room and demanded, "Something wrong?"

"No." She forced the image of his leering face from the nightmare from her brain. "Bonzi woke me."

Hearing his name, the dog finally turned to look over his shoulder and then, whatever enemy he'd thought he'd sensed no longer snagging his attention, wandered around the end of the bed and waited for Trace to scratch his ears.

He stared at Kacey for a second. "I'll go have a look around outside."

"No . . . it was probably just some animal. A squirrel or deer or whatever. This place is new to him." She left her post at the window and patted the big dog's head. "Probably just my nerves. I was having a particularly gruesome nightmare."

"You okay?" he asked, and one big hand fell lightly on her shoulder. Warm and steady. She nearly melted into him, but didn't. She didn't have time to fall apart.

"As well as I can be," she said, sliding into her slippers and grabbing her bathrobe off the hook on the back of the door. A thought nagged at her just below her consciousness, something about the women in the dream, how they were linked, but she couldn't quite catch it. "I'll make coffee," she said, then slipped past him as she headed downstairs. The dog trotted after her, and Trace followed last.

It all seemed so normal.

So damned domestic.

Except for the threats, real or imagined, that lay just outside her door. And the hidden microphones. And maybe even the man she was with now, who had been married to a woman who could be her twin, a woman who'd disappeared. He was also linked to Jocelyn, another look-alike who had ended up dead. Murdered.

Whatever fantasies she had about him, she had to push aside, she determined as she snapped on the lights on the first floor.

With one finger, Trace snagged his T-shirt from the back of the rocking chair. Despite her warnings to herself that getting close to him could be dangerous, Kacey watched his muscles work beneath a patch of curling hair that spread across his chest and arrowed lower over tight abs.

Her throat went dry, and she turned toward the kitchen, pushing all images of him out of her head.

She'd already started coffee by the time he, in his sweater and jacket and boots, walked over the old linoleum to the back door. "I'll take the dog and take a look," he said, whistling for Bonzi, who seemed eager to go. "Once I know everything's secure, I'll be on my way."

"Okay. I'll be heading to the hospital after I take care of some chores."

She nodded and glanced at the clock, noting it wasn't quite six.

"And the authorities?" he asked softly, almost inaudibly.

She nodded. She planned on contacting them but wasn't sure exactly when.

While he was outside and the coffee was dripping through the maker, she ran through the shower. Within five minutes she was dry, half dressed, and winding her hair into a quick knot that she pinned to the back of her head. Today she applied only a slap of lipstick, a brush of mascara, then slid into slacks and a sweater before returning to the kitchen. Trace was just stomping the snow from his boots on the back porch. He opened the door, and Bonzi, fresh from relieving himself and, it appeared, running through the snow, bounded inside.

"Nice morning," Trace said as he stepped over the threshold, shaking his head to let her know he hadn't seen anything outside. She poured two cups of coffee and handed him one. They shared their drinks in silence for a few moments, acutely aware of the microphones.

Finishing his coffee, Trace put his cup in the sink. Kacey followed suit as he asked, "You leaving now?"

"Yep." She grabbed her keys. She might not completely trust Trace, but she really didn't like the idea of being alone in her house, Bonzi or no Bonzi.

CHAPTER 26

Water dripped onto the floor of his listening post. Snow melting off his clothes. He'd hurried back from Acacia's, where he'd spent the night watching the back of her house through his night-vision goggles. O'Halleran had spent the night with her! He'd circled around and seen the man's truck while snow came down heavily, obscuring his tracks almost as he made them. He'd circled back and waited, the big flakes silent and cold, a slow, hot fury taking hold inside him at all the things she'd learned and told O'Halleran.

A light had come on in Acacia's room, and he'd quickly moved farther into the brush and jogged to his car. It had been a short drive to his lair, and he'd hurried inside, eager to listen in, but there was nothing more than what he'd heard the night before.

His blood burned through his veins. He wanted Acacia to die. Soon. *Now.*

He ripped out the earbud and threw it down. If only he'd heard more! The first part had been clear, but then they'd turned up the volume on the television and the radio.

Had they guessed? Had they found the tiny microphones? Been aware of him listening in?

Couldn't be!

In frustration he'd left this morning to go to her place, and the only thing he'd learned was that O'Halleran had never left. She had an ally. O'Halleran! Leanna's ex. How had that happened? He wasn't sure, but he knew they had to die together. Somehow.

Leanna . . . He ground his teeth together. Acacia had found a lot of the names of the women. Too many!

And O'Halleran had told her about Leanna.

Leanna . . . who had left her boy with O'Halleran . . .

Her boy . . .

He contemplated that for several moments, calming himself, thinking.

O'Halleran was already concerned the police would look at him as a suspect. He was already connected to Leanna and Acacia, and it sounded like Jocelyn Wallis as well.

He wasn't wrong. Of course he would be a suspect! The rancher was the perfect suspect. O'Halleran could be blamed for all of it. With a little bit of outside help, he *would* be.

Someone just had to push things along in the right direction.

Pescoli drove into the station lot, slid a little in the ice-crusted snow, and swore violently, way out of proportion to the situation. Hearing her words echo back through her mind, she tried very, very hard not to be totally pissed off, at the world in general, and at herself, too.

Bianca had mono. Mononucleosis. Yep. The kissing disease. And though Pescoli had hoped this affliction might be visited upon her boyfriend as well, no such luck, apparently. Chris was as healthy as a horse and as sticky as Gorilla Glue. Chris, who heretofore had shown no interest whatsoever in hanging around the Pescoli home if Regan was there, now seemed to think it was his life's mission to take care of Bianca, and he'd planted himself on the property.

"Go back to school," Pescoli had told him yesterday, when he'd showed up at noon. He'd left, only to return in the evening and hover around while Bianca basically slept on the couch.

But even worse, it had been Lucky's bimbo wife, Michelle, who'd set the wheels in motion by intimating that Bianca hadn't been herself over the holidays, and didn't Pescoli think maybe she should see a doctor? Never mind the fact that Pescoli had already been trying her damnedest to get Bianca to the doctor's office but had run up against a brick wall at even the mention of visiting Dr. Lundell, Bianca's pediatrician.

"I'm too old!" Bianca had yelled at her. "I'm fine. Just leave me alone!"

So, okay, maybe she should have insisted. She'd half believed Bianca had been faking just so she could hang out with Chris. And things were crazy at work, and she'd let it slide. It was no excuse, and she sure as hell felt guilty about it now, but it was the truth. The good news: at least her daughter wasn't on drugs or suffering from some more serious malaise.

But Bianca was home sick, and Jeremy was there, too, doing nothing constructive, and Chris would be on their doorstep again the first chance he got.

She needed to be there, too.

Pulling back her sleeve with a gloved hand, Pescoli checked her watch. Seven a.m. Maybe she could get a couple of hours in before anyone stirred at home. She planned to work as long as she could, then head home and check on things. It galled her that Michelle had been the one to finally make her force the issue with Bianca. And this after Bianca came back in clothes too raunchy for even a street-walker—in Pescoli's unbiased opinion—clothes Michelle had helped her pick out during their trip to the mall. Good. God.

And then Jeremy, with his video-game playing and no plan to do anything else . . .

She stepped out into unrelenting snow. Huge flakes were falling steadily, and she bent her head as she headed up the steps to the station. Her jaw was tight, her thoughts on her son. What the hell did he think he was doing? She wasn't going to just have him home doing nothing. Even Lucky wouldn't be up for that. And if Jeremy didn't get his butt off the couch and *do something* soon, Pescoli was going to go postal. The video games that were his lifeblood were *this close* to being given to charity. She was pretty sure there was some deserving kid out there who would be thrilled with *Kill 'Em Dead* or *Annihilation* or *The End of the World*, or whatever the hell they were called. Something like that. The perfect Christmas stocking stuffers.

Thinking of Jeremy reminded her of Heidi Brewster, which in turn reminded her of the undersheriff and the fact that she'd drawn Cort Brewster's name for a Secret Santa gift.

Stomping snow from her boots, she headed down the still half-darkened hallway toward her desk. She stopped short upon seeing Alvarez already at her workstation, her dark, smoothed hair pulled back tight as she hunched over an area lit by a desk lamp, a small oasis of illumination in an otherwise dimly lit room.

Pescoli flipped the switch by the door and flooded the place with fluorescent lighting, which buzzed and shook and generally made everything look harsh and unappealing.

Alvarez glanced up. "You're in a mood."

"How can you tell?"

She gave Pescoli a look that made her realize she was standing with her feet apart, arms crossed, glaring aggressively into the room.

"How's Bianca?" Alvarez asked.

"Asleep. Hopefully alone, although Chris won't stay away now that he thinks he's appointed himself her angel of mercy."

"Her boyfriend?"

Pescoli made a rude sound, then brought her partner up to speed on Bianca's boyfriend's new desire to be at the Pescoli home 24-7. "Like all of a sudden he's the concerned parent, and none of the rules apply anymore. And then Jeremy . . . if he isn't spending time playing some video game where he has to annihilate legions of futuristic zombie robots, he's *sexting* Heidi Brewster. I got a real surprise the last time Jeremy left his cell phone just lying around for anyone to pick up. Photos. Of Heidi. If a picture's worth a thousand words, these are like a whole new vocabulary. Some of Heidi's are . . . Actually, I don't even have the words."

Alvarez's dark eyes were wide and staring straight at Pescoli, telegraphing messages.

"Brewster?" Pescoli said aloud, figuring he must be standing right behind her.

"You don't have the words," he said tautly.

Pescoli slowly turned on her heel and eyed the undersheriff uneasily. Some of her anger dissipated as she gazed at his stony face. He might not look like it, but she knew he was just barely holding it together, too. "She's fully clothed," Pescoli told him, holding up her hands.

"So, what then?" he challenged.

"Just a major lip-lock between her and my son," Pescoli said. "My son, who I'm about to give a boot to the backside. And that's all I'm saying about that."

He opened and shut his mouth several times like a gasping fish, then showed enormous restraint by merely slapping a hand in the air at her and turning away.

As his footsteps stomped off, Alvarez said, "You didn't have the words, because Jeremy and Bianca were in a lip-lock?"

"There was one of her bent forward in one of those poses where she's looking at the camera and sucking the hell out of a lollipop. A few other similar ones, too."

"Maybe you can frame one and give it to Brewster for your Secret Santa gift," Alvarez suggested.

"There's an idea. So, what's kept you here all night? I'm trying to get out of here early so I can referee at my house."

"I've been thinking about the case."

"Okay."

"We haven't pushed O'Halleran enough. We just accepted his assurances that he and Jocelyn weren't really dating, but maybe he wasn't giving us the whole truth."

Pescoli rolled that over in her mind. "The guy works pretty much by himself, doesn't have to clock in anywhere."

"Not only was he involved with one victim, but his missing wife looks a lot like the other victims."

"So, you want to call him in?" Pescoli asked.

"I think it's definitely time for another interview."

Pescoli glanced at the clock. "It's barely seven thirty. What time did you get here?"

"Couple hours ago. Is that Joelle . . . ?"

From down the hall they heard a woman's voice, Joelle's, singing: "Here comes Suzy Snowflake, dressed in a snow-white gown. Tap, tap, tappin' at your windowpane, to tell you she's in town."

"Did she make that up, or is it really a Christmas carol?" Pescoli asked.

"I think it's a Christmas carol." Alvarez reached for her phone, but it suddenly rang beneath her hand. She threw Pescoli a look, then hit the speaker button and said, "Alvarez."

"Detective Alvarez." A woman's voice came through. "This is Dr. Kacey Lambert."

Alvarez gave Pescoli a "what's this" look, and Pescoli shook her head. "Yes?"

"There are microphones, listening devices, planted in my home. I'm not sure why, but it may have something to do with these . . . recent accidents."

"Microphones?" Alvarez picked out the word that jumped out at her.

"Tiny ones. Secretive."

"You think someone's bugging you?"

"Looks that way."

"You have an idea who?"

"No . . ." Her voice grew uncertain, and Pescoli could tell she was already having serious second thoughts about calling them.

"Can you come by the station?" Alvarez asked. "I'd like some more information."

"Maybe later. I'm at St. Bart's, checking on a patient. I have to go to my clinic. I'll call later and think about this. I just wanted to let you know."

She clicked off and Pescoli repeated, "Microphones?"

"She sounds pretty rattled." Alvarez went very still, then motioned to the computer screen where images of recent victims were displayed. "She kind of looks like them."

"Doesn't everybody," Pescoli said on a groan.

"No. But there's a connection."

Joelle's voice rang out: "If you want to make a snowman, I'll help you make it, one, two, three. If you want to take a sleigh ride, whee! The ride's on me."

Pescoli covered her eyes with her hands and groaned, and Joelle's voice said suddenly, "Would you look at that snow!"

Both Pescoli and Alvarez glanced out the window and watched the flakes fall relentlessly from the sky. Then Alvarez picked up the receiver and put a call in to Trace O'Halleran's cell phone.

Kacey tucked her cell phone back in her purse. Now that she'd started that ball rolling, she felt half embarrassed, second-guessing herself. She wasn't planning on telling the police everything; she didn't want them getting in the way of her own personal discoveries.

But the microphones . . . She wanted them *out* of her house as soon as possible, and she wanted the police to do it.

Shaking off another frisson down her back, she headed to Eli's room. Sticking her head inside, she saw that he was sound asleep. She quietly walked in and pulled his chart from the folder at the foot of his bed, then watched his even breathing a moment. Tiptoeing out, she went in search of the floor nurse, who nodded when Kacey said, "Eli O'Halleran's temperature's down, and he's breathing easier."

"He's feeling much better," the nurse agreed.

Kacey was relieved. "Good. His father will be here soon, and we'll get him released."

"This flu gets bad fast. We've got a few other cases that haven't turned around as quickly."

Kacey commiserated with her for a moment while she wondered if she should stick around and wait for Trace. But with Eli on the mend and her worries about him abated, Kacey decided to head to the clinic. She had a plan formulating inside her head, and she was determined to leave work early today if she possibly could to put it into play. Everything just depended on her afternoon appointment schedule, which had been light the last she'd checked. She hoped that was still the case.

She called Trace on his cell phone and was sent straight to voice mail; he was probably still doing his chores. Quickly, she gave him Eli's update and then said she had called the police and told them about the microphones.

That done, she drove to the clinic, whose parking lot was thick with new snow. Stepping outside, she heard the *scrunch, scrunch, scrunch* of her boots as she stomped through the thick white powder to the front door. Inside, she met up with Heather, who was brushing snow off the shoulders of her jacket.

"It's snowing like a son of a gun out there," Heather said, wrinkling her nose.

"I'm going to try to leave early," Kacey said. "Would you check the afternoon schedule? I don't think I have much, and maybe I can move some people around."

"Because it's snowing?" Heather asked as she sat down at the reception desk and turned on her computer. "It's supposed to quit before the afternoon."

Not even close, Kacey thought, but said only, "I've got some issues to take care of."

"Well, you've got Herbert Long with a possible sinus infection. His wife said he'd leave work early to come by. Around four, maybe. He didn't want to come at all."

Kacey inwardly groaned. "Maybe Martin can take him."

"Maybe. That's the only appointment holding you up."

"Let me know when Martin gets in."

Kacey headed into her office. She wanted to confront Gerald Johnson as soon as possible, and that meant a trip to Missoula, which was a quick trip in good weather, a little longer with the white stuff accumulating outside.

Her mind jumped to the vision of Trace returning to her house from his foray with Bonzi, snow melting in his hair. She recognized something was happening between them, something that could lead to something more. . . . The idea both thrilled and alarmed her. The man was up to his eyeballs with the look-alikes. Was she an idiot to trust him? Was that what the other victims had done?

She didn't believe it. Not for a minute. She trusted her instincts enough to trust Trace, but even so, as she settled into work, she kept running Trace's involvement with several of the victims through her mind on an endless loop.

"So you don't know where your wife is?" the taller detective asked Trace, her eyes never leaving his face. An imposing woman with reddish hair clipped away from her face, she sat on the opposite side of the small, battered table in the small interrogation room at the sheriff's department. Her expression gave nothing away, but her gaze kept traveling to her watch.

"*Ex-wife,* and no," Trace said emphatically. "I've lost touch with Leanna."

Trace had driven to the offices at the top of Boxer Bluff to "answer a few questions" after Pescoli's partner, Alvarez, the shorter Latino woman with the intense dark eyes, had left him a message on his cell phone, asking him to come in.

He'd gotten that message and one from Kacey in short succession. Kacey's had been welcome; she'd told him the antibiotics had taken hold and Eli was on the mend, something he'd seen for himself when he'd dropped by the hospital after he'd fed and watered the stock and taken Sarge for a walk outside in the falling snow.

He'd spent some time with his boy, who did seem much more an-imated, before speaking with the doctor, who had informed him that Eli would be released in the afternoon, as soon as all the paperwork was finished. It just relieved him to no end, and so he'd made his next stop the police station.

Upon his arrival, Detective Alvarez had escorted him to this win-dowless room with its concrete walls, small table, and three molded plastic chairs. After telling him she was recording the session, she'd left, saying she was going to bring them all a cup of coffee, which he assumed was intended to make this seem more like an informal "chat" than a serious interrogation. Fine. He wanted all his cards on the table. And the police to get to the truth. Kacey's theory that the victims were genetically linked, possibly to her, scared him. It scared him to death.

Still, he was anxious to get this interview over. He didn't want Eli staying alone in the hospital any longer than absolutely necessary. He already had some abandonment issues because of Leanna; Trace wasn't about to compound them by not showing up when he'd promised.

Alvarez returned with half-filled paper cups and set them on the table. As she sat down, she pulled a slim manila file from a briefcase positioned near her chair and slid it onto the beat-up table. Trace ig-nored the steaming coffee but was grateful that its aroma blocked out the stench of sweat and cleaning solvent, as if this room had been scrubbed recently, but it couldn't quite mask the scent of fear, desperation, and guilt.

With no holds barred, he told them the story of his brief marriage, losing touch with Leanna, and raising Eli alone. "The marriage was over before it began," he admitted. "I'm still not even sure she was pregnant. I never saw the test kit results or went to the one appoint-ment with the doctor she'd sworn she'd visited. No bill for the exam ever came through, so maybe I was played."

"Why?" Alvarez asked.

"I suspect she was tired of the responsibility of a kid." Trace's in-sides curdled with the admission, but it was his version of the truth. "Leanna wasn't the kind of woman cut out to be a mother."

"What kind was she?" the taller detective, Pescoli, asked.

"Beautiful and self-centered. Friendly smile. Cold, though."

"Huh," Pescoli observed before picking up a paper cup and taking a long swallow of the coffee. "You're her ex."

"You asked," he reminded the detective. "I'm just saying what I think."

Alvarez asked, "So about Eli. He's not your biological son, but she just left him with you? What about the real father?"

Feeling warm in his coat, Trace unbuttoned it. "It's my understanding that he was never in the picture. He might not even know about Eli. But the adoption's legal. He's my son."

Pescoli asked, "What about your *ex-wife's* family?"

"I didn't meet any of them. We were together less than six months. So, why all the questions about Leanna?"

But he knew. And it came as no surprise when Pescoli opened the file on the small desk and showed him pictures of Jocelyn Wallis and one of Leanna O'Halleran, the picture she'd had taken for her Montana driver's license.

"Since you were the last person Jocelyn Wallis was involved with, and she with you," Pescoli said, "we just would like to know more about her, as well as your missing wife."

He didn't bother correcting her this time, understood that she was baiting him a bit, trying to get a rise. If she kept wanting to call Leanna his wife, fine. "Fire away," he told them, and as both detectives tossed questions at him, he answered clearly and concisely. When they got to a question about Elle Alexander, he said truthfully, "I've never met her. Look, can I sign a statement or something? I've been here over an hour. I've got things to do, and I'm picking my son up from the hospital." There was a hesitation, and a look passed between them. "Are you charging me with something? Do I need a lawyer? I've told you everything I know."

Pescoli looked at her watch again, and Alvarez regarded him soberly, as if she were trying to see into his soul.

Even though it wasn't really his call, Trace added, "Actually, there's something more you need to know. I've been . . . seeing Acacia Lambert, the doctor who works at the clinic downtown. You met her at the hospital. She said she called you and told you about the hidden microphones."

Alvarez reacted, and Pescoli's interest sharpened as well. "That's correct," Alvarez said.

"You might notice that she looks like these women." He pointed at the small table, where the pictures of Leanna and Jocelyn were still lying faceup. "And also, Shelly Bonaventure, that actress who died recently, as well as Elle Alexander. Kacey had noticed it, and so had I. When I was over at her place last night, we discovered the bugs. There was a little microphone hidden in her den, in her bathroom, and in her bedroom. I didn't see any in the kitchen and living room, but I could have missed them, I suppose. She was shocked. Someone is listening in on her. She thinks it has to do with this investigation." He swept a hand over the photos.

Alvarez and Pescoli shared a look; then Pescoli said, "She said she would call us later, after she'd thought it through."

No wonder they'd called, Trace realized. "The place needs to be swept of those microphones. Either you or me. But as soon as we do that, somebody's going to know it."

"You brought up Shelly Bonaventure," Pescoli said. "She was in L.A."

"But she's from around here. Born in Helena. Kacey has a theory that there might be more victims and they all could be related."

"Related," Alvarez repeated.

Trace found himself growing impatient. Kicking back his chair, he stood. "I really do have to go. Let Kacey tell you more herself when she calls back."

"You think she's off on some wild tangent?" Pescoli asked, and Alvarez's lips tightened.

"I don't know about that," he said truthfully. "But something's really wrong here, and I'm worried about Kacey."

"And what about your *ex-wife?* Are you worried about her?" Alvarez asked.

He made a sound of disgust. "Hell, no. One thing I know about Leanna—she can take care of herself."

CHAPTER 27

"O'Halleran's not our guy," Pescoli said as she shrugged into her coat and met her partner in the hallway.

"I know." Alvarez nodded. "It couldn't be that easy."

"Never is."

Together they stepped around a shackled man being shepherded by Trilby Van Droz, one of the road deputies.

"I ain't got nothin' to say!" the man with stringy hair and half a week's growth of beard insisted. "I didn't steal no goddamned truck, and that was *my* shotgun. I don't know how that pipe got into the backseat, but it wasn't mine! I don't know what the fuck you're trying to pull here!"

"Keep movin' it," Trilby said, her voice world-weary.

"Give me a fuckin' break, will ya?" the guy wheedled. "It's the holidays."

"In here!" She opened a door to one of the interrogation rooms. "Merry Christmas!"

Pescoli smothered a smile, which faded as they passed the reception area, where winking lights were strewn around Joelle's desk and a fir tree, complete with tinsel, lights, and presents tucked beneath its fragrant boughs, actually spun slowly in one corner. "There's fruitcake in the lunchroom," Joelle called as they reached the front door. Today an elf was tucked slyly into the platinum strands of her hair. "My great-great-*great*-grandmother's recipe!" She offered them a bright smile just as two teenagers swept inside, a gust of arctic wind swirling behind them, along with a wet smack of snow.

"A maniac tried to run me down!" The girl, in braids and huge glasses, was obviously shaken. "Near the Safeway store. He had to be drunk! He just sprayed snow everywhere!"

"He was drivin' a green Honda. Sweet lowrider, and he came around the corner too fast and slid all over the place," her companion, a boy in a frayed stocking cap, said. "Everyone saw it."

"I was in the damned crosswalk! He just took off!"

"Fishtailing," the boy said, moving his hand from side to side.

"If Lanny hadn't pulled me out of the way, I'd be dead now!" the girl cried. She was about to hyperventilate, and Pescoli would have stepped in to help, but Joelle was already pushing a tissue box in the girl's direction and picking up the phone. She made little scooting motions with her fingers, indicating Pescoli and Alvarez could move along.

"Calm down, honey," Joelle said with a motherly smile as the girl dissolved into tears. "It'll be okay. Let me get someone to help you."

Since the situation was under control, Pescoli pushed the door open, felt the sting of the cold air against her face, and walked outside. Alvarez zipped her jacket a little higher and bent her head against the wind and snow as she took a call on her cell.

"Alvarez," she said, keeping up with Pescoli's longer strides and blinking away snowflakes.

Pescoli slid on her gloves, then jabbed her hands deep into the pockets of her coat as they walked the three blocks to a small deli to grab sandwiches.

Only a few pedestrians had braved the weather, and traffic was moving slowly along, the *chink, chink, chink* of chains a different kind of holiday music.

"Okay. Yeah. E-mail would be fine. Thanks!" Alvarez hung up and slid Pescoli a glance. "Shelly Bonaventure's DNA report. Hayes managed to pull some strings and get it rushed. He's sending it over."

"If it means anything."

"We'll find out."

They needed a break, Pescoli thought as they crossed the parking lot of the strip mall where the deli was located. None of the evidence in this case was hanging together. "You think that there's anything to the talk of Acacia Lambert's place being bugged?" Pescoli asked.

"Must be something," Alvarez said.

"I don't get it. I'm going to have to grab this and go check on the kids."

"I'm going to work on finding the ex–Mrs. O'Halleran. See what she has to say."

"Okay. It'll be interesting to hear why she dumped her kid with O'Halleran and took off, if she really did. So far all we've got for it is his word." She shouldered open the door of the small deli. Warm air and the smells of spices and roasted meat hit Pescoli full force. Her stomach growled as she and Alvarez took their place in line to order their takeout.

It took a while as the older couple ahead of them were in no hurry. The man had trouble hearing; the woman was very concerned about her allergies as they finally settled on a tuna melt and ham on rye. But that wasn't the end of it. To complicate matters, they had their grandson, a kid of about fourteen who wasn't in school but was definitely plugged into his music, as he either texted or played a game on his cell phone. For him to grudgingly order a turkey sandwich—"*no* tomatoes, *no* lettuce, *no* onions, but an extra bag of chips"—and convey that message to his grandmother as he fiddled with his phone and listened to music was excruciating.

Eventually, as customers stacked up behind Alvarez, the patient woman behind the counter got the older couple and their grandson what they wanted, then rang them up. Finally, Pescoli was able to place her order. A chicken-spinach salad for Alvarez and some kind of healthy bottled tea, while Pescoli had a Reuben with extra sauerkraut and a diet cola. They carried lunch back to the station, where they parted ways, Pescoli heading out, while Alvarez ate at her desk, checking her e-mail. The DNA report from Jonas Hayes popped up, so she sent it on to the lab.

An hour later Pescoli returned, and she signaled Alvarez to join her in the lunchroom, where, true to her word, Joelle's fruitcake stood proudly on a cake stand. About half of it was missing, a few slices had already been cut, and the rest, complete with candied pineapple rings and bright red cherries, was ready to be hacked to pieces and devoured. Crumbs littered the table, where napkins decorated with smiling Santas had been placed.

"So, how was it?" Alvarez asked as Pescoli unwrapped half her sandwich.

"Bianca was sleeping. No Chris Schultz so far, thank God for small favors. Jeremy was playing video games and wanted half of my sandwich."

"Did you give it to him?"

"Not on your life. I ate half there, brought this back. I made a grilled cheese for Bianca and showed him how he could make one for himself. He'll probably eat hers, but at least she'll tell me. I gotta do something about that kid."

Pescoli bit into the Reuben and ignored not only great-great-*great*-grannie's cake but also the Christmas decorations and the big sign that Joelle had pinned on the bulletin board. The sign was Joelle's way of reminding everyone of their Secret Santas and the party she had planned for the week before Christmas. Plenty of time to figure out what special little gift to buy the undersheriff.

Thank God the limit was ten bucks.

Still too much in Pescoli's opinion.

"DNA report come in?" she asked.

"It's at the lab. So, we'll see. Compare it to Jocelyn Wallis's. I've already told them to put a rush on it."

"And did they tell you to shove it?" Pescoli asked. "They're pretty busy."

"They'll do what they can."

"You think the doctor's a potential target?" Pescoli had trouble wrapping her mind around that. "Just because she looks like the others and claims to have been bugged doesn't connect her."

"Except for O'Halleran."

"Back to him." Pescoli chewed thoughtfully. Some serial killers were known to go after a type. Time and time again, that had proven true. Ted Bundy was a classic case in point. But it was a big leap to think that a killer was after a victim with a certain DNA profile. It was one thing for a wack job to be attracted to long hair or blue eyes or whatever, quite another for him to be looking for women with DNA patterns or common ancestors.

How would a person even go about that? Geez, it was hard enough for the department, with access to a crime lab, to get a DNA profile.

If the DNA was important, then it only made sense that the common ancestry was the key.

"Whether the victims are linked through DNA or an ancestor or whatever, I wonder if we should talk to Grayson about going public."

Alvarez tried to show no emotion at the mention of their boss. How could she? Like it or not, they worked for the guy, but something wasn't right there. "I think we should," she said now. "Talk to Grayson."

"But it's iffy," Pescoli said. So far all they really knew was that someone had been trying to poison Jocelyn Wallis. The other potential victims were an actress in Southern California and a woman whose minivan had slid off the road with a little help, probably by a hit-and-run driver. Nothing concrete to tie the crimes to one killer. Maybe they were getting ahead of themselves. They couldn't even prove that they had a serial killer in their midst, hadn't alerted the FBI.

Alvarez eyed the cake and, as if she'd read Pescoli's mind, said, "I'm checking with other departments, not just statewide. Idaho, Oregon, Washington, and California to start. See if they have any recent suspicious deaths where the victim has connections here or to Helena. I've also got a call in to Elle Alexander's parents to find out if she was really born in Idaho."

"It all sounds kind of thin, doesn't it?"

Alvarez shook her head, unwilling to be sidetracked. "If Shelly Bonaventure is part of this, then our guy moves around a lot. Could be he has a job that takes him to other parts of the country. If so, there might be a trail of victims. Individual accidents."

"And if Bonaventure, who the LAPD are still claiming offed herself, isn't one of our guy's victims?" Pescoli asked, finishing her sandwich.

Alvarez scowled. "Then we're back to square one."

At two o'clock Herbert Long's wife called to say, with a heavy dose of disgust, that her husband was going to have to cancel his appointment. Kacey, who had been unable to get Dr. Martin Cortez to take the appointment as he was already double-booked, pumped her fist in the air. She could drive to Missoula earlier than planned, and though dark clouds were gathering along the ridge of mountains surrounding the valley, the heavy snowfall had abated, just as Heather had said the forecasters had predicted.

After grabbing a bottle of water from the staff room's small refrigerator, she donned her coat and headed for her car. She had managed to choke down a tuna sandwich for lunch but had no real appetite. She'd put a call in to Trace, ostensibly to talk about Eli, and learned that he'd talked to the police about the microphones. "I think they're planning to sweep your house," he said. "Probably dust for fingerprints."

"I should remind them about Bonzi."

"They want you there, too."

"Good. I'll call them later."

She didn't tell him what she had planned, though it was on the tip of her tongue. But he would try to talk her out of it, or join in, and she really wanted to do this herself.

She'd decided to meet Gerald Johnson face-to-face, see what her newfound dad had to say for himself, and try to figure out why her mother held him in such reverent esteem.

Theirs, it seemed, at least in Maribelle's nostalgic mind, was an affair that transcended all others, a star-crossed, tragic love story that was equal to or more intense than Antony and Cleopatra, or Romeo and Juliet.

The incredibly pathos-riddled tale of Gerald and Maribelle.

"Give me a break," she muttered under her breath as she moved her all-wheel drive onto I-90. In her head she mapped out what she might say to the father who, according to Maribelle, had never known she existed.

Great.

Some of her courage seeped away as the tires of her Ford ate up the miles. She'd done her research. All Gerald's legitimate children lived within fifty miles of their parents. No offspring going to college on the East Coast and putting down roots, or marrying and taking a job in San Francisco or Birmingham or Chicago.

No, all of those who had survived still lived close to Daddy and, she suspected, the fortune he'd amassed. She chastised herself mentally for her suspicions as she reached the city limits of Missoula, but she'd done her research: Gerald Johnson was a very wealthy man.

As she'd gathered information on him, Kacey had also learned that most of his surviving children worked for him. The oldest, Clarissa, had an MBA from Stanford, and she was in charge of marketing. Married, with a couple of kids, she'd been with the company for years. After Clarissa, Gerald had sired two sons in three years, Judd and Thane. Both of them were lawyers: Judd worked for the company, and Thane consulted from his own firm. Neither was married. Then came the twins, Cameron and Colt. Kacey hadn't found out much about them, but they, too, lived in the area, and she would bet they were on the company payroll in some capacity. The last of Gerald's children had been the ill-fated Kathleen, who'd died right before her pending marriage.

There had been a few mentions of seven children, however, so Kacey had scoured deeper. When she'd looked through the archived obituaries, she'd discovered an earlier daughter, Agatha-Rae, "Aggie," who had died at the age of eight from a fall. Agatha-Rae's birthday was exactly one week before her own, so she and Kacey would have been the same age, had she lived. Inwardly, Kacey shuddered and gripped the wheel of her car a little more tightly. No wonder her mother had been vague about Gerald's children.

Snow was beginning to fall again, and she flipped on her wipers. Using her portable GPS as a guide, she made her way through Missoula, a larger city by Montana standards that lay in a valley near the river and was rimmed in snow-covered mountains. She drove past restaurants and storefronts, and an old lumber mill turned into several individual shops now, and then finally crossed a wide bridge to discover Johnson Industrial Park. Newly shoveled pathways cut through the low-lying buildings and rimmed a series of icy ponds complete with cattails and ducks. The new snowfall was already covering the cement.

Though the structures seemed identical, they looked to be built in pods, each grouping housing a different piece of Gerald Johnson's empire and connected by breezeways edging several parking lots.

Money, she thought uneasily, easing along the winding road and spying areas marked MANUFACTURING, RESEARCH AND DEVELOPMENT, TECHNOLOGY, and finally, ADMINISTRATION.

"Bingo," she whispered as she pulled into a parking spot marked for visitors and cut the engine. Giving herself one quick, final pep talk, she grabbed her briefcase.

Outside, the wind was brisk, carrying tiny, hard snowflakes that caught in her hair and seemed to cut into her cheeks. Quickly, she made her way along the aggregate walkway to the door and stepped inside to a vast reception area where yards of gray, industrial-grade carpet swept across the floor and the white walls were covered with awards and pictures.

A wide counter separated those who were visiting from the sanctum of inner offices, which was visible through an open doorway leading deeper inside.

"May I help you?" a girl in her twenties asked. With a pixie-like face and short hair that showed off multiple earrings, she was seated at a desk complete with large computer monitor and little else. Her nameplate said ROXANNE JAMISON.

"I'd like to see Gerald Johnson."

The smooth skin of her forehead wrinkled. "Do . . . you . . . have an appointment?" she asked while looking at the computer screen.

"No."

"I'm sorry. You need to have an appointment."

"Please tell him Acacia Collins Lambert is here to see him. And let him know that I'm Maribelle Collins's daughter."

The receptionist lifted her brows. "O . . . kay." She pressed a button on the sleek phone and, with more than a tinge of skepticism in her voice, relayed the message. "Yes . . . here in the lobby . . . of course, Mr. Johnson." She eyed Kacey with new respect, saying, "He'll see you now. I'll show you to his office." She climbed off her desk chair, opened up a portion of the counter that swung inward, then led Kacey down several hallways, past glass doors, and around a final corner to an office with large walnut double doors that were standing open, as if waiting.

Kacey felt an ache of dread in her heart as she followed Miss Jamison inside.

Gerald Johnson sat at his desk, his shirt sleeves rolled over tanned arms, his eyes on the doorway, his silver hair combed smoothly away from his face.

"Mr. Johnson, this is Miss Lambert," the pixie-like receptionist said.

He climbed to his feet. "Thanks, Roxie. Please, close the doors as you leave."

The receptionist did as she was bid, and Johnson, about six feet tall, still square-shouldered, his silver hair just beginning to thin, turned all his attention on the daughter he'd never met. He didn't bother smiling, just said, "Hello, Acacia. I've been expecting you."

His hands were tight on the steering wheel, his heart was pounding triple time, and sweat was dampening his shirt despite the snow he saw falling outside the window as he drove, pushing the speed limit, his Lexus flying over the road.

She knew!

That bitch understood.

She'd realized the maggot who had spawned her was Gerald Johnson, and now they were having a showdown.

He should have killed her sooner!

All of his work . . . about to be destroyed.

All of his planning, how careful he'd been, about to be exposed.

Taking several calming breaths, he told himself that this was just another small challenge, a bump in the road. He could handle this, he could.

He blinked his eyes.

But he didn't let up on the accelerator as he passed a long, nearly empty van marked ST. BARTHOLOMEW'S HOSPITAL heading the opposite way, toward Grizzly Falls.

Within minutes he was forced to slow for traffic as he guided his Lexus through the streets of Missoula.

Pull it together, he told himself as he stepped on the brakes and waited at a light for a woman on a cell phone who barely noticed the waiting traffic as she crossed to the far side, where a storefront, decorated with mannequins dressed in red and green for the season, beckoned.

Inside his driving gloves, his hands were clammy, and nervous sweat dampened his shirt though the temperature in the car read only sixty-seven degrees and outside snow was beginning to stick in earnest on the roads again.

Glancing into the rearview mirror, he saw no car hanging back, as if following him, no sinister driver hiding behind aviator shades. Nor was there anyone in a long trench coat leaning on a lamppost while observing him, no man on a park bench ostensibly reading a newspaper, while, in fact, surveying his every move.

Of course not!

That was just the stuff of movies!

He counted his heartbeats and punched the accelerator the second the light turned green.

The rest of the drive was excruciatingly slow, while his thoughts were flying through his head a mile a minute. Short, sharp bits of mental movies of those he called his siblings, of those who were now dead, and of the bitch who was currently hell-bent on destroying it all.

Forcing a calm he didn't feel, he drove the Lexus into the parking lot of his father's business and spotted her car parked near the administration building.

His stomach clenched, and he had to remind himself that all was not lost.

Yet.

CHAPTER 28

"You were expecting me?" Kacey stared at the man who, if only by the chance of genetics, was her father. Hadn't Maribelle said Gerald Johnson didn't know about her? Then again, hadn't her mother been known to lie? To keep secrets? "So you know I'm your biological daughter? I thought it was all a big secret."

"Is that what Maribelle said?" He almost seemed amused as he waved her into the large office with its oversized desk, floor-to-ceiling windows, and a sitting area complete with leather couch and matching side chairs. Through the glass wall behind him, she saw another duck pond and beyond, rising in the distance, the mountains, where the ridges seemed to scrape the graying sky. Snow had already begun to obliterate the view. All that was clearly visible was the edge of the parking lot, where she caught the noses of a Cadillac SUV, a BMW, and a Jaguar.

Not just a parking lot, she thought, *but the executive lot.*

"She told me that you didn't know that I existed," Kacey said.

"And you believed her."

"Well, yeah. Now you're telling me something else."

He waved her toward him, where two visitor's chairs were positioned on one side of his desk. Kacey removed her coat and draped it over one chair, settling cautiously in the other. On the side wall were awards, certificates, and his medical diplomas, prominently displayed.

"I assume my mother called and warned you that I intended to find you," Kacey said.

"She did."

"So all her secrets, her insistence that you be kept out of it, that was all just what? A smoke screen? Why?"

"Your mother tried to act as if the baby—you—were Stanley's. I didn't believe it, of course. She'd been trying to have a baby for years, and then, after we got . . . close, she became pregnant, so I assumed the truth." He drew a breath and exhaled it heavily. "Our affair was winding down at the time. I was going to move the company from Helena to here and . . . so," he said, leaning forward, hands clasped, forearms on the desk, "I saw no point in trying to keep what we had going. We were both married, neither wanted a divorce, and so . . . we let it die, and I allowed your mother the fantasy that I didn't know about you. It was just simpler."

"For whom?" she asked carefully.

"Everyone. Including you."

"How thoughtful," she said, hearing the anger rising in her own voice. "You don't know anything about me."

"That's where you're wrong. Of course I found out about you, but I didn't let on. Your mother and I were over, anyway, and we were both married, and at least one of us was happy."

Kacey felt her jaw tighten. Gerald Johnson had a pretty high opinion of himself.

He lifted one shoulder. "I thought it was best if I pretended I didn't think you were mine. I had a family, a wife, a company to run."

"And Mom?"

"She got what she always wanted out of the deal. A child." Gerald's gaze held hers. "It worked out."

"Did it?" Her stomach soured as she thought of all the lies that were her life. "What about my dad?" she said. "The one who raised me?"

Gerald's lips flattened a little, and some of his equanimity seeped away. "What? Are you coming to me now because he's gone? You're looking for a new father figure? Or, maybe it isn't even that altruistic. Perhaps you're looking for something else?"

"I don't know what you're getting at," she said, though she did, and it was pissing her off.

"Look around." He gestured grandly.

"Get this straight, Mr. Johnson. I don't want anything from you but the truth. People are dying, and I think you have the answer."

"Dying? Good Lord, you're as melodramatic as your mother."

"Maybe. But it doesn't alter the facts." She stood up, unable to sit in front of him like a sycophant.

Deep furrows cleft his brow. "I don't know what you're talking about."

"Let's start with Shelly Bonaventure."

"Who? The . . . actress? What about her?"

"You don't know her?"

"Of course I don't. Why would I? The only reason I know about her is that my daughter Clarissa reads those tabloids and the like."

"She was born in Helena."

"All right."

She felt herself falter inside a little. Could she be mistaken? He seemed genuinely at a loss. "Did you know Jocelyn Wallis?"

"Jocelyn who? I have no idea what you're talking about!" Then something sparked. "Wait a minute. I read something about a woman who died recently. She fell while jogging?"

"Or was pushed. I don't know the details," Kacey admitted. "Only that her death is being investigated, maybe caused by foul play."

"What does this have to do with me?"

"It's because of the resemblance. See . . ." She pulled the pictures of the two women she'd mentioned from her briefcase and slid them across the desk, faceup. "These two, and Elle Alexander, who was a patient of mine." She found Elle's photo and slid it across as well. "I guess Mom didn't mention this when she called?"

"She said that you were on some mission, but I was busy, didn't pay attention to her ramblings."

"Maybe you should have."

"I assumed she meant you were looking for me to come out and claim you."

"That's not it at all."

"I don't know these women. Never met any of them."

"I think they could be related to me."

"What? These women?" He looked down at the photos again. "Through me?" He let out a short bark of a laugh, as if he expected some dark, macabre punch line. His skin reddened. "Is this some kind of shakedown?"

But there was something he wasn't saying. She saw it in his eyes, a lie he was trying to disguise. There was more here; she just wasn't sure what.

"Are you trying to punish me?" he demanded.

"Punish you."

"For not acknowledging you like I did with Robert." He said it as if it was a cold, hard fact, one they both understood.

Kacey blinked. "Who's Robert?"

"You know."

"I don't."

They stared at each other, and he seemed to be sizing her up again before he clarified, "My son? Robert Lindley? That's what this is really about, right?"

A chill, as cold as the bottom of the sea, settled at the base of her spine. What the devil was he talking about?

When she didn't respond, he prodded, "Janet's boy."

"I'm sorry. Who's Janet?"

His lips twisted a bit. "You didn't do all of your homework, did you? Robert's a few years older than you, and I . . . claimed him, once Janet and her husband split up."

How had she missed this?

"He works for the company, too, like the others. He's in research and development. Great technical mind."

So there was another half sibling in the mix. Her life as an only child seemed suddenly distant.

"When your mother called, I thought you wanted in, to be a part of the family, get whatever it is you think is your fair share of the company."

Kacey snapped back. "Trust me, I'm not here about your company. I'm here for these women," she said, motioning toward the pictures on his desk. "What you're telling me is that you're not their father. You're not related to any of them."

"That's exactly what I'm saying," he responded emphatically, but a guarded look had slipped across his face, a trace of quickly hidden deceit. Though he stared at her as if she'd gone stark raving mad, there was something more, something darker in his gaze. "I don't know what you think you know."

Though he readily claimed a son and now her as his children, he wouldn't associate himself with the women who'd been killed. As if he didn't believe he was related to them.

Had she been mistaken? He didn't have any brothers; she'd checked. And his only other sibling had been a sister who had died in her twenties, so if not him . . . then . . . ?

She glanced to the medical diplomas on his wall, noticed that he'd graduated forty years earlier.

And then, like a ton of bricks, it hit her, the elusive notion that had been nagging at her since last night's nightmare: he didn't know about these women, because he didn't realize he might have fathered them.

What had JC, her husband, bragged about to her years before?

"I should have been a sperm donor, like those other med students. I could have made a fortune. Women are looking for men like me. I could still do it. I've got the pedigree, the intellect, the IQ . . . and athleticism and looks to boot."

Kacey heard his voice in her head as if he were speaking to her now. And Gerald Johnson, nearing seventy, was a strong, strapping man. . . .

"I'm not related to these women," he insisted, but she could hear the faintest trace of uncertainty in his voice.

"You weren't a sperm donor around thirty-five or forty years ago, maybe when you were in medical school?"

"That's ridiculous! Just because these women slightly resemble each other—"

"Not just slightly," she interrupted. "And not just each other. This one"—with one finger she pushed the picture of Jocelyn Wallis closer to him—"looks enough like me that when she was brought into the ER, several of my associates thought something had happened to *me*. Look at them!" She slid the other pictures closer to him. "I've seen pictures of your family. There is an incredible, uncanny resemblance."

A muscle worked in his jaw as he stared at one picture, then the next. He even went so far as to pull a pair of reading glasses from his pocket to study the images. Finally, as if disgusted, he tossed the glasses onto his desk. His lips were pulled into a serious knot. "So why are you here, Acacia? To confirm that I could have fathered these women because of something I did in my youth?"

"So, you *were* a sperm donor."

"You are fabricating some kind of conspiracy theory that someone is killing people—women—who resemble each other and who might have been conceived through artificial insemination? And you're looking at me as the sperm donor?" He was incredulous.

"Someone tried to kill me," Kacey said. "A long time ago. Not rape me. Not rob me, but kill me. I thought it was a random act until just recently," she admitted. "Now, I'm not so sure. Just yesterday I found out my house is bugged. With listening devices and who knows what else? Meanwhile, women who look like me are having accidents. Deadly accidents that, at second look, aren't really accidents at all. Both Shelly Bonaventure and Jocelyn Wallis have connections to Helena. I figure that if I go there, I'll find a fertility clinic where they were all conceived, and probably there are records for Elle as well. She was just born somewhere else." She leaned across the desk. "How many more will I find, Gerald? Five? Ten? A hundred? Five—"

"This is crazy," he snapped. The color in his face rose and turned his cheeks livid red. "There's no serial killer who's intent on killing children conceived at a certain clinic!"

"Only those fathered by you," she said with renewed certainty.

"That's even crazier."

She didn't have an answer for him, but she was convinced she was on the right track. Yet she had to hear it from him. "What's the name of this clinic?" she asked. "I'm going to find out, one way or another. You may as well just save me some time, before whoever is behind this kills me."

"You weren't conceived by artificial insemination. Trust me on this."

"Doesn't make me safe. When I compare my DNA to any of these women," she said, fanning her hand over the pictures, "I'm going to bet that the test results will prove we're related on the paternal side and—"

"Enough!" It was his turn to stand. At nearly six-one, he had half a foot on her, allowing him to look down his strong, straight nose into her eyes. "I was a sperm donor in my youth. Yes. But I have no proof that any of these victims were my progeny. I think your theory is out-landish. More than that, it's slanderous. I met you today because I thought it was high time I acknowledged you, but I clearly was mis-taken."

"Don't you even care to find out about these women?"

"No. I do not. Now, if you're done with your mad accusations, I have work to do. Important work. Not only does this plant employ a lot of people in the area, but our products, many of which I devel-oped myself, save lives."

"And you could save a few more if you helped me locate other women whom you might have fathered."

He was already reaching for the phone. "I think we're done here."

"I'm going to the police."

The back of his neck tightened, but he controlled himself. "They'll laugh you out of the room. You'd better be careful what you say, Acacia, or you may find yourself institutionalized." His smile was cold. "There is a history of mental illness in the family."

A sharp rap was followed by one of the double doors being pushed open by a tall woman, made even taller by her three-inch heels. With high cheekbones, and a nose reminiscent of the man seated across the desk, she swept inside as if she owned the place. "Sorry to interrupt you, Dad, but we had an appointment. Oh! I didn't know you had someone in here. Roxie's left for the day." She rained a smile on Kacey.

Gerald stood. "You're not interrupting anything, Clarrie. In fact, it's probably a good thing you showed up. I'd like you to meet your sister. Clarissa, this is Acacia. Acacia, my daughter Clarissa."

What the hell had he gotten himself into? Trace wondered as he once again checked on Eli, who was curled on the couch, sleeping, Sarge next to him, the huge cone still in place around the dog's head.

Trace had left the police station knowing that the two cops—Pescoli and Alvarez—had been disappointed that they couldn't nail him for Jocelyn's death and Leanna's disappearance. But that was not what was worrying him now.

No, it was Kacey and how she was involved in this mess.

Obviously, she wasn't safe in her own home, dog or no dog, no matter if she did have her grandfather's shotgun. Someone had gotten inside, planted microphones, and listened in. . . . Why? And what, if anything, did it have to do with the other women's deaths?

It just smelled bad.

"So, what about some mac and cheese?" he asked his son. Eli was supposed to drink tons of fluids, but the untouched soda, Gatorade, apple juice, and vitaminwater bottles on the table near the couch were testament to the fact that it still hurt his throat to swallow.

"Not hungry."

"Well, you've got to eat, and you've got to drink, a lot." Trace cracked open the bottle of reddish vitaminwater and held it in front of his boy's nose. "Remember you promised the nurse when you left the hospital. I just don't want to see you have to go back."

"No way!" Eli said with a frown. His voice was hoarse and he still coughed, but he got the message and took the bottle from his father's hands, managing a couple sips from the bottle.

There was homework piling up, compliments of e-mail from Eli's teacher, but Trace figured he'd fight that battle later. First, he wanted his boy healthy. Last night had been scary for all of them.

Now that he had his son home, his mind was working overtime with worries for Kacey, a woman he barely knew but was already fantasizing about.

Eli picked at the macaroni and cheese, drank part of his juice and Gatorade, and generally vegged out in front of the television, which was tuned to his favorite kids' channel. He slept a lot, but each time Trace took his temperature, it had gone down a little bit more and now was hovering near one hundred degrees.

Now, if there were just some way to make sure Kacey was safe, he'd feel a whole lot better. He tried her cell phone, but it went straight to voice mail, so he hung up without leaving a message.

Relax, he told himself. *She's at work.*

He just couldn't quite shake his misgivings. He didn't know what to believe, but the hidden microphones were real. There was no escaping that.

All the wind had been stripped from Clarissa's sails. She stared first at her father, then let her gaze move to Kacey.

"Are you serious?" she demanded, her eyes narrowing a bit.

"What do you think?" For some reason Gerald seemed a little amused, as if he liked pulling one over on his firstborn.

"Dad, really . . ."

"She's Maribelle's daughter." Gerald stated the fact as if his affair with Kacey's mother were a known fact.

"The nurse who worked for you? I remember her. . . ." This time when Clarissa rained her gaze on Kacey, it was more than a passing, dismissive glance. As if she were mentally ticking off the genetic similarities, her expression slowly changed from shock and confusion to revulsion.

"Oh, God, Dad, tell me this is some kind of sick, twisted joke," she said, crossing the expanse of carpet to her father's desk, keeping her gaze focused on Kacey.

"No joke. Acacia's my daughter. As much as you are."

"But . . . no . . . Jesus, does Mom know?"

"Suspects, I'd guess."

"You don't *know?*"

"It was never discussed."

"For the love of God. First Robert and now . . . now you?" Turning, she faced Kacey. "What're you doing here?"

"Looking for answers," Kacey said and added, "Nice to meet you."

Clarissa's eyebrows shot upward. "Excuse me if I forgot my manners. I've kinda had a shock here." To her father, "What's the matter with you? How many more of these are there?"

Gerald inhaled through his teeth.

"Oh, no . . ." Clarissa's gaze fell to the desk, to the pictures that were still lying faceup on the polished mahogany. Her eyebrows slammed together as she picked up the head shot of Shelly Bonaventure. "Isn't this that actress from that vampire series that ran a few years ago? The one Lance was so into?"

"What's Blood Got to Do with It," Kacey verified as Gerald quickly swept up the rest of the pictures. But he was too late. The damage was done.

"And one was of that woman who fell while jogging," Clarissa said, her face drawn. "Who was the third one, Dad?"

"Elle Alexander, a patient of mine," Kacey responded. "Had two kids."

"These women all died recently, didn't they?" Her blue eyes clouded. "What's going on here?" she asked her father, then once again turned to Kacey. "And why are you here?"

Gerald let out a long, low sigh. "We should probably have a family meeting." He was pale, and for the first time since she'd walked into his office, Kacey thought Gerald Johnson appeared his age, the crow's-feet near his eyes deepening, the knuckles of his hands looking larger.

All an illusion, she reminded herself.

"Judd's here today," he was saying. "And Robert, right?"

"I'm not sure," Clarissa demurred. "I just got back from meeting with the accountants, but Robert was in the lab this morning. . . . Both Cameron and Colt are out. Cam was in Spokane, in a meeting with a distributor there, and Colt . . ." She glanced at her watch. "He should have landed by now. He was in Seattle earlier, talking to the head of cardiology at the medical school."

Kacey's heart nearly stopped when she thought of the city where she'd been attacked and the hospital where she'd learned her practice, the place where JC held a position in the cardiology department. How ironic that the man who had spawned her had been a heart surgeon as well.

Just a coincidence, right? Seattle was a big city.

Still, a ripple of unease swept through her.

Clarissa never missed a beat. "As for Thane, who knows?" She glanced out the window and added, "Who ever knows?"

"Tell everyone you can to meet in the boardroom. Leave a message for Colt on his cell, tell him to get here when he lands, and see if Cam can link up through Skype."

"And Thane?"

"Call him, too. See if he can make it or Skype in."

"Thane doesn't Skype," Clarissa reminded, and Kacey had the distinct impression that this brother, third in the birth order and the second-born legitimate son, didn't play by the old man's rules. The rogue or black sheep. Except he hadn't strayed too far away from the old man's company. "What about Mom?"

"Let's keep her out of this for now." Gerald thought for a second, then said, "Let me handle her my way."

"Good idea," Clarissa said sarcastically. "It's always worked *so* well before. If Lance ever did to me what you've done to Mom, I wouldn't be satisfied by publicly humiliating him on *Jerry Springer* or *Montel* or some other let-all-your-dirty-laundry-hang-out TV show. I'd have to eviscerate him. Maybe with a butter knife."

"Compassion has never been your strong suit," her father said dryly.

Clarissa lifted a shoulder. "It's just how I feel, and since someone stole my gun this week, I guess I'll have to stick with disemboweling. Would a spoon be better?"

"Stop it," her father warned.

"I'm just saying I don't let anyone walk all over me, and neither do you. If Mom would have cheated on you or had a gaggle of bastards, you would never have stood for it."

"Your mother would never!"

"You're right. She wouldn't. *She's* at least got a modicum of class." To Kacey, Clarissa added, "Congratulations. It takes a lot to stir up this particular hornet's nest, and it looks like you've done that and more." She marched out of the room as fiercely as a mother bear whose cubs had just been threatened.

Gerald gave a last cursory glance at the photographs of the dead women. "Clarissa's right, you know. I'm afraid you've started something you're going to regret."

Kacey wasn't going to let anyone deter her, not when she'd come this far. "I'm not afraid at all." But that was a lie, and they both knew it.

CHAPTER 29

Gerald Johnson and Clarissa seemed to half forget Kacey was there as they began planning the family meeting. "Excuse me," Kacey said, sweeping up her coat.

"The boardroom is straight down the north hall. We're convening *now*," Clarissa warned her.

"I'm not leaving," Kacey said. *Yet.* "I just need to make a phone call."

They both gave her a hard look as she left the room. And she thought she was paranoid. Maybe she came by it naturally!

She walked in the direction of the boardroom, tried the doors, realized they were locked, so she punched in the number for the sheriff's department, which she'd added onto her cell phone list.

"Detective Alvarez, please," she said when the call was answered by the front desk. "I'm Dr. Lambert, returning an earlier call."

She was put through immediately, and Detective Alvarez answered, "Alvarez."

"This is Kacey Lambert. I know you've talked to Trace O'Halleran, who found the microphones."

"Yes. We would like to come and see for ourselves. This afternoon?"

"Late afternoon?" Kacey asked. "I'm at an out-of-town appointment that may take a little more time. But I would really like to have those microphones out."

"Call us when you're on your way home."

"Thank you," she said, meaning it.

Next, she phoned Trace, who answered as if he'd had his ear to the phone.

"Kacey," he said, and just the way he said her name flooded her with good feelings.

"Hey, there. I'm meeting the police at my house later today, and they're going to take out the microphones, I guess. Look at them, anyway. I want them out."

"Good. Are you at work?"

"I'm not at the clinic. I'm at an appointment," she said, not wanting to go into the whole thing with him just yet. She didn't know how she felt about anything to do with the Johnsons. "I told the police I'd call them when I was on my way home."

"Call me, too."

"You got it."

"Kacey . . ."

"Yeah?"

"Be careful," he said, clearly reading more between the lines than she'd thought she'd revealed.

"I'll see you this evening," she said, then put back her phone in its slot inside her purse and watched with a certain amount of trepidation as Gerald and Clarissa came out of his office and strode down the hall toward her.

"Go check on your kids," Alvarez told Pescoli. "There's nothing happening here till we meet at Dr. Lambert's."

"I'm going home to shoo Chris out of the house, if he's there, but I'll be right back."

Alvarez waved her off. They were in a waiting game. Waiting for the lab results. Waiting for someone to call back. Waiting, waiting, waiting.

She sat down at her desk, and her gaze flew over the notes she'd made, bits and pieces of information burned on her brain that needed some kind of connection. The missing link that would make sense of it all. Flipping through the pages of thoughts, ideas, and doodles, and then the files filled with reports, she decided there was nothing to do but what she'd already done: make phone calls. Push. Hope somebody somewhere was willing to exchange information.

She saw the number for Elle Alexander's parents in Boise. She'd called it twice already and left messages, but no one had phoned back. They were grieving. She understood. Maybe they felt the authorities speaking with Elle's husband, Tom, should have sufficed. Lots of people abhorred police intruding in their affairs, even when it was a necessary evil.

Placing the call, she readied herself for what she was going to say. After a number of rings, she knew she was facing voice mail again; then there was a click, and a woman's voice said cautiously, "Hello?"

"Mrs. Morris?" Alvarez said, glancing down at her notes. Elle's parents were Brenda and Keane Morris, both retired. He was a pilot, and she was a grade school teacher.

"I can tell you're calling from Montana. You've called before. Caller ID says you're with the Pinewood Sheriff's Department. This is about Elle, isn't it?"

"Yes, ma'am. We are investigating your daughter's death."

"You don't think it was just a terrible accident?" Her voice grew very small.

"We don't know. We just want to be sure."

She started crying softly, and Alvarez's heart went out to her. This was the hardest part of the job.

"Can I ask you a few questions?"

"Go ahead," she said, inhaling shakily.

"We interviewed your son-in-law, Tom Alexander. Elle was on the phone to him when the accident occurred."

"Tom loves Elle. He's heartbroken. We all are."

"Tom said your daughter thought another vehicle was driving dangerously. Did he tell you that?" Alvarez asked.

"He said Elle thought the driver was trying to kill her. I don't know. Sometimes, when you're driving, you kind of think those things, you know?"

"Yes."

"He rear-ended her. Tom said she said that. And his lights were really bright. But then, Tom said she must have dropped the phone. . . . He called nine-one-one. She told him to."

"Did your daughter have any enemies that you might know of?"

"Oh, no. Not Elle. Everyone loved Elle. Her best friend from high school, Jayne Drummond, still lives around here, and she stopped by and we talked about how much everyone loved her." Elle's mother's voice was growing thick with tears again. "You can talk to her, if you'd like."

"You have a son, too."

"Bruce. He's married. Lives in Florida. I can give you his number, too."

"Thank you."

Alvarez wrote down the phone numbers for Jayne Drummond and Bruce Morris as Brenda read them to her. The next questions she wanted to ask were going to sound strange, and she wasn't quite sure how to approach her with them. "Mrs. Morris, we're investigating a death in Grizzly Falls of another young woman. She either fell or was pushed over a railing."

"I'm very sorry for her family," Brenda said sincerely.

"We would like to help them get closure, as well," Alvarez said, pushing on. "The woman, Jocelyn Wallis, bore a remarkable resemblance to your daughter. Enough that someone asked if they were related." A little white lie, but close enough to the truth that Alvarez felt no compunction in using it. "Although I suspect this is just the kind of odd coincidence that crops up from time to time, I wanted to ask about the possibility that they were related somehow. Maybe knew each other?"

It was a total stretch, and Alvarez could hear the embarrassed tone of her own voice. Still, those pictures Trace O'Halleran had discussed with them had offered up more questions than answers. If she could connect any two of the look-alikes, maybe the rest would follow.

"No . . ."

"Elle was born in Boise?"

"Yes."

"Does she have any connection to Helena?"

A sharp intake of breath. "No . . ."

Alvarez's pulse jumped. Something here. "I'm sorry, but it sounds like you are thinking of something?"

"It's not . . . I don't . . . I don't understand how it could."

"Could you tell me what you mean?"

"Oh, dear. My husband . . . oh, dear." She sighed. "We learned that my husband could not father any children of his own, so we went to a clinic in Helena. It's no longer there. But it was then, and we went there . . . to find a donor."

"A sperm donor," Alvarez clarified carefully.

"Yes. Yes. Both of my children were fathered by the same donor."

"Elle and Bruce."

"We never told anyone. Bruce still doesn't know, and Elle didn't know. I know I should tell my son, but it never seemed like the right time and now Elle's gone. . . ."

"This clinic. What was it called?"

"I don't know. We always referred to it as the clinic. I can't see that this matters."

"It probably doesn't. I just want to be sure. Can you tell me anything more about it?"

She exhaled and then inhaled and exhaled once more before saying, "This is . . . I don't know. Information you don't need, I suppose, but all I know is the donor's number, seven-twenty-seven. My husband and I always remembered because he was a pilot and that was the type of jet he flew when he worked for the airlines. We always thought it was lucky."

"How did you pick the donor?"

"He was a medical student with dark hair and blue eyes. He was the same height as Keane, and he was athletic. We wanted our children to resemble us both." Her tone said: "Is that so much to ask?"

"I understand."

"This other woman . . . the one who fell?"

Alvarez didn't want to start answering questions since she didn't know where they would lead. Needing to cut her off quickly, she said, "I don't have all the background on Miss Wallis, but I know she was a teacher in Grizzly Falls and very well liked."

"Like Elle." She sighed. "I was a teacher, too. It's all so hard, isn't it?"

"Yes, ma'am. It is." Alvarez meant it, and the older woman heard her unspoken sympathy.

"If Elle was killed . . . if that's true, you'll find them and let me know?"

"Yes. I will," Alvarez promised.

"Thank you," she said.

Alvarez sat perfectly still for several moments after Brenda Morris hung up.

A sperm donor.

Could it be?

Were these women truly related? It was the theory that had been circling around that no one wanted to really believe. Could Elle Alexander and Shelly Bonaventure and Jocelyn Wallis and Leanna O'Halleran and maybe Kacey Lambert, and God knew how many others, actually be *related?* Have the same father? *That* was the connection?

As fast as she could, she grabbed up her cell phone and punched the button for Pescoli, who answered on the fifth ring, sounding pissed.

"Yeah?"

"I've got something."

"Uh-huh."

"No, I've really got something," Alvarez told her. "Can you get back to the station?"

"I have a lot of screaming left to do here," she said abruptly. "A lot of screaming," she yelled loudly to someone or someones on her end.

"Make it quick screaming," Alvarez told her, then clicked off, her mind already spinning ahead.

Could all these women—these victims—have been conceived at the same fertility clinic? Could their mothers have all used the same sperm donor? Donor 727?

But what did that mean? Even if it was true, what did that mean? Why were they dying? Why were they *being killed?*

If . . .

If they were being killed.

But that's what you're thinking, isn't it? There's something here. You know there's something here. Whether Pescoli believes you or not.

She grabbed up her phone and called the lab, annoyed when she was given the runaround. Hanging up with them, she called Ashley Tang direct and said, "I need some DNA results yesterday. Isn't there someone at the lab you can lean on?"

The forensic investigator answered, "They're getting to it. You know how it is."

"I don't care how it is! I need answers."

"Well, I've got one for you. Not DNA, but an explanation of sorts."

"Hit me."

"The poison found in Jocelyn Wallis's system? We believe it was administered in the coffee grounds."

"Put there on purpose? It wasn't something picked up by mistake, somehow."

"Most likely it was deliberate."

"Was it meant to kill her?"

"Doesn't look like it. The dosage was too small at this point, but then, there might be a lot more left in the coffee. We haven't tested it yet."

Alvarez jumped ahead to Kacey Lambert. The microphones. Maybe Jocelyn had been bugged, too? But the killer removed them before her place was examined?

"I'm going to check some other coffee, too," Alvarez said. "Thanks. I'll get it to you."

This time when she hung up, she could feel her pulse racing and her breathing was rapid. Was Dr. Lambert in a killer's sights?

It sure felt that way.

"Pescoli. Get back here!" she said aloud.

"You always overreact," Jeremy declared, glaring at her from the couch. He held up his phone. "It's just a picture. There's nothing wrong with it!"

"If Heidi's dad saw it, I don't think he'd agree," Pescoli responded.

"You showed it to him!"

"How could I show it to him? It's on your phone. But he knows about it. Pay attention here. Sending pictures like that over the Internet is not a good idea."

"There's nothing illegal about it. Nothing!"

"You're putting words in my mouth. I said it's not a good idea. Period."

"It's just on my phone. Mine. Which you looked at without asking. That's an invasion of privacy!"

"Invasion of privacy?" Pescoli swept an arm to angrily encompass the mess surrounding her, the detritus from Jeremy's video gaming: empty soda cups, a plate with the remnants of his cheese sandwich, or maybe Bianca's—that had yet to be determined—several pairs of his shoes scattered haphazardly over the floor. "Everything you do is an invasion of privacy these days."

"Fine. I'll leave." He stomped across the living room and headed down to his bedroom.

"Praise God. He listens."

"Mom . . . ?" Bianca's voice warbled from down the hall. Pescoli walked briskly down the hall and peeked into her daughter's room, where Bianca lay on the bed, big eyes wide and a little teary. "Why can't Chris come over?"

"When I'm here. He can come over when I'm here."

"I want him here now. He brings me water."

"I'll get you a glass of water. Did you eat any of your cheese sandwich?"

"What cheese sandwich?"

"Jeremy!" Pescoli yelled, stomping out of Bianca's room and turning to the stairs that led down to his bedroom.

"I asked her! She said she didn't want it!" he yelled back up at her.

Pescoli returned to Bianca's room. She looked at her daughter, buried in the blankets on her bed. "Is there something that sounds good?" she asked her.

"Soup."

"Campbell's okay?"

"Chicken noodle."

As she headed toward the kitchen to whip up this culinary delight, she heard softly, "Thanks, Mom," and she exhaled a long breath and almost smiled, remembering why she'd had children in the first place.

Thirty minutes later she was back at the station, and Alvarez was just hanging up the phone as she entered the squad room. "What have you got?" Pescoli asked, and her partner told her about the sperm donor theory from top to bottom.

When she finished, Alvarez said, "Well?" and Pescoli nodded, processing.

"Wow," she said. "What does it mean?"

"I'm working that out. But that's the connection. The common denominator."

"If—"

"Pescoli." Cort Brewster's voice barked her name as if it tasted bad.

"Brewster," she responded neutrally, turning her eyes his way.

"Come into my office." Then, as an afterthought, "Please."

"Well, shit," she muttered under her breath as she followed after the undersheriff.

Brewster didn't bother to sit at his desk. He stood behind it and Pescoli did likewise, preferring to stand herself.

"I talked to Heidi. She says there are no pictures."

"Ahh . . ."

"I think she might not be telling the truth," he admitted. Pescoli lifted her brows. This was a surprise. "It's no secret I don't like your son seeing my daughter. He's a dog in heat, and if I could, I'd bust his ass."

"You tried that once before," Pescoli reminded.

"I don't need an unemployed loser hanging around, and neither does Heidi. He's a bad influence on her. You and I don't always see eye to eye, but we have to work together. I'm doing my best to keep things professional. I expect the same from you." He paused, and when Pescoli didn't respond, he added, "That's all."

She turned on her heel and marched out of the room, annoyed, frustrated, and a little overwhelmed. Not that she'd let Cort Brewster see that. Bastard.

She suddenly ached for Joe. Man, it would be good if he were around. Theirs hadn't been a perfect marriage; she could admit it had already been fraying when he was killed in the line of duty. But, oh, she could use his level head now in dealing with their son.

And then she thought about Santana. The man she loved. Maybe she should move in with him. What was she waiting for? Her kids to accept him? Ha. That'd be a cold day in hell.

Shaking off her confrontation with Brewster, Pescoli returned to Alvarez's desk. "Should I call Jocelyn Wallis's parents and ask them if Dad was a sperm donor?"

"I already left a message," Alvarez admitted. "Told them to call. But I think it's time we take this to Grayson."

Pescoli heard something in Alvarez's tone that she probably wouldn't have wanted to be heard. "What's with you and the sheriff?"

"Not a damn thing," she responded with uncharacteristic punch.

Grayson was just leaving his office, but upon seeing Alvarez and Pescoli heading straight his way, he stepped back inside and asked, "What?"

"We think the deaths of Elle Alexander and Jocelyn Wallis are connected," Alvarez said. "And there may be a number of others."

"Should I sit down?"

"I would advise yes," Pescoli said dryly.

Twenty minutes later Alvarez had recapped where they were so far, finishing with, "We have a lot of questions, and we're following up with the relatives of the victims. One thing. Those victims are all women. Brenda Morris, Elle Alexander's mother, said both of her children were from Donor Seven-twenty-seven. Her son, Bruce, is in Florida and presumably alive and well. Is he on the list? Or is it only women?"

"The list . . . ," Grayson said wearily. "That implies there's more."

"Maybe a lot more," Alvarez admitted.

"Every damned Christmas," Pescoli said. "The season for homicidal nut jobs."

Grayson's gaze met Alvarez's, and Pescoli looked from one to the other. Sturgis, Grayson's dog, crawled from beneath the sheriff's desk and stretched and yawned.

"Damn it all," Grayson said. "Get me some more information. If we've got another serial killer on the loose, I'm going to have to call the FBI."

"We're meeting one of the look-alikes later today." Alvarez looked out the window.

"You think she's on 'the list'?" Grayson asked.

Alvarez looked at Pescoli, and Pescoli looked back at her.

"Yeah," Alvarez said. "I do."

CHAPTER 30

The boardroom was decorated no differently than the rest of the building. A sea of the same industrial-grade carpet was crowned by a long glass-topped table that was surrounded by ten black leather chairs. On one wall was a slim, low cabinet, above which a bronze sculpture of flying geese had been hung. Two other interior walls were of glass, with shades, pulled down, while the only exterior wall was all windows with another commanding view of the surrounding mountains. This part of the building projected over the sloping earth, so that those inside the boardroom had the feeling that they were on the second level, as the ground below fell away dramatically and leveled off at another pond, where snow was gathering on the frozen surface.

If the muted colors and dramatic view were offered to inspire calm or peace, that aura was shattered as Gerald Johnson's offspring entered and joined Kacey, Clarissa, and their father around the table. A few glances were cast in Kacey's direction, and though some were curious, none seemed surprised.

No doubt Clarissa had warned them all. She sat in a chair directly to her father's right, like the apostle John in da Vinci's *The Last Supper*. She opened her computer case and pulled out her laptop, just as if this were a regular business meeting and she were about to take notes or share information she'd gathered.

She glanced at Kacey, seated across the table from her, and there was more than a glint of displeasure in her gaze. Well, yeah. She was the epitome of the bitchy, take-charge firstborn, and a few moments with Kacey carlier weren't going to change any of that. Clarissa's short hair wasn't just near black; it was streaked with an underlying tone somewhere between bloodred and purple, a little more hip than her choice of black suit and knee-length skirt.

Before a word was exchanged, two men stepped into the room, one before the other: the twins, who'd been out of the office, had arrived. They were dressed in slacks, dress shirts, and sports coats. The first, hair unkempt and sporting a five o'clock shadow across his boxy jaw, came up and offered Kacey a warm smile. His nose wasn't quite straight, as if it had been broken at least once, possibly twice. "Colt Johnson," he said, as if he were getting ready to go into a sales pitch. "I hear you're our long-lost sister."

"Not exactly," Clarissa said, but he ignored her.

With his trademark blue eyes and slightly wavy hair, he looked a lot like the old man, just a little more refined; the sharper features he'd received from his mother. "Don't let Clarrie get to you," he warned, and she let out a snort of disgust as he grinned, showing off the hint of a dimple.

"I'm Kacey Lambert." She shook his hand.

Colt lifted a thick eyebrow. "Well, Kacey, you've found yourself one helluva family."

"Have I?"

"Oh, yeah." Colt took a seat next to Kacey as the second twin, right on the heels of the first, introduced himself to her as Cameron. Though he looked exactly like Colt, he'd just shaved and his hair was neatly in place.

"Just for the record, I'm the smarter twin," he said, and his brother barked out a laugh.

Clarissa's jaw tightened. "This isn't really funny."

"Sure it is," Colt said. "It's a goddamned sideshow. Welcome to the Johnson family circus."

Cameron half smiled and nodded.

Clarissa's mouth thinned.

"Having fun yet?" Cameron asked, but not just to Kacey; his remark seemed to be directed at everyone.

Gerald shook his head. "Just take a seat," he suggested. Cameron slid into a chair one seat away from Clarissa and directly across from Colt, just as the fourth sibling arrived.

Judd.

She recognized him from the pictures she'd seen.

He was the tallest so far, his shoulders broader than either of the twins'. While they were built like baseball players, he had the physique of a star quarterback. His hair was neat, so black as to be blue; his face clean-shaven. He wore a black business suit, crisp white shirt, and looked every bit the corporate lawyer, though she did note his tie was loosened slightly. When he looked at her, there was a restlessness to his gaze, an edge, and his eyes were a startling shade of blue.

Gerald said, "Judd, this is—"

"Acacia. I know." He shook her hand. Much more serious than either of the twins, he said quietly, "I guess I'm supposed to welcome you to the family, but I'm not really sure that's such a good idea."

"Yeah?"

One side of his mouth lifted laconically. "You'll see," he said, taking a seat to his father's left.

Gerald checked his watch and looked at his daughter. "Did anyone get the word to Robert?" he asked, but before Clarissa could answer, the door opened again, and a man Kacey didn't recognize rushed inside.

Obviously the missing Robert Lindley.

Gerald made a quick introduction. "Robert, this is Acacia Lambert. She's your half sister."

"I heard." Robert nodded at her before sliding into a seat next to Clarissa, and though he did resemble his half siblings, there wasn't a hint of the refinement to his features that was evident in most of Noreen Johnson's children. Robert's forehead was larger, more pronounced, his hairline receding slightly, though there wasn't any gray in the coffee brown of his hair. His eyes were blue, too, that family brand evident, but his nose was a little broader than those of his half brothers, his eyebrows thicker and more pronounced, his skin a little paler. His physique was more like Judd's than the twins'. He was tall and thick muscled, as if he worked out whenever possible.

"Where's Thane?" Gerald asked, clearly anxious to get the meeting under way.

"Your guess is as good as mine. I left a message on his cell," Robert said.

"He was here," Judd said. "I saw him less than ten minutes ago, locking his car in the lot."

"He'll show up when he shows up." Clarissa was obviously fed up with her younger brother's antics. "Let's get down to it. As you know, Acacia Lambert"—she motioned to Kacey—"is our half sister. Her mother is Maribelle Collins, and until recently, she claims she didn't realize our father was the same as hers."

"I think I should handle this, Clarissa," Gerald interrupted. To the group at large, he explained about his affair with Kacey's mother, revealing that he knew about Kacey and applauded her decision to become a doctor, even admitting to knowing her ex-husband, the noted heart surgeon J.C. Lambert. All of the information made Kacey squirm inside, especially the surprise about her ex, but she forced an impassive expression, though everyone around her was growing more and more tense. Gerald apologized to his children and swore he would make it right with their mother, though he didn't obviously include Janet Lindley, Robert's mother, in the mix of baring his soul and offering up his regrets.

It was odd listening to him, and Kacey wondered how much was heartfelt, how much was an act. All of them appeared to be reining in their emotions, Kacey included, showing only a passive expression while her insides were roiling with anger for a man she'd never known existed until a few days earlier.

"And Acacia didn't just come here to let me know that she'd found me, and you as her siblings. She's got another concern." His face tightened as he withdrew the pictures of the dead women from his pocket and slid them onto the table. "These women all look alike. In fact they look quite a bit like Acacia, and some of their facial characteristics are similar to yours as well.

"Acacia believes these women, too, might be your half siblings and intends to prove it. I want you all to know, this could be technically true, though there were no other affairs during my marriage to your mother. Yes, I had girlfriends before I married, but because of the ages of these women, it's likely, if I'm proven to be their father, that it's the result of my donation to a local sperm bank."

His children, already primed by Clarissa, showed very little shock at his statement, and when he explained further, none seemed to care at all. It was only when he brought up the fact that Shelly

Bonaventure, Jocelyn Wallis, and Elle Alexander might have been murdered that their backs straightened, their eyebrows lifted, their jaws tightened.

Kacey took stock of all the changes in expression but found none that indicated they were privy to the information prior to today.

Clarissa suddenly held up a manicured hand as if she were stopping traffic. "Does she . . . do you," she corrected, focusing those blue eyes across the table, her gaze boring into Kacey's, "do you have some kind of weird theory about this? That some bastard, some killer, as yet unknown, is taking out a bunch of turkey-baster kids? Maybe my dad's turkey-baster kids?"

"Clarissa!" Gerald said through his teeth.

Before Kacey could respond, the door to the room was pushed open and Thane, the missing son, strode in. He was built like Judd, just not quite as tall, and judging by his body language, he seemed a little less somber. "Sorry I'm late," he said as if he didn't mean it, then slid into a chair at the opposite end of the table to his father. Spying Kacey, he said, "You must be Acacia."

"I go by Kacey."

"Kacey, then."

Clarissa said, "She's Maribelle Collins's daughter with Dad."

Thane lifted a shoulder. "You said so on your message."

"Well, there's more." Clarissa pinned Kacey under her sharp gaze again. "She's got some screwball theory that Dad, who, it turns out, was a sperm donor in med school, has a bunch of 'kids'"—she made air quotes with those long, red-tipped fingers—"and they're being knocked off in some diabolical scheme. Why she, Acacia, felt compelled to bring this to us is the big mystery and why we're all here."

"Is that so?" Thane said, an amused twist to his thin lips. Dressed in jeans and a sweater, his hair still wet from melting snow, he didn't bother hiding the fact that he found the situation either ludicrous, funny, or a bit of both.

"Essentially, yes," Kacey said. "The pictures on the table are of women I think were fathered by Gerald. They're all recently dead, probably murdered."

"I know this one!" Thane suddenly said, pointing out Shelly Bonaventure. "I saw her in a film years ago."

"You and one other person," Clarissa snarked.

Thane frowned. "I thought she committed suicide."

"That's the official version," Kacey said.

"So is the official version untrue?" Judd asked. "Is that what the police are saying?"

"Not the L.A. police, but the local sheriff's department, and these women"—she indicated the pictures of Elle Alexander and Jocelyn Wallis—"are from around here. Jocelyn and Shelly were born in Helena, and I'm double-checking about Elle."

"Just because people resemble each other doesn't mean they're related," Cam said.

"Have the police connected the deaths? Are they considered homicides?" Judd wanted to know.

Robert agreed. "I doubt it. If the police had put this all together the way she has, then they would be here instead of her." His eyes never left Kacey's face, and she felt it, the hatred burning there. Somehow she'd stepped her foot into waters he'd claimed as his, and Robert Lindley didn't like it.

Nor did anyone, it seemed.

The discussion heated up, with every one of Gerald's kids expressing skepticism about Kacey and her theory. They were, for the most part, suspicious, expecting her to make demands, she supposed. While Clarissa was hostile and Cameron biting in his comments, Judd was solemn, the one who, though distrustful, listened while she spoke, his questions pointed, but without the same harsh judgment as his sister or Robert Lindley.

Thane didn't say a lot, was probably the most welcoming as he quietly observed the sometimes volatile exchanges. Sometimes a smile would tug at a corner of his mouth, but beneath his laid-back, I-don't-give-a-damn exterior, there was a restlessness to him. He, too, doubted her.

Robert continued to vent. "This is a ridiculous idea," he said, impaling her with his cold gaze. "How would anyone know if these women were Gerald's? Without DNA testing, or some kind of private information leaked from the clinic, how would a killer even know who to choose?"

"More to the point, why?" Judd asked.

Gerald took the floor again. "The clinic's been closed for years. Who knows where the records went?" Though his children listened to him, they all had their opinions about Kacey and what she'd brought to them.

None of them liked it.

She felt their resentment coming off in waves, and for a few minutes even she doubted her own theory.

"What have the police got to say about this?" Cameron asked her, and she felt every eye in the room turn her way.

"They're investigating. That's all I know."

"So, they'll show up here, too!" Clarissa made a disparaging sound. "Just what we need. Now that the patents have expired, we've got competition crawling up our backs, and what we don't need is some bad publicity, any reason for our clients to take their business elsewhere!"

"This has nothing to do with business," Gerald said. "It's personal."

"Tell that to the Internet and the blogs and the local newspaper. This is a publicity nightmare."

"I thought all publicity was good, that there was no bad press," Cameron said.

"Yeah, well, you're a moron." Clarissa didn't back down for an instant. A businesswoman with a master's from Stanford, firstborn in a family of male siblings, she was definitely tough.

Colt straightened in his chair. Rather than come to his twin's defense, he turned the conversation back to the women who had died. "Are there any other victims?"

"I think so," Kacey said but couldn't back it up.

Judd put in, "The first order of business is the DNA tests. We can sit here all day and argue theory, but until we can prove that these women"—he thumped a finger on the table, next to the photographs—"are actually Dad's biological offspring, then all other conversation is moot."

"Judd's got a point," Colt agreed.

The rest of his siblings weren't so inclined to agree and were vocal about the fact that they thought Kacey had come to stir up trouble, make a claim on the estate, or both.

"So what was the point of coming here? To check us out? Or warn us . . . or accuse us?" Cameron asked. "I don't get it."

"There's nothing to get," Clarissa said with a scowl. "She knows about the company."

"That's not it," Kacey said clearly. "I felt you all should know that someone may be killing off people with a genetic link to you."

"And who would that be? Who would go to the trouble of finding Gerald's supposed sperm-bank babies and then killing them off in apparent accidents?" Clarissa said as she slid her laptop into its case. "That's nuts. Makes you sound like you should check yourself into the nearest psycho ward."

"Hold on," Gerald said. "Let's not get nasty."

"Does Clarissa know another way?" Cameron asked. "If so, I've never seen it."

"Enough!" Judd cut in, his anxiety finally showing. "We don't need to insult each other." He turned in his chair so he could watch Kacey's expression. "So, you wanted to forewarn us."

Her stomach knotting still tighter, she brought her temper under control. "I did want to meet you, too. I was curious about the father I'd never known, and since I grew up an only child, the idea of siblings fascinated me."

Clarissa shook her head, as if she had much more important things to deal with and Kacey was wasting her time.

Colt and Judd were quiet, listening.

Cam looked bored, and Robert's jaw was so tense, the bone showed white beneath his skin. Gerald, too, was feeling the pressure, putting up a good, patient front, but one fist was clenched on the table and his lips were flat over his teeth.

Kacey said, "The reason I found out about you all is because there were so many women who looked like me in and around Grizzly Falls. I never met anyone who resembled me remotely when I lived in Seattle, but I move here and it's like they're everywhere. Two . . . three . . . four. It's really out of the norm. I wouldn't have even thought about Shelly Bonaventure. Even though I've seen her face, noted that we resembled each other, she lived in L.A. Just a quirky little coincidence, right? That's how I saw it, even when people made comments. But the others . . ." She looked at the photographs on the table. "They were what motivated me." She explained about being mistaken for Jocelyn Wallis in the ER and how Shelly Bonaventure was her doppelgänger, and how worried she became when they started dying. Intuitively Kacey left out the part about her house being bugged, or that she felt she'd been followed. Already some of them thought she wasn't playing with a full deck; she didn't want them to consider her completely paranoid.

When she finished, Clarissa, a pissy expression twisting her features, said, "So what now? You've come. You've met us. Introduced yourself to Dad. Messed up our mother's life immeasurably, especially concerning that she'd never really accepted Robert as our half brother."

Robert glowered a bit but didn't argue.

Clarissa went on, "I suppose you're going to want to hire on with the company, here, along with the rest of us. Or are you planning to come over for Christmas dinner? That might be interesting in an absurd way."

"More than a little," Cameron added.

Kacey stood. "All I wanted was validation, I guess. To find out a little more about myself and let the rest of you know what's going on, that people related to Gerald Johnson are dying."

"Still just a theory," Robert reminded.

She turned her attention to him, the one most like her, not really part of the family. "I really don't have anything else to say. Contrary to what you think," she added, looking directly at Clarissa, "I do have a life. My own life and it's pretty good. I'd just like to keep it that way."

She was about to walk out when a knock sounded on the door the moment before it was pushed open. A tall man, probably six-two or three, poked his head inside. Handsome, with bladed features and eyes a shocking blue, he looked around the room, his gaze landing on Clarissa.

"I thought we were meeting with the builder this afternoon," he said, obviously displeased.

"Family emergency." Clarissa's lips were tight, but she gathered her things together, zipping her laptop's case.

Gerald added, "It'll just be a minute more, Lance."

Lance? As in the husband Clarissa would "eviscerate" if he was ever caught cheating? That would be quite a feat, Kacey thought, as this man looked tough as nails. Maybe tougher. Like someone who bow hunted and rock climbed and participated in Ironman competitions just for fun. There wasn't an ounce of fat on his large frame and not the hint of a smile in his even features.

Kacey headed to the boardroom closet, where she'd hung her coat. "I'm done," she said to no one in particular as she slipped her arms through her sleeves. "You can keep those photos," she said. Lance, eyeing her speculatively, gave her a wide berth as she walked through the door and into the maze of hallways connecting the rooms and buildings of Gerald Johnson's empire.

It was really just a company, after all, she thought, but the way her siblings acted about it, the corporation could just as well have been called GJ's Holy Roman Empire rather than G. Johnson, Inc.

She felt slightly tired. Nothing really had been accomplished today, except that now Gerald and his children were more than two-dimensional pictures on the Internet to her; they were real, and she felt as if she understood them a little more, which wasn't all good.

But at least they now knew of her and of her mission. She'd warned them, though she wasn't certain any of them were targets. Briefly, she wondered if one of them could be the person who had bugged her house, or possibly even the killer, but it seemed unlikely. Even if the man central to the mystery were Gerald Johnson.

Clarissa was right about one thing; she'd certainly stirred up a hornet's nest. No telling what would come of it, but she doubted there would be any family ties established.

"What'd you expect?" she asked herself as she walked along the pathway to her car. Her boots sunk into an inch and a half of new snow. Had she really thought she'd be welcomed with open arms? Or that she'd be able to pick out which of Gerald's biological children was crazy enough to commit murder?

And why would that be?

Or were the individuals she'd left arguing in the conference room targets themselves?

Blaming her sour stomach on a severe case of nerves, she climbed into her SUV, put the Edge into gear, and backed out of her parking space. A few minutes later she called Detective Alvarez and left a message that she was on her way home. Then she phoned Trace and told him the same thing. Then she asked about Eli. Trace said he was coughing, still a little listless, but definitely improving. The neighbor had come over and was "keeping the boy company" while Trace did the chores. When Kacey was assured that all was as well as it could be with Eli, she launched into the tale of where she'd been and whom she'd seen.

When she was finished, Trace said, "I wish you'd told me where you were going. Sounds like a nest of snakes."

"Vipers," she corrected, and he chuckled, the sound warming her from the inside out. "I just needed to meet him by myself." After spending part of the afternoon under the icy scrutiny of her half siblings, it was a relief to be talking to a man who seemed to trust her, care for her.

"Do you want me there tonight?"

"No, I'll let Detective Alvarez and the rest of them take care of it."

"I can be there. If Tilly will stay with Eli, I'll meet you at your house. If you want me to."

From the background an older woman's voice yelled, "You don't have to twist my arm, Trace. It's time I showed this young'un a thing or two about checkers!"

"I want you to," Kacey said.

"See you soon," he said into the phone.

"Okay." Again her silly heart soared, and again Kacey reminded herself to keep her feet on the ground, her head out of the clouds. Two weeks ago she hadn't even met Trace O'Halleran or his adorable son.

Two weeks ago her life had been normal. In a rut. Then women who looked like her started dying.

Now, at least, with Trace on her side, she wasn't fighting this battle alone.

As she turned off of the main highway toward Grizzly Falls, she glanced in her rearview mirror, glad to see no one appeared to be following her through these snowy hills. Turning on the radio, she was relieved to be leaving the sick tangle that was her newfound family far behind.

CHAPTER 31

Calm down.
Pretend nothing's wrong.
So the bitch went to Gerald? So what?
It was inevitable. As are the police.
And things are only going to get worse when they find the other one. . . .

Glancing down at the screen of his GPS tracking system, he realized that Acacia had driven home from Gerald's company in Missoula, which was exactly what he'd expected. And yet he couldn't help but worry, his hands sweating in gloves, his teeth sinking into his lower lip as he thought of everything that could go wrong.

He'd been so diligent. . . .

He was on the move again. There was just so much to do, and time was his enemy.

He'd switched license plates on the truck, just in case, putting on the set of stolen Idaho plates.

His windshield wipers wiped off the snow as he thought about yesterday and how he'd surprised another one. She had been cross-country skiing on a trail that was one of her usual haunts. He'd had to wait several days in the empty parking lot, hoping she would appear.

Finally, yesterday, as he'd pretended to be checking his own equipment, the nose of her Honda had appeared. After she'd parked, she'd geared up and he'd offered a hand in greeting as she'd snapped on her skis and taken off.

He'd waited until she was around the bend and through a copse of pine before he'd taken off after her, his strides strong and swift. She was athletic, and he was surprised how long it had taken to catch up to her, but he'd kept her red jacket in his line of vision until she'd started up the incline that ran along the creek.

He'd accelerated then, pushing himself, feeling the cold wind permeate his ski mask as it rattled the trees.

Swoosh, swoosh, swoosh!

His skis skimmed over the thick powder.

He dug his poles into the soft snow with smooth, sure regularity and gained on her.

She was thirty feet ahead of him and gliding through the sparse stands, her skis smooth near the creek bank, the wires from her iPod now visible.

Twenty feet.

Up another short incline. *Perfect.*

He dug in, pushing harder.

Sweating.

Closing the distance between them.

Ten feet.

Behind his ski mask, he grinned. She hadn't heard him, didn't know he was following. So into her music and the beauty of the fresh snow in the wilderness, or some such crap, she skied innocently.

Unaware.

Closer still.

Now the tips of his skis were nearly touching the backs of hers. They were heading into a thicker grove, where birch and pine quivered with the wind. One gnarly pine, with a thick trunk and several broken branches, caught his eye.

Perfect!

As she curved around the bend in the creek, he pulled up beside her. They were skiing two abreast.

She caught a glimpse of him because, just as the tree with its broken branches loomed, she flinched. She turned her head, eyes round in fear, mouth pulled back to scream, as he shoved her.

Hard.

Into the rotting pine.

Now, as he remembered the horror on her face, the sickening sound of her body slamming into the bark, the thud of her head cracking against that jagged, protruding broken branch, he grinned again.

One less Unknowing walking the earth.

And now, he thought, bringing himself up to the minute, he would take care of the one he should have dealt with years before. His scar seemed to throb as the wipers swatted away the snow and some inane Christmas song rolled through the speakers.

"Three Kings, my ass," he muttered, and he felt that little zing sizzle through his blood, that spark of anticipation, as he thought of what was to come.

Acacia.

God, he'd like to fuck her. Just to show her what he could do . . . Then again, he'd settle for killing her. Watching her eyes widen in surprise when she recognized him, seeing her pupils dilate in terror, witnessing her understanding that he would snuff the life from her.

He felt his cock twitch and stiffen. With a moan, he let out his breath slowly, loosening his fingers as they gripped the wheel. He had to park out of sight again and snowshoe in, which was perfect, and the falling snow would make an excellent cover, get rid of his tracks.

Smiling, he drove into the foothills.

He knew just the right spot.

"So that's it?" Alvarez said into the hands-free device of her cell phone as she drove. "Black paint that you can buy anywhere?"

"Sorry," Gus said without an ounce of apology in his voice. "It is what it is. And what it is . . . is Premium flat black number three-oh-eight. It's been the same formula for nearly fifteen years."

They were talking about the paint marks retrieved from Elle Alexander's van, and instead of the paint that was transferred belonging to a certain make and model of car, it was from a spray paint can, the kind that could be bought all across the country and was used to paint anything from outdoor furniture to model cars or barbecues.

"Great."

"Hey, I gave you what I had."

"I know. Thanks, Gus." She hung up and considered how many stores in the Grizzly Falls area had sold that particular brand in the past fifteen years. Would they get lucky and find someone who had purchased it lately? And what if the paint had been bought in Spokane or Boise or Missoula or who knew where?

At least she had the information on the coffee grounds. Alvarez was alone. Pescoli had received a call from Jeremy just as they were leaving. He'd told her that Chris Schultz was over, so she'd had to head home again. Alvarez had told her not to bother, but Pescoli had made it clear she would deal with the matter and show up as soon as she could. It seemed Pescoli had been half annoyed, half glad that Jeremy had decided to rat out his sister's boyfriend. It was almost a sign of maturity.

Alvarez found Acacia Lambert's address and turned into the long drive that led to the house, following a couple of sets of fresh tracks. To her unwelcome surprise, Trace O'Halleran was waiting for her as she pulled up beside his truck. The tech crew had already arrived as well, parked to the side of the garage. One of the guys, Rudy, was outside the department-issued van, smoking a cigarette and talking to Trace. Rudy's partner, Eileen, was inside the vehicle, keeping warm as the van's engine idled, exhaust fogging in the air.

Alvarez considered Trace. He wasn't the killer; his alibis had proved that. But he was in this thing up to his sexy eyeballs; she just hadn't quite figured out how.

Yet.

What was it with him and the women who might just have all been sired by Donor 727?

There was no time like the present to find out.

As she opened the door of her Jeep, she heard another vehicle in the drive and saw the play of headlights in the snow. Seconds later Dr. Acacia Lambert herself had parked her car in the drive, behind Alvarez, and had walked over the mashed snow to the group, just as Eileen climbed out of the van.

They discussed the plan to sweep the house. They were to find the bugs, try to locate the exterior source, but leave everything as it was. Kacey and Trace would talk as if they were the only ones in the house, catch up on the day, while the techs combed each room for listening devices and perhaps cameras. Afterward, they would dust for prints.

Clearly Kacey had been hoping the mics would be immediately removed, and Alvarez couldn't blame her. But she saw the wisdom of keeping them in place, and so they all headed toward the house.

If Trace had made a mistake and there were actually cameras in the house as well, they were screwed and would tip off whoever had bugged the house. Then again, if the guy was nearby, there was a chance he would see them, anyway, and probably figure out they were on to him. Even though the house sat back from the road, he could have an observation point.

They made their way to the back porch but stopped short when a deep-throated dog started barking from within. "Hey, Bonz, it's me! Hush!" Kacey ordered, but the animal kept up the ruckus until she was inside. Only then did his hackles lower and his tail begin wagging in wide arcs as he happily greeted everyone. Though he looked as if he were aggressive with predominately pit bull genes, he lowered his head and waited to be petted by everyone filing inside.

Kacey let him outside, then fed him near the back door before heading into the den as planned.

While Rudy and Eileen worked, Trace and Kacey turned on several televisions to mask some of the noise, then played their roles in the den.

Alvarez snapped on a pair of latex gloves, collected some of the coffee grounds, as well as the beans still in the canister and grinder, and placed them all in plastic bags. She didn't expect to find any fingerprints from whoever had planted the bugs, but she believed in being thorough. Who knew? They might get lucky.

Finding the evidence that the creep was targeting Acacia Lambert, playing with her, listening in on her life, went a long way to proving her theory that the deaths were connected. Could Acacia Lambert also be the progeny of Donor 727? Alvarez planned on asking the woman but was waiting till this debugging was over.

While Kacey and Trace played their parts at the computer in the den, the dog curled at Kacey's feet, Alvarez scratched out a quick question on a pad, then placed it in front of the doctor: *Have you been feeling ill?*

Trace O'Halleran frowned, looked from one woman to the other.

Kacey hesitated and frowned. She wrote back: *Stomach.*

Alvarez wrote back: *Maybe poison. Arsenic found in Wallis stomach contents.*

"From what?" Kacey mouthed.

Alvarez wrote: *In the coffee. Most likely a small dosage.*

"Damn it," Kacey's voice was barely discernible, probably wouldn't be picked up on the mic. Her expression turned from concern to anger, and she wrote quickly: *We need to talk.*

Nodding, Alvarez scribbled back: *My car.* She then turned up the television to the point that nothing else could be heard and, carrying the coffee, pot, and grinder, all bagged and tagged, walked through the kitchen and outside.

The wind was blowing hard, snow slanting sideways at times, a tree branch banging against one of the gutters on the second story. She unlocked her car and climbed in. Trace and Kacey showed up a few moments later.

"Okay, it's safe here," Alvarez said as she turned on the engine and ignored any banter or crackling on the radio. Trace was stretched across the back; Kacey in the passenger bucket seat. Alvarez adjusted the heater, to blow out the condensation, then let the wipers swipe off an accumulation of snow. "I think you may have been poisoned, though probably not more than enough to make you sick. And the reason I think so is because we found traces of arsenic in Jocelyn's blood. The guy was toying with her. He'd put it into her coffee somehow."

"Sick bastard," Trace said.

"You think he put it in my coffee, too?" Kacey asked.

"I'll find out."

"I think this 'sick bastard' could be related to me," Kacey said slowly, picking her words.

"How so?" Alvarez asked.

Kacey then, somewhat reluctantly, launched into a story about being the love child of her mother and one Gerald Johnson, a doctor who had invented a certain type of heart stent. She told of her findings that afternoon in Missoula, at Gerald's place of work, summing up her impressions of him and his children, then dropped the bomb that Gerald Johnson as a medical student had been a sperm donor to a now-defunct clinic.

Alvarez took a long moment, savoring the feeling of a case breaking wide open. "We were already on the sperm bank angle," she told Kacey, surprising both her and Trace. "From Elle Alexander's parents." Quickly, she recapped what she'd learned, then gazed at Kacey seriously across the dark interior of the car. "But you have to cease and desist. Give me a statement back at the station, then disappear, hide out. At least until we determine if you're a target and what the story is with Johnson and his kids."

"One of them is like me. Robert Lindley. His mother was another of Johnson's mistresses. And another one of his children, a girl named Kathleen, died in her twenties in a skiing accident."

"Another accident," Alvarez said.

"You think she was a victim?" Trace asked.

"Maybe."

"What about his other kids?" Kacey asked. "Kathleen died years ago. And Agatha, when she was eight. The rest of them, as far as I know, haven't had any brushes with death."

"That's just it. As far as you know. For now, though, you have to quit playing detective. It's too dangerous." Alvarez was adamant. "It's our job. We'll handle it from here."

"Jesus," Pescoli muttered, stunned as she knelt on the snow near the corpse, a cross-country skier who had apparently slammed into the snag of a pine tree perched on the banks of the icy creek. Pescoli had been on her way to the Lambert house when she'd gotten the call.

The dead skier was a woman with reddish hair, and though her face was mangled from her crash with the pine and blood had frozen over a shattered cheekbone and eye socket, Pescoli felt a shiver of dread run through her.

The accident victim's features, though discolored and frozen, were similar to those of Jocelyn Wallis, Elle Alexander, and even Shelly Bonaventure.

"Son of a bitch," she said as the body was photographed, then bagged and driven to the medical examiner's van, which was parked in the lower lot, next to the red Honda, which was registered to Karalee Rierson, who lived ten miles east.

What were the chances?

She spent time talking to the couple who had found her, newly married twentysomethings who had been snowshoeing and happened upon the dead body. They'd nearly missed seeing her as she'd been half buried in snow, but the man had caught a glimpse of something red beneath the fresh snow and investigated.

They had been terrified but, having cell phones with them, had called 9-1-1. Kayan Rule had taken the call and been dispatched to the scene. When he'd seen the victim, he, in turn, had phoned the station again, requesting a homicide detective. Pescoli had been the detective closest, and she'd driven her Jeep up to the lower lot and snowshoed in a quarter mile to the area where the victim had lost her life, in an apparent accident.

The crime scene crew had arrived and was combing the area for trace evidence, but Pescoli figured they wouldn't find much. The weapon of death was the tree; bloodstains on a particularly vicious eye-level snag were still visible.

It could have been an accident, she supposed. A careless or startled skier, maybe. But Pescoli wasn't buying it for a minute. She figured that the dead woman now on her way to the morgue would prove to be yet another victim of a killer who had a vendetta against the offspring of Donor 727, whoever the hell he was.

No, the killer was even more precise in his intentions than that. So far, all the victims had been women. Elle Alexander's brother, Bruce, was alive and well according to her parents.

A mistake?

Probably not.

Now, as she snowshoed back to her Jeep and waited for the truck to come and tow Karalee Rierson's little Honda, she flipped open her cell phone and called Alvarez. When her partner didn't answer, Pescoli left a short message: "I think we've got another one." Then watched as the frozen Honda, with snow piled over its hood and dirty icicles dangling like long, snaggy teeth along the wheel wells, was winched onto the flatbed.

Another "accident."

Another dead woman.

Probably related to good old 727.

Whatever the hell that meant.

CHAPTER 32

*P*oisoned?

She'd been poisoned, and she hadn't even realized it?

With Trace at her side, Kacey was seated on a folding chair in the interview room at the sheriff's department while listening to Alvarez, from the other side of the small, battered table, describe finding arsenic in Jocelyn Wallis's coffee grounds. Kacey thought of her own symptoms, how she'd never considered that there was a toxin running through her veins. She was a doctor, and she would have noticed if the symptoms had become violent, the pain more intense. Still . . .

It all made sense.

Now.

Already the interview was well into its second hour. Detective Alvarez, after warning them to stay out of the investigation, was now doing this by the book.

Trace, though he tried to appear relaxed, was antsy, his jaw, beneath a darkening beard shadow, tight, his lips flat, his eyes serious. Twice during the conversation, he'd stepped outside of the room to call Tilly and get an update on his son. Though he didn't really need to be here and Kacey had encouraged him to go home, he'd stayed.

Alvarez had listened to Kacey's theory about the dead women being related to Gerald Johnson twice so far, once at Kacey's house, and a second time now. When her partner, Pescoli, arrived, Alvarez quickly brought her up to speed.

"Gerald Johnson," Pescoli repeated, shaking her head. "Think this is his work, too?" She offered up pictures that looked as if they had been taken digitally, then printed out. Kacey inwardly cringed as she looked at the graphic images, not so much from the woman's injuries—she'd seen worse in medical school and her practice—but because of what she saw beyond the battered, bloody features. The victim's hair, poking out of a blood-encrusted cap, was a deep red-brown, as close to Kacey's own color as it could be, and the one eye that was open, pupil apparently fixed, was a green shade that wasn't quite as blue as her own but was definitely in the color spectrum of all the victims.

Had her face not been so battered, this woman, too, would have resembled Kacey enough as to have been her sister.

Which, she thought sadly, was probably true.

"You know her?" Alvarez asked.

Kacey shook her head. "I don't think I've ever seen her in my life."

"I was talking to him." Alvarez hitched her chin toward Trace, her dark eyes holding his.

His jaw was clamped shut, and irritation caused a muscle to work in his jaw. "No." He slid the pictures back toward Pescoli, who was still standing near the table.

Kacey asked, "Who is she?"

Pescoli thought for a moment and said, "I guess we can tell you, considering the situation, but keep it to yourselves. Next of kin is being notified as we speak. Her name is Karalee Rierson. She's local. A nurse. Divorced. A couple of times. No kids. Lived in Oregon for a while." She paused a moment, as if thinking things over, then said, "She grew up in Helena."

"Dear God," Kacey whispered, sick inside. Who was behind all these accidents? Why was he killing?

"Dr. Lambert went to see Gerald Johnson today," Alvarez said, then nodded to Kacey, who explained again about getting her mother to come up with the truth, then forcing herself on Gerald Johnson and his family.

"Did you go to see Johnson and his clan to try and flush out the killer?" Pescoli asked, her expression stern. She stood leaning against the far wall, below a camera mounted near the ceiling.

"I actually went to meet them, show them the pictures, tell them what I knew. I wanted to see their expressions, especially Gerald's, as he seems to be the link to all of this." She felt cold inside again, just remembering his reaction and those of her half siblings. Though she didn't really know them, she realized she would never be close to any of them, might, in fact, never see them again. Her curiosity was satisfied, though; as far as she was concerned, they weren't part of her family. "Gerald was concerned when I showed him the pictures of the dead women, and even though I don't think he wanted to, he owned up to the whole sperm donor thing, which bothered most of his kids."

"I'd say," Pescoli muttered.

"From now on, stay away from them," Alvarez advised.

Trace asked, "You think they're dangerous?"

"I think it's police business." Pescoli was firm. "Not that we don't appreciate the fact that you found out who our sperm donor is. We only had a number."

They discussed the meeting with the Johnson clan, and then Kacey told the detectives about Gloria Sanders-O'Malley, the instructor at Fit Forever. "She looks like the rest of us, and she was born in Helena."

"I've seen her at the gym," Alvarez said, her expression growing tense. "She does resemble the others."

"For the love of God, how many victims and potential victims are we talking about?" Pescoli broke in. "This is nuts!" She shook her head. "I'm sorry. Go on."

"Once I figured out there were more people like me, those with Gerald Johnson as a father, I went to meet him, see what he was like. I wasn't sure I'd meet his kids, but once Clarissa barged into his office and figured out who I was, they called a family meeting."

"You should have come here first," Pescoli said.

"What would I have come with? Some half-baked theory about people who looked like me getting killed off? A few days ago I didn't even know that Stanley Collins wasn't my biological father." The newfound anger and sense of betrayal that had been with her ever since her mother's confession still burned bright.

"You know of any other potential victims?" Alvarez asked.

"I have a friend looking through state files. I'm not going to give up their name," she said, instinctively covering for Riza. "And I believe, from what I've learned, that there may have been others already killed. . . . It's as if the guy started out years ago working in a wide circle, then slowly tightened it, until he's now concentrating here, in this corner of Montana. From as far away as Detroit to all along the West Coast, Seattle and San Francisco, women have been having accidents. I haven't had time to look into them all, but I've got names and addresses and dates of death." Reaching into her purse, she found a manila envelope that contained the information from Riza. She slid it across the table toward Alvarez, but she didn't take her fingers off the end of the envelope closest to her.

Alvarez frowned and placed her fingers on the other side of the envelope. Inside the envelope were copies without any information about Riza or the state offices from which they came, but it would be a simple enough matter for the police, if they were so inclined, to figure out where they had come from, and a simple search into Kacey's background and her schooling would connect her to Riza. She had to come clean. "A friend of mine risked their job for this. You have to promise me that they won't get into any kind of trouble. None."

"This is a sheriff's department investigation," Pescoli reminded everyone in the room.

Kacey held fast to the envelope. "*Women* are dying. As far as I know, no men have been killed, which is really odd, since Gerald Johnson has fathered a number of males, too."

"No one will lose their job or get into serious trouble," Alvarez promised, and Kacey let go of the envelope.

"I'm going to have someone get right on this," Pescoli said and left the room quickly.

Alvarez continued the interview. When she asked if Kacey had ever felt stalked or if things were strange, Kacey was reminded again of the attack in Seattle and mentioned it. Then she remembered the accident and Grace Perchant's warning. "This is probably nothing," she said, "but I was in an accident, or almost an accident. Less than a fender bender. The roads were icy and another car lost control, I had to swerve to miss it, and when I did, I slid into the other lane. A big truck, going the opposite direction, clipped my bumper. It seemed like on purpose. Even though it was obviously my fault, the other driver took off, rather than stop and swap insurance information."

Alvarez, who was taking notes, asked, "You didn't get a look at the driver?"

"Just a quick glimpse, but other than seeing it was a man with dark hair, no." Kacey shook her head and, out of her peripheral vision, saw Trace tense, the muscles in his neck tighten. "For the most part, his face was averted. I had the impression I'd seen him before, but . . . I couldn't place him. He did look like some of Gerald Johnson's sons I met today, but I might be pushing that."

Alvarez asked, "Do you know the make or model of the truck?"

"I was too busy trying to stay on the road. It was big, probably domestic—Chevy or Ford, I think—but I'm not sure. What I did notice was that it had a huge bumper guard of some kind on it, looked like it was steel, but painted black, and even though I didn't get a good look at the plates, I had a feeling that they weren't from Montana. One of the numbers was either a three or an eight. Or, maybe it was a *B?* The back plate was really dirty, and there wasn't time to get a second look. It all happened in just a few seconds."

"Any chance there was some paint transfer? From his vehicle to yours?" Alvarez asked, suddenly more interested.

"Maybe . . . I saw black marks and a bit of a dent on my bumper."

"We'd like to keep your car. Try and get at some of those black marks, see if they're paint." Alvarez was all business. "Is there anything else you remember?"

"Not really . . . oh, but, there was a witness," Kacey said. Why hadn't she thought of this before?

Because it was random. You didn't really think the accident was connected to anything else. The driver hadn't intentionally tried to run you down, she thought. Now, though . . .

"Grace Perchant, she was out walking her dog, the one that's part wolf."

"Did you talk to her?"

Grace's warning ran like blood through Kacey's brain: *You should never speak to him. He is evil. He means you harm.* She'd tried to dismiss the pale woman's message, but it had stuck with her, invaded her dreams.

"She told me not to try and chase him down, that the driver was 'evil.' When I asked her who he was, she couldn't come up with a name, just that he meant me harm."

"Sounds like Grace," Alvarez said. "We'll check it out."

Fishing in her purse, Kacey came up with her key ring, then removed the key to her Ford and handed it to Alvarez. "I'll need the car back soon."

"Tomorrow," Alvarez promised, scooting back her chair, indicating the interview was finally over. "And I'll get hold of Grace Perchant."

Trace had listened to most of the interview without saying too much, but as the discussion had worn on, he'd become more and more concerned for Kacey's safety. After learning that she had possibly been poisoned and then viewing Pescoli's gruesome pictures of Karalee Rierson, the most recent accident victim, he'd made up his mind.

As he held the glass door open for her, then followed her outside, he said, "You're coming to my place."

"Oh, I am?" Outside the snow was thick now, still falling, a wind blowing off the mountains. Night had fallen in earnest while they were in the police station. Streetlights glowed, offering a thin blue light to the powdery landscape.

"You're sure as hell not going home alone. Dog or no dog."

"Yeah?" she asked, but even in the semidarkness, he saw that she was teasing, her eyes a deeper green. Turning the collar of her coat against the wind, she followed a trail of footprints along a footpath leading past a flagpole, where chains rattled and the flags had already been taken down for the night. As Trace jogged to catch up with her, he noticed snowflakes settling onto her shoulders, sparkling like glitter in the dark strands of her hair.

"I don't like what's going on," he said seriously.

"Me, neither."

"So, no arguments?"

She studied him for a second. "None from me, but we have to pick up my dog and a few things, and then, in the morning, I'm going to need a way to get to work."

"I think I can handle it. My neighbors, Tilly and Ed Zukov, are watching over things at my place until I get back."

During Trace's last conversation Tilly had assured him that Ed had taken care of the horses and cattle and she was already frying chicken. Trace had heard the sizzle of the meat cooking and the blare of the television, as Ed was more than a little hard of hearing. Satisfied that his son was safe and feeling well enough to ask Tilly to bake him brownies, Trace had relaxed a little.

But his sense of ease had been short-lived as the interview had worn on. He didn't know who was behind the "accidents" of the women who'd died, but the fact that Kacey looked like a target was enough to convince him that she shouldn't be alone. Someone had gotten into her house without forced entry, had possibly poisoned her, was privy to her private conversations, and knew when she was alone.

Trace's back muscles tightened just at the thought of someone listening in.

Was it possible that the person behind the surveillance equipment was the killer?

You bet. In Trace's mind there was no question. None whatsoever. He unlocked the truck, waited as she climbed into the cab, then closed the door.

She smiled at him through the passenger window, and he felt that now familiar little tug on his heart that he felt whenever he was around her. In another time and place he might think he was falling in love. Right here, right now, he couldn't even go there. Not while women who looked like her were dying.

As he slid behind the wheel, she voiced second thoughts. "I don't know if staying with you is the answer," she said.

"Eli would love it."

"That's not what I'm thinking about." She slid a glance his way. "And you know it."

He realized suddenly how close the cab of his truck was, how their breaths had fogged the glass. "Yeah." To break the mood, he flipped on the defrost.

He jammed the truck into reverse, backed out of the parking spot, then switched gears to drive. Slowing so that he could ease into the steady stream of traffic heading out of the town, he inched forward, feeling her gaze upon him as he slid into a spot behind a flatbed truck with a load of Christmas trees.

"It's just that I have to know that you're safe, okay? So I want you to stay with me."

"You want to protect me."

"Something like that."

She half smiled, and it was about the sexiest gesture he'd ever seen. "You know what, O'Halleran? Maybe I'll end up protecting you. Or something like that."

"I want to surprise Gerald Johnson and see what he has to say for himself," Pescoli said as she and Alvarez walked to her office.

"Okay. I was doing some research earlier. Let's follow up some more and then take it to Grayson, so he can contact the FBI."

"FBI, my ass," Pescoli muttered.

Alvarez grabbed up the information she'd already pulled from the Internet, and then she and Pescoli spent time searching for other women born twenty-five to forty years earlier in Helena who'd died accidentally. There was a raft of them, but they chose about a dozen.

"This is just so bizarre," Alvarez said.

"Beyond bizarre. And there are a lot more to sift through. If this is our guy, he sure as hell got around."

"Which means he had money and free time."

They looked at each other. "One of Gerald Johnson's kids?" Pescoli asked.

"Not the youngest. He would have only been six when the first fatal 'accident' took place."

"Unless the first accidents really are accidents or aren't our look-alikes . . . These deaths really started piling up around fifteen years ago, about the time the youngest of Johnson's kids, the twins, were twenty-two, which is about the same time they would have graduated from college if they went."

"And ended up on Daddy's payroll?" Alvarez thought aloud. "But why? And how would whoever it is know where to find the daughters of Seven-twenty-seven?" She grimaced. "Maybe they worked at the clinic while going to college, got the information that way."

"Could be. Or even bought the information if they found dear old Dad had made regular deposits to the local sperm bank. You know what they say, 'Everything has a price.' That includes personal information." Pescoli thought of her own son and his fascination with the Internet. She'd worried that he was playing games and wasting time, or perusing porn, but what if he was hacking, breaking into private files? "What do you think? Is anyone in Johnson's family a computer geek?"

CHAPTER 33

The roads were a mess, traffic snarled, the storm relentless as it dumped more snow over northwestern Montana. It took over an hour for Trace and Kacey to collect her dog, computer, and an overnight bag. Trace's truck slid twice, but he was able to finally reach the old farmhouse he called home.

She'd never seen it before, this big, square home perched on a bit of hill nearly an eighth of a mile from the county road. Snow was thick on the roof, icicles were dangling from the eaves, and a bitter wind was blowing through the naked trees in a small orchard. Trace pulled into an open garage at the back of the house, where a Dodge pickup, nose facing toward the road, was already parked, three inches of snow piled on its hood. Outbuildings stood in the distance, security lamps offering pale, almost eerie, illumination through the curtain of falling snow.

As he grabbed Kacey's overnight bag, he whistled to her dog, opened the driver's door, and stepped outside. Bonzi scrambled after him, leaping and breaking through nearly a foot of powder, while Kacey hauled her computer case up a path broken through the snow.

They took three steps up to a broad back porch, where they tromped the snow off their feet, then stepped through an unlocked back door. Heat, and the smell of wood smoke and spices, hit them full force as they removed their coats and the dog explored.

"Hey there, fella," a deep male voice from somewhere deeper in the house greeted. "Who the hell are you?" There was a sharp bark, and the same voice said, "Hey, Sarge. Enough! Looks like you've got a friend here." Then a chuckle.

The kitchen was large enough for a full-sized table, its butcher-block counter pressed up to a wide window overlooking the back porch and the outbuildings beyond.

"How's Eli?" Trace asked as he walked through a wide archway into the living area, where a fire burned in the grate and a man and woman were seated in front of a television blasting the news. The woman was knitting; the man had an ear cocked toward the TV set.

"He just conked out after dinner," Tilly told Trace as she stuffed a skein of fuzzy yarn into her bag and gave Kacey the once-over. To her husband, she yelled, "Ed, turn that thing down, would ya! I can't hear myself think!"

Ed snorted, blinked, and did as he was bid, bringing the noise level down several decibels. A large man, Ed Zukov wouldn't need anything other than a red suit and fake beard to play Santa Claus.

Trace made hasty introductions.

"Nice to meet ya," Tilly said, but there wasn't a lot of warmth in her smile. Ed, though, stood and shook Kacey's hand as if he meant it, then settled back into his corner of the couch, his hands fingering the remote control before it slipped off the sectional's arm.

Tilly wasn't finished giving Trace a report on his son. "Poor little thing was plumb tuckered out. Probably the medication," Tilly said.

"I think I'll look in on him," Trace said, peeling off his jacket and dashing up a flight of stairs near the front hallway. Sarge and Bonzi followed closely behind.

"Nice dog," Ed said. "He yours?"

"He is now. I just adopted him."

Ed's whitish eyebrows raised. "Guard dog?"

"Not much." She smiled.

"Hunter?" Ed persisted.

Kacey shook her head. "Bonzi? I doubt it. Probably will never know."

As if he'd heard his name, Bonzi came running back down the stairs and bounded past a coffee table, to place his head near the arm-rest of the couch and Ed's hand. "Yeah, you're a good boy," the man said as Sarge and Trace returned to the living room, too. Sarge, cone surrounding his head, curled up on a rug near the fire.

"Don't he look silly?" Ed muttered with a deep-throated chuckle.

Tilly patted her husband's jean-clad knee. "We'd better get going. The storm's only gettin' worse."

Ed struggled to his feet again and pulled a face as he cracked his neck and tried to keep up with his wife, who was walking briskly through the kitchen. "Ain't gettin' any younger," he admitted as they gathered their things, slid into jackets that had been hung on pegs near the back door, and wound hand-knit scarves around their necks.

Once she was bundled up, Tilly said to Trace, "Now, don't forget, there's chicken in the refrigerator, along with mashed potatoes, green beans, and gravy."

"That would be Tilly's killer chicken," Ed said with a grin. He was rewarded for his compliment with a good-hearted swat from his wife.

"I hate to brag, but he's right, you know." Tilly beamed a little. As an aside, she said, "It's the paprika. The Colonel, he can have his eleven herbs and spices or whatever. Let me tell you, I've got paprika!"

"No one remembers that old herbs and spices thing!" Ed hitched his chin toward Trace and Kacey. "These two, they're too young. Way too young!" He settled his hat on his head and walked to the porch, where his work boots were waiting.

"Thanks for watching Eli and feeding the stock," Trace said.

"Anytime," Tilly answered with a smile, though, when her eyes met Kacey's, the smile faltered a bit. As Ed yanked on his boots, she pulled a stocking cap over her gray hair, then shepherded Trace aside and whispered something to him while she eyed Kacey skeptically.

"Come on, Mother. Let's go," Ed said, opening the door. A blast of cold air swept inside. "Oh, sweet Mary, we'd better get home. I heard on the news there's gonna be a helluva storm, and for once, it looks like they're right. You'd better draw some water in the bathtub and the sinks, just in case you lose power here. No reason to be out of water, too."

They stepped outside, and the door closed behind them with a bang. Through the window Kacey saw the branches of the trees still dancing wildly. Snow was swirling crazily. Already drifts were piling against the side of the house and the outbuildings.

Ed was right. It looked to be one helluva storm, even by Montana standards.

Once the older couple had climbed into their truck and rolled out of the driveway, the taillights of their old Dodge disappearing in the falling snow, Trace locked the back door. Kacey was already removing Tilly's leftovers from the refrigerator. "Let me guess," she said, peering over the top of the refrigerator door. "Tilly pulled you aside to give you the word on me, right? I bet she thinks I look a little too much like your ex-wife."

Trace lifted a shoulder. "And Jocelyn."

"Huh." She kicked the door shut. "Now I'm a type." Placing the containers of food on the counter, she felt immediate contrition when she thought of Jocelyn Wallis and how she'd died. Realizing she was tired, hungry, and her nerves were strung tight as guy wires, she said, "Sorry. Guess that's a little bit of a sore point."

"Tilly's impressed that you're a doctor."

"Well, great." She cringed at how sharp she sounded. "I think I'm hungrier and grouchier than I thought."

"Maybe it's the arsenic," he said soberly.

"No. I'm fine. Even if they find it in the coffee grounds, I haven't had much coffee at home lately. What about you? You drank some this morning."

He shook his head. "Either it's not there or just not in what you served up today."

"That's something to celebrate, then," she said fervently.

"You're right." He grinned then, and it made her heart clutch a little. "Here . . . let me heat this up," he said, reaching for the leftovers.

"Mind if I check on Eli?"

"No. Please. Go."

Though Trace had looked in on his son the second they'd arrived at the house, it had been half an hour or so ago. Bonzi, who had explored every corner of the downstairs and had checked out Sarge, seemed to want to follow her, but the command "Stay" from her and the smell of chicken kept him in the kitchen with Trace. Sarge, too, had taken up a spot under the table and was watching anxiously, hoping Trace would drop a savory morsel. Kacey hated to think what kind of growling, snarling dogfight might ensue if any chicken hit the floor. "Be good," she told her dog.

Kicking her shoes off at the base of the stairs, she hurried up the five steps to the landing, then turned and climbed the rest of the flight to the second story, where an old railing with heavy newel posts prevented anyone from falling down the staircase.

Eli's room was tucked under the eaves on one side of the hall, along with a spare room, used, it seemed, for storage. The door to the third bedroom hung ajar, and she pushed it open a little farther, the light from the hallway spilling onto unused furniture, plastic tubs, and stacked boxes.

The bath was located at the end of the hall; the largest bedroom next to it. She looked inside, saw a neatly made massive bed and a small dresser with a flat screen mounted over it. Trace's room, obviously.

Across the hall, wedged between the bathroom and the room used for storage, a door was open slightly, and she deduced from the trail of toys leading through it that this was Eli's area of the house. Pushing the door open farther, allowing more light inside, she spied Trace's son tangled in the rumpled covers, facedown in his pillow. He was breathing loudly, his arm with its cast flung to one side. She stepped closer, careful not to crush toys on the floor, but a floorboard creaked. Eli moaned softly, then rolled onto his back. Blinking, he looked up and his little face twisted in confusion.

"Mommy?" he asked in a sleep-shrouded voice.

Kacey's throat constricted. "No." She sat on the edge of his bed and touched the fingers sticking out of his cast. "No, honey, it's Kacey. Dr. Lambert. You remember me."

He was still eyeing her, and even in the semidarkness she saw the hope on his face fade.

As the storm raged outside, her heart cracked for the boy, but she forced a smile and pushed the hair off his forehead.

He glanced at the closet, which was dark, its door closed tight, then to the window, as if he were trying to get his bearings. "But—"

"It's okay," she said when she recognized his disappointment. He swallowed hard and bit his lower lip to keep from shedding tears.

Her own eyes burned. "So . . . how're you feeling?"

"Okay."

"You want anything?" *Other than your mother.*

"Nah." He shook his head and flopped back onto the pillow.

"Okay. Then go back to sleep and I'll check on you later. Okay?"

He was too tired to argue, it seemed. Closing his eyes, he burrowed deeper under the covers, and though his forehead was creased with confusion for a second or two, soon he was breathing deeply again, probably dreaming about having a mom nearby. As she observed Eli for a few seconds, Kacey mentally swore that if she were ever to run into Leanna, she'd wring her neck.

Stop it! She could be dead, for all you know.

That could explain why Trace hasn't heard from her, why she seems to have completely deserted her son.

Give the woman a break. Leanna could be the victim of an accident, like the others. There is a chance her body just hasn't been discovered.

A cold chill slithered through her body, but even so, she was angry with a woman who could abandon her child.

Satisfied that Eli was sleeping soundly, Kacey walked back to the hallway and down the stairs, where the scents of Tilly's killer chicken were wafting from the lower level.

Her stomach had the bad manners to growl loudly as she entered the kitchen.

Trace, gingerly lifting a bowl from the microwave, looked over his shoulder. "How was he?"

"Confused. Thought I was Leanna," Kacey admitted. "Kinda like Tilly." She managed a smile as she found plates and set them on the table. "I'm giving your son a pass. He's on medication and just a kid. Tilly . . . I'm not so sure."

"She'll come around," he said.

He served the dinner, and Kacey, seated on a beat-up kitchen chair that looked to be at least fifty years old, had to admit Tilly's killer chicken was the best meal she'd eaten since Thanksgiving with Maribelle, maybe better.

They ate in silence. The chicken was succulent, and the beans were seasoned with soy sauce and garlic. Even the mashed potatoes, tasting slightly of butter and sour cream melted in her mouth and really didn't need the gravy that she'd ladled on, anyway.

"Okay," Kacey admitted, once her plate was nearly empty. "So she can cook. And knit. And didn't you say play checkers?"

"And a lot more. Give her a chance."

"If she gives me one."

"No promises there," he teased. "I'm going out and double-checking the stock. Make sure all the hatches are battened down. Wanna come?"

She glanced out the window just as a gust of bitter wind rattled the shutters. "You know, I think I'll pass," she said. "Stay in with Eli and clean up the kitchen."

"Can't get a better offer than that."

She watched him put on his jacket again, long arms sliding through the sleeves. What was it about him she found so damned attractive? She, who had always been interested in professional men, city guys.

Like JC?

Or maybe a guy who is more like one of Gerald Johnson's sons, not the men themselves, but a man in a suit and tie, with an uptight attitude?

"Nope," she said aloud.

With both dogs on his heels, Trace made his way outside to check on the cattle and horses for the night. Kacey, meanwhile, cleaned the kitchen, then settled onto the couch with her laptop. The TV, turned to an all-news channel, was still at a decibel level loud enough to cause her permanent hearing loss herself, so she scrounged in the cushions of the couch until she found the spot where the remote control had fallen, then softened the volume.

Currently, a weatherman was standing in front of a screen showing parts of Montana, Idaho, and Canada. With a sweeping movement of his arm, he explained how arctic air was blasting down from Saskatchewan and Alberta to dump somewhere between eighteen inches and three feet of snow in the next forty-eight hours. "Looks like we'll be getting that white Christmas a few weeks early," he said happily, then cut to a reporter standing near the interstate, shivering and reporting on the freezing weather conditions as semis rolled down the highway behind her.

A second later the television screen changed, and the image of Elle Alexander was visible. "The Pinewood County Sheriff's Office is asking for your help in locating the vehicle that may have pushed a local Dodge minivan off the road and into the Grizzly River," an anchor said as the screen switched to that section of road, right before the North Fork Bridge, where in the snow, flowers and candles had been left to mark the spot where Elle Alexander had lost her life. Minutes later the news was reporting on the death of a "lone cross-country skier," whose name hadn't yet been released pending notification of next of kin.

She drew a breath, then hit the mute button, hearing the storm outside really start to rage, the wind shrieking, a branch beating against the house. A glance at the clock told her Trace had been gone nearly half an hour. He should be back soon, she figured. After walking into the kitchen, she stared through the window and told herself to relax. Her gaze followed the path broken in the snow as it led to the outbuildings.

There was another path as well, smaller, going around the side of the house and almost obscured by the new snow.

Odd.

But then Tilly and Ed had been here with Eli and Sarge. Perhaps one of them had taken Sarge outside . . . ? Tilly, probably, since the path was thin and she couldn't imagine Ed's size twelves tamping down the snow like that.

Except, of course, the new-fallen snow changed the footprints, softened them, and made them appear smaller.

Huh.

She told herself not to worry, not to let the recent accidents, her own house being compromised, or her supposed poisoning get the better of her. She was safe. Here. With Trace.

And yet the feeling that something wasn't right here hung with her. "Just a new place," she whispered, wishing one of the dogs had stayed in the house with Eli and her. With one last look at the fast-disappearing path, she returned to the living room, where the crackling fire dispelled some of her unease. Curling up on the couch again, she opened up her laptop and did a little more research on Gerald Johnson, his company, and his family.

Your family.

"Never," she said aloud as the lights flickered once and a branch began beating against the side of the house like it was trying to get inside.

Again, she glanced at the back door, wishing Trace would return. Other noises assailed her: timbers creaking, the common sounds of an old house settling, the squeak and soughing of tree limbs rubbing against each other. Telling herself she was letting her nerves get the better of her, she fought a ridiculous panic attack and turned her attention away from the dark night beyond. She Googled everyone in the Johnson family and remembered her own impressions of Gerald and his children.

Her father was an enigma. Strong. Smart. Educated. Hard-edged. A man who solved problems and faced adversity.

Ruthless?

Probably.

As for his firstborn, Clarissa, she was a little more transparent, or at least it seemed so on first look. Bold and arrogant, abrasive and downright bitchy, she was married to the Thor-like Lance. Two peas in a pod. Kacey wondered if either one of them had an inkling about a sense of humor. And yet they had children. Kacey had trouble imagining anyone less motherly than Clarissa Johnson Werner, but she'd only seen her agitated. She couldn't help but think there was something going on with Clarissa, her snarly exterior hiding some darker emotion.

Then there was Judd, next in line, quieter, but the kind of guy that made you think of the old "still waters run deep" adage. Who knew what he was thinking or what he was capable of? He was a lawyer, as was Thane, but Judd was definitely the more uptight, by-the-book corporate type and, from what she had read about him, was divorced from a wife who had moved to Portland. No kids.

Thane was a mystery. Quiet. Friendlier than the rest, slightly amused. The black sheep who hadn't quite run off. Almost a rogue, but not quite. The one person in the group who wouldn't settle for being under his father's thumb. At least not completely. Never married. Of all her half siblings the one she might be able to talk to. The least standoffish. She made a note.

As for the twins, she didn't know where she stood with them. Cameron who had smoothed his hair on more than one occasion in the meeting had been more openly antagonistic toward her. However, Colt hadn't exactly been warm and fuzzy, either. The smiles he'd offered seemed cold, as if he were amused by a private joke at her expense. Or had she imagined that?

Neither twin had ever been married, at least not to her knowledge, but she knew very little about them other than that they were salesmen for their father's company and that their jobs took them all over the country and into Canada.

Was it possible they were the culprits? Perhaps working in tandem? One offering up alibis for the other while their jobs provided the perfect cover as they flew all over the country. Could they both be so perverted and twisted?

"Unlikely," she said under her breath, but told herself to dig a little deeper, find a way to check their business trips and how they could have coincided with other unexplained accidents to unfortunate women who may have been born with the aid of a fertility clinic in Helena, Montana.

"That's nuts," she told herself, and turned her attention to Robert Lindley, the oddball, the one half sibling most like her. He was older than she, and again, she'd found no record of his marriage. Granted, she hadn't had time to dig deeply into any of their lives, but a marriage should have been easily discovered, a matter of public record. Robert, too, had been antagonistic; she'd felt his distrust of her from the second he'd walked into the boardroom.

Did he still feel as if he were an outcast, even though he was a part of the family, at least as far as the company went?

But the ones she'd met weren't all of Gerald Johnson's children. Two of his three daughters had died from separate accidents: Aggie, as a child; Kathleen, when she was still in college.

Kacey wondered about them.

Accident victims.

Was there such a thing when it came to Gerald Johnson's female progeny?

But Clarissa. She's survived. Apparently her father's right-hand woman. How does that make any sense?

"It doesn't," she said aloud as the wind whipped around the corners of the house and the lights flickered again. Her skin crawled and she had to fight the feeling that someone, or something was outside, something malicious, something waiting and watching.

The storm was a bitch! Rattling the old window panes, whistling through the rafters of the barn, causing the cattle to low and move restlessly. The dogs, too, were edgy, whining at the noise. Bonzi, for appearing tough, was really a wimp, it seemed.

"Hang in there," he told all the animals and to the rescue dog, "We'll be fine."

But Bonzi's tail hung low as another blast of wind shook the building. Trace ignored him and began rewrapping some exposed pipes that were freezing. It would take some time, but he wanted to ensure that the cattle continued getting water and that the pipe wouldn't burst.

The lights flickered once, then again . . . *Great,* he thought as he hadn't yet even broken a path to the horses in the stable a few yards away. The last thing he needed was to lose electricity.

Bonzi cowered, whining through his nose, but Trace kept on insulating the pipes as best he could.

Hopefully things would be better when he reached the stable.

So they separated.
How perfect.

From his hiding spot, night goggles allowing him to view the snowy landscape, he watched the house, had seen the old people leave. His eyes followed O'Halleran as he trudged to the barn with both dogs in tow. Aside from the kid, Acacia was alone in the house.

And he could deal with the boy.

Things were finally falling together after the scare earlier today, and the feeling that he was being followed again. He'd seen the BMW that he'd thought he'd caught tailing him the other night. He'd told himself he was imagining things, letting his paranoia rule, but again, today, earlier, he could have sworn someone was following him.

Pull yourself together! Do you see anyone out here? Hear them? Has there been any glimpse of a damned BMW for hours?
No!
You're just jittery because tonight's the night. It's all come down to this. Time for revenge, now, isn't it? Soon, oh, so soon, Acacia's life will be in your hands.

Despite the cold and the wind rattling the icy branches of the surrounding trees, he felt his cock twitch at the mental image of her lying beneath him, quivering in fear, eyes trained on the knife that he would use to slit her perfect throat . . .

No! That's not how it's going down. This is not sexual and there can be no knife. It has to look like an accident. Just as you did with all the others. Don't stop now. Stick to the plan . . . she's one of them, those progeny of Gerald Johnson who are mentally insufficient, even deranged. They all are . . . even Clarissa, probably. She, too, cannot be spared even though she's an ally. Eventually, she will have to die . . . But now, concentrate. First you have to incapacitate her, then you have to take out O'Halleran, get him back to the house and stage the scene. Make it look like murder/suicide and then burn the house to the ground. By the time the volunteer fire department arrives, it will be much too late.

Training his gaze on the windows and the light beyond the panes, he caught glimpses of her walking through the house. Each time he saw her, he felt his blood heat in anticipation, knew he wouldn't have to wait much longer. Now, Acacia was in the kitchen and looking through the window, straight at him. His heart stopped for just an instant.

Then he realized she couldn't see him through the shroud of snow, didn't understand that he was observing her closely while plotting the details of her death. He mentally chastised himself. *Do not unravel. Do not fall victim to your own paranoia! You have a mission. Do not be distracted by lust or fear. . . . Goddamnit, be strong!*

Sucking air in through his teeth, feeling the cold burn through his lungs, he forced his thoughts clear. To center. Then he saw her again, peering through the night and a new power overtook him. It was as if he could talk to her through his mind.

You asked for this, bitch. You wanted to find me. . . . He felt a smile twist the corners of his lips as he eyed the farmhouse with its gabled roof. Most of the windows were darkened, especially those on the second floor. Shifting his rifle from one gloved hand to the other, he realized exactly how he would deal with her.

Another gust of bone-rattling wind cut through him and the lights in the house blinked nervously.

Again, she looked his way, her beautiful face drawn into an expression of worry. Oh, if she only knew. . . .

Get ready, Acacia, he thought grimly, heading through the snow toward the front of the house, where the porch was dark. *I'm coming.*

* * *

Where the hell was Trace? Just how long did it take to check on horses and cattle that Ed had already fed?

"Come on," she said and thought about putting on her coat and boots and plowing her way to the outbuildings. But she didn't want to leave Eli alone. What if he woke up again and called for his mother?

Feeling like an idiot, she decided to call Trace on his cell, and using her own phone, punched out his number and waited.

A phone rang inside the kitchen, and she jumped. Then realized the cell belonged to Trace. He'd left his damned phone on the counter.

He's fine! He has to be!

The lights shivered once more; and this time Kacey was spurred into action.

Remembering Ed's advice, she drew water in the tub of the bathroom downstairs, found buckets and a flashlight in the kitchen. The fire was already blazing, wood stacked near the hearth; as she returned to the living room.

Klunk!

A noise overhead. From the floor above.

"Eli?" she called, her heart hammering. She started for the stairs, had taken two steps when the lights failed. Darkness fell in an instant, only the fire offering a flickering red-gold illumination that cast the room in shifting, uneasy shadows.

She hadn't been aware of the furnace rumbling or the refrigerator humming, but now there was total silence, a frightening quietude broken only by the howl of the wind and that same damned branch beating against the house. Waiting, she hoped to hear a generator switch on, prayed the lights would flicker and hold, the furnace would churn to life.

Nothing.

Now what?

She felt cold as death, as if the wind outside were blowing through the bones of this old house. Her skin crawled as she thought of all the things that could go wrong in the dark, without heat, without light, with a homicidal maniac on the loose. . . .

"Stop," she told herself sternly.

Fumbling her way to the kitchen, where she'd left the flashlight, she banged her knee once, bit back a curse, then automatically groped for the light switch before stopping herself, then finding the flashlight on the counter. She pushed the button; and a weak yellowish light signaled that the batteries inside were nearly gone.

Eli.

He would know where more batteries were; and besides, she needed to haul him and his blankets downstairs so they could stay close to the fire.

Glancing outside to the darkness, where no exterior lights offered the slightest illumination, she said, "Come on, Trace!" The lights had gone off in the barn and stable, too. . . . Surely he'd return ASAP.

In the meantime . . .

Following the weak, thin light from the flashlight, she mounted the stairs. Darkness seemed to sink into her from every corner of this old, unfamiliar house. She rounded the corner of the landing and heard another thud against the house.

What was that?

Eli?

Swallowing back her fear, she thundered up the remaining stairs, swung around the newell post in the hallway, and pushed open the door to Eli's room.

The bed was empty; sheets and blankets had slithered onto the floor. "Eli!" she cried, searching crazily, swinging the beam of her flashlight through the room. "Eli!" She threw open the closet door and found nothing but clothes, then ran through the bathroom and Trace's room, the flashlight growing weaker but giving up no trace of the boy. "Eli!" *Oh, God, oh, God!* Where was he?

Now in a full-blown panic, Kacey was sweating despite the cold, fear clawing at her throat. She looked through the third bedroom, around the draped furniture, under the hems, through the maze of boxes and pictures stacked around the bed and mattress, pushed up against the wall. "Eli!" she called and then, thinking he might be as frightened as she was, said, "It's Kacey, honey. Where are you?"

Oh, sweet Jesus, she'd lost him!

CHAPTER 34

Pescoli drove.

She didn't care that Missoula was out of their jurisdiction.

She didn't give a rat's ass that the FBI was stepping in.

She wanted answers and she wanted them now.

So, while Alvarez was on the phone with one of their junior detectives who'd been left in charge of turning Gerald Johnson's life inside out, Pescoli squinted through the windshield where the wipers were having trouble keeping up with the relentless snow falling from the night sky.

It was times like these she craved a cigarette and if Alvarez weren't such a health nut, Pescoli, who'd learned her glovebox stash of Marlboro Lights was totally depleted, might break down and stop at a local convenience store for a pack of smokes and a super-sized cup of Diet Coke. That's the combo she needed to keep her fired up.

Gerald Johnson lived in a gated community, part of a resort that flanked a private golf club where the buy-in was more than her house was worth and the dues would eat up more than a chunk of her salary. She only hoped the bastard was home.

Armed with Kacey Lambert's theories and Alvarez's sketchy proof, she and her partner were going to see the old man, shake him up. Though she'd come to the party late, disbelieving Alvarez's suspicions that the victims could be related by blood, Pescoli was now on board. She'd finally bought in to the wild idea that women were being killed because they were 727's sperm bank daughters. Why, was another matter. Who, the most critical piece of all.

The weather was a bitch, but then, this was Montana in the winter. What did she expect?

". . . okay, got it," Alvarez said into her cell as the radio crackled with news of a robbery and fleeing suspect on Main Street. "Keep looking. Anything you can find on Johnson, his kids, and the clinic . . . call me back." She clicked off and glanced at Pescoli, her face tense as oncoming headlights flooded the interior with glaring light for a few seconds. "Leona's on it." Leona Randolph was a junior detective who had recently joined the department. Highly skilled in all things technical, Leona had the command of the Internet that amazed Pescoli. Though the girl was only a few years older than Jeremy, Leona was light-years ahead of him in maturity, ambition, and direction. Her son could take a lesson!

"I think the turn-off is about a mile ahead," Alvarez said as the snow blew down in sheets, making visibility almost an impossibility. Pescoli slowed out of necessity. The traffic had been reduced to a crawl. Now, when she felt time was of the essence, that the killer was escalating, that the clock was ticking, she was stymied by the blizzard.

"There's the private road to Cougar Springs," Alvarez said, pointing, just as the beams of Pescoli's headlights washed up against a wide turn.

They plowed through the snow and up a road that wound through the sparse timber of a mountain resort and past a gatehouse where Pescoli flashed a badge at the guard and mentioned Gerald Johnson's name. Once the gate swung open, she put the Jeep into a lower gear and drove it up the steep winding lane. A quarter of a mile in they passed a three-storied glass and cedar lodge, warm lights glowing from windows that climbed to the sharply-pitched, snow-covered roof. Tonight only a few cars, unidentifiable as they were half-buried by the snow, were parked in the lot.

Still upward they drove past forested lots with huge, rambling houses tucked into the hillside. Many of them, the summer homes, were dark, only a few showed warm patches of light blazing from windows—those owned by people who lived here year round or spent their holidays on the nearby ski trails.

"Rough life," Pescoli muttered.

"Boring life," Alvarez added.

"I might be tempted to take a year or two of 'boredom' like this."

"Oh, sure. You'd be climbing the walls inside of a week. Back on the force within two." She slid a look at her partner. "Who are you trying to kid? Me? Or yourself?"

"Both of us, maybe," she muttered.

"What's eating you?"

"My kids. What else?" She would have liked to blame her pent-up anger on the case, and that was part of it, of course, but with Jeremy, who seemed hellbent on being a big, fat zero, and Bianca, whose grades were slipping and was turning increasingly boy crazy, was the real source of her angst. And it didn't help that she was getting pressure from Santana.

"Turn here," Alvarez ordered.

Pescoli cranked on the wheel, slid just slightly, then her tires caught and the Jeep whined up a final bend where the road emptied into a circular drive belonging to Gerald Johnson.

"Showtime," Pescoli said as she parked in front of a garage large enough to house a fleet of vehicles. Gas lights flickered near each of the carriage-style doors mounted on the stone facade. Snow blanketed the walkways, but Pescoli followed Alvarez to the front door. As Alvarez poked a gloved finger at the bell, the door suddenly opened and Gerald Johnson, appearing more forceful and athletic than he had in any of the pictures Pescoli had seen greeted them.

"Officers," he said, "Floyd at the gatehouse called and said you were on your way." He stepped back from the door. "Come in. Ever since Acacia left my office this afternoon, I've been expecting you."

Pescoli and Alvarez were allowed into the Johnson home, and just as they were asking Johnson about the clinic where he'd been a sperm donor, Gerald's wife appeared on the upper landing and then quickly descended the wide staircase.

"Don't, Gerald! I don't know what these people want, but don't tell them anything!"

"We're here because of several recent homicides of women," Alvarez said. "Their deaths, which we originally thought were accidents, have been on the news." She pulled a plastic envelope with the pictures from her pocket. "Elle Alexander whose van was forced off the road, Jocelyn Wallis who, we believe, was pushed over the side of Boxer Bluff, possibly Shelly Bonaventure—"

"The actress in that god-awful vampire series?" Noreen Johnson asked, disbelieving.

Pescoli nodded. "And now, most recently, a local woman named Karalee Rierson."

"Karalee," Noreen squeaked, a hand flying to her lips.

"You know her?" Alvarez asked.

"I know of her."

Alvarez handed Noreen the pictures and she took one look at the photo of Karalee Rierson and almost retched. "Oh, God. She was the nurse at a clinic where Gerald . . ." She turned to him, examining his grim expression.

"We believe they're homicides made to look like accidents," Alvarez said.

"Homicides?" she repeated. "Murder? But what do we have to do with any of this? I . . . I don't know the others. Just Karalee."

Pescoli said, "We have reason to believe they may have all been fathered by Mr. Johnson."

"*What? Fathered* them?" Noreen flapped a hand at them. "That's insane! Gerald, do *not* talk to these people!"

Alvarez watched the woman's features, where a gauntlet of emotions, everything from despair, to denial, to rage, played across her face. Dressed in designer jeans and a silvery knit sweater that covered her hips, she was rail thin, nearly bony, the expensive diamonds at her throat, wrist, and fingers accentuating the bones and sinews that were visible beneath her tanned skin. Her near-white hair was cut boyishly, the skin of her face stretched taut as a drum, her makeup excessive.

"We don't know these women! Barely even spoke to that Kara girl. Gerald, seriously!" She shook her head vehemently and said to the detectives, "We're not talking to you without an attorney present. I know my rights." She slid a slim phone from the pocket of her jeans and punched a single number. "I'm calling Judd." To Gerald she lifted a pointer finger and admonished, "Not another word."

He spread his hands. "They're not accusing me of a crime."

"I don't care. They're tricky. I've seen *Law and Order!*" She had the phone to her ear. "Oh, damn." Meeting her husband's gaze she said, "Judd's not picking up!" Then, looking at the ceiling, she left a message: "Judd? It's Mother. Call me ASAP. It's an emergency!"

"For the love of Saint Peter, Noreen, he'll think I'm in the hospital," Gerald protested.

"Fine!" She hit another speed-dial number, waited, then, rolled her eyes in frustration. "I can't get Clarissa, either! Where the hell is she?"

"Noreen, you need to calm down," Gerald said.

"And you need to not tell me what to do!"

Gerald suggested to Alvarez and Pescoli, "Let's go into the den." He motioned them toward double doors to the right of the staircase where a gas fire hissed, flames reflecting on the windows and the black sheen of a baby grand piano. A huge framed flat screen over the mantel was tuned to a sports network, a half-drunk glass of scotch on a table near a leather recliner. Cut flowers on a coffee table were starting to die, their blooms fading slightly, their scents nearly gone.

"It's Mother. Call me! Emergency!" Noreen yelled into the phone again, as if by raising her voice, whomever she had phoned would pick up. The high heels of her boots clicked angrily as she marched stiffly into the den. "I can't rouse anyone! Where the hell are they?"

"Honey, it would be best if you just chill out a little," her husband suggested. He waved the detectives into side chairs as he settled into the recliner and clicked off the television. The latest sports scores disappeared and the screen briefly went black to be replaced, automatically, by a family portrait.

"I will *not* 'chill out!'" She rotated the slim phone in one hand while she glared at her husband. "Why does it seem like my children are avoiding me? Screening their damned calls?" Her scorching gaze landed full force on Alvarez. "Why are you here?"

"Noreen, please—" Her husband held out his hand, fingers splayed, beseeching her to shut up. "Let me handle this." To Alvarez and Pescoli, he said, "I told you I was expecting you because Acacia Lambert came to my office today. She had the same information you just told me about."

"Who came to the office?" Noreen cut in, pacing back and forth in front of the fire. "Acacia who?" She was shaking her head, obviously not understanding. "What are you talking about, Gerald?" But there was something more than curiosity in her imperious gaze; there was a hint of trepidation. Of fear.

"My daughter," he said softly.

His wife's expression froze. "What the hell are you talking about?"

She whispered the question, her gaze darting to the officers for the briefest of seconds. "*Clarissa* is our daughter."

"Not ours, Noreen. Mine," he clarified and Alvarez could almost see him sweat. "With Maribelle," he admitted.

"Maribelle?" Noreen stopped short. "That *nurse* who used to work for you?" She was nearly shivering with rage.

"Acacia's nearly thirty-five now," Gerald said softly.

Something deep inside Noreen broke. Her shoulders slumped and tears welled in her big eyes. "I knew you two were . . . intimate. Of course I knew, but . . ." Noreen's voice quivered. "And I've stayed your wife. Through that other debacle, when you claimed him, *hired* him, paraded him out like some precious puppy. And I suffered through that excruciating embarrassment." Her nostrils flared and her lips curled back over white-capped teeth. "I've even had your bastard's whore of a mother here, in my house." She pointed a finger at the thick carpet covering the hardwood. "I've suffered through that humiliation as well!" Jabbing her finger at the floor, she started to sob. "But this . . . *another* one?" Tears slid down the severe slope of her cheeks. "Don't do this . . . don't you tell them . . . I can't believe, not after that pathetic Lindley woman and her boy . . ."

"My son's name is Robert and he's a man."

"What's wrong with you? Why have you done this? And with whores! You swore to me, do you remember, *swore on our children's lives,* that you'd broken it off with that wretched Collins woman!"

"I did."

She shuddered and looked as if she might throw up. "But you had a child with her. And she was married, then, too. Probably pawned that kid off as her husband's." When Gerald didn't respond, she said, "What is it with you? You didn't father just one bastard child. That wasn't enough. Now there's another! Do our kids know?" She seemed to shrink from the inside out. "Oh, God, they were there at the office when she showed up, right?" When he didn't answer, she said more loudly, "Right?"

"That's probably why they're not answering their phones," Gerald said. "I told them I was going to tell you tonight." He glanced down at his half drunk glass of scotch. "I just hadn't worked up the nerve yet."

"Funny how easy it is to father an army of children, but you don't even have the spine to talk to your wife!" Noreen said under her breath.

"Just listen, okay," he suggested, and let out a heavy sigh.

Noreen crossed her arms under her small breasts and jutted out her jaw defiantly, but held her tongue as he explained what he knew of Acacia and how he'd stayed out of her life, but when asked, acknowledged being a sperm donor.

"So you knew that he'd been involved with the fertility clinic?" Pescoli asked Noreen.

"That was so long ago," she said. "But yes. I knew that Gerald . . ." She waved one bony hand. "That was different. Clinical. Nothing intimate. Not like having an affair and fathering children with whores!" The tears began again. She found a tissue and dabbed at mascara-stained tears drizzling down her cheeks. "I don't understand. That really doesn't explain why you're here. Even if, even if he did . . . well, sire these women for lack of a better word. How do you even know that?"

"It's the one thing that connects the victims," Pescoli said.

"Victims?" Noreen was torn between horror and disbelief. "Oh God! Why these women? Why now? And what does it have to do with him?"

Alvarez said, "That's what we're here to find out."

Calm down, Kacey told herself. *Eli has to be here. He has to.* "Eli!" she yelled, more loudly. "Eli, honey, where are you?"

Frantic, her heart racing with fear, Kacey searched the house top to bottom once more. Her flashlight was losing power, its beam weak as she moved slowly, room by room, calling out Trace's son's name. Her pulse was pounding erratically in her ears, dread propelling her as she swept the pale light under beds, into closets even, dear God, down the laundry chute to the basement.

Still no sign of him.

"Come on, Eli. Where are you?"

The house was getting colder by the second. Through the upstairs she went another time and there, in the third bedroom, she saw a crack, heard the whistle of air seeping through a window that wasn't quite latched. She tried to slam it shut, but it wouldn't catch.

Throwing her weight into it, she heard . . . *what?* The skin on her scalp crinkled as she caught her breath and listened.

Another noise. From the floor below! Footsteps?

"Eli!" She slammed her knee against an old cedar chest as she raced to the hallway, then flew frantically down the stairs. The flashlight's faint beam bobbed and wobbled, casting shadows.

Around the corner and into the living area she ran, where the fire crackled and hissed and the corners were cloaked in darkness.

"Eli?" she said, her voice sounding loud, even echoing as the wind battered the house. "Honey?"

But she saw no one on the main floor.

Not Eli.

Not Trace.

Not the dogs.

But she *felt* a presence . . . Something different, like the scent of fresh, night air clinging to the darkness.

Don't do this. Don't freak yourself out.

In a flash, the night she was attacked in the parking garage sizzled through her mind. Brutal images of pain and fear.

Pull yourself together! Keep searching!

Where the hell is Trace's son?

Bracing herself, nearly wincing as she passed gloomy corners, she pushed herself through the kitchen and into the stairwell. The steps to the cellar squeaked and her nostrils filled with the dry smell of dust that had collected from years of neglect. Whispery fingers tickled her cheek. "Oh!" She nearly stumbled down the remaining steps as a cobweb brushed against her face and clung to her hair.

Quieting her racing heart, she scraped the barest of light from her flashlight over stacked firewood, the scent of raw cedar faint in the cold space where more old furniture and tools had been left to gather dust.

The flashlight was fading but she forced its thin stream of light under the stairs, and across shelves where old canning glassware and boxes of insecticides hid.

Scccrrratttch!

She nearly dropped the flashlight as a mouse, its eye catching the fading light scurried quickly into a crack in the concrete wall.

"On . . God . . . damn! Eli!" she called again, but heard nothing other than the pounding of her heart and somewhere far off, the sound of chains rattling in the wind and that nerve-stretching *thunk, thunk, thunk* of a branch pummeling the house.

She hated dark spaces, had all of her life. No, that wasn't true. Her real fear of the dark had come after the attack, when her assailant had sprung from the shadows.

Again, a horrid memory flashed through her mind and in that instant her knees nearly buckled. She grabbed hold of a post bolstering the stairs for support and in so doing dropped her flashlight. It rolled away, the light drunkenly spinning across forgotten chairs, exposed beams overhead, and a wall of ancient, dirty cement .

Don't think about him. Push the attack out of your mind! It's over.

But now that the image was planted, she couldn't forget her assailant, how his hard, angry body had been as it pressed her to the concrete, how he'd smelled of some faint aftershave mingled with sweat and a trace of cigarette smoke. He'd been so big and strong . . . built like . . . the men she'd met today, her brothers! Some of them had that same strong, athletic build. Hadn't she thought of Judd as a football player, and even Lance, Clarissa's husband, had that same primal, nearly jungle-cat like quality?

The others?

What about Robert or Thane or the twins?

And they all had those cold blue eyes.

Heart pounding, breathing in shallow gasps, feeling the taste of fear in the back of her throat, she slid down the post, then crawled to the flashlight, scooped it up and after giving herself a quick mental shake, struggled to her feet.

You have to find Eli!

Shaken, she pulled herself together. Up the stairs she climbed.

Maybe he'd gotten out of bed and followed Trace to the barns. Perhaps he'd been disoriented . . . hadn't he called her "Mommy?" There was a chance the medication had caused him to sneak downstairs and outside . . .

How?

Wouldn't you have seen him? Heard him?

This was ridiculous!

She needed help!

She threw on her coat, gloves, and boots, took the time to light the one candle she'd seen in the living room with an ember from the fire, then, with her phone clutched in her hand, she walked to the door and punched out Detective Alvarez's number.

What would she say? She'd lost the kid? Trace hadn't come back from the barns?

That was foolish.

She didn't care.

"Better safe than sorry," she said, looking through the windows, feeling the seconds ticking by as the snow continued to pile and drift. When the detective didn't answer, Kacey hung up, didn't leave a message.

Not yet.

She'd find Trace first, she thought, pocketing her phone and opening the door to the cold, dark night.

As she stepped outside a wall of cold air hit her so hard it seemed to strip any warmth from her body. Her skin chilled immediately and she wished she'd taken the time to grab a scarf and hat. Over the keen of the wind, she thought, again, she heard chains rattling, like those on an empty flagpole, or the clinking sound of shackled prisoners walking.

All in your imagination. Keep moving.

Swallowing back her fear, she followed the trail of footprints she'd seen earlier that were nearly covered now, but she kept after them, not toward the barns, but around the corner of the house, past a snow-covered rhododendron bush to the side of Trace's home where more footprints had clustered.

It was impossible to confirm of course, to make out anything definitive with the snow blowing over the area. Over the wind she heard the branch still battering the house. Looking up, forcing the dying flashlight beam skyward, she not only saw the pine slapping at the siding, she noticed one of those fire-escape ladders hanging from the window of the extra bedroom.

The ladder moved with the wind, its chains rattling like the bones of the dead. Her heart plummeted.

She knew in a heartbeat that Eli, with his broken arm, had somehow slithered down this ladder and disappeared into the frigid, unforgiving night.

CHAPTER 35

Noreen Johnson had sunk onto the piano bench, her shoulders hunched together, but, Alvarez observed, hadn't yet given up the fight. "For the love of God, Gerald, why couldn't you keep your pants up! First Robert, with that awful Lindley woman . . . and of course you had to hire him so that I could be reminded every single day of your betrayal and now . . . now another one? How could you?" Her cheeks flamed red.

"What's done is done," Gerald said wearily. "We can talk about this later. For now, I think the detectives have some questions they want answered."

"It's over!" she whispered. "Our life, the one we knew is over."

Gerald cleared his throat and kept his tense gaze toward Pescoli and Alvarez. "What can I do for you, detectives?" he asked, leaning forward, hands clasped between his knees.

Alvarez took the lead, asking him a series of questions. Gerald Johnson swore he'd never met the victims, hadn't known they could be sired by him, hadn't even guessed it until Acacia had shown up earlier in the day. He had no idea if any of them had any enemies, but he was certain from his children's reaction earlier that they were as surprised as he.

Pescoli was keeping to herself, observing, though more than once, Alvarez caught her partner studying the screen that had appeared when the television clicked off. Maybe it was her way of calming her aggression, but just listening, not interacting was certainly out of character for her.

Alvarez took another quick look at the TV screen. Nothing out of the ordinary. The current photo was of a family portrait taken years before, with Gerald and Noreen twenty-five or thirty years younger, their children spread around them in matching outfits, the boys in white shirts, navy vests, and khaki slacks; the three girls in red dresses. Someone had added their names to the digital picture.

"We have nothing to tell you," Noreen insisted, and sent her husband a silent message. She tried, once again, to call one of her children to no avail. "Where are they?" she whispered and closed her eyes. "Don't they know that we need them?"

Pescoli said, "You had seven children?"

"*I* had seven," Noreen clarified, sniffing angrily. "Gerald obviously had a few more."

"What happened to your daughters? Agatha and Kathleen?" Pescoli asked.

"I'd rather not talk about it." Noreen's voice was a whisper. She closed her eyes, her entire face tensed as from pain.

"Agatha was our late in life baby," Gerald said. "There were complications with the birth and we knew early on that there were issues. She would be mentally . . . challenged. But she was . . ."

"An angel." Noreen glared at Pescoli. "I don't see what this has to do with anything."

"How did she die?" Pescoli asked.

Noreen looked like she didn't want to respond, but then reluctantly said, "It was an accident. I'd run to the store, hadn't been gone half an hour. Clarissa, she's the oldest, was supposed to be watching the younger ones . . ." She sighed and looked up, toward the window facing the front of the house, but Alvarez knew she wasn't seeing the snow falling outside. Her sight was turned inside herself, to a time she would clearly rather forget. "As I understand it, the boys were playing like they do—did—they've always been active. Aggie . . . she was supposed to be asleep. Taking her nap . . ." Noreen blinked and shook her head, dispelling the image running through her brain. "Oh, God, I can't do this."

Gerald took up the narrative. "We don't know exactly what happened, but, as Noreen said, the boys were roughhousing, they had a wooden sword and were running up and down the stairs. Aggie woke up, walked out of her room with her blanket and one of the twins—"

"Cam," Noreen supplied miserably.

"Bumped into her." A muscle in Gerald's jaw worked. "She got tangled in her blanket and . . . she fell down the stairs. It was an accident."

Alvarez met Pescoli's gaze.

It was an accident. Like Shelly Bonaventure accidentally *took an overdose? Like Jocelyn Wallis* accidentally *fell to her death over a railing? Like Elle Alexander* accidentally *slid off the road into the river in her minivan? Or like Karalee Rierson* accidentally *skied into a tree?*

Frightened out of her mind for Eli, Kacey started for the barn.

She'd taken three steps through the knee-high snow, around the side of the garage, nearly at the gate separating the backyard from the barnyard, when she saw movement out of the corner of her eye.

Her heart squeezed.

Eli?

She turned.

No, much too tall, she realized as the dark figure of a man began to take shape, a man emerging from the back porch.

Trace?

Thank God!

Relief washed over her and she started heading his way. "Trace—" she began to call when the sound suddenly died in her throat.

Fear congealed her blood.

Just the way he moved warned her. Caused the hairs on the back of her neck to stand on end. The falling snow blurred the image, but now that he was closer she knew he wasn't Trace. Dressed in black from head to foot, odd-shaped goggles over a ski mask, a rifle in one gloved hand, he started to jog toward her.

No!

She took off at a sprint, running, fast as she could through the thick powder, churning up snow, getting nowhere. She heard him behind her, coming ever faster. On level ground she might have had a chance, but she was breaking the trail and he was following. Gaining.

Oh, God!

Frantic, she yanked her phone from her pocket, hit redial and started to yell over the cry of the wind. "Trace!" she screamed but her voice was lost in the storm.

"Bitch!" he snarled so close to her and she plunged forward, bracing herself, knowing a bullet was soon to crack her spine.

Faster! Faster! Faster!

Adrenaline spurred her on.

"Trace!" she screamed again.

If only she had a weapon, a knife, a rock, *anything!*

Blam!

Pain exploded in the back of her head.

Her knees buckled and she fell forward. Arms flung out, stretched. Her phone spiraled into the air to plummet into a drift. Snow covered her face and her eyes felt as if they were jarred from her head. *I'm dying,* she thought, her brain on fire. *I've lost them all . . .*

Blackness pulled at her consciousness and she expected the darkness to overcome her yet she felt his hands upon her. Rough, circling her ankles, dragging her backward through the frozen snow and ice.

She heard him breathing. Swearing. Ranting.

". . . supercilious bitch . . . ruining everything . . . a doctor . . . yeah, right . . . think you're so damned smart . . ."

She tried to fight, to struggle, but her brain wouldn't engage and she felt him drag her up the steps of the house, her chin bouncing on each icy ledge. *Bang, bang, bang!* Her chin split. Cartilage in her nose crunched. Pain ripped up her face. Tears sprang to her eyes and she moaned. A stinging, as if by a thousand jellow jackets had attacked her, pierced her skin. Blood trailed across the porch, following her into the house.

It was all she could do to stay conscious.

Who was he? she wondered, but knew it didn't matter. The fact that she wasn't dead already meant that he had plans for her . . . ugly, horrific plans.

Think, Kacey, think! Don't give up. Don't let the darkness overtake you! Hang on . . .

He kept dragging her across the linoleum kitchen floor and into the den where the fire burned low, reddish embers glowing in the hearth. Then he rolled her onto her back. She felt the blood staining her face.

"I've waited years for this," he growled and for the first time she realized she hadn't been shot. No way would she have survived a rifle blast to the head. But the butt of his rifle showed red stains and hairs where he'd slammed it into the back of her head. "God damn it, I wish I would have killed you the last time."

In the parking garage, she thought. *This man dressed in black was the same who had attacked her years before! Who the hell was he?*

"But then I wouldn't be able to savor it now." The voice . . . oh, God, he was one of the twins! Cameron? Colton? Did it matter? He looked down at her through his black ski mask and she imagined he was smiling, feeling superior. "Take my time."

She blinked, trying to stay focused.

"You're one of them, you know," he said. "The 'Unknowings.' Those Gerald spawned. *Females,* who are compromised."

What? The pain in her body was agonizing, but she was keeping lucid with an effort, her gaze surreptitiously searching for a weapon, anything she could use against him, though he was still holding her ankles in one big hand, his other clutching his rifle.

He was still railing, "Like Aggie with her 'mental challenges' and Kathleen with her depression. Suicidal, they claimed. But it ran deeper. Much, much deeper. A genetic flaw. The flaw of all of Gerald's female offspring. It might not be evident early, but eventually it comes out."

"That's crazy," she said with difficulty, knowing somehow she had to turn the tables on him. "*You're* insane."

He flinched, then shook it off. "Don't," he warned, shaking his head. "Don't." He drew in a shaky breath and she realized he was unraveling, what little grip he had on his mind was fraying second by second. His fingers tightened roughly over her ankles. "It doesn't matter what you think, Acacia. Never has. Because you're one of them. The ones that could ruin everything. The lunatic females."

He was certifiable. He'd made up some crazy, nightmare fantasy about the female progeny of his father. "What about Clarissa?" she asked, through painful, swollen lips.

"In time . . . it has to be all according to the plan . . . accidents . . . arranged at the right time . . ."

She had to get away from this maniac! She had to save herself and save Eli!

The fire popped loudly.

As if he realized he was rambling, he snapped his head quickly back and forth and the eyes that had been staring at her through his mask glared fiercely. "Enough of this! We're done here. It's over for you!"

Now!

With all her strength, Kacey suddenly twisted her entire body.

His fingers slipped around her ankles. "Shit!"

She was free!

Zeroing in on his crotch, she kicked upward.

Hard as she could.

Her boot connected with soft tissue.

"Oooooh!" She nailed him directly in the groin and he doubled over. "Shit!" He dragged in his breath so that it whistled through his teeth. "You . . . fuckin' . . . bitch!"

Quickly, while he was disabled, she scrambled backward, trying to get to her feet, bumping a shoulder into the edge of the couch, her mind still thick from the blow to her head. Where the hell was Trace? she thought wildly as she forced herself upright and sprang through the archway to the kitchen. She had to get away. Find Trace! Locate Eli! Oh dear God, had this monster already killed them both?

Her attacker was sputtering, muttering crazy invectives, *moving!* She heard his footsteps as she gathered herself.

". . . son of a fuckin' bitch . . . I'll make you pay . . ."

Trace's phone was on the kitchen counter . . . somewhere in the dark . . . if she could just get there . . . snag it and run out into the night, she might have a chance! She could call 9-1-1, or Alvarez or . . . Her head still thundered, her mind was still thick, her face ached, but she lunged forward.

Click!

The distinctive sound of a rifle being cocked echoed through her brain.

"You're not going anywhere," he said, his voice rough. "Not after all the years of waiting."

The phone was less than three feet away!

She felt the cold barrel of the rifle pressing against her back.

"Move and I'll pull the trigger," he promised.

She froze. Heard the moan of the storm outside. Wondered what her chances were. There were knives here . . . sharp, deadly blades . . . If she could just find them in the dark . . .

"A wound here—" The nose of the weapon swirled against her spine, in the small of her back, just over her buttocks, "Will take a while to bleed out. And you'll feel it, the life oozing from you."

She squeezed her eyes shut.

But there wasn't a roaring blast that echoed through the house. No searing pain cutting through her flesh.

Why didn't he pull the damned trigger?

Because he wants to make it look like an accident. Just like the others. A gunshot wound to the back can only mean homicide. So, think, Kacey. You're in the kitchen! The knives are in the block at the stove . . .

"Don't even think about it," he whispered, as if he would read her mind. "If I have to, I'll blow your sweet ass to hell and back."

"Then why don't you just—"

BAM!

Pain exploded through her brain and she crumpled to the floor.

CHAPTER 36

Trace held fast to his pitchfork. His heart was hammering, his muscles tight as his eyes adjusted to the darkness. The smell of dung and urine filled his nostrils. The lights had gone out while he'd still been in the barn, still wrapping the damned pipe. He'd finished the job though it had taken longer than anticipated, then headed to the stable.

He'd noticed the house was dark, getting colder by the minute and he felt the urge to hurry, to get back to Kacey and Eli. He'd hoped she would have drawn the water and brought the boy downstairs, near the fire for warmth.

Then he'd stepped into the stable and felt something was wrong.

More than the damned electricity being out, or the worry of frozen pipes.

No, this was a danger within.

The horses were restless, almost spooked, shifting in their stalls. He heard the sounds of rustling straw, nervous snorts and every so often an anxious whinny.

Sarge, too, was out of sorts. Stiff. He'd growled once and stared at the windowless rooms where the oats and other grain were stored. Bonzi, not knowing the drill, hadn't been all that concerned, but his ears were up. At attention. Aware of an unseen being hidden in the darkness.

The back of Trace's throat went dry.

An animal?

Or human?

His skin prickled under the collar of his jacket and he knew the answer. An animal would elicit a different response from his dog. This threat was definitely a person skulking in the shadows.

He thought of shouting out. Maybe it was just someone who'd come in for shelter from the storm. But why not stop at the house? Someone on the run? Someone scared?

Or someone intent on doing harm?

His heart grew stone cold.

He thought of his rifle, hidden deep in his closet, the ammunition locked away in an overhead cabinet in the kitchen. Then his mind went to Kacey alone in the house with his son.

Sarge growled again and Trace heard a noise . . . the tiniest squeak of the stable's floorboards. Every muscle in his body tensed.

Blood pounding in his ears, he held his pitchfork like a spear and began moving slowly through the darkness.

"You can't die, damn it!" a female voice whispered harshly. "Who's going to take care of Eli? *Who?*"

Oh, Lord, now she was imagining things, hearing the voices of angels, Kacey thought, pain surging through her body. She fought back the urge to vomit, and when she opened a bleary eye, she saw only darkness. Lying on the kitchen floor, the room spinning, she tried to pull herself to her knees.

Agony ripped through her skull. *Get up! Pull yourself together.*

The house was still, aside from the wind outside. Her attacker had fled. But he would be back. She knew it. Just as she knew Eli and Trace were in danger.

If they were alive.

She listened for the voice in her head again.

Heard nothing.

And tried like hell to get to her feet.

At the Johnson estate, Alvarez glanced out to the frigid night. Where was he? Where was the killer who had wreaked so much damage? What was he doing?

"And Kathleen?" Pescoli pressed, bringing up the other Johnson daughter who had died.

"She . . . she was killed in a skiing accident," Gerald said, scowling, as if his own words tasted bitter.

"Skiing *accident*," Alvarez repeated. "Any of her brothers present the day she died?"

"What?" Noreen blinked and fiddled nervously with her collar. "What are you suggesting, detective?"

Pescoli's smile held zero warmth. "Let me guess. Was it Cameron?"

"No!" Noreen said, her face shattering as tears came again. "I mean, yes, he was there. But . . . but so was most of the family!"

"Convenient." Pescoli was irritated as she glowered at this couple whose entire married life had been shrouded in secrets.

Cameron? One of the twins? He was the one Pescoli was zeroing in on? Alvarez thought of the two men who looked so much alike, whose jobs took them throughout the country. Handsome and smart. But deadly? To his mother she asked, "Do you know exactly what happened the day Kathleen died?"

Noreen glanced at her husband and then worried her lip. "Of course . . . Cameron was skiing with Kathleen on that last run, but that doesn't mean . . . there were hundreds, probably thousands, of people on the mountain that day." She sounded as if she were trying desperately to convince herself.

Alvarez was trying to remember everything about Cameron Johnson. He worked for the family business, lived on the outskirts of Grizzly Falls, on the way to Missoula . . .

"Poor, poor Kathleen." Sighing, tears filling her eyes, Noreen added, "She'd finally found a man who loved her despite . . . ."

"Despite what?" Pescoli asked.

"Nothing." Noreen shook her head quickly. "Nothing at all." She beseeched her husband silently but he threw up a hand, his own face a mask of sadness.

"Kathleen battled bipolar disorder," Gerald admitted sadly, one of his hands actually trembling. "I was a doctor, wouldn't believe it. At the time we really didn't know what to call it. We said, 'She had spells' or she was 'manic', or 'depressed.' I couldn't really accept that she was suffering so."

Seriously? Alvarez wondered. The second child who'd died from an accident had mental issues? Was there a connection? Seemed unlikely. Then again, everything about this case was slightly askew.

"Gerald, don't you see?" Noreen interjected. "They're . . . they're saying anything they can. Grasping at straws!" Glaring at Pescoli, her nostrils flaring, she added, "They're insinuating that Cameron killed Kathleen! Can you believe it? Cam!" She was shivering in rage. "And that's not the end of it, they're also trying to pin those other accidents, where the women died, on him. As if he were able to . . . This is unbelievable!" Noreen started pacing again, growing hysterical. "But it's not true. It just can't be!" Spinning on a heel, she pointed at Pescoli. "Get out! Now! Get the hell out of my house. You're despicable. Both of you!" She was crying in earnest now, her eyes trained on the large window facing the drive.

"This isn't over. We're not done," Pescoli said, rising to her feet.

Alvarez took her cue, checking her cell phone and starting for the door, just as headlights pierced the paned windows, washed against the walls. Over the whistle of the storm, the roar of a powerful engine surged through the night.

Noreen's shimmering eyes widened. The faintest of sad smiles tugged at the corners of her lips. "Oh, thank God!" she said, dropping a relieved hand over her heart. "Judd's here!"

Judd?

The oldest son?

Why?

As Gerald got to his feet and tried to stop his wife, Noreen raced into the hallway, her heels clicking on the marble floor as she flung open the door. A tall man, broad in the shoulders, his expression grim, entered. The family resemblance was unmistakable, Judd's bearing and facial features almost identical to his father's. He gave his mother a quick, almost obligatory hug as he surveyed the group in the den.

"What's going on here?" he demanded, his voice low, his eyes narrowing suspiciously as snow melted on the shoulders of his black overcoat. With his mother still clinging to his arm, he strode into the den.

"It's the police," she said as if he were the damned Cavalry, sent to rescue her. "They've come here asking all kinds of questions about those women who died . . ." Noreen was talking fast. "The newest accident victim is . . . is Karalee . . . Rierson. From the clinic. Oh . . . oh . . . no . . ." she was shaking her head as she connected the dots. "I, uh, oh God, I tried to set her up on a date with your brother . . ."

Stricken by her thoughts she looked as if she might buckle. Licking her lips, one hand at her throat, she whispered, "But it . . . it can't be . . ."

"Mother," Judd warned. "Stop talking." To the police: "I'm an attorney. I don't want you to speak to my parents without counsel present and it can't be me. I assume this is something criminal, or you wouldn't be here. I'll get in touch with Herman Carlton, a friend of mine and I'm sure you've heard of him."

Herman Carlton hailed from Spokane, but practiced in Montana as well. Of course they'd heard of him. In Alvarez's opinion, Carlton was a prick of a defense attorney and a miserable human being. But he would be trouble in a court battle, big trouble.

"Hold on," Gerald said. "No one's accusing anyone of anything."

Pescoli interrupted and said to Noreen, "The son that you set up with Karalee Rierson? Which one is he?"

"Mother, don't!" Judd was adamant and Noreen snapped her mouth shut.

"It was Cameron," Gerald said gently, his gaze on his wife's stricken face.

And all the pieces of the puzzle started locking into place.

When Judd tried to say something, Gerald held up his hand, as if to stop the barrage of denials. In a softer voice he said to the detectives, "I overheard my wife talking on the phone with Clarissa about a potential date." As Noreen bristled, her spine stiffening, he added, "It's over, honey. We can't bury our heads in the sand any longer."

"You're a bastard, Gerald," she shot back. "You know that, don't you? A number-one bastard! And I *never* called him." Noreen shook her head. "Cam didn't know that I'd spoken to Karalee."

"Of course he did, because Clarissa would have told him. They're tight," Gerald said. "And if she told him, I'm willing to bet the whole damned family knew!" He stared at Judd. "You?"

Judd's jaw slid to one side; he didn't answer. It was admission enough, at least in Alvarez's mind.

"Come on, son," his father implored.

"Judd?" Noreen pleaded.

With a shrug, the attorney reluctantly said, "Okay, I'd heard." His lips twisted into a deep line of disdain. "Clarissa doesn't know how to keep a secret. Never has."

Noreen, broken, let out a little gasp.

Gerald's sigh was deep with despair. As the fire crackled and the snow continued to fall outside the window, where the gaslights glowed, he said to Judd, "You can't protect him any more."

"Where is he?" Pescoli demanded.

"I don't know." Gerald shook his head. "He keeps to himself."

Pescoli ordered, "Call him!"

"I tried on the way over here," Judd admitted. "He's not answering."

"Try him again!" She wouldn't budge, but Alvarez knew they would get nowhere further. They'd learned more than they'd expected and now they had to act. Fast. To prevent Cameron Johnson from killing again. She said to Pescoli as she pulled out her phone, "We don't have time for this."

"You're right." Her partner threw the Johnson family one last angry look, but she was already starting for the door. "Let's find the son of a bitch!"

Click!

Trace heard the distinctive cock of a gun and froze. No one could see him in the dark. Whoever was inside the stable wouldn't be able to draw a bead on him. He had the advantage. He knew his way inside and out of this old building.

Unless the prick has night vision goggles. Or a scope.

Damn it!

Sarge growled again, low and throaty.

Trace felt the dog tense. His own grip tightened on the pitchfork. He eased toward a post where, at least, he'd have some protection.

Show yourself, you sick son of a bitch.

Then he saw it. The tiniest movement, a shadow in the deeper umbra of the stable. His eyes narrowed, his gaze searching, trying to make out the person. He drew the pitchfork back, ready to launch it through the air, then stopped.

Eli.

What if somehow his son was in the darkness? Hiding? Or . . . what if whoever it was had kidnapped his boy and was going to use him as a shield? His insides turned to water. Then he thought of

Kacey and that made it worse. She could be inside, held with a gun pointed at her head, watching the horror unfold.

Heart thudding he tried like hell to make out whoever it was, but the Stygian darkness was impossible to pierce.

"What're you waiting for?" The voice was deep and male. It taunted. "You think that stupid pitchfork can do any real damage?" And then laughter. Deep. Cruel.

So the bastard could see him. Trace's blood burned.

"Who are you?" he demanded, his weapon still ready to be hurled.

"Does it matter?" A snide, sickly question.

"Eli?" he said.

"No! I'm not Eli . . . oh, your kid?" A pause. "What the fuck are you thinking?"

So he didn't have the boy. *Good!* "Let Kacey go!"

"Now that wouldn't make sense, would it? Not after I waited all this time."

Trace crumbled inside. The madman had her! Intended to kill her, if he hadn't already! A new fury took hold and he searched for something, anything so he could see. But there was nothing, not so much as a match!

"She's waiting for you. So that's why I think it would be better if I kill you up at the house with her. Make it look like she did it! An *accident,* you know."

She was still alive? "You crazy son of a bitch." But not crazy enough to fire a rifle in a closed space where it could ricochet. Maybe.

Sarge growled again from somewhere nearby.

"Tell that mutt to back off!" the voice commanded, "or I'll blow his mangy hide to kingdom come."

"Show yourself!" Trace demanded.

"Not on your life."

"Then go to hell!"

He drew the pitchfork back. Stepping out from behind the post, he threw all his body-weight behind his shoulder and let it fly. It hurled through the darkness as he jumped behind the thin post.

"AAAWwwwwooh!" A horrifying scream echoing through the building. "You fucker!"

Crrraaack!

A blaze of light flashed in front of Trace's eyes. Thunder crashed through the stable, rolling through his brain in harsh, loud waves. Panicked horses screamed! The dogs barked and howled!

A pain as hot as the fires of hell seared Trace's thigh, the impact of the bullet so powerful he fell backward. Hard. His head hit the floorboards with a thud and he momentarily lost consciousness, a soothing blackness luring him under, away from the horror and the chaos within.

Don't give in. You're a dead man if you let the blackness take you! Think of Eli! Of Kacey!

Dust and the acrid smell of burnt gunpowder filled his nostrils as he blinked himself awake. The dogs were going nuts, barking and growling like crazy. Horses still kicked and squealed in fear, scrambling in their stalls while the scent of fear hung heavy, mingling with the thin odor of burning gunpowder wafting from the direction of the killer.

"You fucking son of a bitch!" he growled. Trace heard him writhe and swear somewhere near the grain chutes. The dogs ran in circles while Trace hoped beyond hope that his pitchfork had done serious, tissue-ripping damage.

"You're gonna die, O'Halleran and it's not gonna be easy!" the killer snarled. "You hear me? You're a dead man, cocksucker! You and your bitch girlfriend!"

Kacey staggered to her feet, swaying, struggling to think straight. Her mind was sludge, her face on fire, her head thundering in pain. She held the doorjamb for support. *Trace is out there somewhere and so is Eli and . . . and the psycho . . .* Gasping, she dragged in deep breaths of air to clear her head.

Craaack!

Outside, the sharp report of a rifle split the snowy night.

What? Kacey cut back a scream.

Trace? Oh, God. Eli?

In the darkness, she fumbled across the kitchen table for Trace's cell phone. Please, oh, please . . . her fingers hit something that jangled and fell. His damned keys. But next to it . . . yes! She found his cell phone and dialed the last number in her brain, that of Detective Alvarez.

The call went directly to voice mail.

Damn it! She left a quick message. "The bastard's here! We need help . . . oh, God, please send . . ." She tried to tamp down her rising panic, found the control she'd used with patients. "Detective Alvarez, this is Kacey Lambert. I'm at Trace O'Halleran's place on Old Mill Road. He's here. The killer is here, somewhere. He's attacked me and I just heard gunshots coming from one of the outbuildings. Both Trace and Eli are missing. Please, send help. STAT! I, uh, I don't know the address, but it's only about a quarter of a mile west of . . . of . . . Red Wing Corner, a mile from the county road. Please, send officers!"

Heart clamoring, she dialed 9-1-1. She couldn't wait for Alvarez to respond. When dispatch picked up, she tersely explained the situation and the operator insisted she not go forward. "Keep me on the line," the female voice ordered. "I'm dispatching deputies right now. They're ten minutes away."

"Ten minutes is too long!" Kacey spat. "Tell them to hurry!"

She knew in her heart that there was no way they could make it in time. She clicked off, anxiously peering through the darkness of the house. She didn't dare go into the stable without a weapon. But she didn't want to take the time. What if Trace were wounded? She was pretty sure Trace hadn't fired the gun. No. It was probably the sick son of a bitch who had Eli, who had taunted her with his rifle barrel.

Oh, God, was it possible that either one of them was hurt . . . or worse?

Don't go there. You don't have time for recriminations. Move! Save Trace! Save his son!

In her search for Eli, she'd discovered Trace's rifle, hidden in a closet. Now, pain screaming through her brain, she hurried forward, then up the stairs in the dark, using Trace's cell phone's weak, bluish light as a guide. Fumbling, cursing, determined to save them. Into Trace's room. She cracked her elbow on a dresser corner as she stumbled her way to the closet where she pushed aside clothes and a suitcase. *It was here! I know . . . there!*

Her fingers curled around the shotgun's barrel and she yanked the old gun from the closet. The Winchester was dusty, unused, but she didn't care. Praying that the rifle was armed, she checked the chamber.

Empty!

Of course. He had a kid. Was careful. Frantic, the cell phone winking out every ten seconds, she scoured the closet. There were no bullets nearby, no boxes of ammunition on the shelf, nor in a dresser where she rifled through T-shirts and underwear, socks and jeans. "Come on, come on!" The nightstand, too, was empty, no loaded handgun, no bullets for an ancient rifle.

Precious seconds ticked by.

Her heart was racing, her brain on fire.

"Where . . . oh, God, where?" She didn't dare bluff the killer; knew better than to take an empty rifle to the stable.

Fear spurred her. She hauled the rifle downstairs and through the living room where the fire was dying.

Where would he keep the ammo? Far from the gun, yes, but where it was safe and could be accessed by him, not so easily by his child. Close to the door, because he would only use it outside? Quickly she went through several drawers in the kitchen, opening them, searching them with her fingers, slamming them shut, then seeing, as the cell phone's light faded again, the handle of another flashlight!

Oh, please, she thought, feeling precious time slipping past. Even now Trace could be bleeding, dying . . .

She flipped on the flashlight, and a sure, strong beam lit up the room. Quickly she went to work, searching the remaining drawer, when she spied the tallest cupboard mounted above the refrigerator. The same place her grandfather had hidden his ammunition. Could it be?

Hurrying, counting her heartbeats, she hauled herself onto the counter, then yanked the door open. Next to a nearly empty bottle of whiskey was a metal box. Locked tight. No way could she pry it open. She needed a key . . . oh, God, where? She raked her gaze around the room and spied Trace's key ring that she'd knocked over searching for his cell. Quickly, she pulled the musty box from its hiding place, hopped to the floor and scooped up the jangling keys. With shaking fingers she separated the keys and found one that was tinier than all the rest.

"Please, oh, please." She shook the other keys away from it and threaded it in the lock. *Click!*

Thank God. She popped open the box and found the mother load: a box of shells.

"Take that, you miserable son of a bitch," she said under her breath as she thought of the killer.

Mentally thanking her grandfather for her lessons years before, she loaded the rifle quickly, pocketed an extra pack of shells, and prayed to God she wouldn't have to use either as she headed outside again and into the storm.

"Shit!" Trace's attacker swore loudly, his voice reverberating through the stables.

Who the hell was this lunatic? Not that it mattered. In that respect, the killer was correct. For the moment, Trace just had to figure out a way to stop the son of a bitch before he did any more damage.

Moving slowly, dragging himself toward the wall, Trace tried to come up with a plan.

Over the rage of the wind he heard the distinctive sound of the would-be killer drawing in his breath through his teeth. "Shit!" the man growled again, then let out a yowl accompanied by the soft, whooshing suck of the pitchfork's tines being yanked from his body. "You fuckin' cocksucker!" Pain echoed in his voice. "You're gonna pay for this. You hear me, O'Halleran?"

Trace didn't respond, just kept low, pulling himself with his hands as he slid silently along the floor, edging toward the wall.

The horses were out of their minds with fear, hooves shuffling, shoes ringing against the stalls from slamming feet.

Sarge—or was it Bonzi?—too, was upset, growling deep in his throat. A warning.

No! Don't!

"And the dog," the gunman said aloud. "He's dead, too! Where are you, you mangy mutt?" Now, there was satisfaction in his voice. "Oh . . . there you are, Cujo. Come on, boy," the assailant cajoled as the horses snorted and stomped. "See what I've got for you!"

Fury singed through Trace's brain. If he could just get the drop on this son of a bitch, he'd kill him. He felt his blood flowing, reached down to feel it wet and sticky from his leg wound. But he'd be damned if he was going to lie here while this maniac killed his dog, then went after Kacey or Eli.

No doubt she was the true target. His son, like Sarge and Trace himself, were just extraneous, obstacles that had to be cleared to the killer's main objective: Dr. Acacia Lambert.

Trace scooted backward, felt blood flowing out of his leg, his head slightly dizzy from the adrenaline rush. He reached the wall.

"Here, doggy, doggy . . ." The killer's singsong voice masked a groan of pain. The bastard was hurt worse than he'd admit.

Good. Suffer, you bastard. And while you're at it, die!

Trace reached over his head and felt the handle of the shovel. With a wide, sharp blade it was perfect for scooping manure or shoveling snow, and tonight, he hoped, as a weapon to kill a murdering psychopath.

"Come on, boy—" The son of a bitch made twisted, little kissing sounds as he moved closer, still invisible in the darkness.

Trace's fingers coiled over the smooth wooden handle.

BAM!

The door to the stables banged against the wall.

Horses nickered in terror.

Trace jumped as a rush of cold air swept into the room.

"What the hell?" The gunman turned his attention away from the dog.

No! Trace went into full-blown panic. *Kacey, no!* She was the only one at the house . . . or Eli. And the killer knew it!

"Get away!" Trace screamed.

"Sister," the attacker drawled smoothly, almost gleefully. "About time you showed up!"

CHAPTER 37

Damn it all to hell!
Alvarez listened to her message from Kacey Lambert and mentally kicked herself from here to hell and back. Furious, she punched in the emergency number and talked to dispatch who said there had already been a distress call logged and deputies sent to an address for Trace O'Halleran, that gunshots had been reported. Hanging up, she dialed Kacey's number but was sent directly to voice mail.

"Too late," Alvarez said grimly to Pescoli. "Looks like he's at the O'Halleran place."

"What? No!" Noreen let out a cry that rose to the coffered ceiling. Alvarez, standing just inside the Johnson's front door with Pescoli, threw a look over her shoulder.

"I was afraid of this," Judd said. "You know he's never been right, Mother. Even from the start. When he pushed Aggie down the stairs."

Alvarez held up a hand, stopping her partner from yanking on the door handle.

"It was an accident," Gerald said, sinking into his chair again as Alvarez stepped back into the den with its cheery fire, fresh-cut flowers and simmering lies.

"It was," Judd insisted. "Of course it was an accident. But essentially, that's what happened."

"You told me," Gerald reminded his son, looking up to meet Judd's narrowed eyes, "that Aggie got tangled in her blanket."

"I know. That's right," Judd said smoothly, almost as if he'd practiced the line. "And then Cam ran by and knocked her down. She got wrapped in her damned blanket and fell."

Noreen shuddered.

"To her death." Gerald glared at his son.

"We've got to go," Pescoli said tersely. Alvarez rejoined her as she opened the door and the breath of winter blew through the room, rattling umbrellas on a nearby stand. To Gerald, his wife and oldest son, Pescoli added, "You all stay put! Don't go anywhere."

"It's not Cameron," Noreen wailed, but Judd Johnson's tense face said it all. His mother, appearing far frailer than she had just half an hour earlier, collapsed in his arms. Tears rolled from her eyes and she sobbed against his expensive coat, her voice muted as her shoulders shook. "It's . . . it's not Cameron. It can't be!"

Pescoli was already out the door.

The last look Alvarez caught of Gerald was of the big man seated in his leather recliner near the fire, holding his head in one hand, reaching for his glass of scotch with the other.

"I'll drive." Pescoli was already out the door and Alvarez was only a couple of steps behind. As she climbed into the passenger seat, Pescoli engaged the engine and threw the rig into gear. The Jeep lurched forward. Alvarez pulled the door shut as they reached the end of the circular drive and she'd barely gotten her seat belt connected when they were heading onto the slippery road winding down the hillside.

"What the hell happened?" Pescoli asked.

"Something going on at the O'Halleran place," Alvarez said, thinking of the man whom she was now certain was the killer. "Looks like Cameron Johnson is escalating. And he's starting with the people there."

"And killing his sperm bank sisters?"

"Or anyone who's in his path." Alvarez repeated what she'd heard on voice mail.

In the dark car, her face pale, Pescoli muttered, "The bastard's a raving lunatic!" She drove as fast as she dared, past the lodge and gate house, then cast Alvarez a glance as they reached the main road. "Don't suppose you have a cigarette on you?"

Alvarez sent her partner a "dream-on" look, then punched in Kacey Lambert's cell phone number again and waited.

The call went directly to voice mail once more.

*   *   *

Trace's fingers tightened on the shovel's handle.

"I wondered if you'd show up," the killer said and there in the doorway, silhouetted against the white drifts Kacey stood, feet wide, a gun in her hands. But she couldn't see into the darkness. Couldn't guess where they could be.

Click. The bastard cocked his gun.

What was Kacey thinking?

"Get back!" Trace screamed. Frantic, he yanked the shovel from the nails that held it to the wall. Twisting, the blade of the shovel in front of him, he started scrambling backward to the door to save her, push her away, use his body as a shield, any damned thing to protect her!

"Too late." A brittle, hollow laugh echoed behind him.

"Watch out!" Dragging his useless leg, sensing the streak of blood he was leaving on the floorboards, he forced himself to the doorway. "He's got a gun!"

"So do I," she said calmly. Too calmly. "Stay down!"

Blam!

Her gun's nose sprayed fire, her silhouette slipping away, behind the exterior wall.

Trace had flattened to the floor even before she pulled the trigger, the room spinning around him, his neck twisted as he stared at the doorway.

Craaack! Click! Craaack! Click! Craaack!

The killer fired in rapid succession, sending the timbers of the stables shaking and the horses squealing and snorting, rearing in sheer terror. Steel shot hooves pounded the walls of the stalls.

The dogs, too, were barking madly.

Over it all, he heard a single heart-stopping cry.

Kacey!

He rolled over and tried to get to his feet, to stumble forward, but his leg wouldn't work. The best he could do was drag himself through the smoke and fear that rose to the rafters.

Another horrifying moan. As if her soul was being ripped from her body.

"NO!" he screamed, "NO!"

A crackled, satisfied chuckle behind him; the killer's sick pleasure oozing through the aftermath.

You sick cocksucker, I'm going to get you.

"Trace!"

What?

"Trace!" Kacey's terrified voice reached him, a distant weak cry diluted by the rush of the wind. As if she were truly exiting this world and he was truly losing her.

But she's alive! There's still time!

"Hang on!" he ordered brokenly. "Hang the hell on!"

Using the shovel to drag himself forward, he pulled himself closer toward the doorway, to the frigid air blowing snow into the stable. Somewhere behind him, he heard the uneven footsteps of the killer, but he kept moving, didn't care that the rifle might be trained on the back of his head.

Through the doorway he crawled into the night, the cold a welcome slap to his swirling senses.

He saw her then. Unmoving. A crumpled form lying in the snow just outside the building, strands of her hair being lifted by the wind.

NO! NO! NO!

Oh, dear God . . . let her still be alive.

"Kacey," he choked out. "God, please . . . Kacey." Again he heard a noise behind him. The wounded footsteps of the assassin. Was the bastard going to kill him now?

He thought he saw her move. *Oh, sweet Jesus!* Yes, there it was again: one foot was twitching. He crawled closer, to where he could see the rest of her body, and noticed a terrifying, spreading darkness staining the snow beneath her. "Why?" he whispered, fury tearing through him. Why had she come to his rescue?

"Too late, lover boy," the big man behind him was saying, breathing hard. Far in the distance—too far—sirens shrieked over the howl of the wind.

Exhausted, breathing hard, Trace looked over his shoulder and saw a huge, shadowy shape fill the doorway. The rifle was at his shoulder, night goggles covering his eyes, but he leaned a shoulder against the doorjamb. Trace saw dark splotches begin to color the snow beneath the man's left arm. So the pitchfork had done some damage.

"You're dead now, you son of a bitch," the killer warned, his voice a watery hiss.

That's when Trace noticed the gun in the snow.

Lying at the end of Kacey's fingers, its barrel pointed away from her.

Still holding the shovel as protection, Trace lunged, one arm outstretched. He missed, his fingers brushing the gun's muzzle and causing it to spin, burying deep in the snow.

The killer laughed, a gurgling, demonic sound that echoed through the night. "Nice try, bastard!"

Click!

Trace sprang.

Swinging his shovel, the blade knifing through the air, he landed in a drift a foot from the gun. Snatching up the weapon, he nearly passed out in the process. All he could think about was Kacey. Sweet Kacey. How she'd tried to save him and died in the process.

"Say your prayers, cowboy," the killer ordered, hobbling closer, his rifle aimed straight at Trace. "You're gonna get to join your girlfriend."

A tremendous growl erupted from inside the stables.

The killer glanced back, momentarily distracted.

Both dogs catapulted through the open doorway.

Snarling, ears flattened, heads low, fangs showing, they split: one turning left, the other right. They determinedly circled the killer, and snapped and lunged, like hungry wolves ready to bring down prey.

"Shit." The killer didn't hesitate, just took aim at the bigger dog.

Bonzi!

"No!" Trace yelled, trying to stagger to his feet and falling backward.

Bonzi leapt, exposing his big chest and belly, white teeth flashing against his dark lips.

BLAM!

The killer jerked. Squealed. His rifle spun out of his hands.

BLAM!

Again the assassin's torso bucked, his arms flying wildly.

He dropped, falling onto his knees. Blood bloomed over the front of his jacket. His head lolled and he stared at the growing stain as if he couldn't believe it.

"Where is he?" a woman demanded, her voice stern in the night.

Trace, dizzier still, looked over his shoulder. *What? Who was . . .*

She drew closer, a rifle to her shoulder, the sight of her gun—*his* rifle—centered on the wounded man.

Kacey?

But–?

He looked down at the woman he loved—Kacey—lying pale as the snow that was beginning to cover her as the sirens shrilled more loudly.

"Where the hell is Eli, Cameron?" this new Kacey demanded, holding her rifle on the flailing, injured man. Trace thought he might be hallucinating. Two of them . . .

The newcomer—*Kacey?*—was still advancing.

But it can't be . . . She reached the wounded man and kicked his weapon away from him. The would-be assassin let out a last, gasping groan that rattled, wet in his lungs, then didn't move.

Pulling her gaze from his masked face, she turned, finding Trace's eyes before she saw the blood flowing from his thigh, the snow around him discolored and dark from his blood.

"Oh, Jesus! Trace!"

Woozy now, the blackness pulling him under, he watched, sliding onto the ground, as she ran to him as if in slow motion. Kicking up snow, the rifle in one hand, a flashlight bobbing in her pocket, she crossed the short, powdery distance and fell to her knees at his side. "Oh, God, you're hurt!"

"Kacey," he whispered and reached for her, wanting to wrap his arms around her, to hold her close, feel her warmth, smell her hair . . . But his eyes wouldn't stay open and he was spinning, further and further away . . .

"Wait . . . Let me see how badly you're injured. . . . Oh, dear Christ, Trace . . ." He heard her sharp intake of breath and saw that she was focused on the dead woman lying next to him. "Oh, my God. Who?" she whispered, then clearing her throat, she moved close to the woman who was nearly her twin. Leaning over the body, she searched for a pulse at the woman's neck, pushed her ear next to her nostrils. "Gone," she whispered, then dragged her gaze from the body that was so like her own. Touching him on the shoulder, she said gently, "We have to get you to a hospital!"

He was drifting away, his eyelids leaden, "But Eli?" he forced out. "Where's Eli?"

"I don't know," she said softly, holding him close. He drank in the smell of her, felt her warm, wet cheek against his own as the wintry world, like one of those snow globes turned upside down, seemed to spin around him.

"No," he said, fighting to stay conscious. He had to find his son. Had to!

"We'll find him," she promised over the shattering wail of sirens. "You just hang in. You hear me? Trace? Trace! You just stay with me . . ."

But he didn't. One second he heard her voice, the next he was floating away, wondering how this woman he loved could be two, one dead, one alive.

He sank into himself, heard voices . . . men and women . . . couldn't respond.

Kacey's alive . . . she's alive . . . but Eli . . .

He loved them both . . .

"Don't you leave me, Trace O'Halleran!" she yelled at him from somewhere far off. "Damn it, Trace, it took me thirty-five years to find you and you'd better not die on me. Do you hear me? Stay with me." Her voice broke. "Come on, Trace . . . come on. I love you. Oh, Holy Christ, I love you!"

I love you, too . . .

She was losing him!

Right here, right now, Trace O'Halleran was dying in her arms.

And the woman lying next to him, dead in the snow, she was now certain must be Leanna, his ex-wife, probably another one of Gerald Johnson's sperm bank children, and mother to Eli.

"Hang in there," she ordered Trace as the sound of sirens blasted around them and lights bobbed up the driveway.

She didn't look over her shoulder but prayed the EMTs had the equipment to save him. He'd lost a lot of blood, but she wasn't going to let him die. Not on her watch. Quickly, she stripped him of his pants, yanking out the flashlight from her pocket to get a good look at the bullet wound in his thigh. Blood was pumping out of the hole in his flesh and she suspected his femoral artery had been hit. She crossed one hand over the other and pressed them to the wound just as she heard, "Hey! Over here!" from a deep voice yelled near the house. Then footsteps and heaving breaths and conversation swirled around her in the snow. "We'll take over, ma'am," someone said and she felt a man's hand on her shoulder.

"But I'm a doctor—"

"Holy Christ, there's another one!" He started bending over Leanna's body.

"She's dead."

"Hey! Over here!" A woman shouted from the vicinity of Cam's corpse. "Holy shit, what happened here. Looks like goddamned Armageddon!"

"Here, ma'am . . . I've got him now," the EMT said, turning back to Trace.

"But I'm—"

"A doctor. I know." He was firm. "Hey, Annie," he called over his shoulder as Kacey was vaguely aware of colored lights strobing the night. Red and blue flashes through the ever-falling snow. "I could use some help over here! This one's in shock," the EMT said and glanced up at Kacey.

The O'Halleran ranch was a madhouse.

All hell had broken loose before Alvarez and Pescoli arrived, their Jeep sliding around the corner at the end of the drive and nearly taking out the mailbox. Two department issued vehicles were parked near an open gate and an ambulance too, idled, waiting to transport the injured.

At the back of the big farmhouse while battling the elements EMTs were tending to Trace O'Halleran, strapping him to a stretcher while a search team had been dispatched to find O'Halleran's missing son. Cameron Johnson, dressed in black and wearing night goggles, was dead from two gunshot wounds, inflicted, admittedly, by Kacey Lambert.

Shivering, a blanket thrown around her shoulders, Kacey herself admitted to cutting him down when he refused to drop his weapon. Pale as death, obviously in shock, Kacey swore that Cameron had already killed the woman still lying in the snow in front of them.

A woman who could have been her twin.

"I think it's Leanna," Kacey said, almost numbly, her gaze fastened on the woman's frozen features.

"Dead," one of the EMTs confirmed.

"I need to go with him," Kacey insisted as two burly rescue workers carried Trace on a stretcher through the piling snow to the waiting ambulance.

"You can ride with us," Pescoli said.

"Hey!" Trilby Van Droz, one of the road deputies, cocked her head toward the main road. "Looks like we've got company." Twin headlights glowed at the end of the drive, but Pescoli couldn't make out the vehicle. "Five will get you one, it's the press."

A news van.

Of course. Great. Just what they didn't need. "They have to back off. Until we know what went down," Pescoli shouted and Van Droz began heading down the lane, following the tracks of the ambulance that carried Trace.

"I think O'Halleran is going to be okay," Alvarez said.

"But Eli. We have to find him," Kacey insisted. "Leanna . . . I thought she was in the house with me . . . warning me . . . but the timing probably couldn't be. I thought she was an angel."

Pescoli glanced at her partner. "Let's have a doctor look at her, too."

"I'm fine," Kacey insisted, but her face was pretty bruised, the skin scraped, her chin covered in blood.

"Okay, let's go," Pescoli said. As the ambulance sped off through the snow, Pescoli, Alvarez and Kacey trudged through the drifts to the Jeep. Kacey climbed into the back seat. Her car was still in the police garage, the black paint transferred from her fender bender, not yet analyzed. Alvarez settled into the passenger seat and Pescoli backed up, then rammed the Jeep into gear.

Even though Cam Johnson was dead, Pescoli still felt a sense of urgency, and the missing kid didn't help. Where the hell could he be? she wondered as she flipped on the lights and hit the gas. There were too many loose ends to be tied up, too much evidence to be collected, other stories that had to jibe with what Kacey was saying before Pescoli would be satisfied. Even though the doctor was half-mad with worry about the boy's whereabouts and beyond concerned that Trace O'Halleran might not make it, Alvarez and Pescoli were required to haul her to the station.

After their trip to the Emergency Room.

True, Pescoli thought as she drove onto the county road and saw the news team from a local station huddled in their van, Kacey Lambert had called 9-1-1 as well as left Alvarez several voice mail messages on her phone. It had been the doctor who had drawn the authorities to the scene, but she hadn't played by the book, had ignored the 9-1-1 dispatcher's advice and taken the law into her own hands.

Had she saved O'Halleran's life?

Probably.

But two other people were dead and a kid was still missing.

The sketchy statement Kacey had given coincided with everything the crime scene guys had put together so far, but it was too early in the game. They still had to cross all the t's and dot all the i's.

She headed toward Grizzly Falls.

The night was dark aside from the snow, only a few farmhouses in the area, those with generators, showing any light in the windows. Tow trucks had stopped for a vehicle that had slid into the ditch, and other traffic was slow, battling the storm.

Pescoli had the heater working overtime, the interior of the Jeep as hot as a sauna, yet Kacey Lambert couldn't seem to get warm and was shivering as she told her story for the second time, then worried aloud about Eli.

"If anything happens to him, I'll never forgive myself," she said and stared out the window, her breath fogging the glass. "Never."

Two minutes later, just as they reached the snow-covered sign welcoming all to Grizzly Falls, Alvarez's cell phone jangled. She took the call and listened, the conversation one-sided. "What? . . . Where . . . Thank God." She twisted in the passenger seat. "We've got him."

"What? Who? *Eli?*" Kacey demanded.

"Yes, ma'am. He's safe."

"Thank God!" Kacey's voice broke and she sniffed loudly.

Pescoli's hands held the wheel in a death grip, but she felt a rush of relief, a dam of fear breaking inside her. "Shhh!" Alvarez held up a hand and finished the call. "Yeah, well, bring him into the office. We'll meet you there." She hung up and even her usually icy all-professional facade cracked. "He's fine."

Pescoli glanced in the rearview and saw tears of happiness well in her passenger's eyes.

"Okay," Alvarez went on, "I don't know all the details, but it looks like he was kidnapped by his mother, dropped off at the neighbors—Ed and Matilda Zukov's house—and they've been trying to reach someone ever since. Apparently Leanna O'Halleran cut their phone line and stole their cells to give herself time to fulfill some mission."

"She was after Cam," Kacey said quietly. "She knew."

"Apparently," Alvarez agreed. "We'll be getting more information from the Zukov's. An officer is bringing them into the station, along with the boy."

Pescoli grimaced against the glare of particularly bright high beams as a truck rumbled past. "So she was out of the picture for most of the kid's life, then she suddenly, in what some kind of cosmic mother-instinct rolls into town at just the right moment to blow some nut case away?" Pescoli shot a look at her partner. "What did she know?"

Alvarez shook her head. They might never fully figure it out.

Kacey went over her statement three times and answered a slew of questions, though it was obvious Pescoli and Alvarez, and even the sheriff himself believed her. They'd planned on taking her directly to the hospital but she'd insisted on getting the interview at the sheriff's department over with first. As soon as they got there she took time to head to the bathroom, wash her face, down three migraine-strength Excedrin, and use a slightly too large Band-Aid that the woman at reception had given her on her chin. She'd called the hospital on Trace's cell, but had only learned that Trace was in surgery.

Deputy Van Droz brought the Zukovs and Eli into the room where Kacey was being interviewed just as Kacey had finished another run through of the events that had taken place at the O'Halleran ranch. She threw her arms around the boy, tears filling her eyes. "Thank God you're safe," she whispered fervently and ruffled his hair.

"I saw Mommy," Eli said, biting his lower lip.

"I know, honey."

"She came to pick me up."

"I heard," Kacey answered with a smile that was difficult to muster. Seeing Leanna on the snowy ground, her face gray in the half-light, her eyes fixed, had been like staring into her own grave.

"She signed my cast," he stated proudly.

Kacey glanced up at Tilly, who nodded while Ed looked away.

Proudly, Eli displayed the bold scrawl that said. "Love you, Mom xoxo."

"It's beautiful," she said, remembering how Leanna had saved them all. She wondered if she'd really heard Leanna's voice or if it had merely been a hallucination. It hardly mattered, for either way she intended to take really good care of Leanna's son.

"Wanna get some hot cocoa?" Pescoli asked Eli who, after glancing at Kacey and the Zukovs and receiving hearty "yes, go aheads," eagerly followed after the taller, red-haired detective.

Once the boy was gone, the Zukovs told their tale. Leanna had shown up at their house carrying Eli. She'd apparently trudged through the snow to deliver her son, and then she'd disabled their truck and landline and stolen their cell phones. She'd also taken their computer, so that they had no means of communicating with anyone while she said she was taking care of some "unfinished business."

Tilly went on to say that Leanna had admitted that she knew about the killer who was taking out all of the daughters of Gerald Johnson as he believed most of them had serious mental problems. He was intent on protecting his family name and made up an elaborate plan to take care of the problem. He also had a personal vendetta against Kacey and Leanna because he'd fallen for Leanna, not knowing who she was, and he'd despised Kacey as well for being born to Gerald's mistress. He had bad feelings for Robert Lindley, too, but until he'd eradicated all of the "Unknowings" as he'd called them, he would take his time with Robert.

During the recitation Kacey recalled Cameron's taunts after he'd hit her with the rifle butt. He'd believed she and Leanna and the rest of Gerald's female offspring weren't mentally sound when his own mental illness was the reason he'd targeted all of them.

Tilly wound up by adding that Cameron had admitted his deadly deeds to Leanna when he'd tried to kill her years before, but she'd gotten away and found Trace. She'd left her son with Trace, fearing Cameron would take his sick vengeance upon Eli. But her fear for Eli was the reason she came back, to save the boy everyone assumed she'd abandoned and to stop Cameron in his tracks.

"We were horrified," Tilly finished. "And trapped. We wanted Eli to be safe, but we were worried sick about you all. Ed even tried to start the old John Deere in hopes of getting to the Foxx's, our neighbors to the north and calling the police."

"Dang thing wouldn't even turn over in the cold," Ed admitted. Both he and his wife looked worn out and beleaguered.

Pescoli returned with Eli, who was interested in poking at the fake marshmallows floating in his hot chocolate. She also brought several cups of steaming coffee. Kacey took one, more for the warmth than anything else.

She turned to Ed and Tilly, softly asking the question that was now haunting her, "So . . . Eli is Cameron's son?"

"Not according to her. She was very adamant on that," Tilly said and Ed nodded his agreement.

"I'm my dad's son," Eli put in, blowing across his cocoa.

"Of course you are." Kacey walked across the room and hugged him fiercely, sorry he'd overheard her; she'd thought he was out of earshot. She was so glad that he was safe. She would have to deal with his questions about his mother, she knew that, but she was willing to do it; to be with him and to be with Trace. Her feelings about Leanna were torn, but she couldn't deny that the woman had sacrificed herself for the sake of her son.

Alvarez's cell phone jangled and she looked at the screen. "I've got to take this," she said before walking into an adjoining room.

She was gone about ten minutes and when she returned, she said, "Looks like we can convict Cameron Johnson for more crimes than we know. The team who went to his house found a secret room down in the basement. There are pictures of the victims, information about each of them, many already dead, some who escaped."

Kacey thought of Gloria Sanders-O'Malley, the fitness instructor.

"I'm going to have to call Jonas Hayes in L.A.," Alvarez said to Pescoli. "I think we can tie Cam Johnson to Shelly Bonaventure's supposed suicide."

"He was the creep who attacked me in Seattle," Kacey said. "He admitted as much." She sighed and shook her head. "If we're done here, can I get a ride to the hospital?"

Pescoli nodded. "I'll drive."

Turning to Eli, Kacey said with a smile, "Come on. Let's go see your dad."

As it turned out, Kacey wasn't alone in wanting to go to the hospital. Pescoli and Alvarez planned to question Trace when he woke up and Ed and Tilly, though tired, drove to St. Bart's as well.

But being back in the familiar hospital halls was a little surreal for Kacey. Though everything looked the way it had the last time she'd been here, after all she'd been through, it seemed different. Changed. She told herself that it was because of the fact she'd been hit in the back of the head with the butt of a rifle, but it was more, a deeper disconnect that all had to do with meeting a murderer face-to-face and killing him. Though she felt no regret for taking Cameron Johnson's life as he'd intended to murder Trace, she still felt out of step. She'd dedicated her professional life to helping heal, to save lives, and now she'd purposefully taken one.

Shake it off, she told herself and after leaving a protesting Eli with Tilly and Ed, made her way to the recovery room as she was a doctor on staff. Alvarez and Pescoli were right behind her, but hung back to give her a second's privacy when she headed to the bed where Trace lay.

He was just coming around and woozy, his leg bandaged, his hospital gown askew. His leg had been saved, the femoral artery nicked but repaired. He moaned, his head dark against the white sheets. He blinked slowly awake.

"Hey, there," she said, leaning over his bed as the Recovery Room nurse stepped out to allow them some privacy.

With obvious effort, he tried to focus.

"It's me." She took his hand and her heart squeezed at the sight of him, his hair rumpled on the pillow, his jaw dark with beard shadow. God, she loved him and for a few harrowing minutes she'd thought she'd lost him forever. "Trace?"

One side of his mouth lifted in a dopey grin, but his eyes were far from clear. "Kacey?" he said, his voice rough.

"Yeah, it's me." Her throat nearly closed as his grip tightened over hers.

"Eli?" he whispered.

"He's fine." Tears burned the back of her eyes. "And he's here, waiting to see you. He's with the Zukovs, just down the hall."

He seemed relieved, then goofy again. "Oh. Tilly. Ed."

"Yes." She knew he wouldn't remember much about waking up, maybe nothing, but she couldn't help herself from squeezing his hand. "Trace, I need to tell you something," she said.

"Hmmmm..." He was drifting again.

"First of all, Leanna turned out to be okay. More than okay. I think she saved your life." He didn't respond. Probably hadn't heard. "And there's something else," she admitted, leaning close over the bed. "I love you." She smiled though she felt warm tears slide down her face. "It's crazy and I know it, but damn it, I love you."

"I know . . ." His voice was far away. "You're gonna marry me."

He was still out of it; didn't know what he was saying, but it filled her heart with joy. "We . . . we'll talk about it when you're better . . ."

His eyes opened suddenly and in that split second his gaze was clear. "I *am* better," he said, and reached up quickly, his fingers sliding around her nape, as he lifted his head from the pillow and pulled her close so that their noses were nearly touching. "And you're gonna marry me, Dr. Lambert."

Before she could say a word, he pressed his lips to hers in a kiss that was as crushing as it was desperate. "No arguments," he said when he finally released her and fell back on the sheets, spent, his eyes closing again.

"Faker," she accused.

He didn't respond.

She felt a smile tug on her swollen lips and she didn't say it, but thought, *I am going to marry you, Trace O'Halleran. Count on it.*

EPILOGUE

"Come on, come on . . . we're going to go caroling!" Joelle, wearing ridiculous, red felt reindeer antlers, was herding everyone into the lobby.

Pescoli looked up from her desk where she was studying the death certificates and newspaper reports on the two sisters of Cameron Johnson who had died young . . . in accidents. "I am *not* caroling! *I've* got work to do."

"Oh, don't be a Scrooge!" Joelle admonished before clipping off in her clear high heels that looked like something Barbie would wear . . . well, and Michelle. Yeah, Lucky's young wife would *love* those heels.

It was only a week until Christmas and Joelle was really ramped up for the holiday. Christmas music and cookies and garlands and even the spinning tree with its fake presents stacked beneath it. What more could one woman do to a government office?

Not that Pescoli paid much attention. She'd had more than enough to deal with in her own life. For starters, Santana was pressuring her big time. It turned out that Brady Long had left him part of his immense estate and Nate thought she and her children *and* the dog should move in with him.

As if it were just that easy.

Nope, she thought, clicking through the computer screens.

She wasn't convinced, though a father figure for her kids certainly wouldn't hurt. Jeremy, sick of her nagging and bored with his life, had finally agreed to go back to school come January and Pescoli was crossing her fingers that he wouldn't change his mind again. As for his involvement with Heidi Brewster, it was still simmering, but the kids were somehow keeping it on the "down low," which may or may not be a good thing, depending on how you looked at it.

Bianca, well enough to go back to school, had actually started talking to some other boy who'd stopped by a couple of times, some kid on the basketball team who actually called her *Ms. Pescoli,* rather than ignoring her. Chris was still hanging out, of course, but it definitely looked like that particular romance was dying on the vine.

And none too soon.

As for the entire Secret Santa debacle, Pescoli had decided to play along and give the undersheriff a bottle of wine with its own little knit stocking cap that Joelle, Pescoli was certain, would do back flips over. Pescoli, herself, found it kind of gaggy. But she couldn't come up with anything else. The Oregon Pinot Noir had been on a special sale, keeping under the ten dollar limit, and in Pescoli's mind, the gift was a bit of an olive branch. At least that's what she hoped.

After all, she had to work for the prick.

So life was looking up. Except for Alvarez, who had sunk into her usual Christmas funk. There was something going on with her, just like every other holiday season. She never returned home to Oregon for Christmas and this year she'd said she planned to work over the holiday and let the people with families have the time off. When invited to Pescoli's she'd declined, claiming she wanted to spend her free time with Jane Doe, her newly adopted cat.

Pescoli had tried to ask her partner about her avoidance of all things to do with the yuletide, but Alvarez, as ever, managed to evade the questions or change the subject.

Christmas, as far as Alvarez was concerned, was a taboo topic.

Pescoli glanced out the window, noticed it was still snowing. At least, though, the storms had slowed and the work load at the department was back to a more normal level. As for Cameron Johnson, a sicko serial killer if there ever had been one, the FBI had stepped in and taken all of the files, notes and computer information from Johnson's secret room in the basement of his house and were working the case.

It seemed Cameron had been hell-bent on eradicating the female offspring of Donor 727 for years. In his notes, the deputies had found reference to forty two women, some who lived as far away as New England.

DNA tests had proven the victims around this part of Montana as well as others, including Shelly Bonaventure in L.A., had, indeed, been Gerald Johnson's offspring. Other "accident" victims, the "Unknowings" named in Johnson's notes who were already dead, were being examined. If there were any DNA samples taken before they were buried, they were being compared, or the bodies were now being exhumed. They would probably never know about the few who had been cremated as there was no DNA left behind to be tested.

There was other physical evidence that tied Cameron Johnson to his crimes as well. The black paint on Kacey's Ford and Elle Alexander's minivan had matched the custom-made spray-painted bumper guard that had been hidden in a shed and fit perfectly on Johnson's truck. A cache of stolen plates had been located, which explained some of the difficulty they'd had in ID-ing the damned truck.

Pescoli leaned back in her chair until it squeaked in protest and she heard, muted softly, the sound of voices raised in song . . .

"I heard the bells on Christmas Day . . ."

Pescoli checked her watch. It was almost show time and the stage was set.

A few things about the case still bothered Pescoli and scraped at her brain, tickling her into believing there had to be more than they'd already unearthed, even though all leads pointed to Cameron Johnson. As Kacey Lambert had insisted, Pescoli believed that Johnson had been the man who had attacked her in the parking garage in Seattle years before. And now, rumor had it the good doctor might be moving in with Trace O'Halleran, just like that, when Pescoli couldn't commit to a man she'd been in love with for years.

Now Pescoli closed her eyes for a moment and sighed, thinking hard, running over the loose ends. She was pretty sure she had it figured out. Cameron Johnson had been a whack job with a capital W. No doubt about that. Also, he'd definitely been unraveling, more and more taking risks, but that didn't explain everything. How had he gotten all the information on the clinic and the victims? Had he really uncovered that information himself? She didn't think so.

Another thing: it looked like Leanna O'Halleran had stolen the gun that she'd used that night, and that gun was Clarissa Werner's.

Pescoli had interviewed Clarissa and her husband and they both believed Leanna had specifically taken it as a kind of "up yours" to the
Johnson clan as a whole. And it looked like Leanna O'Halleran's special touch of irony was that she drove a BMW, same make and model
as Clarissa's, to also point a finger in the Johnson's direction.

Maybe. Or, maybe not. But there were other issues about the case
that needed to still be addressed . . .

Glancing at her watch again, Pescoli made a sound of impatience.
Alvarez looked up, her brows lifted.

Earlier in the day, while they were grabbing coffee at Joltz, she'd
asked her, "You're not going to let this go, are you?"

"Nope." Pescoli had sprung for a triple chocolate mocha with a
sprinkle of peppermint, just because it was the holidays.

Alvarez had ordered green tea.

Disgusting.

But Alvarez had been interested then, as she was now. "What are
you planning?" she asked.

"I've already done it. Gerald Johnson is coming in, in about fifteen
minutes, and I think he's bringing his favorite attorney."

"Judd?"

"Um-hmm. And I've got a surprise for him."

"Can't wait," she said.

"C'mon, then," Pescoli said and Alvarez followed her to the front
desk. Right on cue Gerald and Judd strode into the department.
Judd was dressed as if he were going to try a case in court, Gerald in
a sweater, ski jacket, jeans and a world-weary expression.

"I don't understand why you insisted on coming here," Judd was
saying to his father. He glanced at Pescoli and added, "I've told you
everything I know about my brother."

Pescoli led them into an interrogation room and Judd stiffened.

"What's this about?" he demanded.

"The truth." Pescoli turned on the recorder. "I've been doing
some checking. A few things still don't add up. Maybe you can clarify
them."

"Be glad to," Gerald said.

Judd wasn't as helpful. "Dad," he warned his father, his expression
brooking no argument, "I don't think this is a good idea."

Pescoli ignored him and waved them into the side chairs as Alvarez closed the door behind them. "When we were talking about Aggie's accident, years ago, there was some discussion," Pescoli began. "You said she got tangled in her blankets and tripped and fell down the stairs."

"No," Judd said, "I remember Cameron brushing up against her and she fell. No one could catch her."

"You also said that she was pushed," Pescoli reminded, from her chair across from them.

"Well, it was a little of both, I think." Judd's eyes narrowed and his shoulders stiffened slightly. "I don't understand."

"I do," Gerald said. "I came home that night and Cameron was really upset. He said he didn't mean to do it, that he didn't want to push Aggie, but he couldn't help himself. I didn't understand it. Then Thane's version was slightly different. He said that you, Judd, ran into Cameron and he fell against Aggie. And Colt said you pushed Cam into Aggie, but Cam was able to save himself."

"We were kids . . ." Judd explained with a shrug. "It was a long time ago. You can't expect any of us to recall exactly what happened."

Pescoli walked to the door and opened it again. Clarissa Johnson Werner stepped inside. "They called me in," she said as a kind of sideways apology to her brother, but nevertheless stated firmly, "You're wrong. I remember. I was there."

"What is this?" Judd demanded. "You've been listening in."

"Watching on a monitor," she said tersely. "And you're lying. I saw what happened that day and you were behind it, Judd. You probably didn't mean for Aggie to fall down the stairs, but you shoved Cameron hard and he fell against her. I was on the phone, coming out to check and . . . you pushed him."

"Where is this going?" Judd demanded tensely. "It was an accident. Kids roughhousing." But he was beginning to sweat, a tiny bead drizzling down his temple.

"And then on the ski slopes when Kathleen died," Clarissa went on determinedly, "you were there. Skiing with Cam and Kathy. I saw you talking to them and later Cam told me you dared him to race Kathy and to go off trail where the snow wasn't groomed. You told him that Kathy, like Aggie, wasn't normal. That she was crazy, when really, Cam was the one who wasn't balanced."

"What are you talking about?" Judd said, the sweat now collecting on his upper lip. "This is crazy. Nuts. *Old* news and I'm not going to listen to this a second longer."

Pescoli was expecting his reaction. She said evenly, "My partner and I intend to get to the bottom of this. We know Cameron was the killer, and maybe he acted alone. But it seems to me he had some help and at first I thought it was his twin. Colt. What better alibi? But then I discovered that your father's corporation, under the guise of several different companies, bought out the old fertility clinic. And guess whose name is all over the documents?"

Judd didn't flinch. "We buy a lot of companies. Especially small medical facilities."

Pescoli leaned back in her chair. "You want to tell us just what your relationship was with your brother, Cameron."

"My brother was crazy."

"And one sister was mentally challenged, another bipolar. Huh. Looks like mental problems aren't just limited to the women your father sired. I think it only makes sense that Cameron had someone helping him along, giving him a little mental . . . 'shove' you might say."

"You're the one who's out of her mind, detective!" Judd's face flushed red, his one hand clenched into a fist. He kicked out his chair and walked to the door. "This interview is over!"

"We'll be seeing you, Mr. Johnson," Pescoli said.

"The hell you will!" He slammed out of the room and Gerald, looking deeply concerned, followed a few moments later, with Clarissa taking up the rear.

When they were alone Pescoli turned to Alvarez and said, "Well?"

Alvarez half-smiled. "Well. We're going to nail him, aren't we?"

"Count on it."

They walked out of the room together and Alvarez glanced up at Pescoli as they reached the hallway. "Another Merry Christmas, partner."

"Another Merry Christmas."